To my sister, Katharine and my niece, Ellie
You've been through so much
There are no words

I

Lola

The sound of footsteps closing in on me came from nowhere. I'd been making a cup of tea in the staff room when the next thing I knew, a set of strong fingers dug into my upper arm and spun me around before I had a chance to react. When his fist connected with my lower jaw, the force lifted me off my feet, and I fell backwards on to the tiled floor, smacking my head in the process.

'I bet you thought I hadn't noticed you flirting with that guy?' Troy yelled as a curly vein throbbed in his temple.

He stood over me with his fists clenched and his eyes blazing for a few loaded seconds, then he swung his leg back and booted me in the side without giving me a chance to reply. The blow forced the air out of my lungs, so I curled myself into a ball and wrapped my arms over my head as pain radiated through my body. I lay on the floor like a deflated balloon waiting for the assault to stop.

'Answer me, you fucking bitch.' Troy's nostrils flared, and his blue eyes bored into me as he waited for me to reply.

'You've got the wrong idea; I wasn't flirting with anyone. I was just doing my job...' My voice trailed off. I had to clamp my mouth closed to stop a sob from escaping from my lips.

Hot tears sprang to my eyes, but I battled to hold them back. I didn't want to give Troy the satisfaction of seeing me cry. I knew from experience showing my vulnerability made him feel even more powerful. But it was hard not to buckle as pain seared through my body like a hot knife through butter.

'Do you seriously expect me to believe that?'

I felt myself flinch when Troy bent down, grabbed hold of my long blonde hair, and dragged me to my feet, twisting the strands around his fist as he did. I cried out in pain. I couldn't help it; my scalp was on fire.

'You were practically begging for it.' Troy squeezed my face with his strong fingers before he used it as a punching bag.

My lip began to quiver. 'I'm sorry, Troy.'

'You're sorry? When are you going to realise it's not acceptable to behave like a slag?'

The look of sheer fury on his face made my knees buckle. I hadn't done anything wrong, but at this stage, I was conditioned to accept Troy's version of events and would do whatever was necessary to make the beating stop. This wasn't the first time I'd been subjected to physical violence at the hands of my jealous partner. And as usual, his accusations were entirely without foundation.

'Please don't hurt me,' I begged as his blows started to rain down on me.

Once the beating stopped, Troy pulled me up on to my tiptoes. 'Get out of my fucking sight,' he said, getting up in my face before he released me from his iron grip.

Troy didn't need to tell me twice. As I went to leave, he lifted his hand to wipe away the beads of sweat that were glistening on his shaved head. I covered my face with my hands in response. I thought he was going to hit me again as I ran past him. I pressed the button that unlocked the door separating the staff area from the shop floor and tore across the grey tiles. Flinging open the glass door at the front of the shop, I spilt out on to the pavement and tripped over my own feet. I was in a hurry to put some distance between us.

2

Paul

16th February, London

'Do exactly what I tell you, and nobody will get hurt,' I said, after Kevin and I burst out of the darkness and through the door of the warehouse wielding guns.

My heartbeat was pounding in my ears as I aimed my weapon at my friend Finn and his dumbstruck colleagues, who'd instinctively held their hands in the air. They looked as terrified as I felt. My blood was pumping, and I was struggling to think straight. We'd been over the plan a thousand times, but now the moment had arrived, I was shitting myself.

I started the timer on my smartwatch while my brother, Kevin, got to work tying up the members of staff. He made light work of securing the men's wrists and ankles with nylon cable tie restraints then placed gaffer tape across their mouths. My eyes widened as they scanned over the pallet loads of cash sitting in the centre of the outbuilding. No word of a lie; they came up to my waist. But gawping wasn't going to get the job done. Time was ticking; we were allowing ourselves just five minutes to grab as much of the loot as we could carry before we made a run for it.

Kevin and I began stuffing the vacuum-sealed bundles of fifty-pound notes into black holdalls, feeling the weight intermittently while racing against the clock. I would have loved to have cleaned them out, but greed would be our downfall. Tempting as it was, if we made the bags too heavy, we wouldn't be able to carry them. We'd done plenty of dry runs with bricks from the building site where I laboured to condition ourselves to carry a heavy load, so we knew our limit.

Kevin and I rushed in and out of the hangar, loading the holdalls into the armoured van that had transferred the money from the plane a little while earlier. It was parked directly outside, and just as Finn had said, the keys were in the ignition.

'We've got eyes on the building, so don't try and raise the alarm,' I said as the timer went off.

I jumped into the passenger seat, and Kevin got behind the wheel and put his foot to the floor. He drove us to the hole we'd made in the perimeter security fence. Kevin left the ignition running, and we jumped out, grabbed some of the holdalls and paced over to where Mark was waiting in the inflatable boat with the engine idling.

Mark stood below us at the stern of the boat with his arms open wide, ready to catch the bags of loot. He let out a grunt as the first one made contact with him.

'Fuck me, they weigh a ton,' he remarked.

'You should try running with them,' I replied as I threw the next one to him.

Once we'd unloaded all of the loot, Kevin and I jumped into the boat, and Mark opened up the throttle. Even though the first part of the robbery was over, the white-knuckle ride was going to keep my adrenalin pumping. I'd lived by the sea all of my life but had never been that comfortable on or in the water.

'Stop swinging the boat around, you bastard,' I called to Mark, but the wind carried my words away with it, and my protests fell on deaf ears.

If the hull bounced off the grey water much more, my breakfast was going to make a reappearance.

'Paul.' Kevin tapped me on the arm to get my attention.

I turned away from Mark and looked at my brother.

'We've got to check the cash for trackers,' he said over the noise of the engine.

I nodded to acknowledge I'd understood what he'd said. I'd been so fixated on my stomach's contents churning that I'd forgotten the next stage of the plan.

As we sped along, Kevin and I cut open the ultra-strong vacuum parcels that had tamper-resistant closures with the aid of folding pocket knives and began throwing any devices we found overboard. But it was easier said than done while wearing gloves and being battered by a bitter north-easterly.

Once we'd removed all of the trackers, Kevin and I started stripping off our British Airways fluorescent jackets and navy trousers with reflective strips. The biting wind and ice-cold spray stung my bare skin, and I wished we hadn't picked a freezing day when we'd planned the heist. But it had been a tactical move. The airport was relatively quiet at this time of year compared with the height of summer and especially at this unearthly time in the morning. But the darkness was our ally, so I wasn't going to complain about the early start.

Kevin tossed me his clothes and lanyard containing his fake ID. I bundled both sets into a black bin liner so that we could burn them later.

Mark was a keen fisherman and knew this river like the back of his hand. And thanks to his job at a watersports centre, he handled the boat like a pro. My insides might not agree with me, but I knew we were in safe hands. Mark steered the boat through some high-speed manoeuvres as the sights of London whipped past us. It was like an opening scene from a Bond film. The only thing missing was the theme tune. It was a shame I couldn't prise my eyes open long enough to appreciate it.

'Get down,' Mark shouted, but his voice was barely audible over the sound of the wind and the engine.

I caught a fleeting glimpse of the black dinghy with Police emblazoned on the sides in glowing white letters before Kevin and I lay down on the bottom of the boat. The contents of my stomach roiled, but there were more important things to worry about. The dinghy was heading straight for us. Its searchlights bounced off the inky water as it raced out of the darkness, sirens wailing. The sound was getting closer by the second.

3

Lola

16th February, Sheffield

'Lola, is that you?' Mum asked when I opened the front door.

'Oh shit,' I muttered under my breath. I was hoping she'd still be at work.

'You're home early, love,' Mum continued, looking up at the clock above the sink as she washed up our breakfast things.

I stood frozen to the spot in the hallway. A look of horror spread across her face when she looked over her shoulder and clapped eyes on me. She dropped the scourer and mug back into the bowl, grabbed the tea towel on the countertop and paced towards me, drying her hands as she closed in on me.

'What on earth's happened, sweetheart?' Mum took hold of my hands in hers.

I didn't need to answer. It wouldn't take long for the penny to drop.

'You've either had a run-in with an angry customer, or Troy's been up to his old tricks again.' Mum shook her head. 'I've had enough of this. I'm phoning the police.'

Mum turned on her heel and started walking back down the hall.

'I'm not going to report him, so you're wasting your time if you phone them. I'll just say I fell down a flight of steps,' I called after her.

Mum stopped in her tracks, then she turned and looked at me with pleading eyes. 'Why would someone stay with, let alone defend, a man who'd just knocked them senseless?'

'You don't understand,' I replied.

'You're damn right I don't. I'm seriously questioning your sanity, Lola. When are you going to realise you can't keep letting him get away with this.'

Troy's aggression towards me had spiralled out of control recently. The beatings had become more frequent, but it was easy to hand out advice if you were just an observer of the situation. I was the one dealing with the problem. Our relationship was a combination of extreme highs and lows. I'd be crushed by his actions one moment and be on cloud nine the next. The answer wasn't as simple as the difference between night and day. There were all the hours in between to consider. When things were good, they were really, really good. Troy could be wonderful and totally focused on me which made me feel special, so I was facing a complicated dilemma. I knew Mum was trying to help, but her words were coming across as a lecture, and I didn't appreciate that. I'd been through a traumatic experience, and I needed some space to try and process what had happened.

Troy's jealousy was so powerful and overwhelming that it made him react to a situation rather than think things through in a rational manner. He'd flip his lid over the slightest thing but always made me feel like it was my fault he'd behaved the way he had. I'd pushed him too far, so I deserved the punishment. When somebody told you that enough, you started to believe it.

Today was a prime example. We didn't have set breaks at William Hill, and I'd been stuck behind the shop's counter for hours, so I was gasping for a cup of tea. But I couldn't leave the kiosk while there were customers in the shop. I'd almost taken root when a man in his fifties, who'd been sitting in a booth ruminating over his betting slip for an eternity, came over and gave me the handwritten sheet. I'd just been making polite conversation to pass the time while I processed his request. But Troy had obviously been watching me from the shadows, and once the man left and I was free to leave my post, he pounced on me. Troy was convinced I was flirting with the pot-bellied, red-faced man, and there was no way I'd be able to convince him otherwise. He'd flown into a rage and taken his anger out on me.

'I hear what you're saying, but please don't get involved. This is between Troy and me.'

I knew if I kept leaving his behaviour unchecked, it would only get worse, but I was too scared to do anything about it. And so, the cycle of our deeply toxic relationship continued.

Mum walked towards me and gently swept my long blonde hair back from my face. 'Look what he's done to you.

You're black and blue.' Mum spoke with tears glistening in her hazel eyes.

'It looks worse than it is,' I tried to smile, but my face was bruised and swollen. I didn't want Mum to worry, so I was doing my best to hide the pain I was in.

'If you're not careful, he'll end up killing you one day,' Mum said.

Her warning sent a shiver down the entire length of my spine. I hoped her prophecy wouldn't turn out to be true.

'Lola, please, I'm begging you. You're an intelligent girl; you know how this will end. You've got to get away from him before it's too late.' Mum didn't try to hide the desperation coating her words.

Jealousy was a dangerous emotion; it could hijack your mind and ruin your relationship if you let it. Troy's behaviour was getting worse by the day. He had a chilling obsession with control and was constantly monitoring my every move. Internet searches, texts, phone calls, emails and social media, nothing was off-limits. His preoccupation with policing my private life became all-consuming, and every other aspect of our relationship faded into the background.

It hadn't always been like this, but Troy was consumed by jealousy. He saw threats everywhere and anywhere. On the rare occasion I wore something nice, he'd misinterpret that as me trying to attract a new partner. And heaven forbid I should behave in a friendly way to a customer of the opposite sex. Troy saw that as openly flirting in front of him. I couldn't win. He was becoming more paranoid by the day, and the boundaries between his suspicions and the reality of the situation blurred to such an extent that he kept drawing the wrong conclusions. It was making me miserable, but it was easier to stay than leave.

A silent tear rolled down my cheek, and Mum wiped it away with the pad of her thumb. 'Let's get you cleaned up,' she said, realising it was time to back off.

Mum took hold of my hand and led me into the kitchen. I wasn't intentionally ignoring her advice. Anyone could see she was beside herself with worry and couldn't understand why I continued to stand by my man. But I clung to memories of when things were good and tried to block out the bad ones, so that clouded my judgement. I bet if you asked any woman in an abusive relationship what made her stay, she'd tell you the same thing. There was also another issue. Attempting to leave would be dangerous. If I thought things were bad now, they would get a whole lot worse if I tried to walk away. His threats were a powerful deterrent. I felt trapped because he'd told me before if I ever left him, he'd hunt me down and make me pay. I knew Troy meant every word he'd said; he wouldn't rest until he found me.

As Mum applied a cold compress to my bruises, my eyes fixed on the vase of long-stemmed red roses sitting on the windowsill. Troy had given them to me for Valentine's Day, forty-eight hours ago. I never knew where I stood with him. His moods changed with the wind direction. One minute I was his entire world, and the next, he couldn't stand the sight of me. He loved me and hated me in equal measures, which made having a relationship with him almost impossible. I never knew whether to hug him or hide from him. I was constantly walking on eggshells, and the longer we were together, the worse things were getting.

4

Abbie

16th February, London

The warehouse was surrounded by a sea of flashing blue lights when my partner, DC Ed Lewis, and I arrived at London City Airport. By the amount of police presence, anyone would think no other crimes were happening across the capital. But, then again, this was an interesting case, so any available units had eagerly responded to the 999 call. This kind of thing didn't happen every day of the week; it wasn't a run-of-the-mill robbery.

'When we go inside, leave the questioning to me, but take as many notes as you like. You can never have too much background information,' I said.

'Okay,' Ed replied.

I wasn't best pleased to see the additional personnel; extra unnecessary people would cause problems. We'd run the risk of contaminating the scene before we had a chance to protect it. Thankfully, most of the officers appeared to be milling around outside. Only those responsible for the immediate investigation should be present, so I'd take great pleasure in dispersing the rest.

'Who's in charge here?' I said to the first uniformed officer I passed.

'Who wants to know?' the young man replied with a smile.

When I saw Ed smirk out of the corner of my eye, I had to resist the urge to roll my eyes. It obviously amused him that I had to defend my rank. I wasn't surprised by the officer's attitude. It was a typical response. Being a plainclothes detective, I'd been told on many occasions I didn't look like an inspector.

I was a high-ranking female officer and had a tough personality but I also loved being well groomed. I liked to curl my hair and wear nice outfits to work; heels and form-fitting trouser suits were my go-to choice. But taking pride in my appearance and the way I dressed had no bearing on my ability to do my job. I was more than competent even if my male colleagues like to question my authority at every opportunity. It drove me insane that they focused on the veneer rather than on the person within, but I wasn't about to change the way I looked for anyone. It was their problem, not mine.

'DI Abbie Kingsly,' I replied, flashing him the lanyard around my neck containing my ID.

The man's eyes widened, and blood drained from his face. 'I'm so sorry, ma'am, I didn't realise...'

At least he had the good grace to look embarrassed, so I decided to cut in, stopping him mid-flow. There was no point in prolonging his agony.

'Can you cordon off the area, please? There should be one entrance and exit into the crime scene, so place an officer here and take the names of all of the people entering the warehouse.' I gestured with my hand. 'Only authorised personnel can enter the area. We don't want to contaminate it,' I explained, as the officer looked new to the role.

We'd only just arrived on the scene, but while I was speaking, I noticed Ed check the time on his watch, signalling his impatience, and I was tempted to pull him up on it, but I made a mental note of it instead. I glanced over my shoulder to where three members of the force were congregated.

'Which officer is in charge?' I asked.

When the new recruit pointed to a stocky middle-aged man at the back of the warehouse, I strode towards him. Ed followed two paces behind me.

'I'm DI Abbie Kingsly, and this is DC Ed Lewis,' I said to the officer handling the scene. 'Can you please bring us up to speed?'

'Certainly. The robbery happened at approximately 07:30. Two men wearing balaclavas, logoed airline fluorescent jackets, trousers and lanyards burst into the warehouse wielding guns moments after the last pallet was unloaded.'

I nodded to myself. The robbers had impersonated airport staff by wearing their uniforms, so it was pretty clear to me that we were investigating an inside job.

'How long did it take the first mobile unit to respond?' I asked, glancing at my watch. It was 08:30.

'They arrived less than ten minutes from when the 999 call was received. Although the staff were bound and gagged, they managed to raise the alarm almost as soon as the robbers left,' the officer replied.

'Any sign of the suspects?'

The officer shook his head. 'No, they'd already fled.'

'Pity,' I replied, letting out a sigh.

'The men used the armoured van to make their escape. My colleagues are currently taking the names and personal details of the staff who witnessed the robbery.'

'Good. We'll take statements from the staff members in due course.'

I turned my attention to Ed and caught him clock-watching again, which was irritating beyond belief. I was well aware of the Golden Hour; the first hour after any crime was critical, so he didn't need to keep communicating his impatience, reminding me that time was of the essence.

'Any sign of the forensic team?'

'They're on their way. To fill you in on the background, the money the thieves got away with was part of a consignment of three pallets of unmarked notes unloaded from a British Airways flight, which arrived at 07:00 this morning,' the officer said.

I surveyed the huge amount of notes the robbers left. They'd hardly made a dent in the consignment. But there was a limit to how much two people could physically carry. It made me question why they didn't bring a bigger team. Were the men amateurs or highly skilled professionals who knew the importance of not letting greed get the better of them?

'Have we got any idea how much they stole?' I asked.

'Not yet. We're still trying to establish how much was on board; the amount varies from day to day. For security reasons, the airline doesn't provide the ground staff with many details about the shipments. But, judging by the piles of fifty-pound notes left behind, I'd say it runs into the hundreds of thousands if not more,' the officer remarked.

It made sense that British Airways wouldn't share specific information about how much money was shipped in the plane's cargo area with their staff. Even though I was well aware that it happened, I couldn't get my head around the fact that commercial airlines transported millions of pounds worth of cash in their hold. These pallets were stowed away with tourists' bags bulging at the seams with half-used bottles of sun cream, sandy flip-flops and souvenirs from local markets. No wonder the airlines imposed a weight limit on passengers' bags. They wouldn't have the capacity to carry all the money otherwise.

Why would an airline store pallet-loads of money in a warehouse? I instantly noticed some serious security issues. I was amazed that this didn't happen more often, considering cash arrived from overseas on a daily basis. The airlines were taking a real risk allowing their workers to be surrounded by all this temptation with very little security presence from what I could see. Two unarmed guards weren't much of a deterrent. I couldn't imagine freight handlers were well paid; it was a thief's paradise.

'I'm afraid there's not all that much to go on at this stage,' the officer said, breaking my train of thought.

'Thank you for filling us in on the background; we'll take it from here,' I smiled.

It was time for me to look at the bigger picture. I walked over to where the staff were assembled and cast a critical eye over them. If you observed a criminal's behaviour when a police officer drew near, they almost always gave the game away even before they were questioned. The issue of whether police officers possessed certain personality characteristics that made them unique had been the subject of much debate in the staff room over the years. Were we a different breed or not? I was a firm believer that it wasn't a myth, copper's intuition was a genuine thing, and I had bucketloads of it. I was good at reading people. It was a useful skill to have, and I'd honed it over the years. Being eagle-eyed, the slightest twitch didn't get past me. Now, to put it to the test, I had more than a hunch that one of the witnesses had had a hand in the crime and would turn out to be a potential suspect.

'Start taking statements from the cargo workers while I speak to the security guards,' I said.

Ed responded with a nod. Then he whipped out his notebook and gripped the tip of his pen, poised and ready for action. There was no limit to my partner's enthusiasm; Ed reminded me of myself when I'd first started out, but there was one huge difference between us. I was patient; he wasn't. He was on the first rung of the detective ladder and was desperate to prove his worth, but he had a lot to learn. Unless an officer was dealing with a situation posing an immediate threat of death or serious injury, the methodical and measured approach typically produced the best outcome. Detective work wasn't for everyone; the process of solving cases could take months and sometimes years.

'So, what can you tell me about the robbery?' I asked the senior security guard with the Clark Gable moustache, who looked like he should have been put out to pasture ten years ago.

The man's face drained of colour as he began to relive the experience.

'Not that much really; it all happened in the blink of an eye. There were two of them, both male. But I didn't get a good look at them. They were wearing balaclavas and were only in here for a couple of minutes.'

That wasn't what I wanted to hear. But I liked a challenge, and I was good at my job, so I'd leave no stone unturned. I pulled out my notebook and pad and began to write the man's account.

'Apart from the members of staff still here, has anyone else entered the scene?'

'No,' the security guard replied.

'Do you have anything to add?' I said to the other guard.

He was considerably younger than his grey-haired colleague and hopefully more switched on.

'A couple of small things, but I don't know if they'll be any use.'

'Go on,' I coaxed. Sometimes the tiniest detail or snippet of information went on to solve the case.

'One of the guys started a timer on his watch while the other one tied us up. As soon as it went off, they fled. He told us not to try and raise the alarm as they'd got eyes on the building.'

I scribbled down what he'd said in my notebook.

'I'll need access to your security footage,' I replied, noticing the warehouse's camera system.

'Of course,' the senior guard replied.

I took two of my business cards out of my suit jacket pocket and handed them to the guards. 'Please call me if you remember anything else.'

'We will,' they replied.

5

Lola

'I know it's an awkward conversation to have, but I can't ignore it any longer. I won't be a bystander to this,' Mum said as we sat opposite each other at the table.

She'd tried several times to broach the subject, but I'd never felt ready to open up to her.

'Why don't you just finish with him?'

That was the worst thing Mum could have asked, especially as her question came with judgement. I knew she didn't understand, but I wished she would stop trying to simplify an extremely complex situation. If you'd never been through an abusive relationship, you had no idea what it was like. It was hard to leave when you couldn't find the way out.

I didn't want to tell Mum that I'd tried to end things several times before, but Troy had threatened to hurt me if I broke up with him. I was scared of what would happen if I walked away – it might escalate things. I didn't want her to worry more than she already was. I wished I could confide in her; the fear I was experiencing at the moment was very real. But I knew it would pass. Things weren't always bad between us. We'd had loads of good times too. When I was the centre of Troy's world, it was the best feeling ever, so I wasn't sure I was ready to give up on him.

'The problem with you, Lola, is you're too soft-hearted, too kind for your own good, and people like Troy take advantage of your generous nature.'

I couldn't argue with that. I was susceptible to pity and a sucker for a tale of hardship. The sadder, the better. I fell for it every time.

'You're a beautiful girl, Lola; you don't deserve to be treated like this. I would never have put up with your dad doing that to me. I'd have been out of the door like a flash,' Mum said.

'And that would have been your choice.'

Talk was cheap. But if you hadn't experienced the crushing terror for yourself, you weren't qualified to comment. Nobody really knew what they would do unless they were faced with the situation themselves.

I clamped my fingers around the mug in front of me and concentrated my gaze on the tea, half-filling the space so that I didn't have to make eye contact with Mum. She hated my boyfriend with a passion which made things awkward for me. I constantly felt like I was in the middle of the two people I cared about the most.

'I know you're trying to be a loyal girlfriend, but you don't owe him anything.'

I looked up when Mum began to speak again.

'Men like Troy chip away at your self-esteem little by little; he won't stop until he's broken you into tiny pieces.'

Fear was etched into the lines on Mum's face. I could see she was worried sick about the situation.

Troy was a troubled soul; he had deep-seated issues. Both his parents had been addicted to crack cocaine, so his childhood had been lacking, to say the least. Mum reckoned he'd been raised by wolves. I'd been desperate to show him some loyalty. I thought I could fix him by teaching him to love.

'You're a big-hearted girl, Lola, and you'll make somebody a fantastic wife one day. But I couldn't think of anything worse than you ending up with that monster. Your dad would turn in his grave if he knew what Troy had done to you.'

'He's got nobody he can depend on apart from me. I promised him I'd never leave him,' I replied.

I wanted to be the one person in his life who'd kept their word. I'd vowed never to end our relationship, so how could I go back on that?

'Promises were made to be broken. Troy's a bully and a thug; he'll destroy you if you let him.'

The sound of the doorbell stopped our conversation in its tracks.

'No prizes for guessing who's outside,' Mum said.

'Let me go,' I said, pushing my chair back and getting up from the table before Mum had a chance to beat me to it.

Troy was standing on the step with a huge bouquet of flowers in his hands when I opened the front door.

'I'm so sorry, Lola. I don't know what came over me,' Troy said as he held the flowers towards me. 'Please forgive me. I promise I'll never do it again.'

I'd lost count of how many times I'd heard him say those

words. He was always apologetic, spoiling me with gifts and flowers, reminding me how happy we were when we first got together until he won me over. But once I gave in, the honeymoon period became a thing of the past, and he'd start controlling me again.

'I'm sorry I blew up at you.' Troy bowed his head and paused for a moment before making eye contact with me again. 'I love you so much, Lola, I can't bear to think of you with another man. I get jealous sometimes, but that's a normal reaction. It's a compliment.'

'You didn't seriously think I found that customer attractive, did you?' I raised my eyebrows.

'You were flirting with him.' Troy narrowed his eyes as he stared at me.

'I wasn't. I was making polite conversation while I served him. For God's sake, Troy, give me some credit. The man was in his fifties and had a huge pot belly and a bright red face.'

'Well, you looked like you were getting very cosy from where I was standing. How did you expect me to react? Were you deliberately trying to wind me up?'

'No. You've got it all wrong.' I shook my head.

'You know I have trust issues. Why do you keep making me feel insecure?' Troy's gaze was intense and I felt heat rise up the back of my neck.

'I don't do it intentionally.'

'Yeah, right. Admit it, Lola, you love pushing my buttons. It's no secret I've got a short fuse.'

That was an understatement. Troy could blow his top in an instant. His temper was like rocket fuel.

'Can I come in?' Troy asked.

'I don't think that's a good idea,' I replied, knowing how Mum would feel about me letting him into our home.

'Fair enough. Can I give you a lift to work tomorrow instead?' Troy smiled. He was on his best behaviour.

'I think I'm going to need to take some time off,' I replied, pointing to the bruising on my face. 'I don't want to have to answer any awkward questions.'

'Lola, your tea's getting cold,' Mum shouted from the kitchen.

'I'd better go,' I said.

'I love you, Lola,' Troy said before I closed the front door.

'Surprise, surprise,' Mum said when I walked into the kitchen carrying the enormous bouquet. 'Don't let him win you over that easily. He's using those flowers to symbolise an apology, but he's not sorry. They're a trap, and you've just walked straight into it. By accepting them, you've allowed him to get a foot in the door.'

When Mum shook her head and let out an exasperated sigh, I had to stop myself from bursting into tears. I needed her support right now, not her judgement. I felt emotional; my mental state was fragile. If I hadn't accepted the peace offering, who knew what would have happened. It was easier to take the bouquet and close the front door than face the consequences.

I used to be such a strong person, but Troy had reduced me to a shell of myself. I was weak and spineless. Mum didn't need to point it out. She thought she was helping by telling me how to handle things, but she was just creating a barrier between us.

'You're sacrificing your safety to keep him sweet.'

'Please. Mum just leave it. This isn't helping.' My bottom lip began to wobble; I was on the verge of tears.

'Don't give that man another chance. You know as well as I do, there will be a next time. I'm worried he might do a lot more than just hit you if you give him the opportunity.'

6

Paul

'That was too close for comfort,' I said, letting out a sigh of relief when the police dinghy shot past us, and the sirens faded into the distance.

Kevin and I had been seconds away from tossing the holdalls over the side of the boat. We didn't want to get caught with the stolen cash.

'You're not kidding,' Mark replied, looking over his shoulder at me. 'I think I've just aged ten years in the last five minutes,' he laughed.

'Tell me about it,' Kevin agreed.

It was still dark when Mark steered the boat into The Swale, a tidal channel of the Thames estuary which separated the Isle of Sheppey from the rest of Kent. We were almost within spitting distance from where we were going to moor up so that we could stash the money. As predicted, there wasn't a soul around as this stretch of water was a haven for bird watchers, walkers and anglers. None of them had ventured out as yet, so we should be able to unload the bags without the presence of prying eyes.

Mark's parents owned a chalet on a small caravan park, The Elms, next to Elmley National Nature Reserve. They bought the holiday let as an investment in the 1980s, but it was always empty at this time of year. They were barely able to tempt people over the threshold in the height of summer, let alone in the depths of winter. Elmley was the only nature reserve in the UK where you could stay the night and wake up surrounded by wilderness. It offered first-class award-winning accommodation that the camp just couldn't compete with. But you wouldn't hear any of us complaining about the lack of visitors. It suited us down to the ground that it was empty more than it was rented. The four of us used the chalet all the time. It had witnessed plenty of our teenage shenanigans; it was just as well walls couldn't talk.

While Mark moored the boat, Kevin and I walked along the wooden jetty to retrieve the heavy-duty cart we'd left hidden in the bushes, which the camp used to transport holidaymakers' luggage to their accommodation. Between the three of us, we loaded the holdalls on to it, steering it the short distance to the chalet, positioned in a very private spot at the edge of the camp. Kevin and I stood side by side on the decking while Mark unlocked the front door.

'I've taken the panel off the bath, so we'll stash the money in there for the time being,' Mark said.

Once he stepped over the threshold, we followed him inside, ferrying the bags through the living area to the small bathroom at the back of the property. It was back-breaking work, but that was a good sign. It meant we'd stolen a lot of dosh.

Mark managed the place for his parents, and nobody else came near it, so the cash would be safe here until we had a chance to count it later. We'd move it once we'd divided it up. In the meantime, we had to carry on as normal and not change anything about our usual routines, which meant back to the day jobs for all of us.

'Give us a hand to hold this in place,' Mark said after we'd put the bags in the space under the bath.

Kevin and I held either end of the yellowing white plastic panel in place while Mark replaced the screws.

I glanced at my watch. 'I'd better get a move on, or I'll be late for work.'

The site manager ran a tight ship, and if I wanted to be kept on, I had to play by his rules, turn up on time, work my arse off and not moan about the conditions. He reminded his workforce on a daily basis that we were all replaceable; none of us was indispensable. I was sure the same could be said for him.

'We'll meet you back here tonight at seven,' I said.

'No problem,' Mark replied. 'I'd better get the boat back before somebody notices it's missing.'

Kevin and I went off in the other direction towards his car. Mark had picked us up in the speedboat from the campsite, so Kevin had left his trusty Ford Focus in a nearby lay-by. We didn't have time to go home, so he was going to drop me off at work.

The last thing I felt like doing was spending the day doing hard graft in freezing temperatures. Especially as I'd just come into a large sum of money, but for now, needs must. Tempting as it was to go straight back to the chalet and divvy up the spoils before jumping on a plane to Spain, it wasn't an option, not at this moment in time anyway. Maybe one day, Kevin and I would fulfil our dream and be the proud owners of a beachfront bar.

But I shouldn't grumble. I was one of the lucky ones. At least I had a job. It was hard to find work on the Isle of Sheppey unless you worked at the steel plant, the docks, or the prison like Kevin. And if you did, it more than likely paid minimum wage. Opportunities for young people were bleak. My Mum and Dad, like countless others, moved here from mainland Kent to buy their first house. They were lured by the low prices and didn't consider how that might affect their future. Those that made something of themselves moved away again; people who didn't had no option but to stay.

Us Islanders took a lot of shit and were the butt of people's jokes. Whenever an article appeared in the newspaper, instead of highlighting the nice things about the island, it was always derogatory, which did nothing to help the tourist trade or boost the local economy. Sheppey residents were accused of being inbred and called bigger sheep shaggers than the Welsh. Swampies with webbed feet was another delightful term that got bandied about, but my favourite of all time was a report I read that said if you had six toes on each foot and were married to your mother, you would fit right in with the locals!

If Mark, Kevin, Finn and myself hadn't grown up in an area surrounded by so much stigma, we wouldn't have turned into the men we were today. Our collective desire for a brighter future was the driving force behind all of us.

7

Lola

I turned to face my bedroom door when the sound of Mum's footsteps paused outside. A moment later, her knuckles gently rapped on the wood. I let out a loud sigh; I knew what was coming.

'I'm sorry to disturb you,' Mum began, poking her head around the door. 'But I heard you tell Troy you were going to need to take some time off work.'

'Well, I can't exactly show up at the bookies like this and not expect people to ask questions, can I?'

Mum looked a bit hurt by my prickly response, but I hadn't been able to stop the sarcastic tone from coating my words, but it didn't stop her pushing the door open, walking into my bedroom and sitting down on the edge of the bed.

'You need to prioritise your safety and well-being, not your relationship. Aside from the obvious physical abuse you've been subjected to, there's the mental torture to consider.'

I went to protest, but Mum held up her hand to stop me in my tracks so that she could continue talking.

'You can deny it all you like, but Troy's been brainwashing you. Every time this happens, he makes you doubt your own memory so that he can suck you back in. What he's doing is out of order. It's totally unacceptable for a man to hit a woman under any circumstances. He's crossed a line,' Mum said.

'I'm at fault too. Sometimes I make him feel jealous and then he overreacts. But he only does it because he loves me.'

'Loves you? He's got a funny way of showing it. If he really cared for you, he'd show you more respect.' Mum let out an exasperated sigh.

'You can say what you like, I know how Troy feels about me, but he has trust issues, so it's no wonder he doesn't always handle situations well.'

'Trust issues?' Mum rolled her eyes which instantly got my back up.

'Yes, deep-seated ones and I have a knack of making him feel insecure.'

'For God's sake listen to yourself. They sound like his words coming out of your mouth. I'll tell you something, he knows damn well he's gone too far and risks losing you. That's why he's come around here with a huge bunch of flowers. Look what he's done to you, Lola.' Mum reached on to my bedside cabinet, picked up my free-standing mirror and held it up to my face.

I turned my head away when I caught sight of the swelling and bruises. They were worse than before. My left eye was half-closed, and the whole side of my face was starting to turn deep purple. I didn't want to see the damage he'd inflicted because it would force me to face the grim reality. I preferred to stay away from mirrors and prying eyes until I was at the stage where make-up would conceal the worst of it.

'When are you going to wise up to what's happening? This is not going to end well. Your relationship isn't normal; it's toxic. If you let Troy reel you back in, he'll revert to his old ways in no time.'

Mum didn't understand my boyfriend the way I did. I was convinced Troy's dysfunctional behaviour had its roots in his past. I think he'd learnt it from his parents. He didn't talk much about his childhood, but I knew his mum and dad were both addicts and could be unpredictable and abusive. They must have manipulated him into keeping their drug problem a family secret. Otherwise, he'd have ended up in care. Somehow, he'd slipped through the Social Services net. By all accounts, things only got worse when his mother died of an overdose.

I wasn't making excuses for Troy, but his parents had a lot to answer for; his upbringing had damaged him and left him emotionally scarred so it was no wonder he sometimes behaved the way he did. He needed somebody dependable in his life to help him overcome his troubled start.

Mum's opinion mattered to me, but I didn't want to accept that Troy and I had no future together and weren't destined to live a happily ever after.

'Troy's agreed to let you have some time off, so you should use it wisely. This is the perfect opportunity for you to make your escape without him breathing down your neck. He knows he's in the bad books, so the ball's in your court, and you should use that to your advantage.'

'I'm really tired; I'm going to try and get some sleep,' I said, feigning a yawn, giving Mum her cue to leave. She sounded like a broken record.

'I'll let you get some rest.' Mum planted a kiss on the top of my head before she walked out of my room, closing the door behind her.

I'd been doing my best to ignore my thumping headache, but it was getting worse by the minute, so I decided to go and get some paracetamol from the bathroom cabinet. I was on my way downstairs to get a glass of water when I heard Mum talking to somebody. She was trying to keep her voice down, which made me curious. I froze mid-step when I realised she was on the phone to her best friend.

'Honestly, Brenda, you should see the state of her beautiful face. He's beaten her black and blue but she's still refusing to end things with him,' Mum said.

I felt my breath catch in my throat when she started to sob. I couldn't hear Brenda's reply but I could read between the lines and, judging by my mum's response, she'd been none too complimentary about Troy.

'I know what you mean. The man's pure evil. She's in real danger, but she can't see it. It doesn't seem to matter what I say, I can't get through to her. I feel like I'm bashing my head against a brick wall. I'm at my wits' end,' Mum said and then she broke down in tears.

A wave of guilt washed over me. I knew Mum had no time for Troy but I hadn't realised just how badly my relationship was affecting her. Hearing her crying her eyes out and voicing her despair struck a chord with me.

'I feel totally helpless. It's gut-wrenching watching that pathetic excuse of a man destroy my precious daughter, knowing there's not a damn thing I can do to stop it,' Mum said.

I felt silent tears roll down my cheek. Mum's heart was breaking and it was my fault she was suffering.

'Thanks for listening. You're a good friend,' Mum said before ending the call.

I didn't want her to know I'd been eavesdropping, so I went back up the stairs without getting the water. My pounding temples didn't seem that important now. My head was spinning for a different reason. The conversation I'd just overheard was really bothering me.

There was no way I'd be able to sleep, my mind was whirring with thoughts. I needed some time to try and process things. I lay back on my pillows, staring up at the ceiling as Mum's words reverberated over and over again in my head. 'This is not going to end well. Your relationship isn't normal; it's toxic,' she'd said, and much as I didn't want to admit it, it was true. I'd tried my best to help Troy. I'd thought if he was surrounded by love, it would allow him to overcome his demons. But maybe some people were too damaged to repair.

Listening to Mum pouring her heart out to Brenda had really got to me. There was no denying how badly my disastrous love life was affecting her. Guilt began hollowing out my insides, so I decided to take her advice and use the time away from work to think about the future. Troy wasn't in any position to demand that I come back too soon, not after what he'd done to me. He'd agreed to give me sick leave so that my injuries could heal, and hopefully, that would buy me enough time to think things through.

I'd been in this situation before, but something felt different this time. I don't know whether it was the shock of seeing the state of my face or the fact that I'd witnessed Mum secretly sobbing. Whatever the reason, maybe it was time to stop brushing off Troy's behaviour and face up to the fact that I was a victim of domestic abuse. Perhaps I should leave while the bruises were still there to remind me how bad our relationship had become. I'd tried my best to help Troy, but sometimes things just weren't meant to be.

I didn't want Mum to know I was considering ending things at this stage. I needed to give this a lot of thought, and I didn't want her to get her hopes up until I'd made my decision. If Troy sensed he was losing control over me and that I was planning to break up with him, I knew his behaviour would become even more extreme.

Our earlier conversation was playing on my mind. Mum had said, 'they sound like his words coming out of your mouth.' Suddenly, it was like somebody had switched on a light; Mum was always trying to convince me to end things with him, but I'd been reluctant to take the next step. Now I realised that Troy had got so far inside my head that he'd brainwashed me into repeating everything he fed me in parrot-fashion. He'd stolen my voice and, in the process, he'd made me powerless.

Now that the penny had dropped, I felt ready to start planning a future that didn't include my boyfriend. But a large stumbling block stood in my way. I wouldn't be able to stay in Sheffield. If I ended things, I'd have to put some distance between us permanently and leave everything and everyone I'd ever known, in order to be safe. That would be a huge sacrifice on my part. But even if I managed to find the strength to pack my bags and leave, Troy was never going to let me walk away easily. I was scared he'd come after me and I hated the idea of having to start again all alone.

I was only going to have one opportunity, so there'd be no margin for error. Ending my relationship with Troy would be dangerous. I couldn't let him find out what I was planning. There was no telling what he might do. Before I started developing an escape strategy, I'd have to do my homework. I was going to need specialist support to enable me to leave.

8

Abbie

'So, what did you take away from the scene?' I asked as we drove back to the station.

This was the first case I'd worked on with Ed, so I was still trying to gauge the measure of the man.

'The men who stole the money weren't opportunistic. The raid had been well planned,' Ed replied.

I agreed with my partner but felt his observations fell short. To the untrained eye, the warehouse that housed millions of pounds worth of cash looked like just another airport hangar containing freight being stored before it embarked on its onward journey. The thieves we were looking for were efficient and well organised, but there was no doubt in my mind they'd had detailed inside information to assist them with the heist.

'It's very likely that one or more of the people on duty in the warehouse when the robbery took place were in on the theft,' I said.

'Do you really think the inside source was that close to home?' Ed questioned.

I nodded. 'Yes, I do.'

'Surely they wouldn't be that obvious.'

Ed threw me a look over his shoulder. I didn't like his tone or his attitude, but we were still sizing each other up at this stage, so it was probably natural that he was challenging me to see how much he could get away with. He'd soon find out; I didn't take crap from anyone. I had zero tolerance for people questioning my authority.

'If my hunch is wrong, then the tip-off must have come from somebody else who worked for the airline and held a position of trust. Whichever way you look at it, a person with privileged information has abused their status,' I said.

'The thought of somebody you worked alongside each day putting your life in danger by pulling a stunt like that is unbelievable. You have to put your trust in members of your team, but it just goes to show how devious some people can be,' Ed said.

'Especially where money's concerned. Light-fingered staff cost their employers millions. You can't really trust anyone; you have to keep an eye on them at all times. The security at the warehouse was so lax this job was asking to happen. When an opportunity presents itself like this, you'd be surprised by how many employees would take it.'

I turned to look at Ed when we pulled up at a set of traffic lights. I expected him to trust me implicitly, even though I couldn't say the same about him. I had no reason to. Ed was giving off overly cautious vibes and questioning my theories.

'I'm amazed that in this digital age, banks still ship cash

across the globe via commercial airlines as cargo. You'd have thought they'd have more sophisticated systems in place to move money around,' Ed said.

'Airports have cutting edge security systems and cameras that monitor passengers' every move inside the terminal buildings. It beggars belief that the same doesn't apply on the outside.'

I looked away just as the lights were about to turn green.

'I thought the warehouse had CCTV?' Ed queried as I drove off.

'It did, but the robbers were wearing masks, so the footage isn't going to be terribly helpful,' I replied.

'Where do you think we should concentrate our efforts?' Ed asked.

'We'll start by questioning the men on duty at the time of the heist. Then we'll extend our inquiries to staff that work in that area but were rostered off. We shouldn't rule out former employees that would have known about the practices the airline had in place. Our robbers knew that a pallet-load of cash would be in that building at that moment in time. And they didn't pull that information out of thin air.'

Ed nodded before he opened up his notebook and scribbled something down on a blank page.

'Judging by the amount of money left behind and the fact that a two-man team executed the robbery, my guess would be we're dealing with small-time crooks. But having said that, we shouldn't ignore the possibility that this could be the work of a criminal organisation. They often recruit company employees to gain information about sensitive shipments such as this. Even though they only stole a fraction of the shipment, it still amounts to a huge sum of cash,' I said.

'At least the robbers didn't turn violent and hurt anyone. They were only interested in the money,' Ed pointed out.

'I suppose it's some consolation that no shots were fired, and nobody was injured. But I doubt that will soften the blow for British Airways and the bank that's now several million pounds worse off.'

'They'll have insurance to cover the money that was taken, though,' Ed replied.

I didn't bother to answer him. Ed was a regular know-it-all, and his attitude was well and truly grating on my nerves. I couldn't wait to get back to the station so that I could get away from him for a while. We were the victims of a personality clash, but we'd both been assigned to this case, so we'd have to learn to work together to make a balanced partnership. Workplace conflict was stressful and unpleasant, so Ed better get his act together, or I'd be forced to make his life hell.

I had to admit, I wasn't much of a team player. I like to set the pace on an investigation and expected subordinate officers to follow my lead. He was entitled to have his own opinions as long as he kept them to himself and didn't try to muscle in on the way I was handling things. Ed was struggling to get to grips with the dynamics of our working relationship. Anyone could see he was desperate to take the reins, but I was the senior officer, so he needed to back off, or I'd be forced to pull rank. As usual, I was having to prove myself more than a male colleague would in the same situation. It was just as well I was good at my job.

'Once we get back to the station, I'll get you to complete

a crime report while I try and pin the airline down and find out exactly how much cash our thieves made off with,' I said, glancing briefly at my partner.

I didn't try to hide the hint of a smile playing on my lips. I hated filling in mundane paperwork, as Ed would soon find out. It was my prerogative to assign him work, so he was going to find himself on the receiving end of all the shitty aspects that didn't interest me. I'd cream off all the best bits for myself. That would teach him to get on the wrong side of me, and if his attitude didn't improve soon, things would get a whole lot worse.

I could see Ed scribbling in his pad again out of the corner of my eye. He was too much of an eager beaver for my liking, and I got the distinct impression that he'd like to trip me up the first chance he got. But I'd worked in a male-dominated profession long enough to know that when you had shoulder-length blonde hair and a pair of breasts, your job performance was always under the microscope.

It would take more than a man like Ed to topple me from my throne. I couldn't take him seriously. He bore a striking resemblance to a grown-up, slightly overweight version of Harry Potter. His dark brown hair was cut into a bowl and swept to one side, and he wore a set of round glasses perched on his nose. If I'd been a die-hard fan of the series, I would have been filled with nostalgia right about now, but sadly sorcery, wands and wizardry weren't my cup of tea at all.

9

Lola

I'd just placed the last spoonful of muesli into my mouth when the doorbell rang.

'No prizes for guessing who that is,' Mum said, pushing her chair back from the table.

'I'll go; I want Troy to see the bruising is worse than it was yesterday.'

Mum sat back down, accepting defeat. As I approached the front door, I rearranged my dressing gown, pulling it tighter around me with the aid of the fabric tie.

'I was just on my way to work and wanted to drop these off,' Troy smiled, holding another huge bouquet towards me.

'Thanks,' I replied, taking the flowers out of his hand.

My tone was polite, but I was secretly fantasising about ramming my fist into his perfect white teeth. Where had that come from? I was taken aback by my desire to lash out at him for once. I'd been suppressed for so long it had taken me by surprise. I knew in my heart I'd reached the point of no return. His jealousy was always going to cause problems between us and I'd taken as much as I was willing to take. My mind was made up; Troy would never raise his hand to me again.

'How are you feeling?' Troy asked.

'I've had better days.'

My response seemed to take him off guard, and Troy suddenly seemed keen to put an end to his visit.

'I'll pop in on my way back from work.' Troy stooped to kiss me on the cheek, and I flinched.

After his lips touched my skin, he turned around and walked down the path without giving me a backwards glance. I didn't wait to wave him off when he got into his car. Instead, I closed the door and headed back into the warmth of the kitchen. A new me was starting to emerge now that I'd decided to leave.

'We've got more flowers than Kew Gardens. You shouldn't keep accepting those,' Mum said, eyeing the beautiful blooms with disgust. 'It gives him the wrong idea. He thinks he can beat you to a pulp one day and then win you over the next by showering you with gifts.'

I could feel another lecture coming on, and I wasn't in the mood for it, especially as Mum's words had finally got through to me, and she'd managed to make me see sense.

'I don't want to do anything that might make him suspicious, so I'm behaving in the way I normally would,' I began.

'Suspicious about what?' Mum questioned, narrowing her eyes.

'I had a long hard think last night, and I've decided I'm going to finish with him.'

I felt my shoulders lift as the words left my mouth.

Mum's hands flew up and covered her mouth, and she let out a gasp. Then she jumped up from her seat and rushed around the table to where I was sitting.

'Thank God, Lola. You don't know how happy you've just made me,' Mum said, and her voice cracked with emotion.

I had to look away when I saw her hazel eyes mist with tears. Otherwise, I was going to turn into a blubbering wreck.

'I know you won't want me to do this, but we need to take photos of your injuries before they fade, just in case you need to prove what Troy did to you at a later stage. Treat the pictures as an insurance policy. If you have them, you won't ever need to use them,' Mum said.

She reached for her phone and began clicking away, capturing images of my face from every angle before I had a chance to protest.

'Can you take off your dressing gown so that I can see the marks on your body?' Mum asked without making eye contact with me.

I unfastened the tie on my grey fleece robe and let it slide from my shoulders. Then I lifted the hem of my pyjama top so that she could photograph the bruising around my ribcage.

'You're absolutely smothered in marks,' Mum said as she finished off taking photos of my battered arms.

As her eyes swept over me, I couldn't help noticing the lines on her forehead seemed deeper than usual. My relationship was taking its toll on her health too. She was so stressed out by my situation that I decided then and there to picture the look on her face any time I doubted going through with the breakup.

'This isn't going to be easy; I'm going to need you to help me,' I said.

'I'll be with you every step of the way,' Mum replied, squeezing my hand in a show of support.

'Once I break up with Troy, I won't be able to stay in Yorkshire.' My eyes filled with tears.

'I know that, but you can start again somewhere new,' Mum replied.

'Where would I go?'

The idea of relocating filled me with dread. I'd lived in Sheffield all my life and wasn't exactly well travelled. I'd only been abroad on a couple of occasions, once with the school to Rome when I was fourteen, and last year Troy and I went to Ibiza for a week.

Just the thought of that holiday made me shudder; it had turned into a nightmare. Being blonde, fair-skinned and green-eyed, I was never going to go home with a tan, and I got burned on the first day. Things went downhill steadily. Troy and I weren't used to spending every minute of every day together, and we'd done nothing but argue since we'd got off the plane. At the beginning of the week, I'd been wearing trousers and long-sleeved tops to protect my skin from the sun. Having to cover up in forty-degree heat was utterly miserable, but things were about to get so much worse. By the time our holiday was coming to an end, I was hiding a lot more than peeling, sunburnt skin.

Troy had never been physically abusive to me before that holiday. He had an explosive temper and would throw things around the room and smash up my belongings, but that was where it ended. Being in each other's space twenty-four-seven made our relationship deteriorate, and he started becoming aggressive, pushing and shoving me around. Things soon got out of control, and Troy progressed to punching and kicking me, covering my body with bruises. None of the marks were where other people could see them. I couldn't help feeling that was a deliberate move on his part. I didn't know how to handle the situation, so I kept it to myself. I was embarrassed to tell anyone what had happened to me.

'What about London,' Mum suddenly suggested, breaking the silence.

The sound of her voice brought me back to reality.

'London's a long way from here,' I replied. My shoulders began to sag.

'Exactly, and it's a big place, so it would be easy for you to disappear. There's plenty of work too, so it shouldn't be hard to get a job.'

Mum's face broke into a reassuring smile as she tried to paint a picture that the city's streets were paved with gold.

'Will you come with me.' I looked at mum with pleading eyes.

'I can't.' Mum shook her head.

'Why not? You've got nothing to stay here for.'

I was the only family mum had. My grandparents were long gone, and my dad had lost his battle against lung cancer eleven years ago when I was thirteen. Mum had an older brother, but he lived in Australia, and she hadn't seen him for twenty years.

'What about the house? And my job? I can't just up and leave,' Mum said, offering me a choice of excuses.

I let out a long sigh. So much for being with me every step of the way.

'Why don't you put the house on the market? You'll easily find work in London too. Good cleaners are hard to come by,' I smiled.

'I'm sorry, Lola, I can't. I'm too old to start again. It's different for you; you've got your whole life in front of you.'

'You're fifty years old, Mum; you're not exactly on the scrap heap.'

Mum had a small-town mentality. She never moved outside of the local vicinity, let alone venture further afield than that. Living in Yorkshire, we were blessed with beautiful countryside and coastline on our doorstep, but that didn't mean a person should confine themselves to staying within the county lines. There was a big world out there waiting to be explored. If I could convince Mum to be by my side, I knew I'd be willing to take the next step. But if I had to go it alone, I wasn't sure I would be brave enough to see it through.

'At least think about it before you write off my suggestion.' I left Mum alone to mull over what I'd said.

10

Paul

Finn, Mark and I were sitting at the small wooden table in the kitchen area, beers in hand, when a shadow appeared in front of the obscured glass panel of the door.

Mark pushed his chair back and walked across to the half-glazed UPVC front door. Kevin was standing on the other side.

'What time do you call this?' Mark asked, shaking his head.

'Sorry I'm late. Work was manic. I got away as soon as I could,' Kevin replied.

'Well, you're here now at least.' Mark turned on his heel, and Kevin followed him inside.

'Hurry up and close the door. You're letting all the heat out. It's freezing in here,' Finn griped.

He was sitting inches away from a small electric heater which, admittedly, was doing a poor job of warming the open-plan interior. The chalet needed modernising to bring it into the twenty-first century, but Mark's parents didn't think it was worth the hassle or the cost involved for the limited amount of weeks holidaymakers resided in it. They didn't seem to grasp the concept of spending money to make money. I'd offered my services on the cheap, but they'd turned me down, citing the place was a money pit. I disagreed. Adding all the mod cons and smartening the interior up would work wonders for their bookings, but I'd resigned myself to the fact that the much-needed makeover was never going to happen. Some investment this place turned out to be, I thought.

'Don't be such a pussy,' Kevin replied.

'I was beginning to think you'd come back here while we were all at work, cleared out the money and done a bunk,' I laughed.

'Now, why didn't I think of that?' Kevin replied with a smile on his face.

'Because you're as dopey as fuck,' I joked.

Mark and Finn fell about laughing.

Kevin stepped behind me with the skill of a ninja and slipped the crook of his arm around my throat, tightening his hold until I tapped him on the forearm.

'Now who's the dopey one? You didn't see that coming, did you?'

'I knew what you were up to, but I was just humouring you, letting you think you had the upper hand,' I replied.

'Yeah, right,' Kevin smiled.

'There's beer in the fridge. Help yourself,' Mark said, interrupting our sibling rivalry.

Kevin opened the under-counter fridge and took out a bottle of Heineken. Then he reached across the table for the bottle opener, snapped off the lid and took a large swig.

He placed his bottle down on the table and took a seat in the last remaining chair.

'It's been a long day. I can't wait until I can hand my notice in,' Kevin sighed.

'I think we all feel the same,' Finn replied.

'Now that we're all here, let's get down to business,' Mark said. 'Give us a hand to get the panel off the bath.'

I got up from the table and followed Mark as he walked out of the living area; Kevin and Finn trailed along behind me. It was a bit of a squeeze with the four of us in the bathroom, but Mark soon had the side off of the bath, and he passed the bags out to us.

As I walked back into the living area, I stopped by the full-length windows to check that the floor to ceiling curtains were fully closed. We didn't want any peeping Toms getting wind of what was going on inside the chalet.

Mark was the last to take a seat at the table. 'Let's count each bag in turn,' he suggested before tipping the contents of one of the holdalls out in front of us.

Kevin and I had cut open the ultra-strong vacuum parcels containing the fifty-pound notes while we were in the boat to remove the tracking devices. At the time, my nerves were on edge, and my body was flooded with adrenalin, so I didn't really take in just how much cash we'd got away with. But judging by the amount in this one bag, we'd helped ourselves to a small fortune. Not bad for a bunch of amateurs with little criminal experience.

'Each one of these parcels should contain the same amount,' Mark said, lifting the first pile of cash out of the bag.

After rechecking he'd counted it correctly three times,

we were gobsmacked to find each bundle contained one hundred notes.

'There's five grand in this pile alone. And there are ten of these in each bag.' I could see Mark totting it up in his head. 'That means every parcel contains fifty thousand pounds.'

Finn blew out a whistle.

It was no wonder the banks weighed money or used counting machines to do this labour-intensive job. It was going to take us forever to get through all the piles, but you wouldn't hear any of us complaining.

Once all the cash was counted, we sat around the table in silence, lost in our own thoughts. Kevin and I had excelled ourselves and had surpassed all our expectations. We'd lifted a cool ten million from the warehouse, far more than we'd ever thought possible.

'That was a productive couple of hours work,' I grinned before I took a celebratory slug of my beer. 'I nearly shit a brick when that police dinghy passed us while we were cruising along.'

Mark had been behind the wheel of the inflatable boat as we'd begun to make our way up the Thames, waiting for Finn to give us the nod.

'Tell me about it,' Kevin replied. 'I could have done with a change of underwear.'

'For one horrible minute, I thought we were going to get nicked before we'd had a chance to lift the money,' Mark laughed.

'I'm not surprised they rattled you, but those dinghies fly up and down the river all the time. God knows what they're doing. They never seem to be going anywhere,' Finn piped up.

'Tell me about it. We saw one on the way back too. Kevin and I nearly tossed this lot over the side,' I said, running my hand over a pile of money.

'You two were brilliant, by the way.' Finn beamed with pride.

'Thanks,' Kevin and I both replied.

'It's good to see all the planning has paid off,' Mark said, holding his beer bottle out in front of him for us all to clink.

'Yeah, how lucky were we? The whole thing went without a hitch,' I agreed.

'Even though I knew what was coming, my heart started pounding when you two burst into the warehouse,' Finn said. 'Poor old Stan, I thought he was going to have a coronary when you pointed the gun at him.'

'I felt terrible doing it, but I had to play the part,' I replied.

'I know you did. It was bad enough for me, and we'd been over the plan loads of times, so I knew exactly how things were going to play out. I never expected to be so scared when the robbery was happening in real-time. God knows how the rest of them felt; you two were very convincing,' Finn said.

'That's good to know because I was shitting myself,' I laughed.

'So was I,' Kevin agreed.

'Well, it didn't show,' Finn smiled.

'Waiting on the water wasn't exactly a laugh a minute either. It was the longest fifteen minutes of my life. I tried to make it look like I was tinkering with the boat, but there's only so long you can pretend to be fixing the engine before some helpful soul offers to give you a hand,' Mark chipped in.

'I can't believe we actually managed to pull this off.' My grin stretched from ear to ear.

'I know, we've been talking constantly about it for a year,' Mark said.

'Stealing the money was almost too easy. Spending it without getting caught will be more difficult,' Finn added.

'The last thing any of us should do is start spending the money,' Kevin said. 'We don't want to draw attention to ourselves. We need to lie low and carry on the way we normally would.'

My brother was right. It was common sense. But I knew I was going to struggle to keep my hands off of my share.

'I told Mum and Dad the place could do with a freshen up before the start of the season to give me an excuse to stay here. The dosh should be safe enough, but somebody should keep an eye on it just in case,' Mark said. 'Why don't you come over tomorrow after work, and we can have a few beers?'

11

Lola

'Have you given any thought to putting the house on the market?' I casually dropped in while we were eating dinner.

Mum looked up from her plate of sausage and mash. She stared at me while she continued to chew, and after what seemed like an eternal pause, she began to speak.

'No, I haven't.'

'Why not?' I quizzed, hoping to put some pressure on her.

'I've already told you, Lola, I'm too old to start again.'

I shook my head. I couldn't believe Mum was trying to talk me into relocating on my own to a huge city like London when she could easily go with me. The thought of leaving without her was daunting.

'Aren't you even slightly worried about packing me off to the big smoke on my own?'

'Of course I'm concerned for your safety. That's why I want you to leave Sheffield. It's the only way to put an end to this. If I suddenly put the house on the market, Troy will get wind of it. You know what people are like around here; they gossip about nothing.'

Much as I didn't want to admit it, Mum had a point. Our neighbours were full-time curtain twitchers, and news travelled fast when you didn't want it to.

'This is never going to work. Even if I did manage to get away without Troy realising, I'd never be able to relax and would always be looking over my shoulder.' My voice wavered as I finished my sentence.

'You have to approach this with a positive attitude,' Mum advised.

'That's easy for you to say. I'll be taking this step on my own, and the thought of that terrifies me. I desperately want to break up with Troy, but I'm not sure I can go through with it if it means I have to leave everyone and everything important in my life behind.' My lip wobbled; I was on the verge of bursting into tears.

'You have to stay strong, Lola. You're the most self-reliant young woman I know; that will stand you in good stead in the future. You've got your dad to thank for that. Right now, you've got into such a rut the quality's become redundant, but once you break free from Troy and harness its full potential, it will be a powerful tool. You're not the only woman that's found themselves in a position like this. You won't be on your own. There's help available, but you have to ask for it.' Mum reached over the table and squeezed my hand.

'I wouldn't know where to start.' My shoulders sagged, I felt utterly defeated, and the battle hadn't even begun.

'Maybe not, but that's where I come in.'

Mum didn't usually mince her words, but she seemed to be skirting around what she wanted to say.

'What do you mean?' I didn't have the energy to play guessing games.

'I know you're not going to be happy about this, but when I realised Troy was hitting you, I rang a women's refuge for some advice.'

Mum's words bounced off every wall in the kitchen. I was shocked that she'd gone behind my back.

'Don't look at me like that. I had no choice. You were in complete denial about the situation, and I was at my wits' end. The lady I spoke to was lovely. She said to tell you that there's a twenty-four-hour helpline you can contact in confidence.'

Troy knew all my passwords and pins. He checked my emails and texts and stalked me on social media.

'I need to get a new mobile and fast.'

The bruising hadn't started to fade yet, but once it did, he'd expect me to go back to work, and I'd have lost my opportunity to break free.

'Use my phone to make the initial call,' Mum said, handing it across the table to me. 'At least you'll get the wheels in motion, and in the meantime, I'll pop out and pick up a pay as you go handset for you from Argos. They'll still be open.'

'I'll be back in a minute,' I said, getting up from the table.

'You've barely touched your dinner,' Mum said.

'I'm not hungry.'

My stomach was a ball of nerves, so there was no way I could eat.

Before I made the fateful call, I typed the word refuge into Google, and the definition brought tears to my eyes. It said a refuge was a safe house for women and children escaping domestic violence. As a woman fleeing an abusive partner, I was able to seek shelter from any local authority even if I didn't live in the local area. The address of the hostel was confidential, and no men were allowed in the building. My mind was made up. I knew right then and there I had to dial the number. My call was answered straight away by a member of the support team. She was very sympathetic and listened intently while I explained the situation.

'Would you like me to search for current vacancies and arrange a space for you?' the lady asked.

I felt myself freeze, but I knew what I had to do.

'Yes, please,' I replied.

'Can you give me a telephone number that I can call you back on when accommodation has been found for you?'

I reeled off Mum's number before I ended the call.

'The refuge are going to phone me when they've found me a space.' Tears sprang into my eyes, and I sniffed to hold them back.

'Don't cry, love, or you'll start me off.'

I paced around the kitchen floor while Mum was at Argos. I couldn't seem to sit still. She'd just walked through the door and was taking her coat off when her mobile began to ring.

'Hello.' My voice sounded hesitant.

'Hello. I'm just phoning to tell you that we have secured a place at a refuge for you.'

I swallowed hard as the lady on the other end's words registered.

'I need to find out how you're going to get to the accommodation.'

I felt panic rise up inside me. I'd been so focused on taking the first step that I hadn't given the practical side of the move a moment's thought.

'I'm not sure.'

I felt like a complete idiot.

'That's okay,' the lady reassured. 'I know I've put you on the spot, so I'll give you some time to think about it. You need to choose a safe time to leave so that your partner doesn't suspect anything is out of the ordinary. Are you likely to want your space tonight?'

'I hadn't realised things would happen this quickly, so I still need to pack. Can you hold my place until tomorrow, please? That will give me time to get my stuff together and arrange a train.'

I would soon discover the refuge would offer me so much more than a place to stay.

12

Abbie

British Airways had confirmed that ten million pounds was stolen during the warehouse heist. The theft of so much cash was a big story, and it made it on to the news, which would potentially bring us some new leads. We weren't offering a reward for information at this stage because that always triggered an influx of interest from the public. Some of the calls would be good, but most of them would be useless. We might have to resort to that if the investigation didn't start to gather momentum.

It was frustrating beyond belief. Ed and I had very little to go on; the only solid fact we had was that two men had held up the staff before making off with a large amount of money. We didn't have anything conclusive. I doubted the forensic team would find any fingerprint evidence to link our robbers to the crime. And the news had just come through that the CCTV cameras had been very conveniently disabled on the day of the robbery, so they hadn't captured any footage. We knew the thieves had been wearing balaclavas, so I hadn't been pinning too much hope on what the cameras had captured, but any insight into how the robbery had unfolded would have been better than none.

'Let's bring all the members of staff that were on duty at the time of the theft in for questioning,' I said.

Once we'd conducted interviews with the witnesses, we could narrow down which of them, if any, were potential suspects. Ed and I both had a civic duty to prevent crime and catch offenders. In my experience, most lawbreakers became anxious and fidgety at the first sign of police interest. Very few could hide their unease and hold their nerve. They started to sweat, their pupils dilated, and their heart rate went up, giving the game away. There would be no cutting corners. We were going to get to the bottom of this.

13

Lola

I stood on the doorstep and watched as Troy drove away, hoping that would be the last time I'd ever have to see his face.

'Now that he's done the rounds, you'd better go and get dressed,' Mum said from the kitchen doorway the minute I closed the front door.

Troy had taken to stopping by every morning on his way to work to check on my progress. He'd be back again this evening on his way home, which left me a window to make my escape. I'd had no idea how I was going to be able to pull this off until Mum suggested I contact a shelter for abused women. From the moment I'd made the call, it was all systems go, which was a good thing because I hadn't had time to talk myself out of it.

I ran up the stairs two at a time, dashed into my bedroom and pulled on the clothes I'd selected. I was dressed head to toe in black, hoping to blend into obscurity. I grabbed the handle of my suitcase and carried it down the stairs. Mum was waiting at the bottom, car keys in hand.

'All set?' she asked.

I nodded. I didn't trust myself to speak in case I burst into tears.

'Let's get a move on; you don't want to miss your train.'

Mum turned on her heel and walked out of the front door. I grabbed my black puffer jacket off the coat stand and then pulled a black bobble hat over my messy bun to hide my hair. Thankfully it was bright and sunny, so my dark sunglasses wouldn't look out of place. They'd serve two purposes. I wanted to hide my bruises and travel incognito. I was worried I might bump into somebody at the station who'd recognise me and start asking awkward questions, exposing my plan before I had a chance to put it into place.

As Mum and I sat in silence on the journey, I kept my eyes fixed on the windscreen. I didn't want to look at her and risk the chance of falling to pieces. We'd agreed last night we weren't going to have a long, drawn-out goodbye; it would only make parting more painful for both of us. Anyway, it was only a temporary measure. Once I was settled, Mum had promised to come down to London and spend some time with me, so I would focus on that to help me stay strong.

Mum had a smile pasted on her face, but when she parked the car outside the station, I saw it disappear. The corners of her mouth had turned down, and her bottom lip was wobbling. She'd left the engine idling so that she could make a quick getaway and was now gripping the steering wheel with white knuckles, resisting the urge to cry with all her might.

'I'd better go, or I'll be late for work,' Mum said.

She wasn't due to start her shift for almost half an hour, so I knew that wasn't true. I'd been hoping she might offer to wait with me for a little while, but it was probably better this way. It wouldn't have taken much for me to talk myself out of this.

'Phone me when you get there,' she said without turning to look at me.

'I will,' I replied before I leaned across and placed a kiss on her cheek. 'Thanks for everything. I love you, Mum.'

'I love you too,' Mum replied. Silent tears rolled down her cheeks as I closed the passenger door.

When the car began to pull away from the kerb, I started pacing towards the entrance without looking back. I wasn't short of time, but I couldn't bear to see the look on my mum's face. This wasn't just hard for me; she was suffering too.

I had three-quarters of an hour to kill before my train departed, so I decided to go and get a takeaway coffee from Starbucks. I lifted the paper cup off the counter, and as I turned around, I nearly jumped out of my skin. My heart started hammering in my chest when I came face to face with Ken, one of the regulars at William Hill.

'Sorry, love, I didn't mean to scare you. I thought you were going to throw your drink all over yourself for one minute. I'm not that ugly, am I?' he joked.

He was a nice old guy and seemed concerned that he'd startled me, but I couldn't afford to reply to him in case he recognised my voice, so instead, I smiled at him before I hot-footed it out of Starbucks, dragging my case behind me. I felt rude, but I couldn't take any chances.

My pulse was still pounding when I took a seat at an empty bench in a quiet corner of the station. I could see Starbucks from where I was sitting, and as I was mulling over what had just happened, I saw Ken leave the café, cup in hand and walk out of the exit. I was pretty sure I'd got away with it. Ken knew me by name, so he was bound to have struck up a conversation with me if he'd recognised me.

I was beginning to wish I'd made my own way to the station now instead of accepting a lift from Mum. She'd had to drop me off early before she made her way to work, but all this hanging around was playing havoc with my nerves. The longer I was here, the greater the chance I'd bump into somebody I knew. Mum and I lived in a small village on the outskirts of Sheffield, but I worked at William Hill in the town centre. The branch was open seven days a week, from 8.30 a.m. until 10 p.m. When you spent long hours with your customers, you got to know them on first name terms, which, up until now, hadn't been an issue, but I'd already had one near-miss, and I was terrified of having another.

I checked the time on my watch. My train was due to leave in fifteen minutes, so I started to make my way to platform five as it was some distance from where I'd been sitting. As I tried to negotiate the crowd of people milling aimlessly around trailing trolley cases after them, I caught sight of a tall man with a shaved head and a blond beard at the other side of the station forcing his way through the throng. I was almost too scared to take another look.

My heart started racing, and a gasp escaped from my lips when I realised that Troy was weaving his way along the concourse, his strong neck extended like a periscope as his eyes scanned the crowd. I felt as though the walls of the huge space were suddenly closing in on me. How the hell did he know I was at the station? Ken must have recognised me after all and tipped him off. I should have known this was never going to work.

I attempted to run through the packed forecourt, with my head down, changing direction frequently, to avoid being spotted. The slow-moving pedestrians seemed to have no other purpose than getting in my way. Troy was closing in on me, I was terrified he was going to pick me out in the swarm, but I finally managed to find the right platform and push my way through the barrier.

I didn't waste time looking for the right carriage, I jumped on board so that I'd be out of sight. Once I found my seat, I slumped down in it, keeping back from the window while I tried to catch my breath. My mouth was so dry it was hard to swallow, but I needed to phone Mum. She'd know what to do.

I pulled my new mobile out of my jacket pocket and quickly punched in Mum's phone number. 'Troy's at the station,' I said when she answered the call. The words tumbled out of my mouth.

'I can tell you're frightened, but try and stay calm. Where are you?' Mum asked.

'I'm on the train, but he's searching the concourse looking for me.'

'It'll be okay. It's a busy station, and your train's about to leave,' Mum replied.

'I'm scared.'

'Don't be. He's not going to find you…'

14

Paul

'I've been asked to go to the police station to give a formal statement,' Finn casually dropped in.

We'd been sitting around the small table in the chalet at the time, sipping cold beers.

'Do you think they suspect you had something to do with the heist?' I asked.

Finn shrugged. 'I doubt it. The copper said it was just routine. Everyone on duty when the money was nicked has been asked to go to the cop shop.'

'I'd be wary about attending a police interview without a solicitor. You won't know what to say and what not to say, so you might accidentally incriminate yourself,' I replied, feeling nervous for him. 'What if they trick you into admitting to something?'

'They won't. I'll be careful,' Finn said.

He was a natural-born bullshitter, so if anyone could pull this off, he could. Lying came as naturally to him as breathing.

66

'If they haven't arrested you, they can't force you to talk,' I said, hoping he'd reconsider.

'It's going to look like I've got something to hide if I kick up about this. Especially when everyone else trots in to give their account. And anyway, Stan was saying if we don't go in voluntarily, the coppers might decide to come and arrest us and take us back to the station so they can conduct the interview. I know which one I'd rather.'

I felt my brow furrow as I considered what Finn had said.

'Stop panicking, mate. Everything's going to be fine. If the police lined all of the warehouse staff up in a row and questioned us, Stan would definitely be the one they'd suspect. Seriously, I'm not making this up.'

That was Finn's go-to sentence. I'd heard him utter those words countless times before. He was doing his best to reassure me, but I had a bad feeling about this.

15

Lola

Tears of pure relief rolled down my cheeks as the train started to pull out of the station while I watched Troy scouring the packed concourse for any sign of me. Although I'd been terrified he was going to spot me, it was clearly like looking for a needle in a haystack.

'It's me,' I said when Mum answered the call. My voice came out in a sob. I didn't want to worry her, but I couldn't help myself. 'I'm sorry to phone you at work, but it's important.'

'What's happened? Has Troy spotted you?' Mum asked with more than a hint of panic coating her words.

'No, I managed to get away. The train's just left the station, and he's still rushing up and down the platform like a headless chicken trying to find me.'

'Thank God.' Mum let out a sigh of relief. 'I told you there was nothing to worry about.'

Mum was trying to portray a confidence I knew she

wasn't feeling, but I appreciated the fact that she was doing her best to give me a boost.

'When he finally gives up looking for me, he's going to come to the house to find out what's going on,' I said.

I knew Mum would already have worked that out for herself, but I felt obliged to mention it.

'Don't worry, Lola. I'm not going to tell him anything.'

'I know you won't, but I'm scared of what he might do to you.'

Troy would be absolutely furious when he realised I'd left, and there was a very real possibility that he'd take his anger out on my mum.

'He's not going to do anything to me because I won't be answering the door to him. I'm sorry, love, but I'm going to have to go. I'm not trying to cut you off, but I'm not allowed to take personal calls. Can I phone you later when I finish work?'

'Of course. But, Mum, please be careful.'

'I will,' she replied as she ended the call.

It was a blessing that Mum didn't have a set workplace; she went where the cleaning agency sent her, and that could vary on a daily basis. Some of the jobs were regular and set in stone, but others were ad hoc. At least that was one less thing to worry about; my thuggish ex wasn't going to be able to turn up at her job and threaten her in front of her colleagues.

I hadn't intentionally brought trouble to my mum's door. But it was obvious that Troy would try to get to me through her, which was one of the reasons I'd wanted to talk her into coming with me. That and the fact that we were incredibly close. She meant the world to me; we had a wonderful relationship.

I hoped Mum was going to be able to stand up to Troy. Even though she was the strongest person I knew, she'd have her work cut out for her. He wouldn't think twice about resorting to violence if he got the opportunity to force the information he wanted out of her.

As the train picked up speed, I tore my eyes away from the window and loosened the grip on my case. I'd only just realised I was still clinging on to it and had my backpack in place. I hadn't wanted to let go of my luggage in case I'd had to make a run for it. Everyone in the carriage was engrossed in their own business, so nobody seemed to notice. I slipped my arms out of the straps and placed my rucksack on the seat next to me. Then I walked over to the shelving and lifted my case on to it.

It was going to be a long journey, I had over two hours to kill, so I might as well use them wisely. I settled down in my seat, then unzipped my backpack and took out my laptop. Now was as good a time as any to start applying for jobs. I had a small amount of savings, but they wouldn't last long if I kept dipping into them. I was pleasantly surprised by what I saw when I began scrolling through a recruitment agency's website. The money was good compared to what I was used to, but I knew there was a reason for that. The cost of living was so much higher in London than in Sheffield. I couldn't believe my luck when I managed to secure a room at a women's hostel. There was no way I was going to be able to afford to rent a flat. I'd be sleeping under the arches if I wasn't careful, but the streets were no place for a woman.

I'd switched off my old mobile before I'd left the house

so that Troy couldn't contact me. I'd also turned off the geo-location settings. I didn't want my ex to use them to find out where I was. He'd be going ballistic by now, but there was no way I was going to be brave enough to switch my phone back on and listen to the countless texts and voicemails I knew he'd have left me. The only reason I'd brought it with me was I'd left in such a hurry I hadn't had a chance to transfer my contacts over to my new phone yet.

I'd only just packed away my laptop when the train pulled into King's Cross right on time. It was my first time in London, and I was sure I'd have been excited if the circumstances had been different. But my stomach was twisting and turning as I struggled to suppress my nerves. I'd expected the station to be busy, but when I stepped off of the train, the platform was literally swarming with people. I found myself being swept along on the tide, which felt a bit overwhelming to a Yorkshire lass who'd rarely been out of the county. I swallowed down the urge to cry, reminding myself that northerners were tough; we were made of strong stuff.

Trying to negotiate the London underground when you'd never done it before was a challenge in itself. Once I freed myself from the wall of people, I studied the map crisscrossed by bright colours for a couple of minutes. It was daunting at first, but then the instructions I'd been given started to make sense, and I managed to work out where I was going. I was immensely proud of myself when I not only found the Piccadilly line, but I also managed to get on the tube going in the right direction. I was on a roll, and even though it was a tiny achievement, it felt huge to me and really lifted my spirits. Mum would be proud of me if she could see me now. The thought of that brought a smile to my face. Now all I had to do was get off at the right stop and find my way to the refuge.

I got off the tube at Acton Town and walked the short distance to the women's hostel that was going to be my home for now. It had been easy enough to find the large red brick semi-detached house, which had no visible signs revealing the building was a women's refuge. It looked no different from the other properties on the street apart from the entry panel on the front gate. I was relieved to see the period house had a secure front door and CCTV cameras.

'Here goes,' I said to myself, then I took a deep breath and pressed the buzzer.

'Hello,' a female voice said.

'Hello, I'm Lola Marshall,' I replied.

The gate immediately started to open, and I stepped over the boundary. Then the front door opened, and a woman with brown shoulder-length hair smiled warmly at me.

'I'm Elaine, the refuge manager. Pleased to meet you,' she said, holding her hand out towards me as I drew closer.

As she closed the door behind me, a sense of relief washed over me. Despite the bumpy start, I'd actually made it to safety.

16

Abbie

I hated admitting that almost forty-eight hours had passed and we had no leads. It was time to question the staff, and hopefully, that should kick-start the investigation.

'Thank you for agreeing to come in today. I'm DI Kingsly, and this is DC Lewis. Would you mind if we took a look at your phone? It's a routine procedure,' I asked the young red-haired man sitting in front of me.

'Go ahead,' he replied.

He put his hand in his pocket and retrieved an iPhone before he placed it on the table in front of me.

'Can you tell me what the pin is, sir?' Ed asked before he put the mobile in a clear bag and left the room with it.

'We'll get started in just a moment. I'm going to be recording your statement,' I said, sweeping my shoulder-length wavy hair away from my face.

Microphones would pick up everything said in the room. There were also video cameras installed, recording the actions of all present.

Once Ed reappeared, I turned on the tape and began speaking, recording where the interview was taking place, the date, the time the interview started and the fact that Ed and I were present in the room.

'Please state your full name, address, and date of birth,' I said.

'Finn McCaskill, 15 Trinity Way, Sheerness ME12 1BA, 9 January 1993,' the man replied.

'Thank you. I'd like you to tell me how your day unfolded,' I continued.

'I started the morning with my usual bowl of Frosties,' Finn replied.

Here we go, I thought. We've got a Jack the lad on our hands. I cut him off with a flash of my eyes and fixed him with a look of disdain, daring him to underestimate me.

'Please start your account from when you arrived at work,' I said in case Finn felt the need to share his entire morning routine with us.

'My shift started at six-thirty, and I spent the next half an hour preparing the warehouse for the cargo,' Finn said. 'The BA flight landed on time, and Stan and Norman…'

'Sorry to cut in. Can I just stop you for a moment, please? You said the flight landed on time. Do you recall what time that was?'

I knew the answer to the question, but I wanted to gauge whether Finn's answers were honest or not. That was an interview technique I always used.

'The plane landed at seven o'clock,' Finn replied without hesitation.

'Okay, thank you. Please continue with your account,' I said.

'Stan and Norman went to offload the pallets from the hold like they normally do. When I saw them coming back, I guided the armoured van into position so that we could move the pallets from the back of the van into the warehouse.'

'Does each member of the team have a specific job to do?' I asked.

Finn nodded. 'Yes, we all have our own roles in the operation.'

'Did anything seem different from your usual routine?' I questioned, knowing that the smallest detail could sometimes lead to the break you'd been waiting for.

Finn shook his head. 'No, everything was the same as it always is.'

'Who was driving the van?' I asked.

'Norman.'

'What happened after he'd backed the van up to the loading doors?'

'We use a forklift to put the pallets into position at the back of the lock-up. Then we take the vacuum bags inside a cage and wait for the security staff from the bank to arrive. We'd only just unloaded the last pallet and closed the double doors when two masked men burst in and threatened us with guns.'

'What can you tell me about the men?'

Finn shrugged. 'Not a lot really. They were both wearing black balaclavas, so I couldn't see their faces.'

I had to suppress a smile when I glanced over and saw the look of disappointment on Ed's face. He was leaning over his notebook, pen in hand, poised and ready to capture the case cracking details. I don't know what he'd been expecting Finn to say; we already knew the robbers' faces were covered.

'I believe the men were dressed in British Airways uniforms,' I continued, turning my attention away from my partner.

'Yes, that's right,' Finn confirmed.

'So what happened after the men entered the warehouse?'

'One of them tied us up, and then they both began filling black holdalls with cash from one of the pallets.' Finn cleared his throat.

'Is there anything else you can tell us?'

I rested my elbows on the table and interlocked my fingers while I waited for Finn to respond.

'That's all I can remember; it happened so fast. The men were in and out in a flash.'

'I just have one final question for you, Mr McCaskill. Why is the money taken to the warehouse instead of being transferred directly to the bank?'

'It's a security measure. After the pallets are unloaded from the plane, they're taken to the warehouse, and the vacuum bags are held inside a locked cage. The security firm appointed by the bank send two employees to open the bags and count the cash to ensure that none of it has gone astray on that leg of the journey,' Finn said.

How ironic, I thought.

'Thank you for your time and for answering our questions,' I said before I ended the interview and turned off the recorder.

'No worries,' Finn replied before pushing his chair away from the table.

I glanced at my blush pink crystal-encrusted watch. 'Let's

take a quick break, and then we'll call in the next member of staff,' I said to Ed.

A mug of milky tea later, Ed and I walked back into the interview room. I turned on the tape and went through the motions of recording the necessary information.

'Please state your full name, address, and date of birth,' I said to the older gentleman sitting opposite me.

He lifted his pudgy fingers out of his lap and wiped them across his mouth to remove the beads of sweat that had formed on his upper lip.

'My name is Stanley Harold Brown. I live at 48 Cecil Avenue, Sheerness, ME12 1DX, and my date of birth is 12 August 1956.'

'Please can you tell us what happened after you arrived at work?' I asked.

As soon as Stanley started to give his account, his words ran into each other, and I noticed the pulsating vein throbbing in his temple. His face was flushed, and he was avoiding making eye contact with me, displaying all the classic signs of deception.

Instinct told me this was an inside job, but whoever was responsible, I didn't think it was Stanley. I couldn't work out why he was so nervous. What did he have to hide?

'We asked you to come down to the station to help us with our investigation, but you seem a little agitated,' I said.

'I'm so worried I'm going to lose my job,' Stanley said, looking me straight in the face. It was the first time he'd made eye contact with me since he'd walked into the room.

'Why do you think that might happen?' I asked.

'I was the senior member of staff on duty the day the

money was stolen. So if anyone's going to get the chop, it'll be me,' Stanley replied.

'That doesn't mean the airline will hold you responsible for what happened. You had no choice but to co-operate with the robbers' demands. British Airways won't make you accountable for the loss. They'll know the members of staff on duty will have suffered trauma from the experience. You're entitled to professional counselling. I'd be happy to refer you to a victim support scheme if you'd find that helpful,' I said, hoping I'd put his mind at rest.

'Thank you. Knowing that's taken a weight off my mind,' Stanley said.

'Good. I'm glad.'

'I've been worried sick. I thought they were going to give me my marching orders, and at my age, I'm not likely to be taken on by anyone else, especially if I was sacked.'

Now that Stanley had explained what was bothering him, it was no wonder he wasn't coming across well in the interview. I decided he'd been through enough; he wasn't our man, so I put him out of his misery and rounded off the questioning. Whoever the person on the inside was, one thing was certain, they could lie like a pro.

17

Lola

'Now, first things first, would you like a cup of tea?' Elaine asked when she led me into a bright, white spacious kitchen.

'No, thanks,' I replied.

I had to force the words out; my nerves were getting the better of me. I pasted a smile on my face and hoped it looked more genuine than it felt. Elaine was doing her best to make me feel welcome, so I didn't want to come across as unappreciative.

'Take a seat and make yourself comfortable.' Elaine gestured towards the large table in front of the patio doors.

Dragging my trolley case behind me, I walked across the tiled floor, pulled out a chair and sat down facing the wall. While I waited for Elaine to join me, I glanced out at the garden which had a well-kept lawn framed on either side by wide flower beds. An area at the back had been turned into a children's play area with swings, a climbing frame and a slide. The sight of it made me realise there were people in worse positions than me.

Apart from the kitchen, which was a modern extension added to the rear of the period property, the house still retained many of the original features. The sash windows, cornices and high ceilings gave the place a homely spacious feel.

'So you've come all the way from Sheffield,' Elaine said, looking up from some paperwork. 'How was the journey?' she asked as she put it down on the kitchen table before taking a seat opposite me.

I cast my mind back to the station and felt myself shudder at the thought of what had almost happened.

'It was fine, thank you. My train was on time, and I even managed to work out how to negotiate my way around the London Underground. It was my first time on the tube, and I'm glad to say I survived the experience,' I smiled.

'You deserve a medal for that,' Elaine laughed. 'I remember my first time only too well. I thought I'd never get to my destination, and by the time I arrived, I was close to tears.'

'You're not from London either?'

'No, I'm from Hampshire,' Elaine replied.

I would never have known. Maybe I'd think differently once I'd been living here for a while, but all southern accents sounded the same to me at this stage.

'I'm going to be your key worker while you're here. I'll meet you at least once a week to ensure you're receiving the support you need. Feel free to discuss any concerns you have with me.'

'Thank you,' I replied.

'There's a bit of paperwork we need to fill in before I can show you to your room. It looks like a lot, but they are duplicate contracts. You keep one, and we keep the other. I'll leave you to have a read through it before you sign on the dotted line, and if you've got any questions, just give me a shout; I'll be in my office. It's the glorified broom cupboard to the left of the front door,' Elaine laughed before she walked out of the room.

I picked up the license agreement and started to read the terms and conditions of staying at the refuge. There were rules in place regarding alcohol and drugs to ensure the safety of myself and other residents, which seemed perfectly reasonable to me. There were also codes of conduct that had to be followed to do with the day-to-day running of the house, but again everything looked fine. Residents had to be in by a certain time in the evening so that staff could make sure the refuge was secure for the night. That wasn't going to affect me; it would be a long time before I felt brave enough to venture out at night. I thought implementing quiet times in the house was a good idea. Nobody wanted to be woken up in the early hours of the morning by another resident crashing around. And I wouldn't have any trouble sticking to the rota for the washing machine, I thought with a smile on my face.

I don't know what I'd been expecting, it wasn't as though I was an inmate in prison, but I was pleasantly surprised by the Ts and Cs. When I'd seen Elaine with the sheets of paper, I'd been a bit taken aback and was wondering what I'd let myself in for. But all the refuge wanted was for people to be considerate to others and clean up after themselves. That wasn't too much to ask. And if anyone had a problem with that, they had no business taking a room in a shelter in the first place.

'How are you getting on?' Elaine poked her head around the kitchen door.

I looked up from the paperwork at the sound of her voice. 'That was good timing; I've just finished reading through the last page.'

'Great. Are you happy to sign the license agreement, or is there anything you'd like to ask?'

'No, everything seems quite straightforward,' I said.

I picked up the pen on the table and wrote my signature in the four places the sign here tab indicated. Once I'd finished, Elaine followed suit. She had such a nice way about her; from the moment she opened the front door, she'd instantly put me at ease.

'How many people are living here at the moment?' I asked as I climbed the stairs behind Elaine.

I hadn't seen another soul since I'd arrived, and the house was in silence.

'We're under capacity at the moment. We have spaces for five women and ten children,' Elaine replied without looking back at me.

That didn't really answer my question, but when I thought about it, I was sure her vagueness was down to the fact that she had to protect the other residents' confidentiality.

'I'm sad to say, we're at capacity most of the time, which shows just how many women and children are experiencing domestic abuse. Having a facility like this is a lifeline for people. I'm grateful to be able to offer a safe space to those who need it when they're at their most vulnerable. We pride ourselves on the fact that our shelter is run by survivors for survivors.' Elaine stopped outside a white panelled door at the far end of the corridor. She turned towards me and smiled. 'This is going to be your room,' she said as she unlocked the door.

I walked into the middle of the spacious, high-ceilinged room and cast my eyes over it. It was spotlessly clean and tidy and had been decorated in a modern, minimal way. The single bed was dressed with nice linen, and two towels and some toiletries lay on the end of it.

'All the rooms come with a food pack,' Elaine said, pointing towards a box sitting on top of a chest of drawers in the far corner.

I was overwhelmed by the thoughtful gesture. I hadn't given food a second thought since I'd left the house this morning.

'You can cook meals for yourself or share the cooking with the other women. It's entirely up to you.'

I was lost for words. I knew I should say something to relay my appreciation instead of remaining tight-lipped, but I couldn't seem to string a sentence together.

'We know that some of our residents might not have had a chance to pack before they get to us, so we try to put together some of the things we think you might need for your first few days.'

'You've thought of everything,' I finally managed to reply.

'I'm glad you think so, we try to make the environment as homely as possible. It's my top priority to make the women who come here feel safe,' Elaine said.

Elaine's words were reassuring. Anyone could see that she threw her heart and soul into her job.

'Obviously, you'll have this room to yourself, but the

living room, kitchen and bathrooms are shared. The communal lounge is the hub of the house. It's a large area with lots of soft seating where residents can relax and spend time together. The refuge is your home for as long as you need to stay. You're not a prisoner here, though; you have the freedom to come and go as you please.'

I didn't want Elaine to think I was being rude, but there was so much to take in I was having trouble processing all of the information.

'I'll leave you to settle in unless there's anything you wanted to ask?' Elaine tilted her head to one side while she waited for me to reply.

'I think you've covered everything,' I smiled.

A short while later, Elaine came to check up on me.

'I'm sorry about earlier. You must have thought I was incredibly rude. I barely said two words to you while you were showing me around.'

'Don't apologise. Your reaction was perfectly normal. I know how difficult it is to adjust to life in a new environment,' Elaine smiled.

Everything had happened so quickly. I'd gone from living in a small village to a bustling city literally overnight. It was probably better that way. If I'd had time to really think about it, I wasn't sure I would have gone through with it.

'We try and offer a nurturing environment to help our residents recover from the trauma of domestic abuse and rebuild their lives. We understand what you've been through, so we'll support you and help you to make sense of what's going on. But it's up to you to decide how much or how little interaction you want to have. Everyone deals with things in their own way. Just shout if you need anything,' Elaine said as she closed my bedroom door behind her.

My instinct was to bottle up the awful things that had happened to me, but maybe if I forced myself to pluck up the courage to share my experiences with other women who'd found themselves in similar circumstances, it might help me to deal with the fallout.

18

Paul

'How did you get on?' I asked when Finn arrived at the chalet for our evening get-together.

'It was fine considering it was the first time I'd seen the inside of an interview room, which is surprising, really, as I've done some dodgy things in the past.'

'Haven't we all,' Kevin replied.

Finn's lips suddenly stretched into a broad smile.

'What's so funny?' I asked.

'The female copper was an absolute rocket, but I'm not sure she was that impressed with my account at the beginning,' Finn replied.

'Why not?' I questioned.

'She asked me to tell her how my day had unfolded, so I said I'd started the morning with my usual bowl of Frosties,' Finn laughed. 'It didn't go down too well, I can tell you.'

'I bet it didn't.' I shook my head. Only Finn could get away with playing it cool like that. He loved to act the fool. 'Nerves of steel, that's what I like about you,' I said.

'I don't mind telling you, deep down I was absolutely bricking it when I had to give a witness statement,' Finn laughed.

I very much doubted that. He might be a friend, but you couldn't trust a word he said.

'Of course you were. You don't expect us to believe that, do you?'

'I'm being deadly serious, mate,' Finn replied.

'Yeah, right. You never worry about anything. It doesn't even bother you that you're a long streak of piss with sandy coloured hair,' I joked.

'Strawberry blond,' Finn corrected.

'You're so full of shit. Everyone knows you're a ginger tosser,' Mark chipped in.

'And a scrawny one at that,' Kevin added, and we all began to laugh.

'Just because none of you is six foot two with chiselled features,' Finn countered.

'They're only chiselled because you've got no flesh on your bones,' Kevin replied.

'Do you lot want to hear what happened or not? Or are you going to spend the whole evening taking the piss out of me?' Finn asked.

'Don't be such a tart. We're only having a bit of banter,' I replied.

But I knew Finn wasn't really offended by our comments. The four of us were always the same when we got together.

'The coppers took my phone,' Finn said. His words made the smiles slide from our faces.

'Jesus. Should we be worried?' Mark asked.

'Now, who's being a tart?' Finn questioned.

'The police can find out a lot when they examine a SIM card. They'll know who you've spoken to, which telephone numbers your phone has stored on it and whether any texts have been sent. They can also trace where you've been from mobile phone cell site analysis.' Mark's eyes began darting around the room.

'They're not going to find anything incriminating on my iPhone. And I dumped the burner phone I used to text you guys in the Thames as soon as I'd sent the message,' Finn grinned.

'But all of our numbers are stored on your iPhone. So if they suspect you, it could lead the police to the rest of us,' Mark said.

He had every right to be edgy, and I felt the colour drain from my face.

'Why would they suspect me?' Finn said in a confident tone.

'You did say you were bricking it when they interviewed you,' I pointed out.

'Yeah, I know I did. I might have felt nervous, but I'm pretty sure I hid it well. Don't be fooled by the idea that liars don't ever look you in the eye,' Finn replied.

I knew my friend was capable of that. I'd witnessed him deliver a whopping fib with the conviction of a priest on countless occasions. He could convince a person that what he'd just told them was one hundred per cent gospel when we all knew it was a crock of shit. Ever since we'd been kids, he'd had a loose relationship with the truth and didn't have a strong moral sense that got in the way when he was lying through his teeth.

'Stan, on the other hand, looked like he had as much to hide as a politician's mistress,' Finn laughed.

'What makes you say that?' I quizzed.

'I hung around after I'd been questioned because I knew Stan was up next. He was sweating buckets when he left the station. Even though he had nothing to do with the robbery, he definitely gave off the vibe that he had something to hide,' Finn said.

I couldn't help feeling a sense of relief. It was good of Stan to inadvertently take the heat off us.

'I had a feeling he wouldn't be able to hold it together. When the cops first turned up at the warehouse, it was obvious the woman suspected one of us. Poor old Stan couldn't handle the pressure even though he was completely innocent. Every time she looked at him, he buckled under the weight of her stare. Don't get me wrong, the copper's eyes were pretty intense. They bored into you like laser beams, but you can't let a thing like that rattle you, can you?'

'You have to remember, not everyone has your nerve,' Mark said.

'Stan was squirming like the female copper had his balls in a vice, and that was while all of us were with him. I dread to think what he was like when he was all alone in the room at the cop shop. When he stumbled out of the doors, his skin was so grey, and he was sweating so much I seriously thought he was going to have a heart attack and cark it on the pavement.'

You wouldn't expect an innocent man to react like that. 'Why was he so nervous?' I asked.

'He's scared the airline is going to give him the boot. He was the senior member of staff on duty, so he feels responsible,' Finn replied.

'Poor old sod,' I said, shaking my head.

'It's a good thing he did. He's taking the attention away from us.'

'I'm not disputing that.'

'We should count our lucky stars. That hard-nosed copper will have our nuts too if we let her. If I hadn't held my nerve, today's interrogation could have ended differently,' Finn said.

The pressure was really mounting, so I was pretty certain I had another restless night's sleep coming my way and judging by the look on Mark's face, he did too.

'How did the police leave it?'

I wasn't sure I wanted to know the answer to my question.

'They just thanked me for helping with the investigation.'

'Is that all they said?' Mark's brow furrowed.

Finn rolled his eyes. 'You need to chill out, mate. I'm not a suspect; I'm just helping the police with their inquiries. I haven't been arrested for anything.'

Not yet, I thought, but I decided to keep that to myself. The investigation was still in the early stages, so we couldn't afford to start celebrating our victory prematurely.

'How come none of you seems overly concerned by the police interest in our gang member?' Mark asked with concern etched all over his face.

'There's no point in worrying about things that haven't happened. You'll give yourself an ulcer if you carry on like this,' Finn replied.

'Maybe I should take a leaf out of your book and not get so het up about this,' Mark replied, forcing a smile.

'Yeah, right! As if that's going to happen,' I laughed.

Anyone could see the grin didn't belong there. His stooped posture painted a more accurate picture of a man with the weight of the world on his shoulders. Mark was definitely out of his comfort zone. He was the oldest of the group, two years older than Finn and I, three and a half years older than Kevin. When he was out on the water doing what he loved best, he lived up to his surfer-boy persona, carefree thrill-seeker, but once you took him away from that setting, he sometimes had the mentality of an anxiety-riddled pensioner, not the thirty-year-old man that he was. But we all had different strengths and weaknesses. That's what made us a good team.

19

Lola

I'd left Mum two voicemails and had tried to contact her by text, WhatsApp and Messenger, but she hadn't replied to any of them. I was scared something was wrong, but then I reasoned she was probably still at work, so she'd have her phone switched off. I was probably over-reacting and needed to occupy my mind now that I'd unpacked my things. Sitting in a room on my own was doing nothing to ease my worry. I was getting increasingly concerned about Mum's safety, so I decided to go and see if any of the other residents were about. I'd turn into a recluse if I didn't push myself out of my comfort zone. Chatting to somebody might help to take my mind off things.

It took me almost an hour to pluck up the courage to walk down the stairs and into the communal living room. As I got closer, I could hear the sound of children's laughter, and that brought a smile to my face. I poked my head around the door, and two women smiled over at me. The younger of the two looked a similar age to me and had the most beautiful poker straight brown hair I'd ever seen. It fell over her shoulders like molten chocolate as she stretched out on the L-shaped sofa.

'Come on in,' she said. 'We don't bite.' As the words left her mouth, a huge smile spread over her face.

'Hi,' I said as I stepped over the threshold.

'Hi,' the women replied.

'I'm Millie, and that's Roxanne. And those two adorable little cherubs are her kids, Kai and Poppy.'

The children didn't even look around at the mention of their names. They were too engrossed in the TV.

'I'm Lola, pleased to meet you.'

Millie swung her slim legs off the sofa and patted the seat next to where she was sitting. I crossed the room on jelly limbs and plonked myself down, leaving a spare cushion between us.

'When did you arrive?' Millie asked, tucking a silken strand of her brown hair behind her ear.

'A couple of hours ago,' I replied.

'How are you settling in?' Roxanne asked. As she tilted her head to one side, her corkscrew curls bounced on her shoulders.

'It feels a little bit strange at the moment, but I'm sure I'll get used to it.' Even though everybody had been really welcoming, it was going to take time to adapt to my new surroundings. 'Give me a week or two and then ask me again,' I smiled.

'Honestly, you'll be surprised by how quickly the place starts to feel like home. I didn't know anyone when I came here either, and to my surprise, I settled in very quickly. I wish I'd come here sooner.' Roxanne smiled as she tried to put me at ease.

That was good to know.

'Seeing my children begin to play and smile again has made it all worthwhile for me.' Roxanne glanced over her shoulder at the little boy and girl glued to the TV. They were lying on their stomachs in identical poses with their faces resting in their hands.

'It might seem a bit daunting at first, but we're a friendly bunch,' Millie said. 'Aren't we, Rox?'

'Yeah, there's a nice group of women here, and the staff are lovely too,' Roxanne agreed.

'How long have you been here?' I asked.

'One month and counting,' Millie replied. 'As soon as I can afford to, I'm going to get myself a flat.'

'We'd love that too.' Roxanne glanced over at her children. 'We've been here almost two months now. Where's the time gone?'

We'd only just met, yet it felt strangely comforting to be surrounded by other women who had experienced similar things to myself.

'Lola, have you got a minute?' Elaine asked, poking her head around the lounge door.

I glanced at Millie and Roxanne before I nodded. Elaine had a serious expression on her face, so I hoped I wasn't in trouble.

'Good luck,' Millie said under her breath.

So it wasn't just me who thought I must have done something wrong.

'Is everything okay?' I asked as I walked towards her, trying to pre-empt the situation.

It was only after I rounded the corner that I saw the two police officers standing in the hallway. My heart began pounding when I caught sight of them.

'The police are here to see you,' Elaine said, but I'd already guessed as much.

'Is there somewhere private we can go?' the female officer asked.

She turned to look at Elaine, who nodded before leading the way down the corridor.

'Take as long as you like. I'll make sure nobody disturbs you,' Elaine said, showing us into the empty kitchen.

20

Abbie

'That old boy definitely had something to hide if you ask me,' Ed said after we'd interviewed all of the staff members. 'He was sweating like a pig the whole time you were interviewing him.'

That was true. Usually, if a person looked uncomfortable, I'd probe around it, but Stanley had explained why he was nervous. He was scared his employer would put him out to pasture and replace him with a younger model, and I was inclined to believe his account. I'd narrowed my suspects down to one. The ageing security guard displaying deer caught in the headlights tendencies wasn't the man my money was on.

'I think we should get Stanley back in for questioning. If we apply the right amount of pressure, I'm sure we'll be able to make him crack. He looked like he was on the verge of spilling the beans if you ask me.'

I disagreed with Ed's insightful observations. I was certain he was barking up the wrong tree and didn't see what could be gained by putting the poor man through another interview apart from wasting precious police resources. We needed to identify the inside source so that we could apprehend the thieves; subjecting Stanley to another grilling wasn't going to bring us any closer to solving the case. But Ed was like a dog with a bone; he wasn't going to drop the matter any time soon.

'Why are you protecting him?' Ed asked.

I didn't appreciate being accused of something I wasn't doing. What would I have to gain from that?

'I'm not protecting him, but I disagree with the assumptions you've made. When you've interviewed as many people as I have, you get a feel for who's telling the truth and who's blatantly lying to your face.'

There were subtle ways to tell if someone was being dishonest, like stiff body movements and micro-expressions. I was very good at picking up on the signals. If I thought somebody was guilty, I was usually right. Despite Finn's cool, calm exterior, something seemed off. His body language hadn't given anything away, but in my experience, the simplest explanation often turned out to be the correct one.

'Six people were on duty at the time of the heist; four British Airways freight handlers and two unarmed guards. Have another look at their movements before the robbery and run checks on their backgrounds through the database,' I said when we walked into the incident room.

Ed had written everything down in his notebook when he'd taken statements from the staff, so he could refer back to that and see if it threw up any new leads. The additional checks would provide details of any arrest, caution or conviction that had previously been recorded and that might give us a different angle.

'I'll get right on it,' Ed replied.

He was chomping at the bit. There was no limit to my young partner's enthusiasm. He reminded me of myself when I'd first joined up before the job had taken over my life and destroyed everything in its wake.

The first twenty-four hours were vital to the investigation, but they had long since passed us by. Instead of producing answers, so far, our lines of inquiry had just uncovered more questions. We needed to come up with a working theory and fast. There was no doubt in my mind that we were trying to solve an inside job. Maybe we should start feeding information to the employees and let them in on the secret that we had nothing, so they'd drop their guard and become careless.

21

Lola

'Lola Marshall?' the officer asked once Elaine had closed the kitchen door.

I could barely hear what she said over the pounding of my pulse.

'Yes,' I replied, then tried to swallow down the huge lump in my throat.

'I'm DS Ash, and this is DC Harris.' She gestured with a wave of her hand to her male colleague.

Even though I didn't know what the officers wanted, I could sense the conversation wasn't going to have a good outcome.

'I'm afraid we have some bad news...' DS Ash let her sentence trail off.

As her words registered in my brain, I felt my knees buckle. DC Harris's hand sprang forward, and he grabbed hold of my elbow to steady me.

'Would you like to sit down?' DS Ash asked.

I shook my head. I just wanted her to get on with telling me why they were here.

'Your mother has been assaulted,' DS Ash said, finally getting to the point.

'Oh my God!'

My hands flew up to cover my mouth as my heartbeat pounded against my rib cage like a battering ram. She didn't need to tell me who was responsible. I knew.

'Is my mum okay?'

I held my breath. I was scared to hear the officer's reply.

'She's stable, but she's been seriously injured,' DS Ash said.

I knew I had to go to her even though the chances were that Troy would be waiting for me. I felt responsible for the attack.

'Can you tell me which hospital she's in?'

I couldn't think straight; my mind was whirring.

'The Northern General Hospital,' DC Harris said.

'We'll take you to her. Go and pack a bag; we'll wait while you get your things together.' DS Ash pointed towards the door.

Going back to my home town when I'd thought I'd made it to safety was going to be a scary experience, so I was glad I'd be returning to Sheffield with a police escort. Having two officers with me would definitely make me feel calmer and safer.

I walked across the floor in a daze, but just before I left the room, I turned and looked over to where the officers were standing.

'I only arrived here today. What's going to happen to my room? Will the refuge give my place away?'

'No, I'll explain the situation to Elaine and ask her to hold it for you for as long as you need it.'

That was one consolation, at least. And when I came back to London, I would make sure Mum was with me.

'Thank you,' I said as I raced along the corridor and up the stairs with tears streaming down my face.

'Are you okay?' Millie asked when she bumped into me on the landing.

I bit down on my lip and nodded. 'I'm fine,' I replied, but it was obvious that wasn't the case.

'We saw the police. What's going on?' Millie asked, rubbing my arm with the palm of her hand.

'I've got to go back to Yorkshire. My mum's not well.'

I didn't want to tell Millie what had really happened, even though I got the impression I could trust her. I was a private person, and we'd only just met. Because of what I'd been through with Troy, I was suspicious of everyone I met.

'Oh, that's such a shame. You've only just got here,' Millie replied.

'I'd better go. The police are waiting for me.' I gestured towards the stairs with a nod of my head.

Who would have thought less than twenty-four hours after leaving Sheffield, I would be on my way back to Yorkshire.

'You've obviously been the victim of domestic violence. Please know that you can talk to us about your situation.' DS Ash turned around in her seat and gave me a sympathetic smile.

I felt my cheeks flush in response as her eyes scanned the colourful bruises on my face. I didn't want to get into this conversation, so I looked down at the floor. Silence lingered in the confines of the car like a bad smell. And as it dragged on, a tense atmosphere spread out between us.

'Refuges like the one you're staying at help thousands of women escape abuse every year,' DS Ash continued.

She was trying the softly, softly approach now, but this topic of conversation was still closed as far as I was concerned.

'We don't know what circumstances led you to the refuge, but something bad must have happened to make you flee from your home. Do you have a place to stay while you're in Sheffield?' DS Ash asked.

'Yes,' I replied.

That wasn't the case, but I'd worry about that later. I just wanted to get to the hospital and see my mum.

'You may or may not know this, but the police receive a call for help relating to domestic abuse every thirty seconds.'

My eyes widened. I had no idea so many people were affected.

'It's more common than you think, Lola. One in four women experiences abuse in their lifetime. But anyone can suffer at the hands of their partner. A third of all domestic violence victims are male.'

I was shocked to hear that.

'Being assaulted, sexually abused, threatened or harassed by someone you know is just as much a crime as an attack by a complete stranger, and it often has far more dangerous consequences.'

DS Ash pressed on in an attempt to wear me down. She was making a valiant effort, but this wasn't a subject I talked freely about.

'We want to catch the person responsible for assaulting your mother. Do you think her attacker and your abuser might be one and the same?' DS Ash quizzed.

I felt colour flood my cheeks. It wasn't just me that thought Troy was responsible.

The DS had changed tactics but was still pressing on with her line of questioning even though I wasn't responding.

'I have no idea,' I said, meeting her intense gaze.

I think we both knew my answer was far from the truth. It didn't take a genius to work out that the two incidents were connected. DS Ash could probe all she liked, but I wasn't on trial here, so I was determined to exercise my right to silence at least until I'd heard my mum's side of the story.

'We're going to make every effort to find the man responsible. I just thought you might be able to help us with a description so that we could start to circulate it.'

My head felt like it was about to explode, so I turned my face away from her unrelenting stare and gazed out at the changing scenery as it flew past the window. The night was beginning to fall, which was a blessing in itself as the car's interior would soon be shrouded in darkness, and then the DS wouldn't be able to make eye contact with me so easily. I noticed her turn away and face the front out of the corner of my eye. Relief washed over me that she'd finally got the message. I turned my attention back to the fields beyond the motorway and allowed myself to be mesmerised by the way the car's lights cast the hedges in alternating waves of glare and shadow.

22

Paul

'The tubby copper paid us a visit today,' Finn said as he opened the fridge and took out a cold beer.

It had become an evening ritual that we all met up after work and spent the evening together at the chalet.

'Should we be worried?' Mark asked.

'Nah,' Finn replied before holding the bottle up to his lips and taking a big swig from it.

'What did he want?' I asked.

'He came to collect our DNA.' Finn put the beer down on the table and took his usual seat.

'Why did he need that if you're only helping with the inquiry?' Kevin asked, but before Finn had a chance to reply, Mark cut in.

'That can't be a good sign. The police use DNA evidence to support a prosecution, don't they?' Mark's eyes darted between each of us in turn.

'Yeah, they do, but the copper said he needed the samples

so that we could be ruled out of anything forensic that was found at the crime scene,' Finn replied.

'That makes sense. The warehouse must be full of your team's prints. None of you guys wear gloves when you're handling the cargo, do you?' I quizzed.

'Nah.' Finn shook his head. 'I tell you I gagged when the bloke stuck the swab in my mouth. I've got a very sensitive reflux, and I think he was worried I was going to spew up all over his shiny shoes,' Finn laughed.

'Would have served him right if you had,' Kevin replied. 'Maybe he wouldn't be so keen to keep poking his nose in if he had to go back to the station stinking of vomit.'

The thought of that brought a chorus of laughter from all of us.

'The cop asked us all how long we'd worked at the airport and wanted to know what we'd done for a living before that.'

'Did he say how the investigation was going?' I asked.

'No, not a dicky-bird.' Finn picked up his beer and necked the contents.

'I guess no news is good news,' I said.

'That copper seemed to have an unhealthy interest in Stan, though,' Finn said. 'He was watching the poor bugger like a hawk, and the more he eyeballed Stan, the more nervous the old sod acted.'

Fingers crossed Stan would lead the investigation in the wrong direction. The longer the case remained unsolved, the likelihood was we'd get away with it.

'Norman keeps trying to convince him to play it cool, but Stan's so worried that he's going to be held responsible his words are falling on deaf ears. There's no way I'm going to interfere. I feel sorry for the bloke; all that stress can't be good at his age, but on the plus side, he's keeping the heat off of us. If he continues to do that with any luck, the trail will go cold,' Finn smiled.

'Too right,' I agreed.

23

Lola

Three hours after we'd set off, DC Harris parked the patrol car outside the main entrance next to the ambulance bay. As the car glided to a halt, I pulled my long blonde hair up into a messy bun and then tucked any loose strands under a black bobble hat in an effort to conceal my identity.

DS Ash led the way; DC Harris and I followed closely behind. I slung my rucksack over one shoulder as I approached the sliding doors, keeping my head down as I walked. I didn't dare look around me; I was terrified that I might spot Troy lurking in the shadows. Once we were inside the foyer, the officers hung back while I approached the man behind the counter.

'Please can you tell me which ward Dee Marshall is on?' I asked.

He tapped his fingers across the keyboard before he made eye contact with me.

'She's been admitted to Huntsman Ward 7, along the

corridor to your right,' he replied before his eyes flicked back to his monitor.

My footsteps echoed along the corridor. When the ward was in sight, my pace gathered speed. I barely noticed the presence of the officers behind me as they were maintaining a discreet distance. All I could think about was getting to my mum's side.

The nurse showed me to Mum's bed. I let out a gasp when I saw her. I hadn't appreciated what it would feel like to see somebody you loved battered and bruised because I'd never been in this position before. But now that the tables had been turned, I understood why she'd been begging me to finish with my violent ex-boyfriend for so long.

Mum's face was black and blue; it was so swollen, I hardly recognised her, and her arm was in a plaster cast, so she'd sustained more than just superficial bruises. Troy was a monster. I couldn't believe he'd done that to my mum.

'Please take a seat,' the nurse said, gesturing to an empty chair by the side of Mum's bed.

It was warm on the ward, so I lowered my rucksack on to the floor, pulled off my bobble hat and unzipped my black puffer jacket, hanging it over the back of the plastic chair. Guilt clawed itself up from the pit of my stomach as I watched Mum sleep. It was my fault she was lying in a hospital bed. She'd asked me more times than I cared to remember why I was putting up with Troy's violent behaviour, and now she was paying the price for my selfishness.

Mum looked shocked to see me when she opened her eyes and saw me sitting by the side of her bed. But instead of being overjoyed, a worried expression spread across her face.

'You shouldn't have come, Lola; it's too dangerous.' Mum's voice cracked with emotion, and moments later, tears started rolling down her cheeks.

It was all I could do to stop myself from breaking down, but that wouldn't help Mum; she needed me to be strong for her.

'It's okay, the police are with me,' I said, hoping to put her mind at rest. 'The DS was asking me about your attacker. Did you give the police Troy's name?' I asked.

'No. I was too scared to; he said if I told them what happened, he'd come after you and kill you.' Mum blurted out the words between sobs, but they kept getting caught in her throat.

A shiver ran down my spine. I knew that wasn't an idle threat. It was no surprise that Troy had paid my mum a visit. I knew he wouldn't think twice about resorting to violence and take his anger out on her if he got the opportunity. But she'd assured me everything was going to be okay. Something had gone catastrophically wrong.

'What happened? I thought you weren't going to let Troy in?'

'He was waiting outside the house when I got back from work.' Mum's bottom lip began to wobble.

I reached across the bed and took hold of her hand.

'I didn't notice him at first, and by the time I saw him, it was too late. Before I had a chance to drive away, he pulled open my door and dragged me out of the car. I was terrified, but I didn't go quietly; I started shouting and struggling in the hope that one of our nosey neighbours would hear, but nobody came to help. I put up a fight, but he was too strong...'

Mum was sobbing and gulping for air. I felt bad making her relieve her ordeal, but I needed to know what had happened.

'Would you like some water?' I asked, to give Mum a moment to compose herself.

I'd never seen her like this before. Not even after my dad died. She'd probably been putting on a brave face on my account, but she'd only ever had very small wobbles, nothing on this scale. Right now, she was almost hysterical, and that was heartbreaking to witness.

'Troy frogmarched me up the garden path and forced me to open the front door. He started screaming at me, demanding that I tell him where you'd gone.'

'Oh God,' I muttered under my breath. If Troy knew about the hostel, I'd have to find another place to stay. I wouldn't be able to go back there, or London for that matter.

'He tried to force me to tell him where you were, but it's okay, love, I didn't tell him anything. I told him we'd had an argument, and you'd stormed off, so I didn't know where you were staying.'

'Do you think he believed you?'

'I don't know. He suddenly flipped and started attacking me. He kept ranting over and over again that I wasn't telling him what he wanted to hear. I thought he was going to kill me, but thankfully he left before it went that far.'

When Mum began to cry, my eyes welled up too.

'As soon as the coast was clear, I phoned the ambulance. I told them I'd been attacked by a man on the street. When the paramedics turned up, the police were with them. I'm so sorry, Lola.'

'Why are you apologising? You've done nothing wrong.' I squeezed Mum's hand and smiled.

'I wasn't thinking straight when the police officer asked me if I wanted him to notify anyone that I was being taken to hospital. I gave them your name and the details of the refuge, but I shouldn't have done that. I've compromised your safety.'

'No, you haven't. The police aren't going to tell anybody where I'm staying.'

'I got the fright of my life when I saw you standing there. I wasn't expecting you to come back. I just wanted the police to let you know that I was okay; I didn't want you to worry. I knew you'd have been trying to call me.'

'As soon as I arrived at the refuge, I tried to touch base with you. I'll apologise in advance for the countless messages I left you,' I smiled.

I'd tried to convince myself that nothing was wrong, but I'd had a bad feeling in my gut that there was a reason I hadn't been able to contact Mum. I felt terrible that she'd taken a beating to protect me. I owed it to her to make sure Troy was locked up for a very long time.

'I'm going to tell the police who did this to you.' Mum's eyes widened, and she stared at me with disbelief written all over her face. 'The DS already suspects that the same person was responsible for both of our bruises.'

'You can't tell the police. Troy said he's going to kill you if I stitch him up.'

Mum looked at me with pleading eyes.

'He deserves to go to prison for what he's done to you.'

Mum shook her head. 'Please promise me you won't do anything stupid. I don't want you to speak out on my account. When the police question me about the attack, I'm going to say I didn't know the man responsible. Troy's threatening to kill you, Lola; he wasn't messing around; he was deadly serious. You've put yourself in real danger by coming here.'

As I mulled over what Mum had said, a nurse appeared at the bottom of her bed.

'I'm afraid I'm going to have to ask you to come back tomorrow. Visiting time ended a while ago, and your mum really needs to rest.'

I saw a look of panic spread across Mum's face when the nurse's words registered.

'What are you going to do? You can't go back to the house,' Mum said when the nurse walked back up the ward.

'I'll book a room at the Travelodge, and I'll come back and see you in the morning.'

'Please go back to London. You were safe at the refuge. If you stay in Sheffield, it's only a matter of time until Troy spots you.'

'I will go back to London, but I'm going to wait until you've been discharged. You're not going to be able to work with a broken arm, so I'm not listening to your excuses. I want you to come with me.'

'The doctor said I could be in hospital for a while. They haven't decided if they'll need to operate on my arm or not yet. There's really no point in you staying; you're just putting yourself at risk.'

'I know it took you ages to get here, and that's why I bent the rules and let you see your mum, but you're putting me in an awkward position now. It's well past visiting time, so you need to go,' the nurse repeated, in a firmer tone this time.

'I'm sorry, we're not trying to get you into trouble. I'm going,' I said as I stood up from the chair.

'Don't argue with me, Lola, go back to London tonight. As soon as I'm discharged, I'll come down and stay with you.'

'You promise?'

Mum nodded.

Tears were streaming down my cheeks when I kissed her goodbye. Leaving her behind in the hospital was the hardest thing I'd ever had to do, but I knew she was right. Staying in a place where people knew me would be a suicidal move for both of us.

24

Paul

Kevin turned off the road and followed the dirt track towards the disused outbuilding we'd used to store our hookey gear when we were teenagers. We'd stashed our stolen goods there multiple times until the heat had died down, and it was safe for us to sell them on. We hadn't been near the place in years, but we thought we'd better check it out in case we needed to move the cash from the heist at short notice. Now that Mark was doing the chalet up and injecting a bit of life into it, somebody might surprise us and actually want to rent it. If that happened, we could hardly leave the ten million where it was.

The old stone barn, which had probably housed livestock in a past life, had seen better days. It was only accessible by foot, so Kevin and I had trudged along a boggy path over the marsh for a considerable distance before we'd spotted the corrugated metal roof. I'd been beginning to wonder if it was still there as we hadn't ventured to this part of Sheppey for years.

The outbuilding was located in a quiet, underpopulated part of the island where only a few cottages, a church and a pub broke up the flat landscape. The area was a nature lover's paradise; wild ponies and sheep grazed on the wetlands dotted with birds that over-wintered there. It was a beautiful spot during daylight hours, but nobody ventured there after dark.

Kevin and I wanted to appear like walkers enjoying the scenery to the few people we passed en route while we were doing our recce, so we didn't veer off of the path or pay any attention to the crumbling stone barn that had been a frequent hangout for us in our younger years.

Instead, we carried on walking towards the water as though we were checking out the pub. It was a nice enough boozer; we'd been across the threshold on many occasions, but today's visit was just for show. The Sailor's Haunt was very aptly named, as the centuries-old building sat behind a stretch of water where a graveyard of shipwrecks lined the sand along a tidal channel of the Thames estuary. The publican tried to tout the ships' decaying skeletons as atmospheric to the tourists from the campsites. But if you asked me, seeing shipwrecks looming out of the mist when it rolled in from the sea gave off a decidedly eerie, creepy vibe more fitting for the opening scene of a horror film.

'We'd better get going, or the guys will think we've stood them up,' I said.

'What time do you call this?' Finn glanced at his watch when Kevin and I walked into the pub.

Ever since we'd been old enough to get served, Kevin,

Mark, Finn and I had spent our Saturday afternoons sipping pints in The Rising Tide. Despite its picturesque waterside location, it was a tip of a place. I wouldn't be sorry when the time came for us to break the habit, but for now, we had to go through the motions of following our usual routines. We didn't want to give anyone a reason to suspect us, so we had to go about our daily lives.

'We went to see if the old lock-up was still standing,' I replied.

'So, is it still there?' Mark asked when he came back from the bar carrying a tray of lager.

'Yeah, just about,' I smiled.

'That's good to know in case we need to implement plan B,' Mark said before taking a sip of his Stella.

As we sat around the scratched wooden table in The Rising Tide, my mind drifted back to that grey and dismal August afternoon six months ago when all of this began. We'd been sitting at this very spot, in our usual seats putting the world to rights, wishing we were anywhere other than where we'd all been born and raised, the Isle of Sheppey. As the afternoon turned into evening and the drinks kept flowing, our disillusionment with our lives grew. We were young men, well relatively anyway; Mark was thirty, Finn and I were twenty-eight, and Kevin was the baby of the group at twenty-six, but we were stuck in a rut with dead-end futures ahead of us.

'You're never going to guess what's happened to me,' Finn had said before picking up his pint and taking a sip.

'You won the lottery,' Kevin laughed.

'As good as,' Finn replied. 'I've only gone and landed a

job at London City Airport.' His lips twisted as he tried to stifle a smile.

'Yeah, doing what? Cleaning toilets?'

Finn flashed me an evil look. 'I'm going to be part of the ground operation crew.'

'You can tart the job title up all you like, but that's not going to change the fact that you'll be pushing a mop and broom around all day.'

I wasn't trying to be an arsehole, but we had barely any qualifications between the four of us, so we were only ever going to be offered unskilled work.

'Stop being a wanker; I'm not part of the cleaning staff. I'm going to be working with the ground crew handling the cargo,' Finn said.

'And my old nan's the Queen of England,' I laughed.

'What do I have to say to convince you? Seriously, mate, I'm not making this up. I had an interview with British Airways yesterday morning, and they phoned me last night to offer me the job. I start next week.' Finn beamed from ear to ear.

'Why didn't you tell us you'd applied for a job?' Kevin narrowed his eyes.

I could see he was unsure of whether or not to believe Finn's good fortune. I wasn't the only one that was sceptical, but who could blame us? Finn was a wind-up merchant and the prankster of the group. He was always playing tricks and practical jokes on us, so we were half expecting him to say he'd made the whole thing up once he'd reeled us all in. Fabricating stories was one of my friend's favourite pastimes, and he had a very vivid imagination.

'So come on then, answer Kevin's question. Why didn't you let us in on your little secret?' I pressed on.

Finn would have found it virtually impossible not to spill the beans.

'Because I know what you lot are like. I didn't think I'd get an interview, let alone be offered the job. I haven't got any experience in that line of work, so I didn't want you bastards taking the piss out of me if they turned me down,' Finn explained.

'Did you see that?' Kevin's eyes were wide as he pointed out of the window at the night sky.

'No,' we all chorused, glancing around the table at each other before returning our attention towards Kevin, who was still gawping at the glass with his mouth open.

'What was it?' I asked, thinking it must have been something good to have provoked a reaction like that out of my brother.

'A pig just flew past the window. I can't believe you lot missed it. It's the most exciting thing that's happened all year,' Kevin laughed.

Finn flicked his beer mat across the table at Kevin. 'Stop taking the piss out of me. I'm deadly serious, you fucker.'

Kevin, Mark and I were close to the bottom of our first pint when Finn walked into the pub the following Saturday. He was dressed in a fluorescent jacket and navy trousers with reflective stripes running down the sides and across the ankles. I felt my mouth drop open when he came into view.

'We'd been wondering where you'd got to. So you weren't having us on, after all,' I said.

Finn put his lanyard with the British Airways logo on the table in front of us. He'd held down a succession of dead-end jobs since leaving school, so we'd all thought he was bluffing when he told us about his new role.

'Fair play to you. I think we owe you an apology,' I continued, holding my hand out towards him.

'Stuff your apology; I think you owe me a pint,' Finn laughed, shaking me by the hand.

I got up from my seat and walked over to the bar. 'Four pints of Stella and a large rum and coke, please.'

'Do you want ice in that?' Neil asked.

'No, thanks.'

'Hey, where's mine?' Kevin asked when I put the pint and short down in front of Finn.

'What's with the preferential treatment?' Mark added.

'I think he deserves it. We gave him such a hard time, didn't we? Anyway, congratulations,' I said, picking up my pint and holding it towards Finn.

'Thanks, mate,' he replied, clinking my glass.

Fast forward a week, and we were back in The Rising Tide, making our way towards the bottom of four pint glasses.

'How's the job going?' I asked.

Finn had barely said a word since he'd walked into the pub, which was out of character for him as he suffered from an incurable case of verbal diarrhoea.

'It's fine,' he replied before lifting his pint to his mouth.

Something didn't add up. I'd been expecting him to bore us rigid with every detail, but his lips were sealed. I wasn't sure I could ever remember a time when he'd given me a two-word answer before.

'You haven't gone and got the sack, have you?'

The thought suddenly popped into my head, and the words were out of my mouth before I could stop them. Tactfulness had never been my strong point.

Finn's sandy-coloured eyebrows shot up to his hairline. He was clearly shocked by my suggestion.

'No, it's nothing like that,' Finn replied.

'Why are you being so cagey?' I quizzed. 'I've never known you to say so little.'

'You are being a bit tight-lipped,' Kevin agreed. 'What's up, mate? Aren't you enjoying it?'

Finn let out a long sigh and then hunched himself over the table, gesturing to the rest of us to follow suit.

'I've been agonizing over this since my first day on the job, but I can't keep it to myself any longer,' Finn began, looking at each of us in turn so that he could pause for effect.

'Don't keep us in suspense then,' I said, realising we must have looked suspicious huddled around the table like we were discussing something top secret.

'When I accepted the job, the airline made me sign a confidentiality agreement. My line manager made it crystal clear to me when he did my induction that if I broke the terms, it was grounds for immediate dismissal, so if I tell you, you can't say a word to anyone. Can you promise me you'll keep this to yourselves?' Finn's blue eyes bored into each one of us in turn.

'Yes,' I said.

Mark nodded, and Kevin pretended to zip his mouth closed as both of them agreed to Finn's request.

'For fuck's sake, get on with it, or we'll have died of old age before you get around to telling us.'

I have to admit, I'd never been a patient person, but Finn's stalling would challenge most people's tolerance. He had a habit of longing out a story, stretching every single detail to try and create maximum suspense. But more often than not, it had the opposite effect, and we lost interest in what he had to say before he got to the end of his tale.

'Now that you've got us all hyped up, this better be worth the wait and not a huge anti-climax,' I said as frustration started to build up inside me.

'Well, if that's how you feel, maybe I should keep it to myself.' Finn folded his arms across his chest and glared at me, his face reddening.

'Get on with it, you big tart,' Kevin said, flicking a peanut at Finn and hitting him right between the eyes to lighten the tension.

'Hey, that could've taken my eye out,' Finn protested, turning his ruddy face away from mine and towards Kevin's.

'Are you going to tell us or not?' Mark asked, hoping to steer the conversation back on course.

Finn nodded. 'I knew handling cargo was going to be the main part of my job, but I hadn't realised what the cargo was until my first day,' Finn said in a low voice, and we all leaned in a bit closer. 'The team I'm working with handle pallet-loads of cash.'

Kevin let out a whistle, then shook his head from side to side.

Finn slumped back in his chair, and a smile spread over his face. Once he moved back from the table, we all did the same. As I straightened my posture, I looked around the pub to see if anyone had overheard what he'd just said, but there was nobody within earshot. And just moments ago, I was wondering why Finn was being so secretive. No wonder he'd wanted us to huddle together.

Finn gave us a moment to digest what he'd told us before he stooped over the table again. This time he didn't need to gesture for us to do the same. We were all eager to hear what he had to say and closed in around him.

'British Airways regularly fly large amounts of unmarked notes from Europe to London City Airport.'

Finn's mouth lifted into a smile, and his blue eyes seemed brighter than normal.

'How come?' Mark asked the question I was sure we were all thinking.

'When British tourists exchange UK notes for foreign currency, the cash gets left behind in that country, so banks have to fly the money back,' Finn explained before sitting back in his chair.

And to think, I was convinced Finn was going to be working as a cleaner when he'd first told us he'd got a job at London City Airport.

'I'm amazed you didn't tell us sooner,' I said.

'Believe me, mate, it's been killing me,' Finn admitted

He never had been very good at keeping things to himself. If you wanted something to remain a secret, he was the last person you should share it with.

25

Lola

DS Ash and DC Harris dropped me at the station just before nine so that I'd be able to catch one of the last trains to London. It had been one hell of a day, and I was completely exhausted, but after what had happened, I knew I wasn't going to get much sleep tonight anyway.

'Take care of yourself,' DS Ash said, handing me her card while giving me a half-smile. 'Please phone me if you ever want to talk.'

'Thanks for everything,' I replied before closing the back passenger door.

I hurried into the station, which I was glad to see was almost deserted. I didn't have time to try and negotiate my way around hordes of people as the train was leaving shortly. I made my way to the only booth that was open and bought myself another one-way ticket. Hopefully, this was the last time I'd have to do this journey.

*

'How's your mum?' Elaine asked when I opened the front door.

'She's okay,' I replied. 'Thanks for asking.'

I felt a bit guilty being so cagey as Elaine was going out of her way to be nice to me, but I didn't feel comfortable discussing my mum's health or the reason she'd ended up in hospital with her. I was worried she was going to ask me what had happened, and then she'd put two and two together like DS Ash had done.

'I'm surprised you're back so soon...' Elaine let her sentence trail off, no doubt hoping I was going to fill in the blanks.

'The doctors don't know how long Mum's going to be in hospital. I was going to book a Travelodge, but she was determined she didn't want me to stay in Sheffield. Mum literally begged me to get the train back to London.'

I forced out a smile, but I had a horrible feeling it looked as fake as it felt.

'I'm inclined to agree with your mum. It's probably for the best you didn't stay. Now that you've made the move, you should try to keep as much distance between yourself and your ex as possible. He could still be a danger to you.'

Elaine's words bombarded my brain like missiles as an image of my battered and bruised Mum popped into my head.

'You're working late. I thought you'd have gone home by now,' I said.

I was desperate to change the subject so that I could force the distressing thoughts out of my mind.

'The police phoned me to tell me that you were on the

train, so I decided to hold on and make sure you got back okay.'

Elaine went above and beyond the line of duty. I don't think I'd ever met anyone so dedicated before, and the experience was humbling. I felt my eyes mist over with tears as my emotions threatened to get the better of me.

'You look exhausted, love.' Elaine rubbed the side of my arm.

'It's been a long day,' I replied, stifling a yawn.

'Why don't you go up to your room and get some rest.' Elaine offered me a sympathetic smile.

'That's a good idea. I think I'll try and get some sleep.'

26

'How did you get on with the background checks? Did they throw up anything interesting?' I crossed my arms and fixed my eyes on Ed.

'Not really. None of the men had anything on file, but that's not really surprising. I wouldn't have expected the two security guards to have any previous convictions or the cargo workers, for that matter. I'm sure the airline does thorough background checks on prospective employees before they hire them to ensure they don't have a criminal history. You wouldn't want dishonest people handling pallet-loads of cash, would you?'

That went without saying, but one of them wasn't as squeaky clean as they appeared.

'Employee theft is a huge problem for businesses. It costs them billions of pounds every year.'

Ed threw me a doubtful look. 'I'm not disputing that, but this sort of thing doesn't happen every day of the week, Abbie.'

'Maybe not, but companies do regularly hire people they think are trustworthy who sometimes turn out to be as dodgy as they come. That's a fact.'

Ed held his tongue, but I could tell he wasn't happy by the way he was chewing the inside of his lip.

'If we're going to get to the bottom of this, we need to find out what motivated our inside source. Any number of things could have led to their actions; a disgruntled employee might use theft as a way to pay back the company,' I said. 'Have any of the team been involved in disciplinary procedures?'

Ed pushed his glasses up his nose before he flicked through his notebook.

'Not as far as I know,' he replied after a slight pause.

'Contact British Airways Human Resources department and see if they have anything on file.'

Ed started scribbling notes down on the page. I gave him a moment before I started talking again so that I had his full attention.

'There are other reasons we should consider. Maybe one of the team was passed over for a promotion. Check that out as well. People get hacked off by the slightest thing sometimes. The staff in the warehouse do shift work; our inside man might have been unhappy about having to work over a weekend or annoyed that they weren't given time off when they requested it. There are countless reasons the employee could use to rationalise seeking revenge. If their employer had done something to hurt them, they could easily justify doing something to get back at them. And let's face it, nothing hits a company harder than theft.'

'That's true, and we're not talking about a bit of pocket

money here. The robbers got away with a life-changing amount of money,' Ed said.

'You never did say what you found out about the men,' I prompted.

Ed hadn't been particularly forthcoming about the results of his information gathering.

'Both of the guards have worked at London City Airport for over ten years. They've been farmed out to different airlines during that time, but they're both employed by the same security firm,' Ed replied.

That was a good sign, I thought. This was the first robbery of its kind at the airport. If either of those two employees had been involved in the heist, they must have resisted the temptation for a very long time before they put their plan into action. In my mind, that placed both of them low down on the list of suspects. Unless of course, they'd recently been passed over for a promotion or had tired of working unsociable hours. I should keep an open mind at this stage. It might become apparent that they did in fact have a motive for taking revenge on their employer.

'What did you find out about the other members of staff?'

'The cargo workers came to the airport from a variety of different fields. None of them had done this line of work before. But there was nothing remarkable about any of the background checks. They'd all been employed in various low paid jobs, having left school straight after GCSEs with little qualifications. Their employment histories were pretty much what you'd expect for manual workers.'

'What did you find out about Finn McCaskill?'

Ed let out a loud breath, glanced at his watch, then started twiddling the pen he was holding in his right hand backwards and forwards before he crossed his arms over his paunch.

'Sorry, am I holding you up from something?'

I found Ed's impatience infuriating, so I'd decided to call him out.

'No, but I think you're focusing on the wrong man.'

Ed's attitude left a lot to be desired, and he set my anger on fire without warning. I could feel my blood start to boil.

'I'm the senior officer here, and you'd do well to remember that. Just answer the question, Ed.'

My partner glared at me with a look of thinly veiled contempt on his face before he tore his eyes away from mine and started leafing back through his notebook.

'Finn McCaskill's twenty-eight, and he was born and bred on the Isle of Sheppey...'

'The Isle of Sheppey's a long way from London City Airport,' I said, cutting Ed off mid-flow.

Ed glanced up from his pad and threw me a look. It was clear he wasn't happy that I'd interrupted him, but I didn't really give a shit about what he thought.

'It must be at least an hour and a half by car. God knows how long by public transport. Find out how he gets to work.'

Ed didn't reply but carried on reading from his notes instead. 'As I was saying...'

A smile crept on to my face. I bet he would have loved to have added 'before I was so rudely interrupted', but he didn't have the balls to do it. That spoke volumes about Ed's personality as far as I was concerned.

'... Finn went to junior and senior school on the island

and left after his GCSEs. Up until six months ago, he'd been employed by various local companies.'

'Doing what?' I questioned, running the risk of incurring Ed's wrath again.

'He'd worked as a labourer on a building site for a good few years, and more recently, he was employed at the steelworks.'

'Can you expand on that? What was his job title?' I coaxed. Getting information out of Ed was like getting blood out of a stone.

'He was driving a forklift and working in the distribution area,' Ed replied.

That was a similar role to the one he was doing at the airport. Why would you leave a near-identical job right on your doorstep for one that was a ninety-minute commute? Unless British Airways paid big bucks, he was likely to be worse off now than he was before. Even if you ignored the financial side of things, the extra time added to the daily grind of travelling to work and back would have been enough to put somebody off accepting that offer of employment, I would have thought.

'Something doesn't add up here. Find out how much Finn was earning at the steelworks and how much his current role pays. How long did you say he'd been working at London City Airport?'

'Six months,' Ed replied.

That rang alarm bells to me.

'You said the guards had been there for over ten years. What about the rest of the team?'

Ed's finger swiped at the pages of his notebook in slow motion.

'The other three cargo handlers have been there eighteen months, nine months and four months, respectively,' Ed replied without tearing his eyes away from his notes.

'So they have a relatively high turnover of staff.'

It was a simple fact of life in some industries, but it gave rise to security concerns. Companies with unskilled workers and younger staff members tended to see higher turnover rates, but that wasn't good news for the investigation. It blew my theory out of the water. The person we were looking for might not currently work for the airline after all. But I wasn't going to let Ed in on that thought. How many people had left London City Airport knowing that airlines regularly flew in with millions of pounds stowed in their cargo? It would be a logistical nightmare trying to trace all the possible leads.

'Contact Human Resources and get a full list of employees who've worked in the warehouse for the last two years. We'll need to carry out background checks on all of them.'

27

Lola

I'd woken with a start after a fitful night's sleep and realised daylight was piercing the thin fabric curtains. While lying on my back, I gazed around the room. It took several seconds for my brain to register where I was. I scrambled out from under the quilt and sat on the edge of the bed. Reaching across to the wooden bedside cabinet, I checked the pay as you go mobile I was using to see if Mum had messaged. Nothing had come through since last night, so I decided to go and get some breakfast. I'd barely eaten anything yesterday, and my stomach was rumbling.

'Did you manage to get some sleep?' Elaine asked when I walked into the kitchen.

'Yes. It took me a while, but I eventually dropped off.'

'That's good. Take it easy for the next couple of days, and as soon as you feel ready, we can help you with a range of practical issues, such as registering with a local doctor and applying for welfare benefits,' Elaine said.

'Thank you,' I replied, forcing out a smile.

'You don't have to do this on your own. Professional support and counselling are available if you want it. But it's not compulsory.'

It was a nice offer, but I didn't feel ready to start sharing my troubles with a stranger.

'Our aim is to give you the help you need to rebuild your life free from fear. We're here to guide you. We're not here to judge you or tell you what to do.'

The kindness of Elaine's words caught me off guard, and my eyes filled with tears. I barely knew this lady, and yet she was so incredibly sympathetic and supportive that it sent my emotions into overdrive.

'I'm sorry. I don't know what came over me,' I said, hoping to excuse my sudden meltdown.

'Don't apologise. You've got nothing to be sorry about. You've been through a rough time, so if you feel the need, don't hold back your tears. Let them out. It's no good bottling up your emotions. I don't know about you, but I always feel better after a good cry.'

I dabbed at my eyes with the tissue I had balled up in my hand. Elaine was right. Moments ago, I'd been like a pressure cooker about to explode, but I already felt calmer.

'I've been in your situation myself, so I know how difficult it is to deal with the barrage of emotions you're experiencing. If you want to talk about what happened, I'm a good listener; you have to be to succeed in this job. But there's no pressure either way. I'll leave you to it, but you know where I am if you need me.'

I knew Elaine was only trying to be helpful and had my best interests at heart, but I couldn't concentrate on anything apart from Mum at the moment. I kept picturing her lying in the hospital bed with her arm in a plaster cast and her face battered and bruised. Guilt was eating away at me; it was my fault Troy had assaulted her. I should never have put her in that position. Now I owed it to her to do the right thing even though she didn't want me to.

I abandoned all thoughts of having breakfast; I'd suddenly lost my appetite. Once I was back in my room, I pulled my rucksack on to the bed, unzipped the front pocket and took out the business card DS Ash had given me. I sat staring at it for several minutes before I plucked up the courage to dial the number.

'DS Ash, speaking,' she said when she answered my call.

'It's Lola Marshall,' I replied.

'Hello, Lola. It's lovely to hear from you. What can I do for you?'

A voice screamed inside my head, willing me to do the right thing, but I couldn't seem to form the words.

'Is everything okay, Lola?' DS Ash asked when the silence between us stretched on.

I'd been about to make up an excuse so that I could end the call. I'd suddenly lost my bottle. It was difficult for me to admit to another person that I'd been abused. I'd kept the secret to myself for such a long time it felt alien to talk about it. I'd constantly make excuses for his behaviour. Troy had a vicious temper, but when he unleashed it on me, I'd convince myself that I must have somehow unintentionally provoked him.

Now I had the added guilt that the same man had put my mum in hospital. No wonder I was having trouble opening up to the police. Even though I hadn't inflicted Mum's injuries on her, I felt responsible for them. It wasn't that I didn't want to report him; I was terrified of the consequences if I did.

'I can't help you if you don't tell me what's wrong. Has this got something to do with your mum?' DS Ash questioned, paving the way for me to spill the beans.

'Yes,' I admitted.

It was only a one-word answer, but I'd just taken a huge step in the right direction. My body began to tremble as I tried to pluck up the courage to speak to the detective.

'What would you like to tell me?' DS Ash asked.

My reluctance to speak must have been frustrating for her, but her patience was going to pay off. Determination started growing inside me like a vine, forcing its way into every fibre of my body. I could literally feel it spreading through my limbs like the branches of a tree.

'I need to talk to you about my mum's attacker.'

'Go on,' DS Ash prompted.

'When we were on the way to the hospital, you asked me if I thought Mum's attacker and my abuser were the same man...'

I suddenly clammed up. It wasn't out of loyalty. My words had evaporated through fear.

'Yes, I remember.'

I took a deep breath. It was now or never.

'I couldn't be one hundred per cent certain until I'd spoken to Mum, but you were right, my ex-boyfriend Troy Jacobs attacked her because she wouldn't tell him where I'd gone.'

'I'd thought as much,' DS Ash replied. 'I need you to give me as much information as you can. We're dealing with a very dangerous individual, and the sooner we take him into custody, the better for everyone.'

'Troy's twenty-six, and he's the manager at the Sheffield city centre branch of William Hill. He should be at work now, but if he's not, he rents a flat in Victoria Street.'

The words tumbled out of my mouth in a continuous stream, and I didn't come up for air until I rattled off all the information. I was scared to pause in case I didn't pluck up the courage to continue. Reporting my abusive ex was a massive step and one I never thought I'd take, but that was before he took his anger out on my mum. He deserved everything he got as far as I was concerned. I was glad Mum made me take photos of the last beating he gave me now. They would help to back up her case.

'Leave this with me,' DS Ash said.

As soon as I ended the call, I burst into tears. Although I felt relieved, I hoped I'd done the right thing.

28

Paul

August, Six months before the heist

Finn hadn't been working for British Airways long when he dropped the bombshell, and from the moment he'd shared the fact that he handled millions of pounds worth of used notes with us, none of us could think about anything else. Saturdays couldn't come around soon enough for my liking. Hearing the latest news from London City Airport was the highlight of my week.

'Did you get your grubby mitts on any huge piles of cash this week?' I asked as I took a sip of my pint.

'Yeah, several in fact. I can't believe how much money arrives at the airport on a regular basis,' Finn said with a smirk on his freckled face.

'You'd think someone would have been tempted to steal it,' I said, putting my thought out there to see what reaction it got.

'My line manager made it clear when he was training me

that BA take theft very seriously and they safeguard against it. If an employee gets caught with their hand in the cookie jar, their contract is immediately terminated,' Finn replied.

'Surely every company adopts that policy. No employer is going to be seen to stand back and let their staff get away with stealing from them. It doesn't mean it doesn't happen, though,' I replied.

'How much cash do you think arrives in one go?' Kevin asked.

'It's difficult to say; the amount varies. Strangely enough, British Airways don't provide us with details of how much money's being shipped for security reasons,' Finn replied.

'Now there's a surprise,' I laughed. 'You guys are just the minions that handle the dosh; you don't need to concern yourselves with anything else.'

'Too right; we wait in the wings while Stan and Norman rock up in the armoured van, offload the pallets of cash from the cargo area of the plane and then transport it back to the warehouse. Then we get the honour of putting the sealed bags in the cage until the bank arrives to collect it,' Finn said.

'Imagine if we could work out a way to intercept the shipment,' Mark said as though he'd just read my mind. 'Considering how valuable the cargo is, it doesn't sound like it travels with a lot of security.'

'It doesn't,' Finn confirmed. 'The banks put trackers in the vacuum bags with the money, and although security staff move the cash from the plane to the warehouse, neither Stan nor Norman are armed.'

'Why not?' Mark asked.

'They're not allowed to carry weapons as they're not cops,' Finn replied.

My ears pricked up at the sound of that. Stealing the shipment sounded almost too easy, too good to be true. The more details Finn gave us, the more tempted I was to try and nick the money.

'I don't know about you guys,' I said, scooting my chair in closer to the table. 'But I'm absolutely itching to get my hands on that cash.'

We'd all been a bit light-fingered when we were younger, so I was pretty sure the thought had crossed their minds too.

'You're not the only one,' Kevin agreed.

'To be fair, I think it would be tough for even the most morally upstanding person to walk away from an opportunity like this,' I grinned.

'It's literally fallen into our laps,' Mark piped up.

'I know it sounds easy enough, but if it really was that simple, why hasn't anyone done it before?' Finn questioned.

'Maybe the other members of staff aren't as enterprising as us,' I smiled.

'It's tempting, but I'm not sure we're up to it.' Finn scratched the side of his face as he considered the idea.

'Why not? We've dabbled in the past,' Kevin replied, referring to our teenage years when we'd do anything to make a bit of pocket money.

'That's as maybe. But nothing on this scale.' Finn's eyebrows knitted together, and he clamped one hand around his pint. 'We've only ever handled goods that fell off the back of a lorry. None of us has any experience of actually doing the robbing.'

Finn had a fair point. We didn't do the nicking, we just dealt with the goods after they'd been lifted, so it wasn't exactly in the same league, but if all of us were up for it, what was his problem? It seemed like too good an opportunity to ignore if you asked me.

29

Lola

I lay on my bed, curled into the foetal position crying my eyes out when gentle knocking on the door stopped my tears in mid-flow. I quickly dried my cheeks with the pads of my fingers before I walked across the floor and opened my door. Millie was standing on the other side. The smile slid from her face when she clapped eyes on me.

'What's up, Lola? You look like you're upset. Do you want to talk about it?'

Millie had given me the green light to open up to her, so it would be stupid of me to ignore it. I nodded and stepped away from the doorway so that she could come into my room. We took a seat on the edge of my bed, and that's when I began letting out all the details of mine and Troy's relationship. Millie listened without interrupting, allowing me to get it all off my chest.

'You poor thing,' she said when I finally came up for air. 'It sounds like you've been to hell and back.'

'I just hope I've done the right thing. My mum was

adamant that she didn't want me to report Troy to the police. She was worried it would fuel his anger. But I'm fed up of covering up for him and suddenly felt the need to make a stand. I wanted to show Troy I wasn't a pushover. I was a force to be reckoned with. Now I'm doubting myself again.'

'Well, don't. I've been in a similar situation myself. I thought long and hard about going to the police before I told them about my ex, but it was the best thing I ever did. He beat me so badly I had to have my eye socket rebuilt with a metal plate,' Millie said, running her fingers subconsciously over a scar by the side of her left eye. 'In some ways, he did me a favour. Having time away from him while I was in hospital made me realise I could never go back to him. I filed a police report, and he was charged with grievous bodily harm. He's currently serving five years in prison. The judge also gave him a restraining order which runs indefinitely and prevents him from contacting me ever again.'

Talking to Millie was inspirational. She was only a month ahead of me in her recovery, but she was doing so well, fingers crossed the same thing would happen to me. After she left, I sat on the edge of my bed, reassured that I'd found the courage to speak out, but the feeling was short-lived.

'Lola, I've spoken to your mum, and I'm afraid she's insisting that she's not going to press charges, so there's nothing more we can do,' DS Ash said when she phoned me a few moments later.

'Let me give her a call and see if I can talk her into it,' I replied, feeling buoyed up by Millie's experience.

'You had no business phoning the police,' Mum said in a

curt tone. She didn't try to conceal her bluntness. 'I thought I made it clear when you came to the hospital that I didn't want to report Troy. Have you forgotten what he said he'd do to you?'

'All the more reason to have him put behind bars. That's the only way either of us will ever be safe. You have to reconsider pressing charges.'

'And if I do, the next thing we'll have is a missing person report, a recovered body and a young man on the run. He's going to destroy our family if we go after him. You know that as much as I do. I've got to go now, Lola, it's hurting my face to talk.'

Mum's words were like a blow to the stomach.

'I'm sorry to say she was having none of it. Mum's determined she doesn't want to report Troy. If I go back to Sheffield, I might be able to talk her around,' I said when I phoned DS Ash back.

'Leave it with me; I'll try to put some pressure on your mum. It's far too dangerous for you to even consider going home while Troy's still a free man,' DS Ash replied before we ended the call.

30

Abbie

I'd grown up rubbing shoulders with some very suspect characters who'd made a living out of dubious means. My upbringing undoubtedly played a pivotal role in helping me crack cases, but I wasn't having a lot of luck this time. We hadn't had one credible lead since the start of the investigation, and something told me today would be no different.

'I've completed the background checks on all the employees who've worked in the warehouse in the last two years,' Ed said when he walked into the incident room.

'And?' I questioned.

'There's nothing to report,' Ed replied without filling me in on a single detail.

'Really? Nothing at all?' I found that hard to believe.

Ed shook his head. 'We've hit another dead end.'

'How many employees are we talking about?'

'Twelve,' Ed replied.

That was more than I'd thought. The list of possible suspects was growing, not diminishing.

'And all of them are decent law-abiding citizens without a single conviction or caution between them?'

'You guessed it.'

'Let me have a copy of the background checks.'

I wanted to see them for myself in case Ed had missed something. He wasn't as organised as I was; I like to compartmentalise information. Trying to work out the connection between the robbers and their inside man had kept the cogs of my brain turning long into the night, and judging from the dark circles residing under my partner's eyes, it had disturbed his sleep too.

Robbers could be classified as amateur or professional based on the characteristics of the crime. Our thieves used weapons and disguises, so they weren't opportunistic. They had arranged for the security cameras to be disabled and had a sophisticated means of getaway in place, which made me think they had done this before. Unlike Ed, I wasn't as keen to write the list of employees off without further investigation. We needed to do some digging if we were going to uncover a clue that would help us solve this case.

'The men we're looking for would have spent months, if not years, planning a heist like this,' I said.

'Which brings me back to my prime suspect.'

Ed wasn't about to shift his thinking any time soon. He shot me an irritated glance. I responded by taking a deep breath and counting to ten to let my anger pass. I wondered if he'd twigged how much I disliked him. Just the mention of his name got my hackles up. Working with my pig-headed partner was the most jarring experience. We didn't see eye to eye on anything.

Ed was completely blinkered by the fact that Stanley was guilty and was hell-bent on finding a reason to frame him for the robbery. Whereas my gut told me Finn was our man even though I couldn't prove it. I had a nagging doubt that wouldn't be silenced, and in a situation like this, I always let my gut guide me when there was nothing else to go on.

Although firearms were used in the heist, our robbers didn't discharge a single bullet which might have given us a lead. When a gun is fired, a shell case is left behind. It could serve as valuable evidence to identify the weapon if we were able to seize that at a later stage.

Ed paced the room, hands in pockets, deep in thought. He appeared tense. Then he leaned against the wall, crossed his arms over his chest and glared at me.

'I think we should bring Stanley Brown in for further questioning.'

'And I think you should concentrate your efforts on something more worthwhile.' I threw my words over my shoulder as I walked out of the incident room. I needed some space from Ed.

31

Lola

'You seem a bit brighter today,' Elaine said when I walked into the kitchen. 'Did you sleep well?'

'Not really. I find it hard to switch off when I've got things on my mind,' I replied.

'Well, you know what they say, a problem shared is a problem halved,' Elaine smiled.

I was desperate to confide in her. Keeping all of this to myself was stressing me out. I'd only known Elaine for a short time, but we were already forming a strong bond.

'I reported my ex to the police last night.'

I felt a sense of relief when the words left my mouth. Taking the first step was always the hardest bit.

'Good for you. You should be proud of yourself.'

Before I'd arrived at the refuge, I'd felt beaten down and worthless, so I was glad I'd finally found the courage to speak up. When you'd spent as long as I had being controlled by somebody, you doubted yourself in everything you did.

'Thanks. It wasn't easy. Troy used to tell me that there

was no point in going to the police because nobody would believe me.'

'When you're in that situation, it's impossible not to buy into the lies your abuser feeds you,' Elaine said.

'I know he had me convinced that I was the cause of the arguments and that I pushed him into reacting the way he did. Over time, he wore me down.'

I cast my eyes towards the floor. I could feel my chin begin to tremble as I fought to hold back my tears.

'Troy was trying to break your spirit, and along the way, he caused you a great deal of despair,' Elaine said. It was clear she knew exactly where I was coming from.

'The worst thing is it took my mum being attacked to make me see sense. Did you know it was Troy that landed her in hospital?'

'I guessed as much. When you work in a refuge for abused women, you get a feeling for this sort of thing,' Elaine said.

'She was only trying to protect me. If I'd acted sooner, this wouldn't have happened.'

My eyes welled up with tears. The weight of my guilt was unbearable.

'Don't think like that,' Elaine said. 'Focus on the positive. You've reported him now, and that's all that matters.'

Elaine always seemed to say the right thing and never made me feel pressured into talking which was probably why I felt comfortable opening up to her. But until I'd felt ready, she'd been the height of discretion even though she'd had her suspicions.

'Once Mum found out the truth about our relationship, I found myself defending him. Can you believe that?' I shook my head, unable to comprehend why I'd done that. 'I didn't want to admit that anything was wrong. I used to blame myself for the arguments because he'd convinced me that I triggered his aggression by acting in certain ways.'

'The abuser always conditions the victim to carry the blame and shame.'

'When I lived back in Sheffield, Troy had access to my phone and was always checking the search history.'

'That's a huge red flag,' Elaine said.

'I knew something was terribly wrong, but I didn't want to admit it, even to myself. Troy had been trying to convince me to move in with him just before we split up.'

'It's just as well you didn't let him sway you. It would have been even harder for you to get away if you'd been living together,' Elaine pointed out.

'My relationship with Troy created a lot of tension between Mum and myself, and we sometimes argued over it. She never believed the cover-up stories I used to spin her when she saw me with bruises, so I found myself withholding information from her. I'd say whatever it took to get her to drop the subject.'

'You're in good company, all the residents here have been in the same boat as you at one time or another, so they'll understand where you're coming from.'

'The entire time we were a couple, I was convinced that love would conquer all. How ridiculous does that sound?'

'It sounds perfectly feasible to me,' Elaine said. 'I'm sure all the ladies here hoped their situations would get better if they gave it more time. I know I did.'

'Once our relationship started to break down, it collapsed like a house of cards, gaining momentum and turning to rubble in the blink of an eye.'

'The same thing happened to me. In all the years I've worked here, I haven't heard of one abusive relationship that became healthier the longer it continued. Not one. Not with therapy. Not with prayer. Not with any other form of intervention,' Elaine replied.

'I was weak and spineless for not leaving sooner.' I swallowed down the lump in my throat as an image of Mum's battered face popped into my head.

'Don't ever let me hear you say that about yourself. Strong women are the ones most likely to be targeted by certain abusers. They look for qualities they don't have themselves; empathy and compassion make a person vulnerable when it's used against them.' Elaine was an expert on the matter.

Wasn't that the truth?

'People often wonder how somebody ends up in this position, but we both know abusers don't reveal their true selves on the first date. If they did, they wouldn't get as far as a second one.' I could see Elaine felt passionate about this subject.

'That's so true. Troy didn't hit me in the beginning. I fell in love with a nice person; it wasn't until later on that he turned into a monster.'

'The same thing happened with my ex-husband. He swept me off my feet and put on an overwhelming display of affection at the beginning of our relationship. I thought I'd bagged myself a real gentleman, but in reality, he needed me to fall hard and fast before his mask slipped. Our situation reached an all-time low after my son was born. He wanted me all to himself. And when that didn't happen, he became increasingly violent.' Elaine's eyes misted up briefly, but then she pushed back her shoulders and replaced her sad expression with a sunny smile.

'Thanks for the chat,' I said.

'Anytime. I'm glad you felt ready to share your experience with me,' Elaine replied.

'You put me at ease when you started telling me about your past,' I admitted.

'I'm glad it helped. Empowering women to overcome violence and rebuild their lives is so rewarding; I love seeing the change in our residents even after a short amount of time. Women arrive here frightened and reserved; they soon learn to take control of their lives again. You'll be a different person before you know it, and when you get to know the others better, you'll realise how much you have in common.' Elaine smiled then squeezed my hand before she left me with my thoughts.

The day was getting better and better. My relentless nagging had paid off, and I'd managed to convince Mum that she was just as much a victim in all of this as I was. I was elated when she phoned and told me that she'd given a statement to the police and that Troy had been arrested.

'We're going to carry out checks on Troy's background and lifestyle. If we can show he had a history of violence, it will strengthen the case against him,' DS Ash said.

She'd called me moments after I'd put down the phone from Mum.

Surprising as it may seem, I knew Troy didn't have any previous criminal convictions, and I was partly to blame for that. If I'd listened to my mum and reported him to the police when he'd beaten me black and blue on countless occasions, we might not be in this position now.

'I might be able to help you with that. I've got some photos of injuries Troy inflicted on me. Would you like me to email them over to you?' I asked.

'It depends how long ago this happened. There's a time limit of six months for a charge to be brought against an offender,' DS Ash replied.

'The assault falls within the time frame.'

'Send them over then, please. My email address is on my card,' DS Ash said.

I was glad Mum had insisted on taking them now. She'd copied them on to a USB for safekeeping. I was more than happy to give them to the police if they would help Troy's conviction stick.

32

Paul

The Rising Tide, Five months before the heist

Since Finn had landed a job at London City Airport and now worked for British Airways as part of their ground operations team, we'd become fixated by the serious security issues surrounding the transport of millions of pounds worth of cash. It beggared belief that the money was held in a loading dock protected by unarmed guards until the bank collected it.

'Let's get down to business. We've been chewing the thought over since last weekend. Have we come to a decision?' I asked when Kevin came back to the table with a round of drinks.

'Yes,' my younger brother replied as he lifted the pints of Stella off of the tray.

Mark and Finn nodded in agreement.

'I'm in,' I said to start the ball rolling.

'Me too,' Kevin replied.

'And me,' Mark piped up.

Only Finn was silent. But if he wasn't on board, robbing the warehouse would be a non-starter. We wouldn't be able to plan the heist without him.

'What about you, mate?' I asked when the silence dragged on.

'I'm in too,' Finn finally said with a face as long as the queue outside the benefits office.

'You don't look too happy about your decision.'

I sat back in my chair and waited for him to reply.

'If you want to know the truth, it's not that I don't want to nick the money, it's just I'm scared shitless about doing it,' Finn said.

'I think we all are,' I said, answering for Mark and Kevin. 'There's a lot riding on this, but we'll never amount to anything if we carry on the way we're going.'

We all had the ambition to succeed if we were given a chance. Mark wanted to open his own watersports centre somewhere he didn't need to wear a wetsuit. Finn fancied himself as a property developer, but the price of houses in the UK was so high his dream was never likely to become a reality. And Kevin and I hoped one day we'd be the proud owners of a beachfront bar in a location where the sun put in an appearance and lifted the mercury into double figures.

Even though I was sure we'd miss a decent cup of tea and fish and chips, none of us wanted to stay in England. We all had our hearts set on sunnier climes. We'd watched enough episodes of *A Place in the Sun* to know how much further your money stretched if you were brave enough to take the plunge and make a new start abroad.

Don't get me wrong; I'd miss Sheppey. It was a fantastic

place to live and was the perfect place to raise a family. Residents prided themselves on the sense of community, and there weren't many areas in the UK where the postman could leave a parcel on the doorstep while you were out at work, and it would still be there when you got back. But my home town was one of them.

Kevin and I had had a happy childhood on the island. The issues only surfaced when we'd left school. Neither of us had been interested in furthering our education, and the one thing our birthplace didn't have was good job prospects. We'd probably never have been tempted to leave Sheppey if we'd been at the stage in our lives where we didn't need to make a living. But lack of opportunities made people resort to things they wouldn't normally do. Pulling off a heist was a big undertaking for a handful of inexperienced guys, but when you had nothing, you had nothing to lose.

We might have been apprehensive, but all of us felt the same about this. None of us needed to have our arms twisted. Thieves never came from wealthy backgrounds. People were driven to do things because of their circumstances. Finn landing a job handling millions of pounds worth of used notes felt like fate.

We knew what the consequences would be if the plan failed. There were three prisons on the island. We'd grown up surrounded by a large concentration of inmates in a small area and knew only too well what happened to people that broke the law, but we were so desperate to succeed we were willing to take the risk.

'Now that we're all agreed, we'll need to start doing our homework. If we meet up later at the chalet, we can get some beers in and a takeaway curry and binge watch some armed robbery films,' I said.

We were complete novices, so we'd need to learn everything we could.

'Eat your heart out, Butch Cassidy,' Kevin grinned.

His smile slid from his face when I looked daggers at him.

'What? I was only joking.' Kevin held his hands up in front of him.

'I've got to head off, but I'll see you guys later.' Finn got up from the table. 'I'll bring the popcorn,' he said over his shoulder before he walked out of the door.

33

Lola

'How are you settling in?' Roxanne asked when I walked into the communal lounge with a mug of tea clamped in my hand.

'I'm getting there,' I replied. 'Where are Kai and Poppy?'

'They're at school,' she smiled, then did a happy dance, which brought a smile to my face.

'I took a big step and reported Troy to the police,' I said.

I'd decided to seize the opportunity to tell her what had happened while she was alone. I'd taken on board what Elaine had said about us all being in the same boat and reasoned the more people I opened up to, the easier the process would become.

'Wow! Good for you, girl,' Roxanne said before high-fiving me. 'I bet you feel relieved.'

'I do, but part of me is terrified I've done the wrong thing.'

'You haven't. I felt like that at the start, but as time goes on, you'll realise holding Troy accountable for the trauma and abuse he's put you through is the only way to stop the cycle. The final straw for me came when my ex-husband broke my nose while my children looked on in horror. He headbutted me because I'd burnt the toast! Imagine doing that in front of two young kids. What an arsehole.' Roxanne shook her head.

'Oh my God.' I was so glad I'd got out before Troy and I had had a family.

'Everyone was shocked when I left him because to the outside world, he put me on a pedestal. He'd tell anyone that would listen that I was the best thing that had ever happened to him. He loved and adored me one minute, and the next, he'd be belting me black and blue. Everybody thought we were a perfect family, but nobody knows what goes on behind closed doors,' Roxanne said.

'Troy was obsessed with the idea of me having exes even though he was the only serious boyfriend I'd ever had. I tried to put his mind at rest, but it was impossible to get through to him when he wasn't in a rational state.'

'Jealousy's an ugly emotion. It sounds like your ex had a lack of confidence, which he tried to camouflage by being a bully.'

Roxanne's assumption was correct. It was good to speak to someone who understood what I'd been through. At the time, the fog of the situation was so dense, I'd lost sight of my compass. But now I found myself questioning why I'd fought so hard to keep the abuse a secret. I knew the answer. I hadn't wanted to let Troy down.

'I'd been desperate to make things work; all I wanted was to have a happy relationship. But all I got was a load of misery.'

'Tell me about it. Bruises fade, but it's the internal damage that's left behind that's everlasting. The trauma I've been through has left scars on my heart and soul. But for my kids' sakes, I'll learn to live with them,' Roxanne said.

I felt humbled speaking to her. However bad I'd thought my situation was, there were people worse off than me.

'My ex-husband was determined to destroy my life when I left him. He tried to strip me of everything and even tried to take my children away from me. Do you know what that experience taught me?' Roxanne asked.

'No.'

'I realised I had to be assertive even if I wasn't feeling it. You can teach yourself to use your tone of voice, posture and facial expression to portray confidence. You'll be surprised how powerful that can make you feel,' Roxanne smiled.

I smiled back. That was another lesson learned on my road to recovery.

34

Abbie

We needed a break, or we were never going to catch the men responsible. What was I missing? I'd spent much of the day poring over documents, photographs, and files, but I was stumped. There was no way I wanted Ed to pick up on that fact, so I'd put some distance between us.

I'd been a detective long enough to know it didn't matter what entry point you started at, there was only one exit, so maybe it was time to look at the heist from a different angle. If I focused on how the thieves had made their getaway, it might throw up some clues and avenues that I hadn't yet explored.

I trawled over what we knew so far. The robbers had taken advantage of the airport's close proximity to London's Docklands when they made their escape, dumping the armoured van they'd used in the heist alongside a hole they'd cut in a perimeter fence. I'd get Ed to check out whether any of the members of staff either owned a boat or had knowledge of how to drive one. That might throw up a lead.

Usually, I loved the problem-solving aspect of my work, but this case was testing my resolve, making me question whether my heart was still in my job. It wasn't the first time I'd felt like this. Six months into the role, I folded up my uniform and placed it with my warrant card on my inspector's desk. The long hours and constant jibes from male colleagues had taken their toll on me. He was astonished that I was going to throw the towel in and said, 'I never had you down as a quitter.' His words struck a chord and jolted me back to my senses. I picked my uniform up, put it back on and went back to doing the job my family said I wasn't cut out for. The inspector and I never mentioned the incident again. It was a turning point in my career. From that day on, whenever I doubted myself and felt like throwing the towel in, I reminded myself of that conversation.

I'd spent long enough procrastinating; it was time to get back to the job in hand. I knocked back the dregs of my coffee, then threw the paper cup into the bin on my way out of the deserted staff canteen.

Ed was leaning back in a chair, legs akimbo with a pen clamped between his teeth, when I walked into the incident room. The sight of him made me bristle, but I'd have to try to move past the obvious personality clash. It wasn't going to be easy. The man had no redeeming qualities. I'd rather stick pins in my eyes than spend time with him. But I should be grateful for small mercies. At least he wasn't the SIO on the case, so I didn't have to answer to him.

'I need you to do some more digging,' I said.

I couldn't bring myself to exchange pleasantries. Ed definitely brought out the worst in me. I wasn't usually this hostile.

Ed took the pen out of his mouth and gripped it in the pudgy fingers of his right hand. We became locked in an eyeballing contest before he decided to reward my patience with a reply.

'Would you care to elaborate?' he asked.

Ed's curt response immediately got my back up, and I felt my blood pressure take a sharp rise. I was silently fuming and had to bite down on my lip so that I wouldn't be tempted to tell him what I really thought of him. Remain professional at all times, I reminded myself.

Ed crossed one stumpy leg over the other while glaring at me with his beady brown eyes. Then he unbuttoned his suit jacket, and in doing so, he exposed the brightly coloured lining. I couldn't help thinking he was attempting to give off the impression that underneath the thirty-something Harry Potter exterior, he was a lot more interesting than he looked. It would take more than some jazzy fabric to convince me.

'We know that our robbers used a speedboat to make their getaway, so I want you to check whether any of the staff members past and present have a boat or access to one,' I replied.

Ed let out a loud sigh. 'Is that really necessary?'

'Yes, it is,' I replied through gritted teeth.

Whether he realised it or not, my partner was on the verge of lighting my fuse.

'Surely, it's much more likely that the thieves just hired a boat to use in the robbery.'

Ed had a valid point, but on principle, I wasn't going to acknowledge that. He wasn't the senior detective, so he had no business questioning my orders.

'If you put as much effort into doing what I asked instead of resisting my requests all the time, we would have a much smoother working relationship.' I didn't try to disguise the fact that my words had a barbed edge to them.

Ed was showing me zero respect, so he couldn't really expect me to treat him any differently.

'Let's call it a night. You can get started on that in the morning,' I said after checking the time on my watch.

It had been a long day. I couldn't wait to get home and pour myself a large glass of chilled Pinot Grigio.

35

Lola

March, Two weeks after arriving at the shelter

'How did you get on?' I asked when Millie walked into the communal lounge.

Judging by the smile she was wearing that stretched from ear to ear, I was certain I could guess what her response was going to be.

'Really well; they offered me the job. I start the day after tomorrow.'

'That's fantastic!'

I jumped out of my seat and threw my arms around her shoulders, congratulating her with a big hug.

'I wasn't expecting to get it. I've worked in my local Londis since I left school, so I don't know the first thing about what goes on inside a casino,' Millie said. 'But I assured the lady who interviewed me that I was a quick learner and a hard worker. She said that wasn't a problem. If anything, it was an advantage.'

'Really?' I questioned.

'Yes. I can't quite believe it myself.'

Millie had landed on her feet by the sounds of it. I'd been trawling through multiple employment agencies' websites looking for work. Almost every advert stated that the applicant needed to have previous experience in the role to apply. It was soul-destroying. My savings were dwindling by the day, and I was going to be in real trouble if I didn't find a job soon.

'You sound like you might be interested,' Millie said.

'I am. I desperately need a job. I haven't been able to apply for anything yet; everything I've seen requires experience.'

'Tell me about it. I couldn't believe my luck when she said it didn't matter because the company provided the necessary training. She said sometimes it was better to employ people that were new to the role so that they hadn't got into any bad habits, and she personally preferred to work with a clean slate. Do you want me to call her and see if they have any more vacancies?' Millie asked.

'Yes, please,' I replied, and then my lips spread into a grin.

I was swirling the teabag around in the mug ten minutes later when Millie walked into the kitchen. I let go of the spoon so that I could give her my full attention.

'Did you manage to get hold of her?' I questioned.

Millie stood facing me with a blank expression on her face, giving nothing away. She nodded, and then her lips spread into her trademark grin.

'Cassandra Peterson would like to see you tomorrow morning at eleven.'

I clasped my hands together and let out a squeal before I could bring myself to speak.

'Oh my God, you had me going there for a minute. I thought it was going to be bad news. Thank you so much. I owe you one.'

36

Paul

Four months before the heist

Plotting how to pull off the perfect robbery had given us a new purpose in life, and we'd started spending every spare moment we had in each other's company. We hadn't spent this much time together in years, and it made me feel nostalgic. Being at the run-down holiday park took me back to my youth. Nothing had changed for years, even the arcade games were the same. It was like living in the land that time forgot.

As I walked over to the chalet from the main car park, memories of our younger days came flooding back. When the holiday accommodation was full, it doubled the island's population. Mainlanders often remarked that Sheppey was a giant caravan park. Nobody could argue it did have its fair share of campsites providing a bolthole for Londoners looking for a holiday retreat.

Hanging around the campsite during the summer months

when there was a sudden influx of teenage girls on holiday with their parents was our favourite pastime when we were at school. Mark wasn't as tall as Finn, but he had a great physique and a pretty much year-round golden glow to his skin from working outdoors. The ladies seemed to love the blond surfer look, so he always got first pick.

Kevin and I were the smallest in the group at five foot ten. We both had brown hair, blue eyes, and the same square jawline with a dimple in the middle. We were like two peas in a pod, so with nothing separating us in the looks department, I like to pull rank on my younger brother and take second pick.

It was a source of great entertainment for Mark and me that Kevin and Finn got to battle it out between themselves so that they didn't get left with the moose. Happy days, they seemed like a lifetime ago now. We'd had quite a good success rate considering none of us looked like Brad Pitt or had his bank balance. We couldn't do anything about what we were born with, but hopefully, the latter would change for the better. Dreaming how to spend money that we hadn't yet acquired wasn't a very sensible thing to do, so I forced myself back to reality.

The outline was starting to take shape. Right from the off, we'd been careful to do any internet surfing regarding the heist on the public computer in the library. We didn't want anything dodgy showing up in our search histories if our laptops were seized at a later stage. Apart from an initial couple of times, we also didn't have any conversations in public about our plans, preferring to wait until we were behind the safety of the chalet walls to discuss the details. This was a huge undertaking for such a small crew, but we deliberately wanted to keep it that way; the fewer people who knew about the plan, the better. We were all sworn to secrecy. I knew I could trust my friends; we'd known each other for years.

We'd decided to wait until February to make a move. Finn had found out the airport wasn't as busy at that time of year. Once the Christmas and New Year rush had subsided, the airport laid off a lot of the temporary staff that had been drafted in to deal with the seasonal influx of passengers. We all agreed that the fewer potential witnesses that were around, the better.

'I've started to work out the timings by pacing out the route you guys are going to take,' Finn said when we got down to business.

'You know what I'm like, I'm sceptical by nature, I'd love to see the layout for myself,' I replied.

'It's not going to be possible to carry out surveillance without potentially exposing our plan, so I'm afraid you're going to have to take my word for it,' Finn said.

'Make sure you take into account that Kevin and I don't have the same inside leg measurement as you when you go striding around the tarmac on your flamingo pipe cleaner pins. We're just average-sized blokes,' I laughed.

Finn rolled his blue eyes before he continued talking. 'I'm going to steal two BA uniforms for you guys to wear.'

That should help us to blend into the background.

'Where the hell are we going to get the guns from?' Finn continued.

Mark's eyebrows shot into his hairline.

'I'll have a word with Randal the vandal, one of the guys from the wing. His family's into all sorts of dodgy stuff. I bet he'd be able to get hold of a couple of weapons for us if the price was right,' Kevin replied.

Kevin worked at HMP Standford Hill, an open prison for men, one of three prisons that formed the Sheppey Cluster, along with HMP Elmley and HMP Swaleside.

'You guys don't even know how to fire a gun,' Mark pointed out.

'I'm sure we can find out what we need to know from YouTube,' I countered.

'Do you really think you need to use real weapons? Couldn't you just get hold of replica guns?' Mark asked. 'The sentencing for armed robbery is so much higher if you get caught.'

'That's what I like about you, mate; you always look on the bright side of things,' I laughed before taking a bite out of a slice of pepperoni pizza.

'I'm just saying, do you really think it's worth taking the risk?'

'Of course it is. We need to look the part if we want to be taken seriously. You'll be asking us to turn up at the loading bay with a cucumber in a Tesco bag next and pretend we've got sawn-off shotguns aimed at the warehouse staff. That's not going to be very convincing, is it?'

Finn, Kevin and I fell about laughing, whereas Mark looked like he was chewing on a wasp.

'Think about this for a minute; the staff aren't going to let us help ourselves to the cash if they don't feel threatened by the situation, are they?' I said.

I took Mark's silence as a small victory when he didn't disagree.

'We're going to need some ammunition as well. Can you

ask Randal to get hold of that as well, Kev?' I added. As my words registered, I saw Mark's face visibly pale. 'Don't look so worried. We're not going to shoot anyone, but we need to be armed as a precaution. If anyone steps out of line, we might have to fire a couple of bullets to get the situation back under control, but we'll aim them at the ground.'

'I hear what you're saying, but I still don't like it. Things have a habit of getting out of control where loaded guns are concerned.' Mark's frown deepened.

'This isn't up for discussion. You can't expect Kevin and me to try and pull off a robbery and not be armed. We're not exactly going to put the fear of God into them if we turn up wearing balaclavas and have nothing to threaten them with. We'll be completely outnumbered. What's to stop the cargo team from overpowering us and calling the police? The game would be over before it had even started. Is that how you want this to pan out?'

Mark let out a loud sigh.

'I don't know why you're getting so het up about this. It's not as though we're asking you to use one of the weapons. None of this concerns you anyway. You'll be in the boat far away from all the action. Do us all a favour and settle down. It's stressful enough without you constantly bleating on about it.'

37

Lola

I sat outside the door with the silver plaque bearing the name Cassandra Peterson willing my nerves to subside. In an attempt to calm down, I kept asking myself what the worst outcome would be. I wouldn't be offered the job, which would be disappointing, but it wouldn't be the end of the world.

As I was giving myself a pep talk, the heavy wooden door opened, and a glamorous well-groomed brunette stood in the doorway smiling at me. My breath caught in my chest at the sight of her as I hadn't heard her approaching. The woman, who looked to be in her early thirties, was dressed in a well-cut grey trouser suit. Her long dark hair hung in loose curls and tumbled over her shoulders. I couldn't help thinking it wasn't a wash and go sort of hairstyle; it was much more high maintenance. She looked like she'd just stepped out of an expensive London salon.

My heart started pounding when she began making her way towards me. The thick carpet silenced her footsteps as she walked across the hallway. She stopped in front of me and reached out her hand.

'I'm Cassandra Peterson. Nice to meet you.'

I stood up from the chair and smoothed down the black pencil dress Millie had lent me.

'Hello. I'm Lola Marshall, pleased to meet you too,' I replied, shaking her kitten-soft hand. Her skin was so smooth it felt like she had never washed up a pot or done a day's hard work in her life.

'Please come with me,' Cassandra smiled.

I followed her into the office, decorated more like a bedroom than a working space. Vases of highly scented pastel-coloured flowers rested on shiny surfaces in the light and airy room. Pale pink carpet, the colour of cherry blossom, covered the floor. It was so springy underfoot I felt like I was walking across a wall-to-wall layer of Victoria sponge cake. Cassandra took a seat behind a huge mirrored desk like a dressing table and gestured for me to sit opposite her in the pink upholstered chair.

'What did you used to do for a living?' Cassandra asked as she kicked off the interview.

'I worked for William Hill,' I replied after clearing my throat.

'The bookmakers?' Cassandra questioned.

'Yes,' I confirmed while holding eye contact with her. I was trying to discretely wipe the sweat off the palms of my hands on the sleeves of my cardigan.

'Oh, that's interesting.' Cassandra's lips stretched into a smile, exposing her bright white teeth. 'What was your role?'

'I was involved with every aspect of the business. I can't

imagine it's the same in the casino, but our customers were mostly working-class men who favoured horse and greyhound racing. The majority of them were retired and used to pop in most days, usually on their way to or from the pub,' I replied, doing my best to give a diplomatic answer.

Working there wasn't exactly a riveting experience, but I didn't want to tell her that. Apart from at certain times of the year, when the stars aligned and the betting Gods came together to allow the schedules of major global sporting events to combine, the hours were long and tedious.

'What was a typical day like for you?' Cassandra asked.

'I'd start preparing the shop for trade by turning on the gambling machines and checking that each of the coin and note slots were functioning properly. Then I'd arrange the form guides from the Racing Post on magnetic display boards, fill the coupon trays, alternate the posters in the windows to attract passing trade from the street. I had to monitor the amount of money in the coin trays, in the till, and in the safe. At the end of the day, I emptied the machines of takings before we closed for the night. That sort of thing,' I smiled while trying not to shudder as a vision of Troy dragging me through the empty shop popped into my head.

'Did you have much customer interaction?'

'Yes, I dealt with customers all the time and had to watch the door in case someone too young or too unsavoury-looking tried to enter.'

'Really? You had to deal with that yourself? That sounds dangerous.'

If she only knew the half of it, I thought.

'Didn't you have a bouncer?'

'No, just a locked door that separated the shop floor

from my service area. But I couldn't stay closeted away all of the time. I had to keep an eye on the electronic gambling machines. They sometimes broke down. I've fixed a few of those in my time.'

'So you have some experience of the gambling industry then.' Cassandra tilted her beautiful face to one side and fixed her dark eyes on me.

My pulse began pounding in my wrist. I remembered Millie saying that this lady preferred to work with a clean slate, and I hoped I hadn't just blown my interview.

'I'm not exactly a blank canvas. I do have some knowledge of the industry.'

There was no point trying to deny the obvious. Now I'd have to dig myself out of the hole and hope I could convince Cassandra to cut me some slack.

'But I'm technically underqualified as I don't have the right experience. I've worked in a betting shop, so I have first-hand knowledge of gamblers, but I've never even set foot inside a casino, let alone know how one operates. I'm completely clueless when it comes to the rules of the games. I can barely shuffle a pack of cards, and I wouldn't know a winning hand if it jumped up and bit me on the arse.'

Oh shit! Why did I say that? My nerves were definitely getting the better of me, and my mouth was running away with itself. I was about to apologise when Cassandra threw her head back and started roaring with laughter. She had a voice like smooth satin and a laugh like a dirty old man. An image of Sid James in the *Carry On* films suddenly sprang into my mind. My dad used to love them. I could still picture him sitting in his favourite chair, beer in hand, howling away at the capers the cast used to get themselves into.

'I like you, Lola; you're down to earth. I've just got one more thing to ask you, and then we'll wrap this up. Why did you leave your last job?'

It was the question I'd been dreading. My head felt like it was going to explode as Cassandra's words bounced around in my brain. There was no way I could tell her the truth, but I hoped the lengthy pause that had stretched out between us hadn't just given away the fact that I was trying to cover something up.

'I didn't like dealing with aggressive customers. Sometimes they'd take their anger out on the machines and destroy them if their winning streak took a turn for the worse. I was on duty when a man went ballistic and smashed up the machines with a stool. He went nuts and completely lost his head because he'd gambled away his rent money. It was really scary. I was the only person on-site at the time.'

Cassandra raised her perfectly arched eyebrows. 'That must have been a nightmare. Every woman has a right to feel safe in the workplace.'

'The betting shop had CCTV cameras, a steel-framed front door with a magnetic lock and the service area had an employee panic button under the counter. It was like a fortress, but I still felt nervous when certain customers walked through the door,' I said.

'That must have been awful,' Cassandra replied.

'It wasn't fun dealing with a drunk customer or trying to get an undesirable to leave. People sometimes drifted in on a whim with no intention of placing a bet, just needing to shelter from the outside elements.'

'Your security should never be an issue.'

'Some customers threatened you, but I tried to block it out. One of my colleagues told me about a private Facebook group called 'I no longer fear Hell' … I've worked in a betting shop, but I haven't joined it. I'm too scared to hear the stories. Apparently, some people had been stabbed and shot,' I said.

Cassandra pulled a face. 'Were the premises ever robbed?'

'Not while I worked there.'

'That's good. I'd heard betting shops get targeted all the time.'

'They do. When I voiced my concerns to my manager, he told me that all they wanted was the money. If I was ever in that situation, all I had to do was hand it over, and then everything would be fine. It was unlikely the robbers would hurt me as long as I did what they said.'

'Seriously? Your manager sounds like a complete idiot,' Cassandra pointed out.

'Tell me about it. I said we should get danger money, and his response was that it was no different to working in a petrol station or corner shop. Any job that handled cash came with a risk.'

'That's true, but a good employer has systems in place to deal with it. Safety in numbers springs to mind. Did you often work alone?' Cassandra seemed concerned by what I'd just told her.

'Yes. Our branch was short-staffed, only the manager, myself and a part-time cashier worked there, so one person manned the shop for periods of the day and after 6 p.m. when it was quiet.'

'Let me guess, that was a cost-cutting exercise?'

I nodded.

Cassandra shook her head.

Work was hard to come by so I wasn't in a position to be choosy.

'I think you'll fit in really well in the team,' Cassandra smiled.

'Aww, thanks,' I replied grinning from ear to ear.

'So with that in mind, I'll get your references checked.'

I felt the smile slide from my face as my heartbeat went into overdrive. My eyes were glistening with tears. I knew I was on the verge of breaking down. I'd been hoping Cassandra hadn't noticed, but when she reached across her desk and pulled a tissue out of the box before getting up, walking over to where I was sitting and handing it to me, I knew that wasn't the case.

'Is everything okay?' Cassandra asked, fixing me with a look of concern.

My bottom lip started to quiver.

'Oh, Lola, please don't get upset.' Cassandra rubbed the side of my arm with her velvety fingertips. 'If you tell me what's bothering you, I'm sure we can find a solution.'

I wanted to believe her, but I didn't want to tell her that my manager was also my psycho ex and I couldn't ask him for a reference because then he'd be able to track me down.

Just the thought of Troy finding out where I'd gone threw me into a pit of despair and my tears started rolling down my cheeks before I could stop them. I frantically dabbed at my eyes with the tissue Cassandra had given me to try and stop them mid-flow but they just kept coming.

'Listen, Lola, nothing or nobody is worth getting this upset over. Let's rewind a little bit, shall we?' Cassandra smiled before she turned on her heel and walked back over to her desk. 'Your previous manager sounded like a total dick if you ask me.'

Cassandra's description of Troy was spot on and that brought a smile to my face.

'Is it going to cause you a problem trying to get a reference from him?' Cassandra got straight to the point having worked out the issue.

I felt panic crawl up from the pit of my stomach. I wasn't sure how to answer the question. If I said yes she was bound to want to know the reason, but if I said no I'd have to be prepared to give her Troy's details. Unless I could bypass him completely and go straight to Head Office. I let out a loud sigh when I realised that wouldn't work either as I hadn't officially resigned from my position. While I battled to reach a decision, my stomach began twisting and turning making me feel physically sick.

'If you don't want to ask your boss at William Hill, do you have a previous employer you could approach for a reference?' Cassandra was the first to break the silence.

I shook my head. I didn't trust myself to speak. I was worried my words might come out as a sob, but Cassandra had been so patient with me, she deserved an explanation, so I'd have to dig deep and force out a response.

'I've only ever worked at the bookies, so I don't have any other employment history.'

Cassandra crossed her arms over her chest before biting down on her bottom lip. I could see she was mulling over my reply. I could feel the opportunity slipping through my fingers so I decided to go into a little more detail.

'I didn't have a good relationship with my boss,' I began. Wasn't that the truth! 'So I'm reluctant to ask him for a reference because I'm not sure he'd give me a good one.'

'I understand.' Cassandra offered me a sympathetic smile.

'But I can assure you, I'm a really hard worker.' I threw in for good measure.

'I don't doubt that.' Cassandra drummed her fingertips on the desk for a couple of seconds before she continued speaking. 'I like you, Lola. I have a good feeling about you and I think you'd be an asset to the firm, so I'm going to waive the usual protocol. There's no point in being in charge of the hiring and firing if you can't bend your own rules, is there?'

That sounded positive, I thought, but I didn't want to get my hopes up.

'I'd like to offer you a job. How soon can you start?'

I only became aware that my mouth had dropped open when I went to speak. My jaw felt like it was frozen in time.

'Thank you so much,' I finally managed to utter. 'I was so nervous I thought I'd messed up the interview.'

What the hell was I doing. It was as though I was trying to talk Cassandra out of the offer.

'It's an advantage that you know how betting works. It's one less thing you'll have to learn.'

'That's true, but I don't have the faintest idea of how a casino operates. I hope I won't be out of my depth.'

Why did I say that out loud? Was I on a self-destruct mission?

Cassandra's guttural laugh put in another appearance.

'You'll be fine. We make sure our staff are fully trained before we let you loose on the punters. I promise you, being inexperienced won't be a problem. You'll soon get the hang of life inside a casino.'

38

Abbie

'I've checked out all the members of staff past and present, and none of them owns a boat or has access to one,' Ed said when he walked into the incident room.

I looked up from the notes I was reading and trained my eyes on him. I'd been hoping that might throw up a fresh lead, but it looked like Ed was right, the thieves must have hired a boat to use in the robbery. We were going around in circles. We'd carried out criminal records checks on all the employees, and that had brought back nothing. The forensic team had thoroughly examined the scene, but they hadn't managed to collect any evidence. All we had were the statements from the staff, which Ed had carefully documented. I'd been hoping that as time wore on, more witnesses would come forward since the story had made it on to the news. The theft of ten million pounds in cash was a big story. But the fresh leads we'd been hoping to follow up hadn't materialised; so far, nobody had come forward.

We hadn't offered a reward for information that might

lead to the capture of the culprits at this stage because that always triggered an influx of interest from the public. But the investigation wasn't gathering momentum, so I was considering making an appeal on TV for help with the unsolved case. If that didn't work, we might have to resort to reconstructing the heist in an attempt to catch the offenders.

Being in financial trouble would be the most obvious motive for why somebody would want to steal a huge amount of unmarked notes.

'Did any of the staff have money worries or large debts?'

'Not that I'm aware of,' Ed replied.

'Well, do some digging and get me a definitive answer. Also, find out where Finn McCaskill banks and get copies of his account transactions for the last twelve months.'

39

Lola

Just as I was about to go to bed, I received a call from DS Ash.

'Hi, Lola is now a good time to talk?' she asked.

'Yes,' I replied.

I didn't want to tell her that I'd been hoping to get an early night so that I would be fresh for my first day at work tomorrow. I knew she wouldn't have called me unless she had some news; this wasn't going to be a social chat.

'Is everything okay?'

'Not really,' the DS said, and my heart sank. 'We arrested Troy for assaulting your mum, but she's refused to testify, so the CPS has decided not to prosecute him, and the charges against him have been dropped.'

'You can't be serious.'

I suddenly came over light-headed, so I gripped on to the headboard for support. My knees felt like they were going to buckle. This was so unfair. Mum and I were the victims, but I was now living in exile and could never go back home, whereas Troy was able to walk around as a free man.

I knew my mum was scared, but I thought I'd talked her around. She'd obviously got cold feet at the last minute. She might have made things a whole lot worse in the long run. Now Troy was free to carry out his threat. I couldn't help feeling I was in more danger than ever, even though hundreds of miles were separating us.

'Listen, Lola, the last thing I'm trying to do is scare you, but women are much more likely to be killed in the weeks after they leave their abusive partner than at any other time during the relationship.'

DS Ash didn't need to tell me that. I was only too aware of the statistics; I'd read them for myself on one of the women's aid websites when I'd been working out how I could leave. Before I'd even made the call to the refuge, I'd thought long and hard about whether or not I was doing the right thing.

'Keep your wits about you at all times, and don't hesitate to call 999 if you feel like you're in danger,' DS Ash said.

'I will. Even though it wasn't what I wanted to hear, thanks for letting me know,' I said before I ended the call.

I know DS Ash was only trying to warn me about the dangerous position I was in, but she was scaring the shit out of me. I'd be sleeping with one eye open tonight. As I sat on the edge of my bed, taking it all in, I began to tremble. I was barely holding things together. I needed to speak to my mum and hear her side of the story.

'I've just spoken to DS Ash...'

I knew my tone was frosty, so I decided to let my sentence trail off. I didn't want to go in all guns blazing without giving her an opportunity to explain why she'd done a complete U-turn.

'I'm so sorry, Lola. Don't be mad at me,' Mum said in a strangled voice. I could tell she was trying to hold back tears.

'I can't believe you backed out. I thought we'd agreed that you were going to testify against Troy.'

'I changed my mind. I couldn't go through with it. You knew I didn't want to involve the police, but you didn't take the blindest bit of notice, you kept pushing me into it,' Mum fired back.

The tears that had been threatening to put in an appearance were a thing of the past. She was riled up and ready to do battle.

'Now we're worse off than we were before,' I said through gritted teeth.

'We wouldn't be in this position if you hadn't insisted on going out with that psycho in the first place.'

Mum's words stung like a slap on bare skin. Talk about giving me a huge dose of tough love. There was no point in continuing this conversation. We were just trying to point the finger of blame at each other and were going around in circles. We weren't achieving anything apart from hurting each other.

'Thanks, Mum. Why don't you tell it like it is?'

I hadn't thought it was possible to feel worse than I already did, but I was wrong. After I ended the call, tears started running in tracks down my cheeks as I sat staring into the middle distance, feeling sorry for myself. I'd never felt more alone than I did at this moment. I desperately wanted somebody to tell me that everything was going to be all right, but that wasn't going to happen. It was too late to bother Millie with this now, and Elaine had left for the night.

So much for my bright new start. I should have realised it was too good to be true. Every time I took a step in the right direction, an obstacle from my past seemed to land in my way.

As I tried to drift off to sleep, my conversations with DS Ash and Mum played over and over on a continuous loop in my head. I tossed and turned for hours, so when the alarm went off at eight o'clock, I felt like I'd only just closed my eyes.

'I'm so proud of you girls,' Elaine said with a tear in her eye as Millie and I were about to leave the refuge for our first day at the casino.

'Don't you dare cry, or you'll start us all off,' Millie replied.

I was already on the verge of tears, so it wouldn't have taken much to start me off. After what had happened last night, I didn't feel like going in today. But if I didn't turn up to training, everyone would want to know why and I didn't feel like explaining. I needed this job, so bailing out wasn't going to be an option. It was probably a blessing in disguise that we were starting work today. Keeping busy would stop me from dwelling on the situation.

'I've never done anything like this before, have you?' Millie asked as we walked towards the station.

'You must be joking. We didn't even have enough money in the budget for staff, so there was never any development or training.'

Millie and I got on the tube at Acton Town, and around twenty minutes later, we arrived at Piccadilly Circus. It was an easy journey, less than thirty minutes door to door as the casino was just a few minutes' walk away from the station. It felt good to be in the thick of things. The West End was buzzing with activity. Passers-by were too busy to take any interest in a nobody like me, but that didn't mean I wasn't keeping an eye out for my ex.

'Is everything okay? You've hardly said a word since we left the house.'

Millie tilted her head to one side and fixed me with her brown eyes.

'I'm not feeling too great; my stomach's doing somersaults. I'm struggling to keep the first day nerves at bay,' I replied.

That wasn't a lie. I was shitting myself. But the reason I didn't feel like talking was more to do with me trying to get my head around the fact that Troy had got away with assaulting my mum if I was honest about it. I couldn't concentrate on anything else. I'd tell Millie what happened at a later stage; now wasn't the right time to bring it up. I needed to try and push it out of my mind.

'I know the feeling. What are we like? We should be gassed that we've been given this chance. We shouldn't be fretting about it. I'm glad we've been given the same start date. It'll be good to have a friendly face on the training programme,' Millie replied, and a smile spread over her face.

I smiled back at her, but mine wasn't genuine. I'd come to London to get away from my past and my violent ex-boyfriend. I'd been off to a good start by landing myself a job. I'd been sure if I played my cards right, I could do very well for myself. This city offered so many opportunities. But now, I felt like I'd never be free of him, and that thought was undermining my confidence.

I'd been a bit alarmed when Millie had said the casino was in Soho. Having never been to the area before, I didn't know what to expect. I'd thought it was well known for being a red-light district, so I'd imagined women standing behind red-lit glass doors, dressed in fancy underwear like they did in the window brothels in Amsterdam. Instead, Soho had a quirky, cool vibe with lots of restaurants, pubs, nightclubs, theatres and, of course, casinos.

Millie and I stopped outside the sleek modern building and gazed up at the large three-dimensional letters spelling out the casino's name, Rolling the Dice. When we pushed the handle of the glass turnstile door, it swept us from the pavement to the foyer in a matter of seconds. The pewter and silver colour scheme of the interior was effortlessly classy.

'Good morning, I'm Adam,' the man in his forties said as he approached us. 'Are you here for the staff training?'

'Yes,' we both replied.

'I'm Millie.'

'And I'm Lola.'

'Nice to meet you both. If you'd like to come with me, we'll get started.'

Adam led the way across the cloud grey tiles and down a long corridor with doors on either side. He turned and smiled at both of us before he opened the furthest door on the right.

'Take a seat wherever you like. It's just the two of you on the programme,' Adam said as he made his way over to a state-of-the-art drinks machine in the corner of the room. 'Can I get you a tea or coffee?'

Millie and I both declined the offer.

'So I gather neither of you have worked in a casino before?' Adam smiled, and the lines at the corners of his eyes deepened.

'No,' Millie and I replied.

'There's a lot to teach you, so let's dive straight in. We offer world-class gaming; blackjack, roulette and baccarat tables, as well as slot machines, electronic roulette and poker. There's a restaurant and cocktail bar on the rooftop. It's a covered terrace so that it can be used all year round, but it's been designed in such a way that the glass walls can be opened up in the warmer weather. I'll give you a tour later on; it offers spectacular views across the London skyline.'

Talk about information overload, but I was glad of the distraction as it took my mind off what was going on with Mum and Troy.

'How are you getting on?' Cassandra asked when she walked into the boardroom. A waft of expensive perfume followed her into the room.

'They're doing really well. They seem to be picking it up brilliantly,' Adam replied on our behalf.

We both grinned at the thought of being A-star students for a change. That was a novelty for both of us. I was glad he was pleased that we were making progress, but I was having real trouble concentrating on what he'd been saying, and my mind kept drifting off. A lot of the things he'd told us had gone over my head. I was glad he'd given us a set of printed notes to take away with us. At least I'd be able to read over them in my own time.

'In that case, I think you should call it a day. We'll see you back here at the same time tomorrow,' Cassandra smiled before she disappeared out of the boardroom.

The lack of sleep, the situation with Troy and the argument with my mum had affected me badly, and I wasn't able to give the training my all as I'd intended. But this was just a bump in the road. Cassandra had been good enough to give me a chance, so there was no way I was going to let her down. I just needed to get my head together so that I could refocus. Tomorrow was a new day.

40

Paul

One month before the heist

Labouring on a building site was a young man's game. I couldn't picture myself doing this job in ten years' time. Kevin and I needed to get some money behind us, or we'd still be living at home with our parents when we were in our forties. Don't get me wrong, I loved them to bits, they were the salt of the earth, but we'd got to an age where we needed our privacy.

If we wanted a brighter future, we had to get our hands on some money, but we were stuck in a vicious circle. It was virtually impossible to save when you worked in a low-paid job. We'd had the same problem our whole lives. A lot of the work on Sheppey was seasonal. When the holiday accommodation was full, it doubled the island's population. It was easy enough to pick up work on one of the numerous parks in peak season, but that dried up as soon as the tourists headed home. As teenagers, we'd been forced into making pocket money by other means when there were no legitimate forms of employment. We'd all been involved in petty crime when we were young; nothing hardcore, but we'd been known to handle goods that fell off the back of a lorry, selling the stuff to anybody we could shift it to.

Kevin worked in the kitchen at the prison and had met some interesting characters over the years. He'd got to know some of the inmates very well, and they'd filled his head with stories of how to commit the perfect crime. He'd picked his contacts' brains discreetly and managed to gain access to some insider information which would hopefully help us when it came to pulling off the heist. One of Randal the vandal's relatives was a wannabe gangster based in Sheerness. He'd set himself up as an illegal arms dealer, so we'd got hold of two weapons from him on the quiet.

The closer we were getting to the heist, the more a nagging doubt kept appearing in my head. If breaking the law was really that easy, why were they all banged up? I wasn't sure any of us would be able to hack being locked up for an extended period of time. The inmates had also told Kevin enough horror stories about life behind bars to last me a lifetime. The tales kept bombarding my brain when I was drifting off to sleep at night. I'd been so certain about everything, but now I was beginning to question whether we were really going to be able to go through with this.

Having extra manpower might make the job easier in the short term, but in the long term, the more people that were involved, the more likely we were to get caught. Somebody was bound to slip up, and then we'd all go down. Once one of the gang got caught, it would have a domino effect on the others. God help us if Mark became a suspect; the game would be up. I hoped for all our sakes that he never got picked up by the Old Bill. He'd sing like a canary and take the rest of us down with him. Not that he wasn't loyal, but he didn't handle pressure well and would cave in if the thumbscrews were put on.

'What's up?' Kevin asked. 'You don't seem yourself tonight.'

'I'm fine. I just had a shit day at work, that's all,' I lied.

I didn't want the others to know I was having second thoughts or the plan might fall apart. I'd been the instigator and the driving force behind the idea, and I was sure it wouldn't take a lot to talk them out of it if they realised I'd got cold feet.

'For one horrible minute, I thought you were going to pull the plug on the heist,' Kevin laughed.

My brother knew me better than I cared to admit.

'Nah, nothing like that. I'm looking forward to it. The day can't come around soon enough for my liking,' I replied. Now I just needed to get my shit together and start believing what I'd said.

Sometimes you had to take risks in life in order to better yourself, and although we'd be getting a leg up the ladder illegally, it would be a means to an end. We might get caught, but then again, we might not. It was a chance we had to take to get out of the rut we were in.

41

Lola

The casino was open twenty-four hours a day, seven days a week. Millie and I were contracted to work thirty-six hours, but because the shifts were twelve hours each, we'd only be working three days with four days off.

'I've taken on board the reason you left your last job. Being face to face with aggressive customers must have been terrifying, so I wondered if you'd like to train as a cage cashier instead of being out on the floor. You'll still be in direct contact with the customers, but you'll be behind a protective screen at all times,' Cassandra suggested when I arrived for my final day of training.

'I'd love that,' I replied.

My nerves were in tatters at the moment, knowing that Troy was free to roam the streets. I felt much happier knowing that I'd be working behind a toughened glass panel so any disgruntled customers couldn't take their anger out on me. I knew from experience that all you could do was stand by and watch when people took their fury out on the machines. There was nothing you could do about it, and if you tried to intervene, you ended up putting yourself in the firing line. When customers were in that frame of mind, they weren't thinking straight and would happily turn their aggression on to you. It wasn't unheard of for customers to smash up the shop. I'd witnessed that first hand.

I hadn't liked the idea of being in close proximity to male customers, especially if they'd been drinking, but I needed the money, so I knew I was just going to have to get on with it. I hadn't mentioned my concerns to Cassandra, so I wasn't expecting her to come up with a solution. I could already tell that staff satisfaction was high up on her list of priorities.

'I think you'd make a great croupier,' Cassandra said, turning towards Millie.

'Sounds good to me,' Millie smiled. 'Not that I know what that entails. I could have just lined myself up for anything.'

'You'll be the person in charge of a table. You'll collect the bets and pay the winnings out to the customers who've won,' Cassandra explained.

'I can't wait,' Millie replied.

'It's an interesting role. Gambling comes as naturally as breathing to some people. They're born risk-takers, and the casino's full of them. These people like high stakes drama and thrive on the adrenalin rush that walks hand in hand with winning or losing. Some of the odds are fifty-fifty, so there's a fine line that separates the two,' Cassandra said.

'It sounds like it.' Millie tilted her perfectly symmetrical face to one side, and as her head moved, the over-head spotlights bounced off her super shiny hair.

'Once this week of training's over, I'll start both of you

off on the day shift. I always do that with new members of staff to break them in gently. The casino's quieter during office hours; it really comes to life after the normal working day has finished,' Cassandra said.

She wouldn't hear me complaining. I couldn't speak for Millie, but that suited me down to the ground.

Cassandra glanced at her diamond-encrusted watch. 'I'd better get back to work. I'll leave you in Adam's capable hands.'

Millie and I started work at the casino the following Monday. We'd arrived ten minutes early for our eight o'clock shift, and we were standing in the deserted lobby dressed in white shirts, black flat fronted trousers with no pockets and black waistcoats. The outfits were a bit on the masculine side, but they were free, so I wasn't about to complain. It could have been worse; some companies had terrible uniforms. McDonald's had had some shockers over the years. And anyway, it took away the stress of finding something suitable to wear to work each day. Having staff clothing provided was an absolute blessing as I hadn't been able to bring much with me, and I certainly didn't have the money to waste on buying myself a new wardrobe.

'Good morning, ladies,' Adam said when he appeared. 'I'm afraid I'm going to have to split the two of you up. You'll be spending the first week undergoing training for your specific roles.'

I would have accepted any job I'd been offered, but I was glad I wouldn't be in close proximity to the customers. I knew only too well how tempers could flare when a bet didn't go the way the person had expected. Mum hadn't liked me working in the betting shop. She didn't think it was a safe environment for a young woman and the pay was crap. I couldn't think of any other minimum wage job that carried the same amount of risk.

Cassandra was just running through my day-to-day duties, explaining that I'd sell and receive casino chips, release jackpot payments and process cards and credit applications when a tall man with a huge frame walked up to the other side of the glass. I jumped when I caught sight of him. He had thinning black hair swept back off his face in a Count Dracula style, and although I was sure he was intending to be friendly, the grin on his face looked sinister if you asked me.

'Aww, look who it isn't.' Cassandra's face lit up at the sight of the tall man with intense dark brown eyes who was wearing stonewashed jeans with a shirt, sports jacket and shiny slip-on shoes.

I stood there gawping at him because I didn't have a clue who the man was.

Cassandra opened up the booth and greeted the man with a kiss on the cheek. As he snaked his arm around her waist, the links on the chunky bracelet he was wearing on his right wrist moved like scales. When he leant towards her, I was fully expecting him to sink his fangs into the side of her bare neck, but he didn't. He rubbed the tip of his nose against hers instead like some kind of gothic Eskimo. I wasn't sure if it was sweet or cringy.

'Lola, I'd like to introduce you to Zac Peterson, my husband. He's the casino owner,' Cassandra announced and then stood there beaming with pride.

I had one of those faces that didn't deal with surprises very well. People could read my expressions like a book. I gave away everything I was thinking and feeling, so I was sure I hadn't hidden my shock. I realised they had the same surname, but I'd presumed because of the large age difference between them that he was her father, not her partner.

'Pleased to meet you, Lola,' Zac said.

'Likewise,' I replied. My features felt like they'd frozen.

Zac checked the time on the limited-edition Rolex he was wearing on his left wrist, made his excuses and then left Cassandra and me alone.

Cassandra closed the booth door and then turned to me with a smile playing on her lips. 'Your expression was priceless,' she said.

'What do you mean?' I replied, trying to act all innocent, but I could feel heat rising up the back of my neck.

'You thought Zac was my dad, didn't you?' Cassandra's loud laugh echoed around the small space.

'No,' I lied. As the words left my lips, I felt my cheeks flush as if to confirm my guilt.

'It's okay, you don't have to look so embarrassed.'

Cassandra smiled, which confirmed my worst fear; she didn't believe me. I shouldn't have been surprised, I was a terrible liar.

'It's an easy mistake to make. Everybody always thinks we're father and daughter. I think it's hilarious, and it doesn't bother Zac as much as it used to.'

'Oh my God. I'm so sorry.'

There was no point in trying to carry on with the pretence, so I decided to apologise instead.

'No harm done, but seriously, your face was a picture. I don't know how I kept my laughter in.'

Cassandra was lovely. It made a refreshing change to have a supportive manager who put me at ease instead of one with an unpredictable temper. I used to have to walk on eggshells to avoid making Troy angry.

'Let's get back to training. How are you finding the job so far?' Cassandra asked with a smile on her face.

'I'm loving it,' I replied, smiling back at her.

42

Abbie

'I've checked out the staff members' accounts, and none of them have any large debts they're struggling to repay,' Ed said when he walked into the incident room.

Being in financial trouble was the most obvious motive for stealing a huge amount of cash, so I'd been hoping to uncover something by checking out their spending habits.

'Here are the copies of Finn McCaskill's bank transactions for the last twelve months.' Ed handed me a pile of Santander statements detailing his monthly expenditure. 'I've been through them, but nothing seems out of the ordinary.'

I was eagle-eyed by nature and noticed every detail, so I wasn't about to take his word for that.

'What else did you find out about him?'

'He still lives at home with his mum and dad,' Ed replied.

'So he doesn't have a mortgage or any large overheads then?'

'No. I guess, like most people in that situation, everything he earns goes on himself. He probably spends most of his money on socialising and takeaways.'

I remembered those days well, but they seemed like a distant dream to me now.

'Some parents ask for a bit of rent towards the housekeeping, don't they?'

Well, mine did anyway. My dad even used to make me hand over a portion of the money I earned from my Saturday job to prepare me for life in the real world. Talk about tough love.

Ed scoffed. 'That's hardly likely to break the bank and land him in crippling debt, is it?'

Ed's sarcasm hadn't gone unnoticed, but he wasn't going to get a rise out of me today, so instead, I gave him a black look as a warning.

'What about his phone records?'

Ed opened the folder he was holding, rifled through some paperwork and then passed me a bundle of A4 sheets.

'Again, nothing stood out for me. You've got tunnel vision when it comes to Finn McCaskill, but I think you're barking up the wrong tree. I still think the old fella's our man.'

I fixed my gaze on my partner and only narrowly managed to resist rolling my eyes.

'If you think about it logically, everything points to Stanley Brown. He's part of the company pension scheme, but his payout isn't worth much. It's little more than a pittance, and he's nearing the end of his working career. So he'd really benefit from a massive windfall. Especially if he moved abroad, his money would go much further.'

I couldn't help feeling Ed seemed to have put a lot more time and effort into checking out Stanley's background, blatantly ignoring what I'd asked him to do. His mind was already made up; now, Ed just had to make the facts fit around the crime he was convinced Stanley had committed, even though he didn't have any concrete evidence to back up his theory. Talk about being innocent until proven guilty.

'I can see why you think he might have a motive, but there's no way a man like Stanley would get involved in something like this. Anyone can see he doesn't have the right kind of disposition. Being scared of your own shadow isn't a quality armed robbers would look for when they were selecting a potential inside source. Their person would need to be dependable and have the ability to remain calm in dangerous or difficult situations, not fluster easily. Possessing nerves of steel would be essential,' I said, hoping we could finally put this to bed and get on with catching the real culprits.

'You say that, but being a nervous wreck would make him the last person you'd suspect.'

Ed had an answer for everything. But that was the most illogical thing he'd said since the start of the investigation. If that was the kind of theory he was going to come up with, he might as well not bother turning up to work tomorrow.

'I really don't get where you're going with this.'

And to think Ed had the cheek to accuse me of having tunnel vision.

'The robbers might have chosen Stanley for exactly the reason you're discounting him, thinking we'd never suspect a man who fell to pieces as easily as he does. He was literally shaking in his shoes when we asked him to come into the station to answer some questions, and he hadn't even been accused of anything.'

Ed and I were never going to agree on this.

'And I was surprised you fell for that sob story he fed you.' Ed shook his head.

'What sob story?'

It was clear Ed was hoping to provoke a reaction.

'When Stanley told you he was worried the airline was going to put him out to pasture. Just because he's old, it doesn't mean he's not guilty. Nobody would take the blindest bit of notice if he resigned from his position because he was traumatised after being held at gunpoint. Then he'd be free to skip off into the sunset with his share of the millions and start a new life like one of the Great Train Robbers. Meanwhile, he'd be having the last laugh because nobody suspected the doddery old boy,' Ed said with smugness in his voice.

43

Lola

'I can't believe how far you've come,' Elaine said as I was about to leave for work. 'When you first arrived at the refuge, I was worried about your mental health. I could see you were struggling, but you were reluctant to talk to anybody about your troubles. These days, you're in a completely different place.'

'A lot of that's thanks to you,' I smiled. Elaine was amazing; she'd been like a second mum to me.

'I can't take the credit for your mindset change. That's down to you,' Elaine replied.

Now that I'd tasted freedom, I was more determined than ever to be in control of my life. I'd landed on my feet when I got the job at the casino, and it was doing wonders for my confidence. I was like a different person. I knew if I dug deep enough, I'd find the girl I used to be lurking somewhere inside the shell that I'd become. Everything about Troy was toxic, and like acid, he'd eroded my self-confidence and destroyed every fibre of my personality until very little of it was left.

'I hardly recognise myself. It looks like life is finally on the way up. I'd better go. I don't want to be late.'

I took a deep breath before I pulled open the door and stepped inside. The casino was like a labyrinth of machines and tables that all looked the same. It had been cleverly designed like a giant maze, intentionally set up so that customers got lost in it. As I made my way to the cashier's booth, an explosion of colour hit me; flashing lights were coming from every direction, and the sound of bells and alarms assaulted my senses. I was sure I'd get used to it in time. But I couldn't wait to be behind the protective screen that would keep the noise and the customers out. I'd feel much happier once a barrier was between me and the outside world.

Cassandra was already behind the counter; she looked up from the desk when I approached and gave me a warm smile.

'How are you feeling?' she asked when I took a seat next to her.

'I'm not gonna lie; I'm a bit nervous,' I replied.

'Don't be; you're going to be absolutely fine. I'll stay with you to shadow you until you get the hang of things, but remember, your safety isn't an issue. The booth is monitored by cameras, and there's always a security guard stationed right opposite you.'

Knowing I was surrounded by surveillance was reassuring. I couldn't allow my experience at the betting shop to put me off. And just as Cassandra had promised, the casino was virtually empty at this time in the morning. Compared to what I was used to, this was going to be a breeze providing things stayed this way. The phrase money for nothing sprang to mind.

I was grateful for the slow start. It would give me a chance to get used to things instead of being bombarded from every angle. Not many businesses handled as much money on a daily basis as a casino. They were set up to maximise profit and separate customers from their hard-earned cash.

'There are double locked metal boxes under every table on the floor, which are emptied daily, and the contents are brought to the count room, which is divided into two separate areas. One for counting banknotes, we call that the soft count and one for counting coins, that's the hard count,' Cassandra explained.

'So a customer doesn't have to get their chips from me?'

'No. I should explain what happens when a player sits down at a table, they can hand over a note and get chips back in return. The dealer places the customer's cash into a slotted box located below the table. At the end of the dealer's shift, a drop team, which consists of two members of staff from the count room and a security guard, exchange the box for an empty one to be used by the next dealer. The box is then taken to the soft count room.'

My mind was buzzing. There was so much to take in.

'Because Rolling the Dice is in central London, we get a lot of tourists milling around the place, but you'll soon start to recognise the die-hard regulars that treat the casino like a second home. Zac's office overlooks the floor. He likes to keep an eye on things from up there,' Cassandra pointed to a set of windows spanning the wall over the entrance. 'He can see us, but we can't see him.'

I wasn't sure why that made me feel uneasy as I had no intention of doing anything underhand, but all the same, the thought of Zac watching me gave me the creeps.

'Do people sometimes try and beat the system?'

'Yes, we get our fair share of hustlers through the doors. There's a lot of money at stake, so there's always going to be somebody brave enough to try their luck. The croupiers are trained to never take their eyes off the dice. Scam artists will try and distract them from what they're doing by spilling a drink or getting into an argument. That's why we have the eye in the sky,' Cassandra said.

'I've heard the term before, but I'm not really sure what it is,' I said. I was here to learn, so there was no point trying to bluff my way through things.

'Years ago, a small team armed with binoculars viewed the floor below for signs of suspicious activity. Now hundreds of closed-circuit television cameras do the job instead. They cover every square inch of the casino, including the tables, the count room, and, as I said earlier, the casino cashier. The network operates twenty-four hours a day, seven days a week.'

Although it was reassuring to know there was a good security presence, the fact that our uniforms didn't have pockets, and Millie told me that she had to clap her hands under the security camera to show she wasn't carrying any chips away with her any time she left the table, made me realise employees were under just as much surveillance as the customers.

'It's sad to say the biggest amount of theft happens behind closed doors by sticky-fingered employees, not from players trying to cheat the system. A lot of money goes in and out of the casino on a daily basis. So it's crucial we keep track of the winnings. All the cash that's funnelled through ends up in the count room. The vault and all the secure offices are in the basement casino. In fact, let me show you where it's taken while we're not busy,' Cassandra said.

She led the way out of the booth, weaving her way past row upon row of slot machines. The bright flashing lights made my eyes go funny, so I turned my face away from them until the unmistakable sound of coins tumbling into a metal tray attracted my attention. The bells that announced a win were intentionally noisy. As I turned to look, the old man sitting in front of the machine glanced over his shoulder towards me, wearing a grin that stretched from ear to ear. That will make his pension go a bit further, I thought.

The casino was like a warren. Everything looked the same to me, but Cassandra negotiated the huge space effortlessly. It must have taken her years of practice to find her way around. She waited for me to catch up before she pressed her fingertip against a panel on the wall next to a door marked private. When it clicked open, she led the way into the sterile-looking corridor and down two flights of stairs.

'Now for the technical bit. Zac went all out and installed a biometric door access control system so that only authorised personnel can enter the count room,' Cassandra said.

Then she looked in a facial recognition camera. It was at least a minute before the time-delayed metal door in the brightly lit basement clicked open.

It took a moment for my eyes to adjust to the contrast. The windowless space we'd walked into was clinical with harsh strip lighting. It was so different from the casino floor, which was a kaleidoscope of bright colours.

Steel shelving lined one wall of the room, and a row of clear plastic tables ran down the centre of the solid concrete floor. Plain stick chairs made from the same material as the table were pushed underneath it. There was no way anyone would be able to stash some cash under a loose floorboard or beneath a chair cushion or inside the upholstery. I could see everything had been done with transparency in mind.

'This is the soft count area. Do you remember I told you the metal box was swapped over at the end of every dealer's shift?' Cassandra asked.

'Yes.'

'This is where the drop team bring it. The count team then empties the box in the centre of the table. One member sorts out the currency by denomination and places them into stacks. Then a second member counts the notes and records the information on the soft count sheet. A third member does a recount and compares the figures. If the two amounts are the same, then it's recorded on a table summary sheet. There's no room for human error here,' Cassandra said.

Then she placed her finger on a panel which read her print, and after the door opened, she led us through into another room.

'This is the hard count area. The coin drop buckets are removed from the slots and brought here. It works in pretty much the same way. But instead of counting by hand, the coins are separated by denomination into containers and weighed using large scales programmed to automatically derive the value of the container's contents from its weight. The handler then wraps the coins and prepares them for either a bank drop or a trip back to the gaming floor,' Cassandra smiled. 'Have you got any questions?'

'Not that I can think of.'

'Let's get back upstairs then,' Cassandra said.

Moments later, Cassandra used her fingerprint to release the private door. When we stepped back on to the casino floor, I was surprised by how many customers had arrived in the short space of time we'd been downstairs. A group of young men were huddled around one of the slot machines, cheering loudly as the sound of tumbling coins filled the air.

'The beers are on you,' one of the men said as he slapped his friend on the back.

I walked past them with a smile on my face. I had a feeling I was going to like working in this adrenaline-filled atmosphere.

44

Paul

The night before the robbery, we met at the chalet to run through the plan and timeline of events one last time. It had been a long time coming; in the morning, it was all systems go. I doubted any of us would get much sleep tonight; nervous tension was filling the air.

'Has anyone got any questions?' I asked when we finished the run-through, then I lifted my bottle of beer off the table and sat back in my chair.

Finn, Kevin and Mark all shook their heads.

'Right then, I think we should call it a night. We've got an early start in the morning.'

I was taking the lead because I'd masterminded the robbery. You couldn't really blame us for wanting to steal the money. When you put temptation in people's way, not everyone was able to resist.

*

'Are you still awake?' Kevin asked in the early hours of the morning.

'I was just dropping off,' I replied, but that wasn't true.

Having your sleep disturbed by another person was one of the many downsides to sharing a bedroom, but the list was endless when you got to our age.

'So much for getting an early night; I've been tossing and turning for hours,' Kevin continued.

He didn't need to tell me that. I could hear the springs in his bed creak every time he rolled over. I didn't want to get caught up in a conversation. I needed my mind to be clear for the morning. If Kevin was having doubts, I'd rather he kept them to himself.

'Good night, Kevin,' I said, hoping he'd get the message.

I'd been accused of being blunt and to the point on many occasions, but at least you knew where you stood with me.

'I'm tempted to just get up,' Kevin prattled on.

'Don't do that. Mum and Dad might hear you, and then they'll wonder what the fuck's going on. Do us both a favour and stay where you are. You need to rest even if you can't sleep.'

Kevin and I crept out of the house like a couple of cat burglars at 5 a.m. I felt like death warmed up from the lack of sleep. My body wasn't accustomed to the early start.

'So far, so good,' Kevin said as we tiptoed up the front path.

The first stage of the plan was complete. We'd managed

to get out of the house without waking mum. That was the hardest bit, so the rest should be a doddle.

'She must be losing her touch,' Kevin grinned as we walked along the icy pavement towards the car.

Mum had had ears like a bat when we'd been teenagers and were trying to sneak in after a night out. The memory of her standing in the hallway with her hands on her hips saying, 'What time do the two of you call this?' brought a smile to my face. We'd always be the worse for wear, but she wouldn't let us get to bed until we'd apologised for waking the whole house up. A slight exaggeration on her part as she was the only one we'd disturbed. Neither of us dared mention the fact that we could hear Dad snoring through the paper-thin walls, and the dog hadn't even bothered to raise his head when we stumbled past his basket. He was out for the count, dreaming of catching rabbits.

Kevin had left his car at the bottom of the road, which was a distance from the house, so Mum wouldn't hear the sound of the engine warming up. When Kevin unlocked his trusty Ford Focus, I put the bag containing the BA uniforms in the boot. Armed with a couple of scrapers, Kevin and I got to work removing the frost from the windscreen.

As Kevin drove towards the coast, I sat in the front passenger seat, rubbing my hands together, trying to stifle the yawns that kept coming one after another like waves crashing on the shore. A few moments later, we parked in a secluded lay-by on the outskirts of the camp. We couldn't risk bringing the car on to the site in case the cameras at the entrance recorded Kevin's number plate. We'd have to walk the rest of the way on foot. But first, we needed to get changed.

It was bitterly cold, and our breath swirled in the air around us as we paced towards the jetty. We were running a little ahead of schedule, but Mark was already waiting in the boat. He mouthed, is everything okay to us, and we gave him the universally recognised thumbs-up in response.

Under cover of darkness, Mark removed the lines securing the boat to the dock, and then, with the use of the aluminium oar, he pushed it away from the shoreline as quietly as possible so as not to alert any witnesses. As the boat glided through the inky water, a wave of trepidation washed over me.

'Are you all right?' Kevin asked. 'You look a bit green around the gills.'

'I was expecting the boat Mark borrowed to be a bit more seaworthy than a flimsy little dinghy,' I replied.

'I'll have you know, this little beauty is built from the highest grade marine PVC; she's light and fast, so she's easy to manoeuvre. Don't look so worried, mate; she's tougher than she looks,' Mark reassured.

But it would take more than his words to convince me. I'd nearly drowned when I was a kid, so now I avoided the water at all costs.

'It would freeze the bollocks off you this morning,' Mark said as we cruised along.

'Ain't that the truth,' Kevin replied, blowing into his hands and then rubbing them vigorously together to try and keep warm.

It had been cold enough on land, but being on the water had added to the chill factor. There was a bitter north-easterly blowing, whipping up sizeable waves that kept smashing into the low-sided boat, adding to my discomfort.

The wind dropped considerably, and the water became much calmer once Mark turned on to the Swale.

Mark took advantage of the favourable conditions and opened up the throttle. As the engine sprang to life, his shoulder-length wavy hair billowed out behind him like golden seaweed. The sudden noise disturbed a flock of migrating birds that had been resting overnight on the nearby nature reserve. The sound of their flapping wings startled me when they took off into the sky. My heart started pounding in response; my nerves were on edge.

'Bit jumpy aren't you, mate,' Mark noted.

'I think I've got good reason to be,' I replied, but my words were carried away on the breeze.

I was bricking it, but Kevin looked as cool as a cucumber. He was sitting at the front, on the inflatable seat, with his arms stretched along the edge of the boat, admiring the scenery like he was on an excursion. I couldn't work out how he was managing to stay so calm. I was crouched down on the middle seat, clinging on to the underside of it, hoping my bowels wouldn't open.

Mark throttled back the engine once we started making our way along the Thames. The closer we got, the worse I was getting. I'd been the brains behind the plan, so I hoped I wasn't going to bottle it at the last moment. My nerves were one of the things I had no control over. It probably didn't help that I hated being on the water. Bouncing around in the centre of an inflatable boat was making my stomach churn without stress of the highest order being thrown into the mix.

Mark moored the boat at Thamesmead, a stone's throw from the airport, but far enough back so that we didn't raise suspicions while we waited for Finn's call. He was going to ring us on a burner phone as soon as the plane landed, which meant we had approximately fifteen minutes to get into position.

The timing needed to be perfect. Once the airport security guards arrived with the vacuum-packed cash, a forklift moved the pallets and placed them inside a cage. The staff then waited for the bank's representatives to collect it. Kevin and I had to grab the money after the last pallet was unloaded and before the armoured van arrived. Simple really. Who was I trying to kid?

Waiting for Finn's call was harder than I thought. I must have checked the time on my watch a hundred times while we sat in silence in the boat, lost in our own thoughts. When the phone eventually began to ring in my hand, it took me by surprise, and I nearly threw it over the side of the inflatable.

'The plane's just landed,' Finn said before he ended the call.

Now it was all systems go. I blew out a breath before I passed the message on, but the others knew what he'd said without me having to relay it.

Mark started the engine when there were five minutes to go.

'Good luck, guys,' he said.

As he opened up the throttle, his blond hair became airborne and danced around his head like a lion's mane.

'Thanks,' Kevin replied.

I couldn't speak; my tongue was stuck to the roof of my mouth. Even though I was chilled to the bone, my hands started to sweat. After all those months of planning, the moment had finally arrived, but I was paralysed by fear and on the verge of bottling it.

'Put your gloves and balaclava on,' Kevin said before he pulled his down to cover his features.

I fumbled in my pockets with frozen digits trying to find mine. I got to them just as Mark pulled up alongside the perimeter fence. Kevin jumped out of the boat as I rushed to put my balaclava and gloves on, but I was all fingers and thumbs. My brother had almost finished cutting through the heavy-duty wire by the time I joined him. Without saying a word, he passed the bolt cutters back to Mark, then he ducked down and scrambled through the hole he'd made. Watching him lead the way fired me into action. We'd always been fiercely competitive with each other ever since we'd been kids, so I'd have to buck myself up and play my part. Anyone would think Kevin had done this a hundred times before. He looked like a true professional, and I wasn't about to be outdone by my younger brother. One-upmanship sprang to mind.

45

Lola

'Can you both come down to my office?' Cassandra asked when Millie and I walked into the foyer at the start of our shift.

My pulse started pounding so I glanced over at my friend for reassurance, but Millie seemed as worried as I was. This couldn't be good, I thought.

'Please don't look so concerned. You haven't done anything wrong. I just want to have a quick chat while the casino's still quiet.'

Cassandra turned on her heel and led the way along the corridor. When she opened the door, the sweet smell of lilies wafted out of the light and airy room. Cassandra walked across the cherry blossom carpet and took a seat behind the mirrored desk, gesturing for Millie and me to sit opposite her.

'How are you settling in?' Cassandra asked.

'Really well. I'm learning something new every day,' Millie jumped in before I had a chance to speak.

'That's good. What about you, Lola?' Cassandra turned her face towards me.

'I feel like part of the furniture already. I love working here,' I replied.

'Considering neither of you had any experience, you're both doing brilliantly,' Cassandra smiled.

She was looking at Millie and me like a proud mum and I felt my shoulders drop as the tension slid away. A moment ago, I'd thought she was going to give us our P45s but now I was grinning from ear to ear.

'Millie and I should thank our lucky stars that you were prepared to take us on,' I said.

'Everybody deserves to be given a chance. When I first met the two of you, I had a feeling you'd had troubled pasts,' Cassandra said.

Her words startled me and put me on edge. The palms of my hands started sweating. I suddenly felt uncomfortable and started to squirm in my seat.

'Was it that obvious?' Millie asked filling the awkward silence.

'Not to the untrained eye, but I'm a professional at recognising the signs. My first proper relationship was with my brother's friend. Matthew didn't hide the fact that he wasn't keen on Julian and me becoming an item. I couldn't see what the problem was and put his concern down to the fact that he didn't want to share his bestie with his little sister. But he rubbished that idea. Matthew insisted he was just worried it would make things awkward for him if Julian and I split up. But of course, I didn't listen. I was too smitten to see sense.' Cassandra shook her head.

I had a strange feeling I could guess what was coming next.

'Matthew and Julian had been friends since primary school. He was always over at our house, so I thought I knew him. But he was a Jekyll and Hyde character. To give him credit where it's due, he hid it well. I swear to God the man was a nut job. One minute, he'd be incredibly loving and the next he'd be beating me senseless.'

Now that sounded familiar. All the bad memories of Troy suddenly came flooding back and threatened to sweep me away, so I took a deep breath to try to calm my racing pulse.

'Are you okay, Lola?' Cassandra asked. 'You look very pale.'

'I'm fine,' I lied before pasting on a false smile.

'I'm sorry; I'm being insensitive rambling on about an old boyfriend without thinking how my story might make the two of you feel. I just wanted you to know I understand what you've been through and I'm here to help you in any way that I can. I promise I'll shut up now.' Cassandra gave us a burst of her infectious laugh.

'Please don't stop on my account. I'd really like to hear how things turned out.' I glanced over in Millie's direction to see her reaction.

'So would I,' Millie agreed.

'In that case, it would be rude not to finish. I'd hate to disappoint you. Things went south pretty quickly, and Julian started hitting me. I felt obliged to hide that from my brother. I kept it a secret for the longest time. But in the end, Matthew worked it out for himself and just as he predicted, he fell out with Julian over it.'

'I would never have imagined you'd been in the same position as us,' Millie said, which brought a smile to Cassandra's face.

I had to agree. It was hard to believe Cassandra had suffered at the hands of a former partner. She'd clearly come a long way.

'What happened after your brother found out? Did the two of you split up?' I asked.

'Yes. That was ten years ago. It was hard to get my life back on track at first, but then I became Zac's PA and everything changed. He hired me, despite me not having the right experience for the role. Zac's also a true believer in giving people a chance. It might surprise you to know that Zac spent some time in a women's refuge when he was a young child. His mother ended up in a hostel when she left his abusive father so he understands exactly what we've been through.'

It was strange to think the four of us had all been living in a safe house at one time or another. I'd completely misjudged Zac. Just because he was a huge man didn't mean he was a threat to me in any way, shape or form. Cassandra made him sound like a pussy cat and a huge-hearted one at that.

Cassandra and Zac were an unlikely couple and I was curious to know more about how they'd ended up together but I couldn't exactly ask. I got the feeling she'd just read my mind when she continued speaking.

'Zac's the kindest man I know; he really is a gentle giant. I was completely broken when I met him, but he put me back together and turned me into the woman I am today. So now I like to repay the favour. Helping others get back on their feet brings me a lot of pleasure.'

Cassandra was inspirational and exuded such confidence. I hoped one day, I'd follow in her footsteps.

'Somewhere along the line, I fell in love with Zac, although it took me a while to convince him to go out with me. Six months in fact,' Cassandra threw her head back and her trademark laugh resonated around the room. 'Zac was worried people would think he was a cradle-snatcher and was taking advantage of me. He was also reluctant to get involved with an employee because he said it wasn't ethical. He had a list of excuses as long as my arm, but I'm delighted to say I eventually managed to wear him down.'

Zac Peterson might not have been a Disney version of Prince Charming, but it was very clear he was Cassandra's knight in shining armour.

Cassandra glanced at her watch. 'Apologies for boring you rigid with my life story, but I wanted you to know my background. I think it's important for survivors like us to stick together and support each other. The problem is, I feel so passionate about the matter I get a bit carried away. I'm sure your ears are bleeding at this stage so I'll let you get back to work,' Cassandra said, giving Millie and me the cue to leave.

It was just before the end of my twelve-hour shift when a balding man in his mid-forties approached the cage. The sight of him dragging the woman he was with along behind him almost made me go into a meltdown. My pulse started jumping around in my wrist, and I had to battle to keep horrific flashbacks from my time with Troy bombarding my brain. The tension was heightening. I shook my head, hoping to dislodge the unpleasant memories, but they were here to stay. The woman looked through the glass and fixed me with bloodshot eyes as two rivers of mascara ran down her cheeks. My heart went out to her.

'I need to cash these in,' the man said, firing some chips into the under-counter tray.

'Certainly, sir,' I replied, not forgetting my manners even though he apparently didn't have any.

As I counted out the money, I saw the woman's face crumple.

'Is that all we've got left? We were meant to be winning, not losing,' she said.

The man's head snapped around, and he glared at his partner before the corner of his lip lifted into a snarl.

'Shut the fuck up,' he said, getting right up in her face.

The woman flinched as he spat the words at her.

I'd been really enjoying working at Rolling the Dice, but I couldn't get out of work soon enough this evening. By the time I'd got my jacket from the staff cloakroom and was walking towards the station with Millie, I was on the verge of having a full-blown panic attack.

'Are you okay, Lola?' Millie asked. 'You don't seem yourself.'

'I just had a bad experience, that's all,' I replied, still trying to dislodge unpleasant thoughts of my ex from my mind.

'Difficult customer?' Millie quizzed.

'Some guy was being a dick to his partner, and it brought back memories of a time I'd rather forget.'

'Let me guess. Was it a balding guy in his forties with a huge beer gut?'

I nodded.

'He was an absolute pig. They were on my table, and she kept trying to stop him from gambling, but he wasn't having any of it. He just kept putting more and more chips down even though he wasn't winning anything back. I felt sorry for her, but there's nothing you can do in a situation like that. It's not your place to intervene,' Millie said.

'I know, but it's horrible to watch. It was weird seeing things from the other side.'

Millie and I sat in silence on the train. I couldn't speak for my friend, but I was mulling over what had happened. I bet that poor woman was being beaten black and blue right about now. I'd felt her pain when she'd looked at me through the glass. I'd been in the same no-win situation as her. Any time Troy and I got into a confrontation, everything was always my fault. We'd get into huge arguments over something trivial, and it would blow out of all proportion. I'd do anything to avoid one of the ugly conflicts we'd end up in, which could drag on for days until I was practically on my knees begging for Troy's forgiveness just so that we could put an end to the episode.

To avoid World War Three breaking out in the first place, I'd sometimes admit I was in the wrong even though I didn't think I'd done anything out of turn. But if Troy was in the mood for an argument and I tried to apologise, he wouldn't accept it. I couldn't win.

Troy had mastered the art of gaslighting, getting me to question myself and the part I played in him losing his rag. I'd doubt my version of events and become unsure of what had actually led up to the latest episode to take the heat off him. He always made me feel like I was responsible for his actions. It was my fault he'd reacted in the way that he had. He'd tell me I'd baited him into it. Troy's mind manipulation was so powerful I sometimes questioned my sanity. Over time he chipped away at my self-esteem. It took me a long while to realise what he was doing. Troy would accuse me of being too sensitive when I was pretty certain my reaction was somewhat normal.

I kept hoping that Troy would change. He was always very sorry after he'd blown up at me and begged for forgiveness, promising that he'd never do it again, but of course he always did. He'd convince me that everything would be different from now on, telling me he felt terrible that he'd hurt me. Troy would keep his word for weeks and sometimes months before he became abusive again. But instead of getting better, things got worse the longer I put up with it.

I'd thrown everything into our relationship. While Troy and I had been a couple, I'd spent an endless amount of time trying to get to the bottom of what made him behave the way he had. I'd wanted to find an explanation for why he'd kept hurting me and was convinced the reasons lay in the past. Fast forward twenty years, to deal with what had happened to him as a child, he'd taken his anger out on me. It was a destructive pattern. I'd been desperate to help Troy bury the ghosts that still haunted him and hoped he'd be able to lock the bad memories in a box and throw away the key. Sadly, that never happened. Nobody could deny he'd had a rough start, but that didn't give him the right to make my life a living hell.

I hoped the woman I'd met at the casino earlier found the strength to leave her abusive partner. I wished I'd had five minutes alone with her to tell her things didn't need to be that way. There was help out there for her; she only had to ask.

46

Abbie

I found everything about my partner jarring, and if I didn't put some space between the two of us, I couldn't be responsible for my actions.

'I'm calling it a night,' I said before I scooped the paperwork back into the file and headed for home.

I wasn't much of a team player; I like to set the pace and needed some peace and quiet to go through Finn's bank statements. I wasn't going to get that if I stayed at work. There were too many distractions at the station, so it was time to take myself out of the equation.

My ultra-modern flat, on a new development in Greenwich, was my haven, even though it was full of bittersweet memories. It had been two years since Ryan had left me for another woman. I'd never experienced pain like it, and I never intended to do so again. His sudden departure from my life had broken me in more ways than one. It wasn't just the emotional fallout I'd had to deal with, it was the financial implications too. Without his lawyer's salary in the pot, I'd struggled to pay the mortgage and the bills. But my home was all I had left, and I wasn't going to let him take that from me too.

My heels clicked across the tiled floor of the communal lobby. I'd normally take the stairs, but it had been a long day, and I didn't fancy walking up six flights, so I decided to call the lift instead. When the doors opened, I stepped inside and pressed the button for the penthouse; my apartment was up in the gods, which I loved. There was a snobbery attached to owning a property on the highest floor of the building, but I didn't care what people thought; I kept myself to myself. The penthouse apartments had luxury fixtures and finishes and were far superior to the other units in the building; the view from the wrap-around balcony was amazing. Being on my private terrace surveying the world beat having to sit in the communal gardens with the other residents any day. Making small talk with people I barely knew didn't feature high up on my list of favourite pastimes. I didn't like casual acquaintances knowing about my private or professional life. Revealing I was a member of the force always met with mixed reactions.

When the lift came to a stop and the doors glided open, I stepped out and walked along the corridor to my front door, a stylish flat-fronted charcoal-grey composite door with a long chrome handle. It took me a moment to locate my keys, which had fallen to the bottom of my black leather handbag. I let out a contented sigh when I pushed the door open.

I swapped my Karen Millen heels, the last present Ryan had bought me, for a pair of comfy slippers I'd bought from

Asda as soon as I stepped over the threshold. The best way to keep a clean and hygienic house was to leave shoes at the front door. The soles carried bacteria from the outside in; I didn't want to spread germs around my flat. I worked long hours and didn't have the time or the inclination to do housework, so I took every opportunity to avoid it. And I certainly didn't trust anyone enough to allow them to be my cleaner.

I pulled a chair out from the S-shaped glass table then spread the paperwork over it. Taking my notebook and pen out of my bag, I started scanning through the rows of transactions on Finn's bank statements. By the time I'd reached the bottom of the fourth page, a bottle of chilled white wine had started calling to me from the fridge. Having a drink while I was working probably wasn't going to help my concentration, but I was off-duty, and it would definitely break up the monotony of the job, so I wasn't going to feel guilty about pouring myself a large glass.

Considering Finn was a young man, he didn't lead a very exciting life. Judging by his debit card transactions, he seemed to spend every Saturday from lunchtime to closing in The Rising Tide. I made a note of the name; it had to be worth paying his local a visit to see if there was anything I could find out about him. Little details could lead to big breaks. It was in the forefront of my mind that cases over twenty-four months old usually stayed unsolved.

47

Lola

'Seeing the way that guy was treating his partner has really affected me,' I said when Millie and I walked home from the station.

'I could tell. You've hardly said a word since we left work.'

'I wanted to reach out to her and tell her to be brave. Feeling like you're trapped in a relationship with no way out is the pits; uncertainty hovers over every decision you try to make. Well, it did in my case.'

'Mine too,' Millie agreed. 'My ex was so jealous and possessive he'd monitor and track my movements and messages, and he used his temper and intimidation to frighten and control me.'

'That sounds familiar. It wasn't just me Troy took his anger out on though, customers felt the lash of his tongue on many occasions, but he stopped short of physically abusing them. It always amazed me how he managed to control his temper when it suited him. Pity he never showed me the same courtesy.'

'My ex was the same. He saved the violent outbursts for behind closed doors. Before he started hitting me, he subjected me to verbal, emotional and psychological abuse worse than anyone could imagine.'

Millie had a haunted look on her face, and I felt guilty for bringing the subject up. But I knew exactly what she meant. Words didn't leave bruises, but they did a lot of damage to a person's self-esteem.

'It's all about power and control with these men,' Millie shook her head.

'With any luck, after the disastrous day that couple had on the tables, they won't bother darkening the doorstep of the casino any time soon,' I said. 'Do you fancy watching a film later?' I asked to veer the conversation off in a different direction. I could see Millie was just as troubled by the encounter as I was.

'Yeah, why not, as long as it's something light-hearted, but not a cheesy rom-com,' Millie replied.

I was a romantic at heart before Troy had destroyed my faith in men, which was partly why I'd put up with my situation for so long. I'd thought we were a match made in heaven because we'd both lost a parent and craved the same things from a relationship. Having a special connection with my partner was my number one priority; for me, looks and money didn't come into the equation.

It hadn't taken long for things to start to unravel. I seemed to have a knack of unintentionally pushing his buttons and making him lose his rag. He could change like the flick of a switch. But instead of apologising, he'd turn the situation around and make me feel as though I was somehow at fault. Once he'd convinced me to accept the blame for his actions, he'd calm down and act as though nothing had happened.

I was powerless to stop the cycle. I was terrified of him and stuck in an unhappy, toxic environment. Back then, I wouldn't have dared even think about reporting him to the police. I kept focusing on what Troy had been like at the start of our relationship. I'd hoped if I stayed, things would go back to how they were at the beginning. But some people were beyond fixing. Just because Troy had had a bad start in life, it didn't give him the right to take it out on me. I was so glad I'd plucked up the courage to leave.

48

Paul

March, One month after the heist

Finn had come up with a genius idea. He'd convinced his GP he was suffering from PTSD and had been signed off work for the foreseeable future. When the time came, it would make it easier for us to split if he didn't have to work his notice. After what he'd been through, the airline wasn't in a position to argue.

Before we met up at the chalet, I'd scoured every news channel and trawled through social media sites looking for any mention of the airport heist, but nothing new was being reported. That was a good sign, I thought. With any luck, the trail had started to go cold. So far, everything had gone to plan, so all we had to do was sit tight.

'Am I the only one that's getting bored of going through the motions?' Kevin asked before shovelling a huge forkful of sweet and sour pork into his mouth. 'The money's burning a hole in my pocket.'

'Well, you're going to have to resist the urge to start spending. We have to carry on as normal and not change anything about our usual routines,' I replied.

'How much longer are we going to have to keep this up?' Kevin shook his head.

'I don't know, but at least until the trail runs cold.'

'Surely we're already at that stage. The story hasn't been on the news or in the paper for weeks now,' Kevin replied.

'I had to phone HR today to give them an update on my condition. While I was on the blower, I asked how the case was going. The police have to keep the airline updated on how the investigation is going, and people love to gossip, don't they? The woman I spoke to said it was going nowhere,' Finn said.

Whether Finn's interpretation was right or not, none of us knew for certain.

'Why don't we start trying to launder small amounts of the money through a casino?' Kevin suggested.

'I think it's too risky. It's not as though we could stay anonymous. Casinos have to verify the identity of every customer. We've come within an inch of success; we don't want to balls it up now,' Mark replied.

He was the cautious one of the crew. We'd only ever planned to store our stolen cash until the heat died down, and that seemed to be the case, so what were we waiting for?

'You can do what you like with your share. But if we don't try and clean the money, we'll never be able to use it,' Kevin said. 'I was earwigging on a conversation earlier when one of the guys on the wing was talking about how he used to wash the cash he earned drug dealing. He'd go to a casino and convert the money into chips. Then he'd gamble a small amount of it on the tables before changing the chips back into cash. He reckons it's almost impossible for anyone to trace it. Why don't we start off gently and build up to larger amounts?'

The idea of using a casino to break the chain of traceability appealed to me. I wasn't a regular player, but I'd been to Rolling the Dice before, so my details were in the system.

'Who fancies heading up to London and going to a casino this weekend?' Kevin asked.

Kevin loved being behind the wheel, so he'd volunteered to be the designated driver. Mark had finally come around to our way of thinking and was sitting in the back of Kevin's Ford Focus, sipping away on a bottle of Bud to give himself some Dutch courage even though it was only ten in the morning. We were all in high spirits on the journey and looking forward to the trip up to London. Going out in the capital made a pleasant change from Sheppey.

'It's going to cost most of the proceeds of the heist to get my car out again,' Kevin said when he pulled up alongside the barrier at the NCP car park and saw the tariff board displaying the hourly rate. 'I don't know anywhere that charges for parking on a Sunday. Talk about daylight robbery.'

'Stop being such a tightwad; it's not as though you can't afford it,' I replied.

London was full of casinos, so we could have split up and all gone to different ones, but we decided it would make it look like an authentic boys' day out if we all hit the same one. There was also the added bonus that if we were betting against each other, it would minimise the amount we lost as we'd decided we were going to pool the winnings at the end of the trip. We were all in this together, so that seemed like the fairest way.

I pushed open the revolving glass door and stepped out of the drizzle. Kevin, Mark and Finn filed in behind me. We walked across the foyer and made our way to the casino floor. The place looked like it had been refurbished since I'd last been here; it was a lot posher than I remembered, but I'd been three sheets to the wind at the time, so my recollection might not have been that accurate.

There were a few customers milling about, but it wasn't busy, so I was able to walk straight up to the cashier's cage.

'Hi, can I change up some money, please?' I asked the beautiful green-eyed blonde sitting behind the counter.

'Of course,' she replied, flashing me a smile. 'How much would you like to exchange?'

'A thousand pounds, please.'

I placed the bundle of fifty-pound notes into the under-counter tray, and a moment later, the young woman scooped it out from the other side with her slender fingers. She glanced up at me to make sure I was watching before she started to count the cash to verify the amount. There was no way I wouldn't have been looking; she was absolutely stunning, and I was mesmerised by her. Even after she finished serving me, I could barely tear my eyes away from her.

'Are you coming to hit the tables, or are you going to stand there gawping instead?'

Kevin threw his head back and laughed when the words left his mouth. He loved nothing more than embarrassing me and took every opportunity he got to do so. I'd been hanging around by the side of the booth so that I could watch her for a bit longer while my friends were being served. I'd thought I was being really subtle, but that obviously wasn't the case. Kevin hadn't even bothered to wait until we were out of earshot to humiliate me.

'I wasn't gawping; I was just waiting for you guys to get served,' I replied.

I was too embarrassed to own it, so I tried to gloss over it instead. By the way my friends dismissed my response, I knew there was no point in trying to deny I'd been checking out the cashier.

'Yeah, right. Of course you were,' Finn said, raising his eyebrows up and down.

'Give the guy a break. You can see you're embarrassing him.' Mark tried to put an end to my agony, but his statement unintentionally made me feel ten times worse.

'You'll have to excuse my friends,' I said to the attractive blonde behind the counter. 'They're a bunch of morons and don't go out in public very often, so they don't know how to behave when they're let out of the asylum for the day.'

'No need to apologise,' she replied with a smile on her face.

After ordering a round of drinks at the bar, we took a seat at the roulette table. The croupier gave us a moment to settle ourselves down. Then she said:

'Place your bets.'

Kevin put his chips on eleven black; Mark chose twenty-four black, and Finn placed his on nine red. He was born on the ninth, so it was his lucky number. That just left me to decide. I opted for twenty-one red. We'd purposely chosen numbers away from each other's, but it was anyone's guess where the ball would land.

'No more bets,' the croupier said.

The dealer with the waist-length brown hair spun the wheel. All eyes were fixed on her when she threw the small white ball in the opposite direction. As it raced around the outside rim of the circular track, I glanced across at Mark. He was in a trance-like state, but it wasn't the ball that had his attention as it ran around the circumference of the wheel, it was the young woman in charge of the table. The ball dropped down from the rim when it eventually started to slow down and travelled towards the centre of the wheel. My heart was in my mouth when it scattered chaotically across the inner section, bouncing over the pockets, losing more and more speed. The atmosphere around the table was tense while we waited to see where it would land. When it came to a stop and fell into twenty-one red, my mouth dropped open. I couldn't believe what I was seeing. A loud cheer went up from our table.

'You lucky bastard,' Finn said, slapping me on the back.

'It's a fix,' Kevin called out.

The girl with the shiny hair looked taken aback by his outburst.

'I can assure you it isn't. Roulette is a game of chance. The pockets are all the same size, and the probability of the ball landing in any one of them is equal.'

I couldn't help thinking her answer was well rehearsed.

I could see why the roulette wheel was a favourite among casino customers. It was highly addictive and the croupier had us all under her spell as she released the ball over and over again. Our purpose had been to launder some money and make our visit look like a legitimate boys' trip, but we were winning more than we'd arrived with, so it was time to put an end to the thrilling roller coaster ride.

'I don't know about you lot, but I'm going to quit while I'm ahead,' I said, scooping my winnings up and making my way over to the cashier's cage.

Kevin, Finn and Mark followed my lead, and we formed an orderly queue. I made sure I was the last in line so that I could admire the view for as long as possible.

'How would you like the money, cash or bank transfer?' the young woman said before fixing me with her green eyes.

'Bank transfer, please,' I replied.

In a few days, my winnings would be deposited into my Santander account, leaving the all-important paper trail behind. The thought of that brought a smile to my face.

'I told you filtering the money through the casino to make it look legitimate was a good idea,' Kevin said. He turned to look at me as he drove us towards home.

'I know you did, but I wasn't the one you had to convince. Mark was the one sitting on the fence. But I don't think we'll have any trouble getting him to tag along next time, now that he's got his eye on the dealer.'

'You're a fine one to talk,' Mark laughed.

49

Lola

Working in the casino had done wonders for my confidence. It had opened windows of opportunity all around me. Now that I had money coming in, I'd started to save for a deposit on a flat. Millie and I had decided, as soon as we could afford it, we were going to rent a place together. Who would have thought I'd have come this far in such a short space of time? I'd arrived with virtually nothing but hope for a brighter future. I hadn't been expecting much. I'd resigned myself to the fact that even if I was dealt the longest odds, they would be a vast improvement from the ones I'd left back home. I wasn't expecting a pot of gold to be waiting at the end of the rainbow.

I hadn't known the meaning of the words job satisfaction before. When I'd worked at William Hill's, I'd had to psych myself up each morning so that I could pluck up the courage to press the button that unsealed the shop's magnetically locked front door. Opening for business always filled me with trepidation as I never knew what the day would bring.

Sometimes the place was dead. It wasn't every day of the week that a football final, title fight, horse race, golf tournament and the Grand Prix all coincided. But occasionally, they did. And when that happened, all hell broke loose. We needed a bouncer on-site to deal with the aggressive gamblers, but Troy had ignored my repeated request. He used to get a lot of pleasure bringing lairy customers into line. But they terrified me, especially as I was often alone on the premises.

Working three twelve-hour shifts seemed like a breeze compared to the long stints I'd previously done. I felt like a part-timer now. It wasn't just the hours; everything was so much better. I didn't miss the customers one bit. They tended to fall into two groups. The older generation favoured horse and greyhound racing, whereas the younger ones preferred to bet on football or try their luck on fixed-odds arcade-style games instead.

Customers used to accuse the shop of rigging equipment when they lost a lot of money. Fifty pounds could be fed in and gambled on some machines every twenty seconds. People sometimes blew their hard-earned cash in a matter of minutes, hoping to strike it rich. That was asking for trouble in a working-class environment if you asked me.

These days, I walked into work with a spring in my step. The management were so supportive, and I got on well with my colleagues. With the exception of the balding bully I'd had to deal with, the customers were in a different league too. A few weeks after I'd started working at Rolling the Dice, I'd met Paul and his friends. He always bowled up to the cage with a bright smile on his face, and his easy manner never failed to lift my spirits whenever he came in.

'I love your accent, by the way. Where are you from?' Paul asked after I'd changed his cash for chips.

I felt heat rush to my cheeks, and I hoped it didn't show.

'Yorkshire,' I replied, not wanting to be too specific. My experience with Troy had made me wary of everybody.

'What made you come down south?' Paul asked, fixing his blue eyes on me.

My pulse speeded up in response to his question.

'Work.'

I realised my one-word answers must be coming across as rude, but I was in a blind panic and couldn't think straight.

'It was nice chatting to you, but I'd better let you get on,' Paul said as he walked away from the counter and caught up with his friends.

The afternoons were always busier than the mornings, but there wasn't much going on today, so I had plenty of time to dissect the conversation I'd had with Paul, or lack of it on my part anyway. I felt bad that I'd been so frosty to somebody that was just trying to be friendly and decided to make more of an effort when he came to cash in his chips. But he didn't come back to the booth before my shift ended, so he'd either cashed out while I'd been on my break, or he was still inside the building somewhere lost in the maze of machines and tables.

'I never thought I'd hear myself say this, but I really like Mark,' Millie said. She was sprawled out on the sofa in the communal lounge in her Mickey Mouse pyjamas. 'I can feel myself falling for him.'

I wasn't into long hair on men, my ex used to shave his head, so Mark wasn't my type. But I could see why Millie had a soft spot for him. He had a toned torso and golden skin, which made me think Viking blood flowed through his veins. I had a feeling he wasn't short of admirers. He was the sort of man who sets hearts racing.

'I'd never have guessed. You're hiding your true feelings so well,' I joked.

Millie flipped her glossy hair over one shoulder, tilted her head to one side and fixed me with her brown eyes. She seemed confused by what I'd just said.

'The faraway dreamy look you've been wearing just recently suits you, as does the twinkle in your eye,' I laughed.

'Oh my God, please tell me I'm not being that obvious.' Millie looked horrified by the thought.

'I'm only teasing you.'

'Even so, do you think he's noticed I fancy him?' Millie swung her legs off of the sofa and sat bolt upright, chewing on her thumbnail.

'I doubt it.'

'I'll be mortified next time I see him.'

'Don't be. I didn't mean to make you feel paranoid. I'm really happy for you, Mills. And for what it's worth, I hope the feeling's mutual. I think the two of you would make a lovely couple,' I grinned.

'Aww, shucks.' Millie wrapped her arms around herself, and a huge smile lit up her face. 'What about you? Has anyone caught your eye?'

I felt myself blush in response which pretty much answered the question for her.

'Maybe,' I replied, knowing there was no point in trying

to keep the truth from my friend. 'I've taken a bit of a shine to Paul.' As the words left my mouth, I felt my lips stretch into a grin. But then I realised I was being stupid, so I let my smile slide. As if he was going to fancy me.

Millie's eyes sprung open as if that was news to her. 'Oh, fantastic. We can double date.'

'I think you might be jumping the gun a bit. I hate to point out the obvious, but they haven't asked us out,' I laughed.

'That's just a small technicality,' Millie replied.

'I have to say I love your enthusiasm. I hope it's infectious.' But I somehow doubted it. My relationship with Troy had scarred me and my self-esteem had taken a knock. I wasn't sure anyone else would ever want me. I was damaged goods. Aside from that, I'd never been a jump straight in sort of person, and I wasn't convinced that was about to change any time soon, especially under the circumstances.

50

Abbie

April

This was the first time I'd ventured across the bridge to the Isle of Sheppey. I hadn't really known what to expect. It had a reputation for being a large campsite, but I wasn't getting that vibe at this stage. I hadn't seen a single mobile home yet. The first thing I noticed was the sewage works and paper mills that greeted me on arrival. I'd heard the island was a landscape of prisons and marshes, but I'd have to reserve judgement for now.

If first impressions counted for anything, I was pleasantly surprised. It was a beautiful warm spring day; there wasn't a cloud in the sky. The sun was beating down on the stretch of water beneath me, making the surface glisten as oystercatchers waded through the shallows hoping to find their next meal. The blue expanse looked very inviting, peppered with small boats.

The Rising Tide had a prime waterside location, along the coast from Sheerness Beach, close to Barton's Point. I'd had high hopes as I drove towards it, but when I arrived, the place was a bit of a let-down; it didn't have much kerb appeal. From the state of the exterior, it looked like it hadn't had a coat of paint for donkey's years. I pulled into the empty car park and made my way across the pothole-riddled frontage towards the pub entrance.

I pushed the brass handle on the half glass timber framed door, expecting it to be locked. It was so dark inside, I wasn't sure whether they were open. I stepped inside the deserted pub, walked up to the bar and flashed my ID card at the man behind the counter.

'I'm DI Kingsly. I was hoping to have a quick word with the landlord if he's about.'

'That would be yours truly. I'm Neil,' the tall man replied, holding his hand out towards me. 'What can I do for you?'

'I believe Finn McCaskill is one of your regulars.'

'That's right.' Neil's eyes lit up.

'What can you tell me about him?'

'What's he been up to?' Neil's tone resembled that of an old woman's when she was about to get hold of a juicy piece of gossip.

It never failed to amaze me how some people got a real buzz from the thought of another person's misfortune.

'Has he been a naughty boy?'

'No, nothing like that.'

I could tell instantly that Neil wasn't a man who could be trusted with confidential information, so I couldn't afford to give anything away. If he knew why I was interested in finding out information about his customer, he'd go running back to Finn at the first opportunity to tip him off in true busybody style.

'Finn comes in here every Saturday lunchtime with his three friends Mark, Paul and Kevin. They always sit at that table.' Neil pointed towards the far corner of the pub.

I looked over to where he'd indicated before casting my eye around the interior. Everything was shabby but not in a chic way; the table legs were scratched, and the tops bore the battle scars of heavy use and drunken nights; the upholstery on the few chairs that had any left a lot to be desired. It was stained and coming away from the seams in places. The pub was in need of a full renovation, but judging from the lack of customers, it was lucky to still be open, so spending money he didn't have on fixtures and fittings wasn't Neil's top priority.

'You said Finn comes in here with his friends. Do you know their surnames by any chance?'

'Mark Gibson and Paul and Kevin Best, they're brothers,' Neil replied. 'They're nice enough lads. They don't give me any hassle.'

I wrote that down in my notebook. I was glad I'd paid the publican a visit now. He'd been extremely helpful and was turning out to be the fountain of all knowledge where my suspect and his possible accomplices were concerned.

'The lads generally drink pints of Stella or the occasional rum and coke. Once they've sunk a good few, they usually order burgers and chips, then wash the grub down with more booze,' Neil laughed.

I wasn't sure why he was laughing, but I suppose the joke was on them if they were stupid enough to want to frequent a place like this. They were braver than I was. It looked like it was a health inspector's paradise. I'd noticed the hygiene rating on my way in was two. I was surprised Neil was displaying the sign. I wasn't tempted to have a drink out of a sealed container while I was there, let alone put my lips near anything that came out of the kitchen. Finn and his friends deserved a medal for propping up the failing establishment.

'From what you've told me, I've established that Finn and his friends are good customers.'

'They're the best. You won't hear me complaining about them. It's people like those lads that see me through the dark days when all the tourists have gone away at the end of the summer. If it wasn't for my die-hard regulars, the pub would have closed long ago.'

Having to rely on seasonal trade to make a living was a stark reminder that we weren't in London now. It must be virtually impossible for a business to stay afloat.

'Is it usually this quiet?' I gestured to the sea of empty tables spreading out in front of me.

'Yes, this is pretty much a standard day at the office for me.'

Neil laughed. If that was the case, I was surprised he could afford to stay open. But then again, judging by the state of his red face, he looked like he drank any profit he made.

'You wouldn't recognise this place during the summer. When the holiday parks are full, it doubles the island's population, so it's standing room only and three people deep at the bar trying to get served. We're rushed off our feet.'

I couldn't help feeling that was wishful thinking on Neil's part.

'Sheppey comes alive during the summer months. The island has a lot going for it which is why it's a popular holiday destination. The open spaces and beaches are second to none.'

I didn't doubt that.

'I'm proud to say I was born and bred here, as were my parents and grandparents,' Neil said with a smile on his face.

The conversation had started to digress, so I glanced at my watch to give the publican a subtle hint that he was rambling on about something that wasn't relevant. I was keen to wrap up our chat sooner rather than later. Neil was nice enough, but I didn't want to hear his life story or about his heritage. He could obviously sense my departure was imminent, which more than likely prompted his next question.

'So, is there anything, in particular, you want to know about Finn?'

It was clear I'd more than piqued Neil's curiosity. He was desperate to know what was going on and was falling over himself to help me. I got the distinct impression being questioned by a detective about one of his regular customers was the most excitement he'd had in a long time. Getting him to talk wasn't a problem; keeping him from veering off on a tangent was proving to be more of a challenge. Neil loved the sound of his own voice. I'd surmised he was the type of character that was an authority on everything, but being able to talk for England was a quality that probably ensured he was a good landlord too.

'I think you've given me enough to go on.'

'You never said why you were interested in Finn.' Neil stared at me with a hopeful look on his face.

'I'm afraid I'm not at liberty to say. Could you please let me know if you hear anything that you think might be of interest,' I said as I handed Neil one of my cards.

'Like what?' Neil quizzed.

'I don't know. Anything that seems out of the ordinary,' I replied.

'Will do, and if there's anything else you'd like to ask me, feel free to give me a bell,' Neil grinned.

'Nothing springs to mind at the moment,' I smiled. 'But thanks for your help.'

It was time to make a break for the door before Neil found anything else to talk about. It wasn't as though he was rushed off his feet; he had plenty of time to kill. There wasn't a single customer in the pub that needed serving, so nobody was going to come to my rescue.

51

Lola

Before Mum had been discharged from the hospital, the doctors had decided she didn't need an operation after all. I'd kept trying to talk her into coming down to London while she was signed off, but she'd gone back on her promise and had refused to come and stay with me while her broken arm healed. All she'd done was give me one excuse after another.

'How did you get on?' I asked. Mum had started back at work today.

'Not too bad, but my arm's throbbing a bit now from all the exertion.'

'Do you think you went back too soon? Why don't you ask the doctor to sign you off for a bit longer?'

'I can't do that!' Mum jumped down my throat. She sounded horrified by my suggestion. 'My boss will throw a hissy fit if I take any more time off. He's been very good to me, so I don't want to take advantage.'

'But you're struggling to do your job, so you obviously

haven't recovered enough to be back at work. If that's the case, then your employer's the one that's taking advantage, not you. It's not too late to come and join me in London, you know.'

'Honestly, I'm fine. I wish I hadn't said anything now.'

'You're not fine; you just said your arm was throbbing.'

Mum let out a loud sigh. 'Drop it, please. I don't want to get into an argument over this.'

'Neither do I, but don't be so narky with me. I'm worried about you, Mum.'

'Well, don't be. I'm made of strong stuff, and now that I'm mopping floors again, it'll build up my muscles in no time.'

'It's not just the physical side of things, though—'

'Please, Lola. Let's not go there,' Mum said, cutting me off mid-sentence.

'You can bury your head in the sand all you like, but we both know that Troy is still a threat to you.'

'He wouldn't be stupid enough to try and hurt me again.'

'I hope you're right.'

'I am, so do us both a favour and put this out of your head.'

Mum was no match for my ex, but she wasn't listening to me and dismissed my concerns. She seemed a lot more confident about Troy leaving her alone than I was. I was seriously worried for mum's safety. She was five foot two and slight like me. Troy was exactly a foot taller than us and well built. The strength of one of his punches used to lift me off my feet; I'd been powerless to stop him. He had virtually no control over his temper. I'd been on the receiving end of it more times than I cared to remember. When he blew, he blew; there were no half measures involved. He had a very short fuse and could turn on you so quickly it made your head spin.

'Anyway, that's enough about me. Tell me how you're getting on,' Mum said, changing the subject.

'I'm doing really well. Everyone's really friendly at the shelter, and I'm getting on great at work too. I love my job.'

'That's good to know.' Mum was trying to sound upbeat, but she wasn't quite managing to pull it off. 'I'd better let you go. This call must be costing you a fortune.'

'It's not. I'm using my minutes.'

But Mum had obviously decided she didn't want to talk any more, so she chose to ignore what I'd just said.

'I'll give you a ring at the weekend. Take care of yourself, love,' she said before she ended the call.

I sat on the edge of my bed, staring into space. I couldn't put my finger on it, but something wasn't right. Mum and I used to chat away for hours on end and still not run out of things to talk about. But the conversation we'd just had was strained. Maybe I was reading too much into it. Mum was bound to be tired after her first day back at work, but I had a nagging doubt at the back of my mind that there was more to it than that.

Troy might have gone quiet for the moment, but that didn't mean he'd given up trying to find me. He was a control freak and was never going to let me walk away without punishing me. He'd turned his well-defined muscles on me when he'd flown into a rage for lesser things.

When we'd been a couple, he'd been obsessed with my phone, wanting to know who I was messaging and who I was spending time with when I wasn't with him. He knew my passwords to social media sites, my email, and how to unlock my phone. I'd felt like I'd had no privacy. Troy was incredibly jealous and constantly accused me of cheating on him. He'd discouraged me from seeing my friends on my own, and on the rare occasions I went against his wishes and did go out without him, he'd constantly be checking up on me, calling me four or five times which raised more than a few eyebrows. By the time I'd plucked up the courage to leave, he'd started making everyday decisions for me, telling me what to wear and controlling what I ate. He might have pulled back into the shadows, but instinct told me I hadn't heard the last from him.

52

Paul

'I wasn't sure if you boys were going to be in today,' Neil said when I went up to the bar to order a round of drinks.

'Why not? We're as regular as clockwork. You know it's Saturday lunchtime without even having to check the time on your watch the minute we appear,' I laughed.

'I know you are, but there was a copper sniffing around here on Tuesday asking questions about the four of you, so I thought you must have been up to no good. I wondered if you'd been banged up by now.'

Neil stared at me with a big grin on his face, clearly delighted to be the bearer of such a tasty little piece of information.

I felt my mouth drop open but quickly closed it again. I didn't want to give Neil any more reason to be suspicious. We'd been lying low for ages; there hadn't been a word about the robbery on the news or in the papers for weeks, so we'd been hoping the trail had gone cold. If the police had been in our local asking questions, it looked like they'd worked out there was a connection between us, which couldn't be a good thing.

'How strange,' I said, hoping to give the impression that I hadn't got a clue why the police might be interested in us. 'What did they want to know?' I quizzed.

'The bird just asked if Finn was one of my regulars,' Neil said.

'Was that it?'

'Pretty much. I hope she comes back again; she was a lovely bit of eye candy. She looked more like a model than a member of the filth and had a set of peepers that made me go weak at the knees. She looked like the picture of innocence with those huge blue eyes, but I bet she's a real goer in the sack. The angelic-looking ones always are.'

I was fairly certain the attraction would have been one-sided. Neil wasn't exactly God's gift to women; the only thing he had in his favour was that he was tall. He had a belly you could rest a pint on, a badly receding hairline, a bulbous nose and a bright red face. I'd seen enough publicans with the same complexion over the years to know it was an unpleasant hallmark of the job and the sign of a heavy drinker.

'I'm intrigued to know what she wanted now.'

'As if you don't know,' Neil replied.

'Honestly, mate, I haven't got a clue.'

'Yeah, right, proper little Pinocchio you are,' Neil laughed. 'Feel free to confess all to me. Then I'll have an excuse to give her a call.'

'I bet that would make her day,' I joked. Neil threw me a black look. 'So the only thing she asked was if Finn was a regular?'

'Yeah, and when I told her you lads came here every Saturday without fail, her ears pricked up, and she asked for your full names.'

I felt my heart sink. 'And let me guess, you told her,' I replied.

'Course I did,' Neil chuckled.

'Thanks for that, mate.' I shook my head as I looked daggers at him.

'What?' Neil threw his palms up as he tried to act innocent.

'I can't believe you gave our names to the police.' I was absolutely fuming.

'What was I supposed to do?'

'You could have said you didn't know our surnames.' The man had shit for brains.

'You just said you've got nothing to hide, so it shouldn't cause you any problems.'

'That's beside the point. This is a matter of principle. Offering up your loyal customers to the filth is a low blow even by your standards.'

'You're sounding more and more like a man with a guilty conscience if you ask me.'

'Well, I didn't ask you,' I said through gritted teeth.

'I don't know what you're getting so worked up about unless there's something you're not telling me.' Neil narrowed his eyes and glared at me.

Anyone would think he was Columbo the way he was carrying on.

'Let me make one thing clear. I don't appreciate you giving our details out to the Old Bill. If it was the other way around, I'm sure you wouldn't want them noseying through your personal business either.'

'Calm down, mate, there's no point in getting your knickers in a twist,' Neil laughed.

His comment was like a red rag to a bull, and I knew I needed to put some distance between us before I made matters worse than they already were.

'Why don't you do yourself a favour and zip it.'

Neil was a slimy fucker. After all the business we put his way, he'd rewarded us by throwing us to the wolves. Who needed enemies when you had a friend like him.

'What does it take to get a drink around here? I'm going to die of thirst waiting for you to pour the pints,' I said.

I'd decided to put an end to the conversation. Neil could talk for England if he got half a chance, and I was keen to get back to the table to tell the others what he'd said.

'Fucking hell, what took you so long? I take it Neil was in one of his talkative moods then, was he?' Kevin asked as he lifted a pint off of the tray.

'I'm glad it was your round and not mine.' Finn laughed. 'There's nothing worse than having your ear chewed off by know-it-all Neil.'

'You know I wouldn't normally entertain his bullshit, but he had something interesting to say for once, so I had to give him air time,' I replied.

'Really? That makes a change. What did old Neily boy have to say for himself then?' Kevin asked.

I leaned forward, then gestured for the guys to scoot in closer to the table.

'He said there was a policewoman in here on Tuesday lunchtime asking questions about us.'

Kevin, Finn and Mark stared at me with horror and disbelief written all over their faces.

'What the fuck!' Kevin's blue eyes were as wide as saucers.

'What are we going to do now?' Mark looked like a deer caught in the headlights.

'We're not going to do anything. We're going to carry on as normal,' I replied. 'If they had anything concrete on us, they would have arrested us. The worst thing we can do now is panic.'

'If you don't settle down, you're going to give the game away,' Kevin said. 'Neil's watching us like a hawk. Let's get off the subject and talk about something else. We can discuss this later back at the chalet.'

'Neil's so fucking nosey. I wouldn't put it past him to have bugged our corner so he can listen in,' Finn said.

It would be our own fault if he had. We were creatures of habit. The four of us always sat at the same table every week.

'Well, it's going to look a bit obvious if we get up and move seats now, isn't it?' I said.

Kevin suggesting that our conversation was being monitored had pretty much finished Mark off. He was a nervous wreck, and the fact that he was shitting himself wouldn't have gone unnoticed by our overly curious publican. Neil had a nose for gossip; he could sniff it out from a mile away. If I didn't know better, I'd think he was part bloodhound.

'Kevin's right; we need to put this to bed for an hour and carry on like we normally would. Otherwise, Neil's going to smell a rat, and we don't want him running back to the cops, do we?'

'I've got one question for you, and then I promise I'll drop the subject. Did Neil say which police officer paid him a visit?' Finn asked.

'He didn't mention any names; he just said it was a woman and a nice looking one at that. He reckoned she looked more like a model than a copper,' I replied.

'It must have been Abbie Kingsly. She's the one that brought us all in for questioning. I have to say for once I'm inclined to agree with Neil. Shocking, I know, but there's a first time for everything. She's a proper sort. I'd love to have a go on her. She looks like she's got that much pent-up aggression, I reckon I'd be in for the ride of my life,' Finn laughed.

53

Lola

Paul walked up to the counter and greeted me with a bright smile. 'Hi, Lola,' he said.

'Hi,' I replied before glancing behind him. 'All on your own today?'

'Yep, Billy No Mates at your service,' he laughed without going into any details.

Every time Paul had been into the casino, he'd come in with his brother and two friends. But I didn't feel I could ask where they were if he wasn't volunteering the information.

'Can I change this into chips?' Paul asked, sliding a bundle of fifty-pound notes into the under-counter tray.

'No problem.'

I started going through the motions of counting out the money, but I already knew how much was there. Paul always changed one thousand pounds.

'Thanks. Wish me luck,' Paul said before he disappeared into the maze of tables.

On quiet days, I'd discreetly while away my shift on

my phone, keeping it under the level of the counter, out of sight of the cameras. As today was particularly dead, I was scrolling through Instagram when Cassandra suddenly appeared in front of the booth. I nearly jumped out of my skin.

'Sorry, Lola, I didn't mean to startle you,' she said. 'Zac wanted me to check whether any of these customers were here today.'

Cassandra handed me a Post-it note with the names Paul Best, Kevin Best, Finn McCaskill and Mark Gibson written on it. I felt my heart sink. Even though I didn't know what the significance was, I had a feeling in my gut that it wasn't going to be good news for them.

I pretended to be looking through the records to buy myself some time. I'm not sure why, but I briefly considered lying. I must have been subconsciously trying to protect them from whatever it was The Count had in store for them.

'Paul Best is here, but the other gentlemen aren't,' I replied, handing her back the note.

'Before Mr Best cashes out, please can you let Zac know. He wants to authorise the transaction,' Cassandra said, then she turned on her heel and walked back the way she'd come.

About three-quarters of an hour later, Paul came back to the cage. Not that I didn't enjoy seeing him, I was hoping on this occasion, he'd leave without coming back to the cashier's desk. Then I wouldn't have anything to notify Zac about.

'Going so soon?'

'Yeah, Lady Luck's not smiling down on me. The one-armed bandits have got it in for me today.'

Paul had only used around a hundred pounds worth of chips.

'I won't keep you a moment.'

'Is there a problem?'

Paul had tried to make his question sound light, but I couldn't help thinking he looked very concerned.

'No. I just need my boss to authorise the transaction.'

'You've never had to do that before.' Paul seemed as confused as I was by the sudden interest.

'I know. It won't take a moment,' I said before I called Zac's extension to let him know Paul was at the counter.

I felt like I'd just thrown him under the bus, but there was no way I could warn him without arousing suspicion.

'Good evening, sir, I'm Zac Peterson, the owner of this establishment,' The Count said a moment later, and his lined face stretched into a smile.

Although his introduction was warm, I knew something was up.

'Good evening,' Paul replied, smiling back at him.

'Would you mind stepping into my office for a moment, please?' Zac gestured the way with his outstretched arm.

'Bye, Lola,' Paul said as he followed Zac across the casino floor.

54

Paul

Zac Peterson was a huge bear of a man. I wasn't exactly short, five foot ten was a respectable height, but he was at least a head taller than me. When he'd arrived at my side and asked me to accompany him to his office, I wasn't in a position to refuse the request and followed him along the carpeted hallway until we reached a set of double doors that spanned the width of the corridor. His name was engraved on a brass plaque fixed at head height on the right. Zac stepped inside the spacious office, crossed the room and took a seat behind a large mahogany desk.

'Please sit down,' he said.

I did as he asked, settling back into the green leather. 'Nice place you've got here,' I replied.

Then I began looking around the room, hoping to appear casual and relaxed, which was no mean feat as two suited heavies had followed us inside and stationed themselves in front of the door, blocking my only means of escape.

'Would you like something to drink?' Zac asked.

'No thanks,' I replied, wishing he'd share his reason for detaining me sooner rather than later before my blood pressure went off the chart.

Zac got up from his desk and walked over to a drinks trolley in the corner of the room. He lifted the lid on a cut-glass decanter and poured a hefty measure of a dark spirit which I assumed by the colour was brandy into a crystal tumbler. Then he replaced the lid, picked up his glass and walked back to his desk. Once he was seated, he took a sip of his drink, savouring the flavour for a few moments before he swallowed it. Talk about eking out the build-up. He was determined to prolong my agony. I was sweating like a lump of cheese on a hot summer's day.

'I'm sure you're wondering why I asked you to join me,' Zac said, fixing me with the most intense set of irises I'd ever seen.

'It had crossed my mind,' I replied in a light-hearted tone to disguise the feeling of dread rising within me.

Zac's dark, beady eyes were shifty and impenetrable. He wasn't giving anything away. I was trying to come across laid-back, but I couldn't take much more of this before I lost my cool. He was a master at using the art of suspense to heighten the tension in the room. Zac surveyed me with the same interest a giant Huntsman spider would its prey. His eyes darted around as though he was waiting for the perfect opportunity to pounce and drag me inside his jaws.

'It's been brought to my attention that you're making a habit of changing a large sum of cash for chips, but you only play with a small number of them before cashing out. When a pattern emerges like that where a customer regularly exchanges far more money than they use, it's a cause for concern,' Zac said, lifting his tumbler to his lips.

I hadn't thought Lola was the type to go telling tales to the boss, but it served me right for falling for a pretty face. That was the oldest trick in the book. There were plenty of casinos in London; I should have mixed things up a bit instead of focusing on just one. But Mark and I had ulterior motives for wanting to go to Rolling the Dice as often as possible, so we'd let that cloud our judgement and made a schoolboy error. Now I didn't know how I was going to talk my way out of this. While I tried to decide what to do, I adopted the struck dumb approach, which allowed Zac time to continue spinning his web around me. He informed me that the casino had recently been asked to overhaul its systems to flag suspicious transactions such as this.

Zac rested his elbows on the desk in front of him and interlinked his fingers. I felt my Adam's apple start to bob up and down in my throat. I couldn't see Zac's heavies as I had my back to them, but I could feel the weight of their stare. The three pairs of eyes fixed on me acted as passive restraints. I quickly realised the game was up. I'd been rumbled.

'Our friends at the government asked the industry to tighten up procedures to put an end to this type of scam. So now, every chip you purchase is embedded with a tag to allow casinos to track their every movement. We know whether they've been played or not, and if somebody steals them, the ID can be added to a database to prevent them from being redeemed for cash. Who would have thought we'd go to so much trouble?'

Zac sat grinning at me for the longest time. I wasn't often lost for words, but my mouth was so dry I wouldn't have been able to speak even if I'd wanted to.

'As you can see, we have a bit of a problem. Laundering money is illegal, so I'm required to report my findings to the authorities, but you seem like a reasonable man. I'm sure we can come to some arrangement. If you want to avoid being arrested and sent down for the crime you're committing, I'll need a slice of the cash in order to turn a blind eye.'

My head felt like it was about to explode.

I had plenty of time to mull over what had happened with Zac Peterson on the drive back to Sheerness. I wished I'd listened to the others now and stayed away from the casino. Neil had put the wind up them when he'd announced that the police were sniffing around. They'd thought it was safer for all concerned if we stayed away from Rolling the Dice for the time being and kept a low profile. I hadn't agreed. It had become part of our regular routine to go there on Sundays, so I'd been keen to carry on and not change our plans.

But I hadn't realised at that stage that Zac was on to us. The guys would go mental, so I couldn't decide whether to own up and tell them what had happened or keep them in the dark. Common sense told me there was no point in trying to lie. The truth always came out in the end.

Kevin, Finn and Mark were watching the match, beers in hand, when I walked into the chalet.

'Oi oi, here comes the high roller,' Fin laughed when I opened the double-glazed door and stepped inside.

'How much did you fleece the casino out of today?' Kevin asked.

'Nothing. I was on a losing streak.'

I walked up to the counter, lifted a tumbler off of the draining board, then unscrewed the lid off of the half-empty bottle of Captain Morgan's and poured myself a large measure. After I knocked it back, I realised that three pairs of eyes were trained on me.

'What's up?' Mark asked.

'Don't ask, mate,' I replied before pouring myself another hefty drink.

'Blimey, it must be bad if you're hitting the hard stuff at this time of the day,' Finn pointed out.

'No mixer either. You must have had a shitty time,' Kevin laughed.

'It's not funny. I got hauled into the casino owner's office,' I blurted out, which subsequently wiped the smiles off of their faces.

'Why?' Mark asked, scooting to the edge of the sofa.

'Zac Peterson's been keeping an eye on us, and it hasn't got past him that we're changing a large amount of money but only playing a few games before we cash out. He wanted to talk to me about it.'

Mark jumped out of his chair and pointed his finger at me. 'I told you we should stay away from the casino for the time being.' He started pacing around the small room, muttering to himself. 'You're going to end up bringing all of us down with you if you're not careful.'

'Sit down and shut up. Panicking's not going to help the situation, and watching you pacing is doing my head in. You never listen, do you? If you had, you'd realised I'd said

Zac has been watching all of us, not just me. He knows your names too.'

One thousand pounds was a fortune to us, but I'd thought it would be chicken feed to a casino, so I'd never expected an amount like that to trigger any interest.

'Start at the beginning and tell us what happened,' Finn said.

'I'd gone up to the booth expecting to cash out as normal hoping it would look as though my luck was continuing. Instead of processing my winnings, Lola asked me to wait a moment and I instantly knew something was wrong. She looked really uncomfortable, so I asked her if there was a problem. She tried to make light of it, telling me she just needed her boss to authorise the transaction. She'd never done that before, so that was a red flag,' I explained.

'Jesus, I'm surprised you stayed to face the music. I think I'd have cut and run,' Kevin said.

'Believe me, I seriously considered legging it. But there's so much security, I wouldn't have got as far as the door before I'd been stopped in my tracks, so I had no choice but to hold my nerve.'

'Rather you than me,' Kevin replied.

'I'm going to go out on a limb and say this isn't the first time Zac's tried to blackmail one of his customers. He was so comfortable with the situation. I felt like a fly trapped in a spider's web when he hauled me into his office.'

'It's just as well you don't suffer from arachnophobia,' Finn laughed.

'I was on the verge of losing it, so I had to force myself to try and play it cool. Zac told me that every chip we purchase is embedded with a tag so that casinos can track their movements. They can tell whether the chip's been played or not.'

Despite my nerves, I'd managed to squirrel away little pieces of useful information he gave me.

'Oh shit! No wonder they were on to us,' Kevin replied. 'They must have changed things since the guy on the wing used to wash his drug money. He reckoned it was almost impossible for anyone to trace it. Or otherwise, he was just chatting shit and had never done it before. You get that a lot with the lags; they like to spin a yarn to try and make themselves look like they were big men on the outside to earn the respect of the other cellmates.'

'I think he was telling the truth, but he must have been going back a few years. Zac said the government had asked the casino to tighten up procedures to end the scam. He didn't seem to have a problem with us laundering money and said we could come to some arrangement. He told me he'd be happy to accommodate us as long as there was something in it for him. He'll turn a blind eye, but he wants a slice of the cash,' I said.

55

Lola

'**H**ow were the guys?' Millie asked when I got home. She'd had to swap shifts to cover another member of staff's annual leave, so she'd offered to cook dinner as she wasn't working. And we were moving out of the hostel tomorrow, so it gave her time to pack. The only downside was she wouldn't get to see Mark.

'Only Paul came in today,' I replied, getting the knives and forks out of the drawer as she dished up some of the pasta bake she'd made.

'That's odd,' Millie remarked. 'I was beginning to think they were joined at the hip. They always seem to travel in a pack.'

'I know what you mean,' I laughed. 'Paul had only been inside for about half an hour when Cassandra came up to the booth and said The Count wanted to know if any of the guys were on the floor. She had Paul, Kevin, Finn and Mark's names down on a list. Then she told me to call Zac when Paul came to cash out.'

'I wonder what that was about.' Millie tilted her face to one side.

'I've no idea. My shift was about to finish when Paul went off with Zac, so I didn't see him again.'

Millie and I were only renting it, but when the estate agent gave us the keys to the two-bedroom flat above the shops in Acton town centre, I felt like the luckiest girl in the world. I'd come a long way since I'd left Sheffield a couple of months ago.

'Thanks for everything,' I said as Elaine handed me the last box from the boot of her car.

'My pleasure. Keep in touch, and if you need anything, you know I'm just around the corner,' Elaine replied.

'Once we settle in, you'll have to come around for dinner,' I smiled.

Elaine had been a huge support to Millie and me, and we were keen to show our appreciation for everything she'd done to help us.

'I'd love that,' Elaine beamed. 'Take care of yourselves.'

The day I moved out of the refuge, I was a changed woman, with a job and a sense of freedom which made me feel empowered. I'd never forget what the staff had done for me. I'd be forever in their debt, having arrived with little more than the clothes on my back. My thoughts immediately turned to Mum. I wished she could see how well I was doing. When I'd left Sheffield, she'd promised to come down to London to spend some time with me, once I was settled. I had a horrible feeling that was never going to happen. Things had been strained between us since Troy had attacked her. And when she'd refused to press charges, it had only made matters worse. We'd always been so close, but these days our relationship was complicated. We didn't have nearly as much contact as I'd like.

'Here's to us,' Millie said, holding her glass of Prosecco towards mine.

'Cheers,' I replied, clinking glasses with her.

We'd left our old lives behind us and completed what we'd set out to do. This was our first night in our own place, which was a huge confidence boost, so we were celebrating in style with a takeaway pizza from the kebab shop and a bottle of fizz.

I'd had many sleepless nights and shed a lot of tears since Troy and I had become a couple. I'd been living under a cloud of confusion. Troy had used manipulative tactics to maintain control over me for the longest time. My reasons for staying had been complex. It was human nature to downplay uncomfortable truths.

I didn't think I'd ever be brave enough to end our relationship. But I had; he'd eventually driven me away. Now I felt like I'd just taken a huge step into a future that would hopefully be free of him. Our flat wasn't exactly the Ritz, but it was all we could afford for now, so it would have to do until we got on our feet.

'Here's to escaping from our controlling partners.' Millie and I clinked glasses again.

I'd definitely drink to that. I took a gulp of Prosecco, and as the bubbles danced on my tongue, my mind drifted back to my ex. In the early days, he used to get angry with me for not telling him my plans. But if I said I was going out with my friends, he'd go ballistic. As time went on, I stopped bothering to go out without him. It wasn't worth the hassle involved; I didn't miss listening to him ranting. Troy relished the role of my tormentor. He invalidated me in all ways possible.

'I didn't think I could top the feeling I got when the court imposed a restraining order on my ex, but moving into this flat has taken me to another level,' Millie smiled.

I knew what she meant. I turned to look at Millie, and my lips stretched into a smile. I was proud of my friend. Come to think of it, I was proud of myself; we'd both come a long way.

'I tell you something, my ex would be doing his nut if he saw me now. He always used to tell me I was bottom rung staff and wouldn't get anywhere without him. He'd beat me senseless, then shower me with presents and beg me to forgive him. Every time it happened, he'd promise he'd change, and I'd believe him, but it was all lies.' Millie's eyes misted over before she pulled herself out of the downward spiral.

Millie's relationship was a mirror image of mine. Seeing my friend's resolve wobble made me think about the way Troy used to reduce me to a crumbling wreck. He'd treated me so badly and like a fool, I'd always put him first. I'd wanted him to get better, so I'd done my best to support him. But he needed professional help. Nobody would be able to reach him if he didn't admit he had a problem. I wasn't sure he'd ever overcome his deep-seated issues. It would be a huge challenge, if not impossible.

Even in the most perfect of relationships, it was normal

for couples to argue. Nobody agreed with everything their partner said. But they settled their differences without violence. Whereas Troy used his fists to bring me around to his way of thinking, and then he'd tell me not to go bleating about it to anyone. He had me convinced that no one would believe me.

'More Prosecco?' Millie asked, already refilling my glass.

I took a bite out of my pizza and lazily chewed it as I glanced out of the window at the street below, bustling with people going about their business. Dusk was just beginning to fall. I loved this part of the day when the sun cast long shadows before it disappeared for the night.

'Don't let memories of the bad times bring you down, Mills,' I said.

'I won't. There's nothing like a bit of people watching to lift my spirits. Look at that lady over there. I've never seen anyone walk a cat on a lead before,' Millie laughed, glancing sideways at me.

'It's a first for me too,' I smiled.

Acton town centre had some colourful residents if the snapshot of the high street we'd just seen was anything to go by. It was going to be very entertaining living here.

56

Abbie

Now that Neil had kindly given me the full names of Finn's friends and told me that they lived in Sheerness, I was in a better position to start probing into their personal lives. Certain cautions, fines, offences and spent convictions wouldn't appear. But if they'd done anything bad, it would stick for life.

I looked up from my desk when Ed walked into my office. 'You wanted to see me.'

Ed couldn't have been more underwhelmed by the thought of being in my company if he'd tried. The feeling was mutual.

'I need you to run a background check on these people: Mark Gibson, Paul Best and Kevin Best.'

'Who are they?' Ed asked, looking up from his notebook. He glared at me, his frown deepening.

'Just do it please,' I replied, holding my ground. I was irritated by the fact that he always felt the need to question everything I asked him to do.

Ed's eyes darkened in silent rage. 'What do you want me to look for?'

I rolled my eyes and tutted. 'You know, the usual. Previous convictions, whether they're known to the police or not, that kind of thing and while you're at it, get copies of their bank statements for the last twelve months as well.' My voice was riddled with undertones of frustration.

'That's a bit over the top, isn't it?'

I didn't bother to give him an answer; he didn't deserve one. Pushing my buttons seemed to be the highlight of his day, and, like a child having a tantrum, the more reaction I gave him, the more enjoyment he got out of it.

It is the reality of police work that investigators were rarely assigned a single case. I would have liked nothing more than to concentrate my efforts on finding the gang responsible for the airport heist. But Ed and I had been given the task of questioning a young guy who'd stabbed a drug dealer he was trying to rob. He was currently being detained in a cell so dealing with him had to take priority for the moment.

'Get the background checks started, and then come and join me in the interview room,' I said as I walked out of my office.

This wasn't the first time Wayne Perry had been in trouble with the law. He'd been arrested multiple times but had only ever been cautioned before. This time his fingerprints were all over the weapon used in the attack, so he was looking to be put away for a long stretch.

The custody sergeant unlocked the cell, and the man, who was a known drug user, stared at me with hollow eyes.

'I need to ask you some questions. Come with me, please,' I said.

Wayne stood up from the bench and began walking towards me. As I led the way along the corridor towards the interview room, the duty solicitor joined the procession. I couldn't help noticing that Wayne looked a mess; he had sores all over his lips, and his clothes were hanging off his emaciated frame.

I opened the door and stepped inside the small, sparsely furnished room. The chairs and table were bolted to the floor to stop less than contented prisoners picking them up and launching them at myself and my colleague when the heat got too hot for them to handle.

'Please take a seat,' I said, gesturing to the stick chair, which would no doubt provide little comfort to his underweight frame. The legal aid solicitor sat down next to him. 'We'll get started in just a moment. I'm going to be recording the interview. This is an opportunity for you to tell your side of the story.'

Wayne plonked himself down and placed his clenched fists on the table. His fingers and the skin on his hands and arms were covered in abscesses. He was so jittery; the vibrations that were coming off of his body in waves were making the tabletop judder.

When Ed appeared, I walked over to the recorder that was tucked into a recess in the wall, turned on the tape and began speaking, stating the names of all those present in the room.

'For the purposes of the tape, can I ask you to introduce yourself using your full name and your date of birth?'

'My name's Wayne Perry, and I was born sixth of the ninth, ninety-three,' he replied.

'Thank you. You were arrested at the scene on suspicion of the attempted murder of Roman Brady. Would you like to explain to me what happened?'

'I had nothing to do with it.'

'Are you denying that you were in Mr Brady's company?'

Wayne glanced at the duty solicitor before he turned his attention back towards me.

'No comment,' he replied. His speech was slurred.

'Why were you in Monk Street, Woolwich, at the time of the assault?'

Wayne shrugged.

Roman Brady was a small-time dealer and lived in one of the high-rise flats close to where he was attacked. The area was a hive of crime, populated by numerous dodgy characters. Stabbings were a regular occurrence in that neck of the woods.

'Let me put this to you. I think you'd arranged to meet Mr Brady with the intention to buy drugs from him.'

'I'd advise you not to answer that,' Wayne's brief piped up.

I had little time for men like him. They were a different breed to the rest of us and made a small fortune defending the dregs of society. I'd never understand how lawyers like him could stand up in court and attempt to get a person off of a crime they knew they'd committed.

'Nah, that's not what happened. It was a coincidence I was in the area, that's all.'

Much to my delight, Wayne had gone against his solicitor's advice and responded to my question. I was aware my lips had stretched into a smile, and I was displaying a hint of amusement that didn't seem appropriate under the circumstances, so I lost the grin before I started to speak.

'There was nothing coincidental about it. A knife was also recovered at the scene.' I showed Wayne a picture of the weapon. 'Can you tell me why your DNA is all over it?'

Wayne's eyes started darting around the room, and his tremors notched up a gear. 'No comment.'

'There's no point in trying to deny your involvement. We both know you were at the scene, and your prints are all over the knife that almost ended Mr Brady's life. Look at this from where I'm sitting. What am I supposed to think?'

'I suppose it looks a bit suspicious, but I swear to you I wasn't involved,' Wayne said.

'I'm afraid I don't believe you. You see, I think you had a motive. Why did you try to kill Roman Brady?'

'No comment.'

Wayne could deny it all he liked, but he couldn't control his body's responses. His eyes had turned glassy, and his sweaty hair was stuck to his head in clumps. I decided to put an end to the questioning for now as he looked ready to collapse.

'Right, let's call it a day for the moment,' I said, concluding the interview for the time being.

Wayne got up from the table and made a break for the doorway on unsteady legs with his brief in hot pursuit. Ed followed suit, but he stopped walking before he reached the door. When he turned to look at me, his expression was stern.

'Do I take it that from the half-hearted effort you've just put in, you're not going to make any serious attempt to investigate the assault on Roman Brady?'

I shot Ed a venomous look. It didn't take much for him to push my buttons.

'Whatever gave you that idea?' I asked through gritted teeth.

'You seem completely disinterested in the case,' Ed replied.

'Well, I'm not,' I snapped.

I was getting a bit pissed off with Ed's short-sightedness. He thought he knew what I was thinking and kept second-guessing what I was going to do next. A lot of planning went into interviewing a suspect, so I needed time to prepare. If I was going to take somebody's liberty away from them, I had to make sure I'd dotted the I's and crossed the T's.

'You could have fooled me. Why didn't you grill Wayne further?' Ed asked with his hands on his hips in a show of defiance. 'You'd barely started questioning him before you sent him off for a break.'

'You saw the state of him. What was I supposed to do?'

'Break him down while he was at his most vulnerable.'

I didn't appreciate Ed's sarcastic tone.

'It might have escaped you, but suspects have certain rights, which include entitlements to breaks and rest periods. Wayne needs a bit of time to sort himself out. And while he's doing that, I'm going to concentrate my efforts on the other case I'm trying to solve. If that's all right with you.'

Ed took a step back as though my words had scalded him. Then he hot-footed it out of my office without saying another word to me. I was glad to see the back of the man and quickly turned my attention to the other matter in hand, closing the net on the armed robbers who had so far evaded arrest.

I'd been resisting doing an appeal, offering a reward for information about the airport heist. I usually reserved that as a last resort when all other leads were exhausted. The aim was to tempt a witness who had never come forward to break their silence. People had their reasons for keeping schtum, sometimes they were scared of the consequences, or other times they simply didn't want to get involved. There was no denying a cash incentive helped to move an investigation forward. Money played a key role in loosening people's tongues. But more often than not, it ended up hampering the inquiry with an information overload. That was a major drawback. But the clock was ticking, so it was a risk I was prepared to take to try and flush out the thieves.

57

Lola

Paul was becoming a regular at the casino, not that I was complaining. He had a nice way about him and was easy enough on the eye. I wasn't looking for a boyfriend, but that didn't mean I couldn't window-shop from afar.

'Being a croupier's a single girl's paradise,' Millie said. 'I don't know how many times I've been chatted up and asked out by the customers. My dickhead ex has got a lot to answer for. It's a bloody shame he's put me off men for life!'

'You and me both,' I agreed. 'My bullshit detector's on high alert.'

'Oh my God, Lola, you crack me up sometimes.' Millie roared with laughter.

'It's good that we can joke about it, but in all seriousness, I'm not sure I'll ever feel comfortable enough to trust a member of the opposite sex again.'

Nobody had any idea how much damage Troy's abuse had inflicted on my mental health. At the moment, the idea of being in a serious relationship made my blood run cold. I hoped it wouldn't always be that way, but my barriers were firmly in place for now.

The smile slid from Millie's face. 'I hope that's not the case. You deserve to be happy.'

'I'm definitely getting there.'

'Me too; slowly but surely,' Millie agreed.

'You can't rush these things. All we can do is take it one day at a time.'

Whether we liked it or not, we were part of an exclusive club. We were lucky to have survived domestic abuse. That couldn't be said for all of the victims.

Millie and I looked up from our plates and stared at the TV screen when we heard the police making an appeal for witnesses regarding the heist at London City Airport. They were offering a ten thousand pound reward to anyone who provided information that led to the conviction of the gang responsible.

'Can you just imagine getting your hands on ten grand right now?'

Millie gripped on to her knife and fork as she stared into space. No doubt deciding how she'd spend such a windfall.

'It would be amazing.'

My bank balance was hovering just above zero. I'd used all my available funds scraping together the deposit for the flat; I'd be holding my breath until payday at the end of the month.

'Do you think this is a wind-up?' Millie asked, interrupting my train of thought.

'What do you mean?'

'That woman doesn't look like a detective. There's no way she could run after anyone in those heels,' Millie laughed.

I was inclined to agree. The detective was wearing make-up, and her blonde hair was sitting in loose waves on her shoulders. She was incredibly feminine and well turned out. When I pictured a policewoman, a short-haired, gruff-voiced geezer bird sprang to mind.

58

Abbie

'Have those background checks come back yet?' I asked when Ed slithered into my office.

'I'm not sure. What's the hurry? I would have thought you'd got enough on your plate trying to convict Wayne Perry of attempted murder without worrying about anything else. While you're distracted by trying to solve the mystery of the missing millions, let's hope the custody clock doesn't run out. Tick tock; tick tock.'

It was a horrible feeling when time ran out on an investigation, but the jury was out on whether Wayne should be given a medal or a prison sentence. It depended on how you looked at things. In some ways, he'd done the police a favour by taking a drug dealer off the street, albeit temporarily. But I didn't bother to share my thoughts with Ed. He'd only disagree with me just for the sake of having a different opinion.

'I thought we'd been over this. I'm working on both cases simultaneously.'

I didn't expect Ed to understand the concept of that. It wasn't a myth; it was a fact that women were better at multitasking than men.

'As you've just pointed out, I've got a lot to deal with at the moment, and time is of the essence, so have you got the paperwork or not?'

Ed seemed startled by the way I'd just spoken to him. My words might have been a little curt, but I wasn't about to apologise. Why should I? A man in my position wouldn't expect to have to defend their tone. Ed shot me a look of contempt before he handed over the file containing the information. Typical; he'd had it all along, but instead of just giving it to me, he'd made me work really hard to extract it from him.

'Thanks. Can you close the door on your way out?'

I wanted Ed to know in no uncertain terms that his presence was no longer required as I buried myself in the case file. I'd gone through Finn's phone records with a fine-toothed comb and identified who the numbers belonged to and how they related to him. I wouldn't normally involve myself in such a tedious job, but I wasn't sure I could trust Ed to do the task correctly.

I was convinced Finn was our inside source, even though I couldn't prove it at this stage. He was a clean skin, an individual with no criminal record who wouldn't normally have attracted the attention of the police. But there was something about him that I just couldn't shake. The trail had gone cold, but I wasn't going to give up. There was too much money at stake. The cogs of my brain kept turning, going over the same details trying to work out the connection between him and the other gang members. I needed a break.

Otherwise, it was unlikely the men responsible would ever be brought to justice.

As I scanned over the paperwork, something caught my eye. Finn and his friends had recently started visiting Rolling the Dice. This could be the break I'd been waiting for. I'd been hoping the robbers would be tempted to start spending the money, and what better way to make it look legitimate than to try laundering some of the cash from the heist through a casino. There were plenty to choose from in London. What a stroke of good fortune that Zac Peterson happened to be an acquaintance of mine. I hadn't paid him a visit for a while now. It was about time I did. I didn't want to get ahead of myself, but this looked like a very promising lead indeed. I arranged to see Zac on Sunday so that I could talk to him in private. I didn't want Ed breathing down my neck while I followed up on this line of inquiry.

I'd arrived early for my meeting with Zac, and when I'd walked into the foyer, my eyes were drawn to four men in their mid-twenties queuing up to exchange money for chips. I quickly realised the tall, red-haired man was no other than Finn McCaskill. Fancy seeing him here. He hadn't noticed me, but the sight of him made my pulse speed up, and I only just managed to stop myself from walking over to him. I needed to stay in the shadows and observe for the time being.

'How lovely to see you, Abbie. It's always a pleasure. I must say you're looking exceptionally beautiful today.'

Zac planted a kiss on both of my cheeks in an overfamiliar manner that didn't sit easily with me before leading the way to his office. As he took a seat behind his desk, Zachary Peterson flashed me a smile that wouldn't have looked out of place on a paedophile. He made my skin crawl, but he seemed oblivious to the fact.

'So have there been any big spenders through the doors recently that I need to know about?' I asked when I took a seat opposite Zac.

'No, nothing to report. People are being a lot more cautious since the crackdown on regulations. It hasn't been good for business,' Zac laughed and exposed his stained teeth.

My eyes were drawn towards them. I'd often wondered why a man with all his money and a glamorous young wife had never bothered to have them fixed. He must have a massive phobia of dentists, I concluded.

'It's not doing my arrest rate any good either,' I replied.

Zac was a handy contact to have. He'd given me plenty of tip-offs over the years when some shady individuals were using the casino to launder their ill-gotten gains, which had subsequently led to the arrest of criminals previously unknown to the Met.

'So you haven't had any new customers who'd be of interest to me?'

I narrowed my eyes and waited for him to respond.

Zac shook his head. 'No, like I said, the changes in regulations have put a stop to any serious money laundering.'

That wasn't the answer I was looking for; it didn't make sense that Zac hadn't alerted me to Finn and his friends. Maybe I was mistaken, and they were just enjoying an innocent flutter. But it seemed like too much of a coincidence. Something didn't add up. I'd been hoping to leave with some evidence, but I'd endured a meeting with Zac for nothing and was about to walk away empty-handed. It was time to wrap this up.

'Can you do me a favour? Let me know straight away if any high rollers pay you a visit.'

The thieves couldn't steal ten million and expect the authorities to turn a blind eye when they started to wash it.

'That goes without saying,' Zac replied. 'I tell you what; I'll go one step further and ask around for you.'

Zac had lots of contacts, so I was sure he'd be able to find out if large sums of cash suddenly started filtering through his competitors' doors.

'I'd appreciate that,' I replied, making my way towards the door so that he didn't have another opportunity to get up close and personal with me.

'My pleasure,' Zac called as I slipped out of the doorway.

59

Lola

I'd just checked the time on my watch; it was coming up to eleven o'clock. The morning was dragging so far. I'd started my shift about three hours ago, but nothing much had been going on. It was the same most mornings and Sundays were no exception. The casino was open twenty-four hours a day, but it didn't really spring to life until the early evening.

I'd been sitting behind the desk, trying to make myself look busy, when all of a sudden, there was a flurry of activity. Paul and his friends walked through the door, and my spirits lifted. While I was serving them, I noticed an attractive woman with shoulder-length blonde hair come into the building. She looked familiar, but I wasn't sure where I knew her from. Then a thought popped into my head. I had a feeling she was the police officer I'd seen on the TV last night making an appeal for witnesses regarding the heist at London City Airport. Millie had noted at the time that she didn't look like a detective. She was absolutely stunning and had the most striking pair of blue eyes I'd ever seen. As she stood in the foyer, I stole another glance and decided it was definitely her. I couldn't help wondering what she was doing here. While I was mulling over the possibilities, Zac came into view. He greeted her like an old friend before the two of them disappeared down the corridor.

'I'm glad you came in today. I wasn't sure if you'd be back after last week. I would have warned you if I'd realised Zac was watching you and your friends, but I had no idea until his wife asked me to let him know before you cashed out,' I said when it was Paul's turn to be served.

'I was a bit surprised to be hauled into the big boss's office. I felt like I was back at school,' Paul laughed.

'We've been told to keep an eye out for people that change large amounts of money into chips and then don't use them on the floor before changing them back again. Be careful how much you try to use at any one time. The casino's put systems in place to catch people out,' I warned.

'Thanks for the tip-off,' Paul replied before taking his chips out of the tray. 'I owe you one. You'll have to let me buy you lunch sometime.'

'I'd like that,' I replied; seeing his blue eyes shining made my heart skip a beat.

The words tumbled out of my mouth before I had time to stop them in their tracks. My head had been saying no, but that wasn't what came out of my mouth. I'd surprised myself when I'd agreed.

Paul's face lit up, and a smile spread across his handsome face. 'What time do you finish?'

'Not until eight, but I get an hour off at two,' I smiled. What the hell had got into me?

'Great. I'll be back here at two,' Paul added with a hint of a smile.

He locked eyes with me; his gaze was loaded, and my pulse speeded up in response. A feeling spread between us, drawing me towards him as if it was a strong magnetic force.

As I watched Paul disappear into the sea of machines, my hands started sweating. I couldn't help feeling apprehensive. What had I just agreed to? If I let down my barriers, I'd make myself vulnerable. When Paul first suggested taking me out for lunch, excitement chased the dark cloud away which had been hovering over me since I'd left Sheffield. But now, my nerves were getting the better of me. I'd have to pull myself together before I talked myself out of it.

60

Paul

I was just deciding which number to place my bet on when I felt a tap on my shoulder. As I clocked Zac looming over me, I had to stop myself from letting out a groan.

'Can I have a word, please?' Zac asked.

I managed to make eye contact with Kevin before following Zac as he headed off in the direction of his office.

'I thought you'd like to know I did you a favour earlier,' Zac said, settling back in his chair.

'That was nice of you,' I replied, knowing there was bound to be a catch. Everything came at a price.

'An acquaintance of mine from the police was here earlier asking questions. She was very keen to know if there'd been any big spenders through my doors recently. Obviously, I lied and told her I had nothing to report. She asked me to let her know straight away if that changed,' Zac grinned. 'There's a lot more at stake for me now that the police are showing an interest, so I'm going to have to increase my cut to make the risk worthwhile. I'm sure I don't have to remind you, money laundering is a serious offence.'

'How much are we talking?' I asked. There was no point in beating around the bush.

'Twenty-five per cent.'

That was an eyewatering amount by anyone's standards and I felt my mouth drop open, but I wasn't in a position to renegotiate the terms of our deal. So instead I reached towards the desk and shook Zac by the hand before I hot-footed it out of his lair.

'Where do you fancy going?' I asked when Lola let herself out of the cashier's cage.

The conversation I'd had with Zac earlier was still in the forefront of my mind, but now wasn't the right time to dwell on it. 'Somewhere local. I have to be back by three,' Lola replied, looking up at me with her beautiful green eyes.

'How about the pub opposite?'

'Sounds great.'

I ordered two BLTs, a pint of Stella for myself and a coke for Lola, then I walked over to where she was sitting with her back against the wall at the far side of the pub.

'So what do you do for a living then?' Lola asked when I took a seat opposite her.

'I'm a labourer on a building site.' I felt my lips stretch into a smile. 'You seem surprised by that. What did you think I was going to say?'

'I don't know?' Lola replied.

'Go on; honestly, I won't be offended, just tell me what you were thinking.'

Lola clamped her full lips shut.

'I bet you thought it was something far better paid,' I laughed.

Lola's cheeks flushed. 'You seem too well off to be a labourer. I would have thought you owned the firm not worked for it.'

She wasn't stupid, far from it. She was as bright as a button and a straight talker too. I could tell she was already suspicious about where the money was coming from, and I didn't want her to get the wrong impression of me. I was desperate to get to know her better. Lola was a great girl, and after what she told me today, I already felt like she had my back. I could sense she'd been hurt in the past, but I wanted to be more than friends, so I was prepared to put in some hard graft. If I confided in her and gained her trust, maybe she would start to open up to me.

'I'm sure you've been wondering where I get all the cash from,' I blurted out.

The others would kill me if they knew what I was about to do, but there was a method to my madness.

'It's none of my business,' Lola replied, throwing me a sideways glance.

That was the best answer she could have given, which spurred me on to say some more.

'I don't want you to think I'm a lowlife drug dealer or anything like that. Those people are the scum of the earth in my eyes. They wreck the lives of everybody they come into contact with. Be honest with me, is that where you thought I was getting the money from?'

'No, I thought you'd robbed a bank,' Lola laughed.

She'd hit the nail on the head, so the least I could do was tell her the truth.

'And there was I thinking I was so mysterious. How did you work that out?' I shook my head, and a smile spread across my face.

'You're not serious.' Lola's mouth dropped open, and her big green eyes grew wide.

'You've got an honest face, so I think I can trust you. If I tell you something in confidence, can you promise to keep it to yourself?'

I hoped I was right about Lola. Only time would tell if my gamble was going to pay off.

'Of course, I can keep a secret,' Lola replied.

That was good to know. 'I was part of the gang that pulled off the heist at London City Airport.'

'Oh my God.'

Lola looked stunned by what I'd just told her.

'That's why I've been coming to the casino. I've been trying to launder the money so that I can start to use it.'

'Did you see the appeal on TV last night?' Lola asked.

'Yeah. The case must be getting cold if the police are looking for witnesses to come forward,' I said.

'This might be a coincidence, but when I was serving you guys this morning, I saw the detective from the appeal come into the foyer and then a few minutes later, she disappeared down the corridor with Zac Peterson, the owner. From the way he greeted her, he looked like he knew her well,' Lola said.

That wasn't what I wanted to hear, and although her words rang alarm bells, I was glad Lola had given me another tip-off. Zac never mentioned the officer who'd been asking him questions was the one investigating the heist.

'Thanks for telling me. You're proving to be worth your weight in gold. I owe you another lunch. Same time next week?' I laughed.

Lola checked the time on her watch. 'I'm sorry about this, but I'm going to have to go back to work,' she said without replying to my question.

'Wait, are you giving me the brush off?'

'No, it's just my lunch break's over...'

The last thing I wanted to do was make her feel uncomfortable, but I could see my comment had rattled her, so I let the matter drop.

'Don't look so worried. I believe you,' I smiled before I got up from the table.

There had been a definite shift in the atmosphere between us, and things were a bit tense when we walked back to the casino. I could see Kevin, Mark and Finn waiting for me in the lobby, so I decided to say goodbye at the door. I didn't want to run the risk of them taking the piss out of me in front of Lola in case it made matters worse.

'I'm going to head off with the guys now. See you next Sunday,' I said.

'No worries. Thanks for lunch,' Lola replied, flashing me a bright smile.

'Why did you get hauled off to Peterson's office?' Kevin asked as he drove us back to Sheerness.

'He wanted to renegotiate the terms of our deal. He said an acquaintance of his from the police had been asking questions about big spenders. He covered for us, but now he wants a bigger cut to reflect the risk he's taking,' I replied.

'That doesn't sound good. How much does he want?' Mark asked.

'Twenty-five per cent,' I said.

'What the fuck?' Finn made eye contact with me in the mirror.

'Then while we were having lunch, Lola told me something very interesting,' I said.

'Don't keep us in suspense,' Finn replied.

'You know the blonde detective who made the TV appeal yesterday,' I began.

'Yeah, what about her?' Kevin asked, turning to briefly look at me before his eyes returned to the road.

'She's called Abbie Kingsly,' Finn piped up from the back, reminding me of the name I'd rather forget.

'She came into the casino this morning when we were queueing up to get some chips.'

'She did what?' Mark questioned, leaning forward in his seat.

'Lola said she spotted Abbie in the foyer when she was serving us.'

'Why would she need to visit the casino?' Mark narrowed his eyes.

'Why do you think?' I turned to look at my friends in the back of the car. 'She was the acquaintance Zac was talking about.'

'I've got a bad feeling about this. What if Abbie works out what we've been up to?' Beads of sweat were now apparent on Mark's upper lip.

'If the police had anything concrete, they wouldn't be making an appeal for witnesses, would they?' Kevin said.

His words hung in the air between us. My younger

brother could be a bit of a dreamer when the mood took him, but he also talked a lot of sense.

'And Zac won't jeopardise losing his slice of the cash by squealing to Abbie about our little arrangement. The big man covered for us earlier when she questioned him, didn't he?' I paused to let my words sink in. 'Just think about this logically for a minute, if Zac keeps schtum, how are the cops going to find out?'

61

Lola

I'd been shocked by Paul's confession. I couldn't fake my body's response. When he'd told me about the heist, it had hit me like a bolt out of the blue. I'd tried to push the conversation to the back of my mind and play it down. Money stolen during an armed robbery would be insured. It wasn't as though Paul and his friends had mugged an old lady.

I was sitting behind the counter wishing a customer would appear to break up the monotony of the afternoon, as his words swam around in my head. I wasn't sure how I felt about his admission. I would never have thought he'd be involved in anything dishonest. He didn't seem the type. But he must have had his reasons. Not everything in life was black and white. There were always grey areas in between. I would love to know what had driven him down that path, but I wasn't about to ask him. I wouldn't be brave enough to broach the subject.

The casino was dead, and with nothing else to do apart

from dwell on the matter, my thoughts drifted back to Paul. In hindsight, part of me wished I'd rejected his offer to buy me lunch, but I hadn't realised he was going to use the opportunity to unburden himself.

Paul could tell I was shocked when he told me he was trying to launder the money through the casino. My facial expressions always gave the game away without me saying a word. Zac had to be on to Paul and his friends. Why else would Cassandra have asked me about them? I'd had a gut feeling at the time something was wrong. And now the police had visited Zac the morning after the appeal for information about the heist. It couldn't be a coincidence. There had to be a connection.

My mind wandered, bouncing different ideas back and forth, wondering what this all meant for Paul. None of the outcomes seemed good. Then something horrific popped into my head. Would I be considered an accessory if the police caught up with him? I'd handled the stolen money and processed the transfer into his bank account, but I hadn't known what I was doing at the time.

I suddenly felt my blood pressure spike when the police officer I'd seen Zac with earlier approached the booth. She'd appeared out of nowhere which startled me, and my breath caught in my chest. My eyes flicked to DI Kingsly's ID as she flashed it at me. I swallowed hard in response. Get a grip, Lola, I told myself. The worst thing I could do was panic. I'd have to try and stay tight-lipped and act young and dumb. That was the only thing I could do.

62

Abbie

'Hi, I'm DI Kingsly,' I said, flashing the green-eyed blonde in the cashier's booth my police lanyard. 'What's your name?'

'Lola Marshall.'

I jotted that down in my notebook.

'I'd like to ask you some questions about a group of customers that visited the casino earlier.'

The young woman looked nervous as she sat behind the desk, but I wasn't too surprised by her reaction. Law-abiding citizens often panicked when questioned by the police, even though they hadn't done anything wrong. People sometimes subconsciously worried that they were going to trip themselves up and put themselves in the frame of a crime they hadn't committed.

'The customers I'm interested in are Finn McCaskill, Paul Best, Kevin Best, and Mark Gibson.'

'What would you like to know?'

'Can you give me the details of their recent transactions?'

'No problem. I'll look up their accounts and get the details for you. One moment, please,' Lola replied.

She handed me a sheet of paper with the men's names, the amount of cash they changed for chips and the value they cashed out with today.

'So they only changed one hundred pounds each?' I questioned.

'Yes,' Lola replied.

My eyes scanned the paper. Finn and his friends had all made a loss before they'd called it a day. If they were the gang members we were looking for, they were going to be old and grey before they laundered the money at this rate.

'Was today a typical day for them, or would they usually play with more than a hundred pounds?'

'I'll just check,' Lola said and then she started tapping away on her keyboard.

I'd been expecting to come here for answers, but instead, my visit was raising more questions.

'I've looked back at the transactions, and they seem to change the same amount every time, but the amount they've won or lost has varied ever so slightly,' Lola said.

'So they're not exactly big spenders then.'

'Hardly,' Lola laughed.

'How long have they been coming to the casino?'

Lola tore her eyes away from mine and trained them back on her screen.

'They've been registered here for a couple of years,' Lola said.

'A couple of years?'

Lola nodded.

That was longer than I'd expected.

'And they play here regularly?'

'Yes.'

Maybe I was barking up the wrong tree after all.

'What are their registered addresses?'

Lola wrote them down on a piece of A4 paper and put it into the under-counter tray for me to retrieve.

'Thanks for your help,' I said. 'Can you please drop me an email every time those gentlemen come in?'

'Of course,' Lola replied.

I'd given up enough of my free time for one day. I wasn't even on duty, but I couldn't exactly slip off to a casino for a private meeting while I was on the clock. If I'd tried to do that, Ed would definitely tag along. Visiting Zac out of hours had been the only option.

Our meeting was playing on my mind. What he'd said made perfect sense. The changes in regulations had been put in place to stop money laundering, so it seemed only right that the measures he was taking were working. I'd been expecting him to tell me that Finn and his crew had started flooding the casino with cash in the last couple of months, but by all accounts, that hadn't been the case. Lola had backed that up when she'd told me that the men only bet a modest amount and had been members for a couple of years.

The facts were staring me in the face. It looked as though nothing untoward was going on here, so why did I still have a nagging doubt in the pit of my stomach? Unless maybe Zac was double-crossing me. I didn't have any proof to back that up, but I couldn't help feeling suspicious. Copper's intuition was a powerful thing.

63

Lola

When the detective fixed me with her intense blue eyes and started questioning me about Paul and his friends, my head felt like it was about to explode. I'd done my best to hide the panic that was flowing through my veins, but not giving away my feelings wasn't my forte. I always did a bad job of concealing my emotions. Half the time, I didn't realise I was doing it. It was something I constantly had to work at. Training my face to stop revealing what my brain was thinking was a difficult thing to master, but I was determined to keep trying. I didn't want people to read me like an open book.

Once I was sure Abbie had left the casino, I pulled up Paul's account and entered his mobile number into my phone. I was involved now whether I wanted to be or not, so I'd call him later on and tell him what had happened.

*

'Is that Paul?' I asked the male voice on the other end of the line.

'Who wants to know?' he replied.

'It's Lola.'

'This is a nice surprise. I'm tempted to ask how you got my number, but I don't really care. I'm so glad you phoned.'

Paul sounded happy to hear from me, but I wasn't sure he was going to like what I was about to tell him.

'I just wanted to warn you that DI Kingsly questioned me this afternoon about you, Kevin, Finn and Mark.'

'What did she ask you?' Paul's good mood seemed to be taking a back seat for now.

'She wanted to know details of your recent transactions, how long you'd been registered at the casino and your addresses.'

'Oh, bollocks,' Paul said.

'Don't worry; I didn't tell her the truth. Well, I did on some of it, but not all of it.'

'Come again?'

'I didn't lie about your addresses or the fact that you've been registered at the casino for a couple of years. But I might have accidentally, on purpose, left a zero off the amount that you guys change into chips. I told her you cashed one hundred pounds, not one thousand.'

I knew I couldn't tell her the truth without raising her suspicions, so I'd hidden the amount they'd been gambling. I was surprised how easily the words flowed off my tongue, considering I'd been thinking on my feet. I'd wrestled with my conscience, but not for nearly as long as I'd expected.

'Thanks, Lola. That was very decent of you, but I don't want you getting into trouble on our account.'

'You don't need to thank me. The DI's got no reason to suspect I wasn't telling the truth. There's one more thing; she's asked me to email her every time you come in.'

I let out a loud sigh. 'Is there any way around that?'

'I'm not sure. Even if I don't pull up your account to sign you in, you'd still have to get past the camera installed with facial recognition software. It's time and date stamped, so if the police ask to look back at it, there'd be a record of your entry. I wouldn't worry too much; after the figures I gave her, I don't think she'll be poking into your accounts any time soon. She definitely seemed shocked that you were betting such a small amount and that you'd been registered at the casino for years.'

'Hopefully, you've thrown her off our trail. You're an absolute diamond, Lola. I won't forget what you've done for us,' Paul said before we ended the call.

His words brought a smile to my face. I wasn't sure why I'd lied to the police to protect somebody I barely knew. In hindsight, I'd probably done a stupid thing, but at the time, I hadn't given it a second thought. I'd instinctively tried to divert the attention away from Paul. If I was honest with myself, I knew that was because I was developing feelings for him.

64

Paul

Lola's call rang alarm bells. We'd hoped the trail had gone cold enough for us to start spending the money, but DI Kingsly was watching us, and if we weren't careful, it was only a matter of time before she worked out the connection between us and the missing millions.

'Jesus Christ! What are we going to do?' Mark asked with a look of fear on his face after I broke the bad news.

'We need to step up the rate we're cleaning the money, or we'll never be able to use it.'

'Are you mad? That's the last thing we should be doing if the police are sniffing around.' Mark shook his head.

'We've got to act quickly before the net closes in on us,' I replied.

It was all very well having two and a half million pounds in cash each, but if it stayed in that form, it had its limitations. Gone were the days when you could rock up to buy a villa in Spain with a suitcase full of notes. If we could just filter a percentage of it into our bank accounts, we'd be able to use it as collateral.

'The police must suspect that Finn had something to do with the robbery. Otherwise, they wouldn't be digging around in his private life,' Mark blurted out.

Finn's blue eyes darted across to Mark. 'What makes you so sure that the pigs aren't doing exactly the same to all the other members of staff working that day?'

Mark was too busy chewing on his bottom lip to reply.

'That's a good point,' I said, filling the silence. They're bound to suspect the heist was an inside job, so it makes perfect sense that the Old Bill would start looking into what the airline's employees got up to when they weren't at work. Lola reckoned the detective was underwhelmed by our gambling habits, so hopefully, that'll buy us some time. We can't afford to sit tight; we've only got a limited opportunity here. Are you on board with my idea or not?'

'Count me in,' Kevin said, glancing over at me.

There were only eighteen months between us, and despite being highly competitive, my younger brother and I shared a close bond. I could always rely on him.

'I think it's too risky,' Mark said, worry lines etched on his forehead.

'We don't really have another option,' Finn said.

We all needed to be on the same page if we were going to succeed. Mark's reluctance made me realise no matter how solid a chain you thought you possessed, you were only as strong as your weakest link. If he buckled, he could take us all down with him.

'If we don't continue going to the casino, Zac will report us. He made me agree to pay him twenty-five per cent to keep quiet. That's a lot of dosh, so he won't take too kindly to being shafted.'

'Stepping up the amount we launder has got to be worth a try,' Kevin said, backing my corner.

'I don't like it.' Mark was going to take some convincing.

'What else can we do?' Finn threw his hands up in frustration.

'I could talk to Lola and see if she can help us,' I suggested.

'Why would she want to do that?' Mark quizzed. 'What's in it for her?'

I didn't want to tell the guys I'd already confided in her. Now wasn't the right time to share that piece of information. Mark would shit a brick if he knew. I wasn't going to feel guilty about keeping them in the dark. Lola had rewarded my trust with a valuable tip-off, which confirmed my belief that opening up to her had been the right thing to do.

'I could offer Lola a cash incentive to help us,' I smiled. 'I'd rather pay her the hefty commission than the big ugly bloke that owns the place.'

'I think we should stash the money in lots of different places to safeguard it and keep our heads down for the moment,' Mark countered.

Kevin and Finn looked at each other.

'I think getting Lola on side is our best bet,' Kevin replied.

'So do I,' Finn agreed.

'Looks like I'm outnumbered.' Mark let out a long sigh.

'Hello.' Lola sounded hesitant when she answered the phone a moment later.

'Hi, Lola. It's Paul.'

'Hi, Paul. I didn't recognise the number, so I almost let it ring off,' she admitted.

'Did you think it was going to be one of those calls asking if you'd been involved in an accident recently?' I laughed.

It crossed my mind that she might not pick up, but I didn't want to risk calling her from my phone now that DI Kingsly was watching me. If she worked out there was a connection between myself and Lola, it would put an end to my plan before I got it off the ground and potentially set off a chain of events.

'I thought it was safer to use a burner phone to call you. I don't want to implicate you in anything, but I really need your help. We need to clean as much cash as possible without raising any suspicions. We'd be happy to pay you for your trouble.'

'I'm sorry; I can't. I'd lose my job if Zac found out.'

'I don't want to put you in an awkward position. I just thought you might be glad of the extra dosh; it's expensive living in London.'

'Thanks for the offer...' Lola let her sentence trail off.

'No worries.' I could sense she was feeling uncomfortable, so I backed off. 'Can I ask you a favour?'

'Fire away,' Lola replied.

Even though she was trying to sound breezy, I could hear the reservation creeping into her voice.

'Get yourself a cheap pay as you go phone and use that to communicate with me from now on. I'll give you the money for it when I come in on Sunday.'

'Sure thing. I'll see you at the weekend,' Lola said before ending the call.

'It's bad news, I'm afraid. Lola doesn't want to help us wash the cash. So it's back to the original plan. We'll have to grease the owner's palm instead. But let's not mess around; let's really go for it before time runs out,' I said.

65

Lola

May

Much as I'd done my best to fight against it, I'd started to develop strong feelings for Paul. I'd felt awful turning him down when he'd asked for my help, but what else could I do? I was in deep enough without wading in any further.

I supposed I could share some insider knowledge with him that might be useful without involving myself too deeply. I was sure I could think of ways he could stay under Zac and DI Kingsly's radar while cleaning as much cash as possible. Casinos were set up to separate customers from their money. Slot machines were the biggest source of revenue, so he should stay away from those unless he wanted to empty his pockets. Playing with a group of friends was a good move, though. A lone customer always attracted Zac's attention.

*

When I answered the unexpected knock on my door and saw DS Ash and DC Harris standing there, a feeling of dread washed over me.

'Hi, Lola,' DS Ash said.

'Hi,' I replied in a strangled voice.

'Can we come in, please?'

I stepped back from the doorway and took a seat on the edge of the sofa. I knew something terrible was coming before DS Ash continued speaking, and I didn't trust my legs to hold me up.

'I'm afraid we have some bad news.'

I felt my face crumple.

'Your mother was found dead at her home a short while ago.'

My breath caught in my chest. I'd thought she was going to say that Troy had assaulted her again.

'Mum's dead?'

I couldn't believe what I'd just heard. A feeling of emptiness burrowed into my chest.

'Yes, I'm afraid so.'

'Oh my God.'

I covered my mouth with trembling fingers and then swallowed to try to ease the dryness in my throat.

'What happened to her?'

I held my breath while I waited for the detective to reply. Mum hadn't been ill recently and didn't have any pre-existing conditions that I knew of. Before I had time to consider the possible causes of sudden death in an otherwise healthy person, DS Ash continued speaking.

'I'm sorry to have to tell you this, Lola, but your mother was murdered.'

DS Ash's words bounced off the inside of my head like a ball released from a pinball machine. My mind was a blur, and it took me several moments to take in what I'd just been told. Troy had to be responsible. Mum had been convinced he wouldn't be stupid enough to try and hurt her again. The biggest mistake I'd made was to assume she was right.

I'd convinced Mum to file a police report when Troy had assaulted her, but the case was dropped because she'd withdrawn her statement. Now she'd been found dead at her house. It was too awful to contemplate. DS Ash hadn't said who was responsible, but in my mind, only one person was in the frame.

'Did Troy kill her?'

'It looks that way,' DS Ash replied.

I knew women were much more likely to be killed in the weeks after they left their abusive partner than at any other time during the relationship. But Troy was my ex, not my mum's. Why had he killed her and not me?

I had a sudden flashback to a time when I'd thought Troy was going to end my life. He'd clasped his strong fingers around my throat and started squeezing. I'd clawed at the backs of his hands with my nails to try and loosen his grip, but he was too strong. My strength had begun to fade as each second had passed. Troy had suddenly released his grip, and I'd fallen on my knees and gasped for air.

'How did he kill her?' I blurted out between sobs. I wasn't sure I wanted to know the answer to my question.

'She'd been repeatedly beaten and suffered catastrophic head injuries.'

That shocked me to the core. DS Ash hadn't sugar-coated the truth, and I felt the contents of my stomach rise.

'Where did he kill her?'

Hearing the details was agony, but I had to know what happened.

'In the hallway of her house.'

The very place she should have been safe from him.

'Your mum's manager became concerned when she failed to turn up for work two days in a row without contacting him, so he raised the alarm.'

Guilt threatened to overwhelm me. Mum had been lying dead, and I hadn't realised anything was wrong.

'Who found her?'

It should have been me. But I'd selfishly cleared off to London and left her to deal with my mess.

'The police. They forced open the front door and discovered Dee lying dead in a pool of blood. Her skull had been smashed in with a blunt instrument.'

A picture of the grisly scene flashed before my eyes, so I buried my face in my hands to try and block it out. I couldn't bear to think about the suffering Mum had endured on my account and started sobbing my heart out.

'Can I see her?' I looked up at the DS as tears continued to roll down my cheeks.

'I'm afraid not. It would be too traumatic. Your mum suffered such severe head injuries she's unrecognisable. You shouldn't be alone at a time like this. Is there anyone you'd like me to call?' DS Ash asked, changing the subject.

I continued to stare at her with my tear-stained face.

'Would you like me to phone Elaine from the refuge?'

I nodded. Millie was still at work. She wasn't due home for hours, and I couldn't bear to be on my own right now.

66

Abbie

I wasn't ready to give up on Finn and his group of friends yet. Although I hadn't uncovered the secrets of the universe during my visit to the casino, I was surprised to learn the men had been regulars for years, so it hadn't been a fruitless exercise.

I decided to dig a little deeper into their backgrounds, and that was when I made an alarming discovery. My persistence was starting to pay off. I felt sick to the stomach when I realised one of Finn's friends worked at a watersports centre. I should have figured out Mark Gibson's job just by looking at him. He had long blond hair and had surfer boy written all over him. Mark would definitely know how to drive a boat, and, more importantly, he'd have access to one.

I took a sharp intake of breath as the realisation hit me. I'd given Ed a simple task, a bit of basic investigation work that a junior member of the force would have been able to handle, and he'd failed miserably. I'd asked him to check out all the members of staff past and present and find out if any of them owned a boat or had access to one as I'd been hoping that might throw up a fresh lead. He'd told me none of them had. Ed had been convinced the thieves had hired a boat to use in the robbery. I didn't know if he'd accidentally missed the connection between Mark and the watersports centre or whether he'd deliberately not bothered to follow orders because he'd thought it was a waste of time. Either way, the end result was the same. He'd well and truly fucked up.

We would have discovered the link sooner between Finn and the potential getaway driver if he'd done what I asked him to do instead of making a half-arsed attempt at finding out the information. The man was infuriating; he wouldn't let go of his theory that Stanley was behind the theft of the ten million pounds even though he couldn't find a single shred of evidence to link him to the crime. Cases fell apart in situations like this where a detective thought they knew who the guilty party was, but they didn't have anything concrete to obtain a conviction.

Stanley had never been out of the UK. He didn't even have a passport, so why Ed thought he was going to turn up somewhere like Cuba, spending the rest of his days smoking hand-rolled cigars and living off the proceeds of his ill-gotten gains, was a mystery to me. As if somebody who had never left the country would suddenly want to up sticks and make a new life in a place they've never even visited before. Stanley had the kind of lily-white complexion that looked sunburnt if the temperature crept above eighteen degrees, and his idea of trying something exotic was probably switching out ketchup in favour of brown sauce on his bacon sandwich. I had a lot of experience in profiling people; Stanley wasn't another Ronnie Biggs; he was a real ale and pork pie kind of man. And the thought of visiting anywhere foreign in place of Bognor Regis just wouldn't appeal to him. I knew that for a fact.

Instead of questioning my authority, Ed should use the opportunity to learn from me. I didn't need to prove myself to him, but I'd seen this kind of attitude before. When you worked in a male-dominated job, you couldn't let it hold you back. I'd been eager to climb the ladder and prove that even though I was outnumbered, I could succeed. I liked to think I had a more creative way of thinking than my male counterparts. I was proud of what I'd achieved.

Without women in the ranks, the force would be too macho. I'd passed my sergeant's exam within four years of signing up. Four years on from that, I was an inspector. But something became glaringly obvious the higher up the ranks I climbed. The number of women dropped off, which was down to family commitments because the more senior you were, the more demands there were on your time. I'd joined the police because I'd wanted to help people and make a difference. But in the process, I destroyed the thing that was the most important to me, my relationship with my ex, Ryan.

'I'm bringing Finn back in for questioning,' I said after Ed walked into the incident room.

When he rolled his eyes and let out a slow breath, I had to stop myself from jumping up from my desk and grabbing him by the throat.

'Is that Finn McCaskill?' I asked, when a young man answered the phone.

'Yes,' he replied.

'It's DI Kingsly here. I wonder if you could pop down to the station tomorrow. I've got some more questions regarding the robbery that I'd like your help with.'

'No worries,' Finn replied as if he didn't have a care in the world.

67

Lola

I looked up at the sound of the bell then dabbed at my eyes with the soggy tissue I had balled in the palm of my hand.

'I'll get it,' DS Ash said before she opened the front door.

Elaine rushed over to where I was sitting, dropped down on the sofa next to me and pulled me into her arms.

'I got here as fast as I could. I'm so sorry about your mum, love.'

I buried my face in Elaine's shoulders as a fresh wave of tears started rolling down my cheeks. My grief was too large to measure.

'We'll leave the two of you to talk in private,' DS Ash said.

I looked up at the sound of her voice.

'Don't hesitate to call me if you need anything or have any questions. I'll be in touch with any developments,' DS Ash continued before heading for the door.

DC Harris trailed along behind her. He offered me a sympathetic smile and then disappeared out of sight.

'What am I going to do?' I looked into Elaine's eyes as she held both of my hands in hers. 'I feel so alone.'

'You're not alone. I'm not going anywhere, and Millie will be home soon,' Elaine said, cradling me and rocking me backwards and forwards. 'I wish you'd let me call her. She'd want to be here with you.'

'What's the matter, Lola?' Millie asked when she walked into the flat a couple of hours later.

'Troy's killed my mum,' I blurted out before sobbing my heart out again.

Millie's eyes widened, and her mouth dropped open.

I swallowed hard before I began to speak again. 'The police found her lying dead in a pool of blood. The bastard smashed her skull in.'

Millie shook her head as she walked towards me. 'I don't know what to say. I have no words right now. But please know I'll help you through this, and I'll hold your hand every step of the way.'

Was this nightmare ever going to end?

'Are you going back up to Sheffield?' Elaine asked.

'No, there's no point. It won't bring Mum back. I can't believe she's gone; I'm going to miss her so much.'

'I thought you might want to see her; it might help you come to terms with things. It's been a terrible shock for you,' Elaine replied.

'The detective said Mum's injuries were so severe; it would be too traumatic. What am I going to do without her? She's been both parents to me since my dad lost his battle with cancer. Now I've got nobody.'

'You've got us,' Millie said. 'We're not going anywhere.'

Elaine draped her arm around my shoulder and gave me a squeeze. 'You poor love, you've been through so much.'

68

Paul

'I've been asked to go back into the station tomorrow for questioning,' Finn said when he breezed into the chalet. 'That doesn't sound good,' Mark replied before leaping out of his chair and pacing backwards and forwards across the floor.

'Should we be worried?' I asked.

Finn shrugged. 'I'm not going to get het up about it.'

Finn was maintaining a calm exterior, but I couldn't help feeling a bit edgy, as though the ring around us was tightening. Was it time to start thinking of other ways to launder the money? Maybe we should invest some of the cash in legitimate businesses. It couldn't hurt to have our fingers in many pies. Our freedom was riding on this. The last thing we needed was for the police to still be sniffing around. I wasn't sure whether we should make a break for it or go to ground.

'Do you think we should get out of here while we still can?' Kevin asked.

'I was thinking the same thing,' I replied. 'But we can't all disappear at the same time.'

That would raise eyebrows in our close-knit community.

'Finn's the only one of us that has a permanent contract and he's signed off sick,' Kevin pointed out.

I used to think doing casual work was a real disadvantage. That was no longer the case. Our employers hadn't thought enough of us to give us full company benefits, so we wouldn't need to feel guilty if we cut and run. In fact, it could turn out to be a godsend as we wouldn't need to give notice. The only thing that would prick my conscience if we decided to scarper before the Old Bill caught up with us would be having to lie to my mum and dad.

'Mark could go first,' Kevin said.

'What if I don't want to?' Mark replied, and his lip curled.

'It makes sense, mate. Your job's seasonal, and the watersports centre hasn't reopened for the summer yet, which gives you the perfect opportunity to disappear without anybody asking any awkward questions.'

Mark snapped his head around and glared at me.

'Do I have any say in the matter?'

'Of course,' I smiled, already hatching a plan.

Mark could take the Channel Tunnel to Calais and then drive through France to southern Spain. It would be far riskier to try and take the cash on a flight. If he was really unlucky, somebody might steal the money while it was in the plane's hold. Imagine if that happened. Karma really would be a bitch, wouldn't she?

'I think you guys are jumping the gun,' Finn said. 'We don't even know what the police are going to question me about yet. We should sit tight until tomorrow and not do anything hasty. We'll only make ourselves look guilty if we shoot through, and if the cops had anything concrete on us, they'd have arrested us by now.'

'For once, the ginger tosser's not chatting shit. He's got a point,' Kevin laughed.

'Who are you calling a ginger tosser?' Finn replied.

Mark and I fell about laughing when he grabbed a tea towel off of the counter, wound it up and flicked it across Kevin's arse cheeks. My brother started screaming like a teenage girl as the fabric whip made contact with his skin.

'Enough, children,' I said as Kevin grabbed another towel and prepared to retaliate. 'Let's sit tight until Finn's questioned tomorrow, and then we can make a decision.'

69

Lola

'I can't believe my relationship has cost my mum her life,' I said to Millie after Elaine had gone home.

How would I ever come to terms with that? The idea made me wrestle with my conscience, and grief threatened to overcome me as my emotions bubbled close to the surface again. I'd thought I was all cried out at this stage, but the tears just seemed to keep coming. My eyes were puffy, and my head was pounding. The only thing I wanted to do was drown my guilt at the bottom of a bottle.

'I need a drink,' I said, getting up from the sofa. I hadn't moved from the spot since DS Ash had broken the news to me and had almost taken root.

'What do you want? I'll get it,' Millie offered.

'Have we got any vodka?'

I was a lightweight in the drink department and usually stuck to Kopparberg ciders, but after the day I'd had, I needed something stronger to help me block out the world.

'I think so,' Millie replied as she disappeared into the

kitchen to check. 'Do you want me to make you something to eat?' she asked when she came back a few moments later, carrying a bottle of Asda's own brand, a can of Pepsi Max and two glasses.

'No thanks,' I replied, taking the bottle and a glass out of her hand.

After pouring myself an enormous measure, I added a splash of the mixer before downing it in a few swallows.

Millie didn't say a word, but she stared at me with a look of concern on her face. By the time I was a third of the way down the bottle, my head was spinning. I wanted to reach out to Paul on the phone I'd recently bought. I'd got such a collection of mobiles now, I felt like a drug dealer. But it didn't feel right to burden him with my problems, so instead, I poured myself another drink. Half an hour later, Millie held my hair back as the contents of my stomach landed in the toilet bowl.

Millie was a true friend. She slept on the floor of my room that night. Even though I'd insisted I'd be fine on my own, she knew I wouldn't be. Every time I closed my eyes, I kept picturing either Troy or Mum's face. It brought me a lot of comfort to look over the edge of my bed and see the moonlight bouncing off Millie's long, shiny hair.

My bed was next to the window, so I scooped back the curtains and let my head rest against the cold glass. The sky was full of black clouds. I trained my eyes on them in an attempt to clear my mind. I was exhausted, but I couldn't sleep. As I thought about Mum, I felt the stab of tears. I was only twenty-four, and both of my parents were dead. The ramification of that hit me like a bolt from the blue. I'd never felt more alone. This was the longest night of my life.

*

'Did you manage to get some sleep?' Millie asked when daylight pushed through the thin curtains.

I rolled on to my side and looked at her.

'Stupid question, right?'

'I feel completely hollow,' I replied.

'That's understandable.' Millie offered me a sympathetic smile.

Ever since DS Ash had broken the news to me, I'd been going over the same details. I felt like I was trying to swim against the tide in an endless sea of emotions. The hours morphed into one as my mind tried to block out the horror.

'I'm not sure I'm going to be able to go into work.'

'Work is the last thing you should be worrying about. I'll phone Cassandra and let her know what's happened. You'll be entitled to some compassionate leave,' Millie said.

As she walked out of my bedroom to make the call, my mobile began ringing.

'Lola, it's DS Ash. I just want to give you an update. We still need to gather a vast amount of information to support any prosecution, but a witness placed Troy at the scene of the crime on the night of your mum's murder. We've prepared an artist's impression from their description, which bears more than a passing resemblance to Troy.'

A shiver ran down my spine.

'It's a good likeness, but he denies any involvement. He said it's not as though your neighbours don't know what he looks like. He reckons he's being framed and maintains the witness has got it wrong. Troy's adamant he was working at the bookies, so he couldn't possibly have been there. As he has an alibi, we have to make enquiries to establish whether or not he's telling the truth.'

'Why is it taking so long to check out whether he was working or not?' The frustration in my voice was evident.

Troy had taken Mum's life to get back at me. And now he was walking around without having to face the consequences.

'Troy's claim is unsupported. He was rostered on duty, but there weren't any customers present during the timeframe in question, so nobody can verify that he didn't slip out of the bookies. He's exercised his right to silence and refused to answer any questions, using the standard no comment response to everything we asked.' DS Ash sounded frustrated too. 'We're still in the early part of the investigation, but I'll be in touch as soon as I have more news.'

70

Abbie

At 10.00 a.m., the duty sergeant called me to say that Finn was waiting for me at the front desk.

'Thanks for coming in. If you'd like to follow me,' I said, leading the way along the corridor that led to the interview rooms. 'Take a seat. My colleague will be with us shortly.' I gestured to the chair.

As I busied myself setting up the tape, I studied Finn out of the corner of my eye. He looked as cool as a cucumber. I was beginning to wonder if my gut instinct was wrong. He didn't look like he had anything to hide. Had I lost my touch? Moments later, Ed walked through the door and flashed me a thunderous look before he took a seat at the table opposite my prime suspect.

'What did you want to talk to me about?' Finn asked, brimming over with confidence.

I interlinked my fingers, resting them on the desk between us to gauge the measure of the man as I prepared to start questioning him. I was tempted to jump straight in and ask him outright, 'Did you steal the money?' I managed to restrain myself. Frustrating as it was, the case had to be proven against him, so even if he was guilty, he wasn't going to admit it.

I'd harboured a desire to be in the police since I was a little girl. By the time I was eighteen, my mind was made up. I knew I wanted to join the force even though my parents were against it. They thought it was too dangerous. But I wasn't having any of it. Sometimes I wished I'd listened. Being an officer wasn't easy.

'There are still some lines of investigation that need exploring, but I want to pick your brains,' I replied, hoping to discover something that would change the course of the investigation.

Crime-solving was a process of puzzles and explanations. We weren't at the stage where every piece locked smoothly into place yet. Being suspicious of something wasn't enough; you had to be able to back it up with a fact. If you couldn't prove it, you'd have to think again. But following the trail of breadcrumbs that kept leading to dead ends was beyond frustrating.

'Fire away,' Finn smiled, taking everything in his stride.

'Have any of your colleagues started behaving differently since the heist?'

'The only person I've noticed a change in is Stanley.'

'In what way?'

'He seems to be permanently on edge these days.'

Ed's ears pricked up at Finn's reply. He gave me a sideways glance as he straightened his posture. I pretended not to notice.

'On edge, you say. Can you elaborate?' Ed piped up, his dark brown eyes as bright as buttons.

I felt like snatching the pen out of his hand as he started twiddling it backwards and forwards. He was desperate to dig up some dirt on Stanley to back up his theory.

Finn shrugged. 'He just seems overly jumpy all the time.'

I would have thought that was a normal reaction after what he'd been through; you couldn't really blame the man for being nervous.

'Can you tell us again what happened on the morning of the robbery?'

'Is that necessary? I've already given my account,' Finn questioned before shifting in his seat.

It was very subtle, but there was a change in his behaviour. When he'd first walked in, he'd had a presence.

'I know you have, but you might remember something else,' I narrowed my eyes and stared at him. Finn didn't seem quite so confident now.

We were trained to use lots of different tactics to obtain confessions and get suspects to cough up information. I wanted to compare what Finn said this time to see if he slipped up and offered me a different version of events, a version that might contain something incriminating.

'I'm sorry, but I don't see how going over my statement will help. Am I free to leave?'

I hadn't been expecting Finn to ask that. Ed and I exchanged a look.

'Yes,' I replied. It was the only thing I could say.

'I told you Stanley had guilt written all over him. I hope you're going to bring him back in for questioning,' Ed said after Finn left the room.

'Not for the moment. I'm going back to my office to look through my notes on the assault on Roman Brady. The custody clock's ticking on Wayne Perry, so I need to gather as much evidence as possible.'

I didn't give a damn whether Wayne was released or not, but I wanted to put some space between myself and Ed so that I could dig into Finn McCaskill's private life. He was able to provide us with an alibi that we could genuinely verify because he was at work at the time, but I didn't know if the same could be said of his friends. It was time to find out.

71

Lola

All the signs had been there, but I'd been determined not to see them no matter how many times mum tried to convince me that Troy was trouble. I'd always been very defensive when she'd tried to point out flaws in our relationship and open my eyes to how abusive Troy was being. Mum always said I was too soft-hearted. She was right. I couldn't resist helping someone in need and didn't think of the repercussions before doing so.

'Lola, it's DS Ash. I've got some news for you. The Crown Prosecution Service has decided there isn't sufficient evidence to charge Troy with your mum's murder. He's been released under investigation and placed on bail.'

'Oh my God.' I closed my eyes as I tried to make some sense of what I'd just been told.

'I'm so sorry. This was not the result we were hoping for,' DS Ash said.

'So, where does this leave us? What if he comes after

me?' I asked, bitter tears spilling down my cheeks as fear nested inside my chest.

'We've imposed conditions on his bail, but they'll only last for twenty-eight days.'

'What are the conditions?'

My mind wandered. I was terrified by how vulnerable I suddenly felt. Mum was being laid to rest tomorrow, so I was heading back to Yorkshire this afternoon. I'd expected Troy to be behind bars when I went home. But he was free to roam the streets, so he'd have the opportunity to finish the job.

'Troy's prevented from contacting you and required to live at his home address. But I urge you to keep your wits about you, especially when you come back to Sheffield for the funeral. Troy Jacobs is a very dangerous young man, so I'd advise you not to stay any longer than absolutely necessary.'

'The CPS have let Troy go. They said they didn't have enough evidence to charge him,' I said when I phoned Elaine to tell her about my conversation with DS Ash.

'I'm sorry to hear that, Lola, but the truth of the matter is, this will happen over and over again until the courts learn to recognise and respond to situations like this. In the meantime, another abuser gets to walk free without facing the consequences.'

'It makes my blood boil,' I replied as my grief turned to anger.

'Mine too. Are you still heading home today?' Elaine asked.

'Yes.'

I was scared Troy was going to come after me, but I decided to keep that to myself. I didn't want Elaine to worry.

'I'm going to drive you back.'

'That's a lovely offer, but I can't let you do that, it's such a long way, and I've already booked my ticket...'

'Do you think it's a good idea to travel alone under the circumstances?'

'I don't want to put you out.'

'Don't be silly; you're not putting me out. I wouldn't have offered if I didn't want to do it. Anyway, Millie and I decided this long before you spoke to the detective. She's coming too.'

'Really?' I felt my eyes brim over with tears.

'Millie and I talked about this, and we aren't prepared to travel by train. When you get upset, and you will, every Tom, Dick and Harry will be gawping at you. I cried for months after I lost my mum, and she didn't die in tragic circumstances like yours did.'

After Dad passed away, Mum had decided to pick out her coffin and take out a funeral plan, pre-paying for everything, which took most of the work out of my hands. Because a lot of the details were already arranged, I hadn't discussed the funeral arrangement with Elaine and Millie, so I hadn't realised they'd intended to go until now. I'd thought Mum was being morbid, but she'd insisted that she was just being practical. In hindsight, she'd done me a huge favour.

'What time do you want me to pick you up?' Elaine asked even though I hadn't accepted her offer.

'I'm not sure. Millie's still in bed, and I don't want to wake her. We had a late night.'

I'd been having trouble sleeping since Mum had been murdered.

'How about one o'clock?' Elaine suggested. 'Does that give you enough time?'

'That sounds perfect. Thanks for offering to drive me back; I really appreciate it,' I replied with tears streaming down my face.

We hadn't known each other that long, so I hadn't felt I could ask Millie and Elaine to attend Mum's funeral, but I'd be eternally grateful to both of them for stepping up and helping me in my hour of need.

It was going to be an emotional journey, so I was relieved I wasn't making it on my own. Mum's death had knocked me for six. Elaine and Millie had been so supportive. I wasn't sure I'd have got through the dark early days without them.

I was sitting in the lounge staring out of the window when Elaine's car pulled up outside.

'She's here, Millie,' I called before getting to my feet.

'Coming,' Millie replied.

I picked up my rucksack and made my way out of the room. Millie was waiting by the front door when I walked into the hallway. She reached towards me and rubbed the top of my arm.

'All set? Have you got everything?'

I nodded then followed her outside.

Elaine threw her arms around me and pulled me close after I placed my bag into the boot of her car.

'How are you holding up?' Elaine asked.

I gave her a weak smile, but I didn't answer. There was

no point in saying I was okay when it was blatantly obvious I wasn't.

Millie sat in the back of the car next to me, holding my hand as tears streamed down my face.

There was no magic fix when coping with the effects of trauma and grief. It was an ongoing process that took time. I was going to have good days and bad days. After Dad died, the slightest thing triggered memories, and when that happened, sometimes grief engulfed me at a moment's notice.

'Let it all out, Lola; it's the best way to let go of some pent-up emotion. After a good cry, you'll feel a bit better,' Elaine said, glancing at me in the rear-view mirror.

72

Paul

'How did it go at the station?' I asked when Finn walked into the chalet.

'Okay,' Finn replied, helping himself to a cold beer.

'Do you think the cops suspect you had something to do with the robbery?' That question had been on my mind all day. Hopefully, Finn was going to be able to answer it now.

'Nah. Kingsly doesn't know that I've been signed off, so she asked me if any of my colleagues had started behaving differently since the heist,' Finn replied.

'What did you say?' Kevin asked, tearing his eyes away from the crap he was watching on TV.

'I used the opportunity to spin her a line and told her Stanley had been very jumpy,' Finn smiled.

'Poor old bastard,' Mark said, shaking his head.

'If it keeps the heat away from us, you won't be complaining.' I threw Mark a look.

'Exactly. Sometimes you have to sacrifice others to save yourself. I don't think Kingsly suspects dear old Stan, but the other copper looked interested at the mention of his name. I played it cool, but I wouldn't be at all surprised if the shit doesn't hit the fan soon,' Finn warned.

'What makes you say that?' I quizzed.

'Abbie asked me to repeat my statement. I got the impression she was trying to trip me up. As if I was going to be able to remember what I'd said word for word.'

Mark's face paled as he took in the information, and the implications sunk in.

'What the fuck did you do?' Mark asked before swallowing the lump in his throat.

'The best way to avoid dropping myself in the shit was to say nothing. I told her I couldn't see how going over my statement would help and asked if I was free to leave?'

'Way to go, buddy!' Kevin said, slapping Finn on the back.

'So what happened?' I asked.

'They had to let me go,' Finn beamed. 'But I think it's time we made a move. I don't want to hang around any longer and risk getting caught. I'll talk to my boss and tell him I'm going to resign as I'm not sure I'll ever be able to return to work.'

'How do you feel about driving to southern Spain with the money?' I asked Mark.

'Why am I the one taking all the risk?' Mark didn't look happy with my suggestion.

'You're the only one who's not employed at the moment, so nobody will notice if you disappear for a bit.'

'Thanks, but no thanks.' Mark's blue eyes flashed with anger. 'I don't fancy a solo road trip.'

I couldn't really blame him for being arsy.

'Well, one of us has got to go,' I replied.

'What about Finn. He's signed off. Why can't he go?' Mark added.

'You could go together,' Kevin suggested. 'I think it'll look less suspicious to the authorities if we travel in pairs. What saddo goes on holiday on their own?'

He had a point. I hadn't thought of that.

'If you don't fancy doing the drive, couldn't you skipper a boat? You've done it before,' Finn said.

Mark's expression suddenly changed. The scowl slid from his face, and he tilted his head to one side as he considered the option.

'You're on a roll today, mate. That's a brilliant idea!' I laughed.

'I'm not just a pretty face, you know,' Finn joked.

'I like the idea of being a skipper again, but it could take time for a job like that to come up, and besides that, I can't sail a boat on my own. I'd need a crew,' Mark replied.

He seemed to be coming around to the idea now that travelling across a huge expanse of water had been put into the equation. I shouldn't have been surprised; he was at his happiest when afloat.

'I'll be going with you,' Finn said.

'And I'd be only too happy to offer my services,' Kevin added, with a cheesy smirk plastered across his face.

'Hang on a minute. I thought you said we should travel in pairs?' I fixed my brother with a glare.

I didn't want to take one for the team and be the only person left behind. Being the last man standing didn't appeal to me at all.

'I know I did, but I thought we were travelling by road. Mark will need a crew if we sail, and we can hardly recruit outsiders,' Kevin replied.

'You could come with us,' Finn suggested.

I shook my head. 'It's going to look too suspicious if all four of us disappear at the same time.'

Aside from that, I hated the water. I'd rather face my chances with Abbie, the sniffer dog on my trail than jump aboard a vessel and head out to the open ocean.

'I don't know why I didn't think of this before, but there's a boat being overwintered at the watersports centre. I could easily stock it up with supplies without anybody noticing, smuggle the money on board and stash it in some of the nooks and crannies. There are loads to choose from. My boss never comes near the place at this time of year, so we'd be long gone before he realised the craft was missing,' Mark said, his blue eyes shining.

I had to admit it sounded like a good plan. My only reservation was being left behind if the cops were closing in on us.

'That's a genius idea. When are we setting sail, captain?' Finn smiled.

'At least think about it, Paul,' Kevin said, looking a bit concerned that I wouldn't be going with them.

I shook my head. 'There's no way I'd be able to travel all the way from Kent to southern Spain on a boat. You know what I'm like when I'm near water.'

The very thought of it made me hyperventilate. I'd had a lucky escape when I was a child, and I wasn't about to tempt fate.

'It's not fair to leave you behind. I'll stay,' Kevin said, his conscience getting the better of him.

'No. I want all of you to go. I think this could work. I'll keep the DI occupied while you get away. But I can tell you now, I won't be far behind you.'

73

Lola

Losing my dad at the age of thirteen had had a profound effect on me. I was young and impressionable and struggled without a father figure in my life which drove me to find a partner at the first opportunity. Troy was in a similar situation, having lost his mum when he was a child. Our common ground drew us together. I'd thought we were the perfect match; I couldn't have been more wrong.

It didn't take long for things to turn abusive; I couldn't believe how quickly everything soured. Mum would have had a nervous breakdown if she'd known what was going on behind the scenes. I wished I'd confided in her, but I'd lost my sense of identity so I'd hidden it. By the time she found out, we'd hit rock bottom.

I'd asked myself on countless occasions what was making me stay. I knew deep down our relationship was doomed, but I clung to it like an emotional life raft. I didn't want to lose the only man in my life, no matter how unsuitable he was. What a huge mistake that turned out to be.

My mind raced on the journey. I stared out of the window the entire time so that I didn't have to speak. When Elaine pulled the car up outside the B&B, the hairs on the back of my neck stood to attention. It was only a couple of streets away from Mum's house, but I couldn't face going inside the front door, let alone staying there after what had happened. Even being back in my home town sent a shiver down my spine. The sooner this was over with, the better. I never thought I'd feel like this, but I couldn't wait to get back to London. I didn't feel safe in this sleepy little village any more.

'Stay strong, sweetheart,' Elaine said.

I tore my eyes away from the pretty exterior with colourful baskets hanging on either side of the shiny black door and met her gaze. She was staring at me in the rear-view mirror with a look of concern on her face.

I'd chosen the first slot in the morning for Mum's funeral. I knew I wouldn't be able to sleep the night before, so it seemed like a sensible thing to do.

'How are you feeling?' Elaine asked as I pushed Weetabix around the bowl. I put down my spoon and looked at her with tears welling up in my eyes. She reached over the table, squeezed my hand and gave me a tight smile.

'It's going to be hard, but we'll help you through it,' Elaine said.

When I started to cry again, Millie wrapped her arm around my waist and gave me a squeeze. A feeling of dread nestled deep inside of me. I couldn't seem to shake the feeling.

'We'd better get going soon,' Elaine said, checking the time on her watch.

I forced air into my lungs, wishing this was over and done with as I got up from the table.

Once outside, Millie put our bags in the boot of Elaine's car before we made the short journey to the chapel of rest. Mum's coffin was already in the hearse when we arrived, a spray of white lilies lay on the top. I got out of the car and stared through the window, hardly able to believe my mum was inside the wooden box. It was all so surreal. The funeral director approached me and offered his condolence. I wanted to drop to my knees and sob, but I somehow managed to hold it together. Millie appeared at my side and guided me back to the car. I sat trembling like a leaf as we followed Mum on her final journey.

The haunting sound of 'My Heart Will Go On' by Celine Dion greeted me at the entrance of the chapel, and my legs felt like they were going to buckle. I was glad Millie had her arm around me, supporting me. She guided me past the handful of friends and neighbours who'd attended. Mum had wanted a simple non-religious ceremony, not an elaborate affair.

My eyes filled with tears when the pallbearers placed the coffin at the front. Mum was almost within touching distance. I laced my fingers together to stop myself from reaching out to her.

'If you'd please stand for the committal,' the celebrant said. 'We are meeting here today to honour the life of Dee Marshall and to comfort her family and friends who have been affected by her death…'

I couldn't face listening, so I let my mind wander to

happier times when Mum was still alive. We'd shared such a close bond I couldn't bear to think about a future with her not in it.

'Here in this last act, in sorrow but without fear, in love and appreciation, we commit Dee Marshall's body to its natural end,' the celebrant concluded.

I looked up at the sound of Mum's name and turned my tear-stained face towards the lady conducting the service. She signalled to me with her eyes that the funeral was over. Millie helped me to my feet. I tilted my chin upwards as we walked towards Mum's coffin, doing my best to be brave and not make a show of myself. We paused in front of the casket so that I could run my fingertips over the polished wood before heading for the exit. Elaine followed two steps behind us.

I stood outside the chapel flanked on either side by Millie and Elaine. As we waited to greet the other mourners who had come to pay their respects, I groaned with despair, then covered my mouth with my hand. Get a grip; I willed myself. I owed it to Mum to hold it together. Millie squeezed my arm in a show of support.

Mum's best friend Brenda was the last to approach me. 'I'm so sorry for your loss, Lola. The world will be a sadder place without Dee in it.'

As I went to reply, I felt my lips begin to tremble. Brenda patted the back of my hand to comfort me.

'It's okay, love, you don't need to say anything, but could I have a word with you in private?' Brenda said.

'I won't be a minute,' I said to Millie and Elaine as I followed Brenda to a quiet corner.

'I don't want you to think I'm trying to lay the blame

at your feet, but I wanted you to know Troy had been harassing your Mum from the moment you left.'

Guilt washed over me like a huge wave and almost swept the legs out from under me. The burden was so huge I buckled from the strain.

'I can see you feel bad about that, and it's not my intention to make you feel worse than you already do, but I think you deserve to know the truth. I hope I know you well enough to be able to say this to you without you taking offence,' Brenda said, and I felt myself squirm.

She'd always been a straight shooter and didn't mince her words, so I steeled myself in preparation.

'Before he killed Dee, that maniac had been stalking her. He kept demanding to know where you'd gone. He said if she didn't tell him, she'd have to pay the price,' Brenda said, and her eyes glazed with tears.

'Why didn't she tell me?' I stumbled over my words.

'You know what your mum was like. She was fiercely protective of you. She didn't want you to worry,' Brenda replied.

'I wish you'd told me what was going on.'

I'd known Brenda all my life. If things were as bad as she was making out, I was surprised she didn't get in touch with me.

'So do I, but she'd sworn me to secrecy. She made me promise not to say anything.' Brenda's voice was full of regret.

I had no right to be annoyed. Brenda was just being loyal to my mum. It was incredibly selfish of me to continue a relationship with such a violent man who didn't have the self-control not to take his anger out on my nearest and dearest when he couldn't get to me.

The lines at the corners of Brenda's eyes deepened before she burst into tears. 'Dee was my best friend. We'd known each other since we were five years old. I can't believe she's gone.'

As Brenda stood in front of me sobbing, my mind drifted back to all the conversations Mum and I had had since I'd moved to London. She'd sworn blind that everything was fine. I could sense she wasn't telling me the truth. I wish I'd trusted my gut and acted on it now. I should have realised that Troy was at the root of it all. If I'd known he was harassing her and making verbal threats, I could have involved DS Ash. She might have been able to put a stop to it, and then there'd have been a very different outcome.

I hadn't seen this coming, but it should have been obvious to me. By the way Troy conducted himself while we were a couple, I should have known somebody would have to pay if he didn't get what he wanted. My biggest regret was that I'd chosen to ignore what was staring me in the face. As Brenda continued to cry, I bowed my head in shame. Mum was the best role model I could have asked for, and I'd lost her forever. But she'd left behind an indelible mark on my heart.

74

Abbie

The people I grew up with had no respect for members of the force, so admitting I was a copper wasn't something I shared openly. The few people I chose to tell never believed me anyway. Being blonde, my IQ was always underestimated by the opposite sex. They assumed I was an air-head, but my mind was razor-sharp.

Police officers were predominantly male, and senior females were treated with suspicion more than respect. It drove me insane that I wasn't equally valued and didn't get the same appreciation as a detective. I'd had to fight for my position on the career ladder; climbing it was no mean feat as, nine times out of ten, a male officer would get promoted over a female one.

I'd been hoping to continue delving into Finn McCaskill's friends' private lives when word came through in the nick of time from the CPS regarding the assault on Roman Brady. We'd been up against the wire. The custody clock had almost run out.

'We've got an answer from the CPS. Can you come down to the custody suite?' I asked Ed.

Wayne Perry was brought out of his cell and stood opposite the custody sergeant as Ed came into view.

'The CPS has decided there's sufficient evidence to charge you with aggravated assault and possession of an offensive weapon,' the custody sergeant said.

'No way,' Wayne said.

I wasn't sure why he seemed so startled by the news. His prints were all over the knife; he was lucky he wasn't being charged with attempted murder.

'What have you got to say about that?' I asked.

Wayne stood in silence, gripping on to the counter with white-knuckled hands as he processed the information.

'It was an accident,' he finally blurted out, turning around to face me.

'An accident?' I crossed my arms over my chest and stared at him.

Wayne nodded. 'I didn't mean to stab him; we got into a struggle when the deal turned sour. I was acting in self-defence.'

That was a typical response. Criminals thought they were at liberty to follow a different set of rules to law-abiding people. There was nothing going on behind his eyes to indicate whether he felt remorse or not.

I was inclined to believe his account, but it made no difference to me either way whether he was telling the truth or not. I really didn't give a damn if the drug dealer he'd stabbed got justice. He was just a piece of vermin that needed taking off the streets anyway, so Wayne had done society a favour as far as I was concerned.

I'd wasted enough time on this case. I had more important things to do than getting bogged down with the ins and outs of it and had no intention of investigating the crime thoroughly. I'd be only too pleased if the case lost momentum.

'Where are you going?' Ed asked, my retreating back.

'I'm following up a lead,' I replied without going into detail.

I pushed open the door and walked out of the main entrance, filling my lungs with air before taking the steps two at a time. Then I crossed the forecourt to where my car was parked. Once inside, I punched the postcode of the watersports centre into my satnav.

I suspected Mark Gibson was the getaway driver of the speedboat, so it was time to pay his workplace a visit and see what I could find out. The traffic was light, so I reached the Isle of Sheppey in good time. It didn't come as a great surprise to find the gates to the car park padlocked when I arrived at the marina.

'Excuse me,' I said to a man I spotted on the jetty. 'Do you know why the watersports centre is locked up?'

'It's not open at this time of year,' the man replied.

It was May, so I'd been hoping to see a bit of activity. I'd have to revisit this line of inquiry at a later date.

'Do you know when the centre reopens?'

'Usually at the end of the month around the Bank Holiday weekend to cash in on the tourists.'

'Thanks for your help.'

That wasn't too far away, I thought as I made my way to the car. I wouldn't bother going back to the station. It would be well past clocking off time when I arrived back in London.

75

Lola

As soon as all the mourners had left, Elaine, Millie and I were heading back to London. I was an emotional wreck, so I couldn't face the thought of having a social gathering. Even though most people expected it, there was no law to say I had to have one. The last thing I wanted to do was sit around a pub table exchanging stories and memories of Mum. It was far too soon for that, in my opinion.

Leaving Mum's coffin alone in the chapel before it was cremated was the most difficult thing I'd ever had to do. I had Millie and Elaine to support me. That was enough for me. I didn't want to be surrounded by well-wishers, so a wake was out of the question. And anyway, DS Ash had advised me to keep my wits about me, especially while I was in Sheffield. Troy was still a threat to me. It would take more than a restraining order to keep him away. The sooner we left Yorkshire, the safer I would feel.

I'd been suppressed for such a long time, but after

Mum was murdered I was determined to emerge from the experience a changed woman. I wasn't about to let Troy ruin my life any more than he already had. It would have been so easy to curl into a ball and give up, but I owed it to Mum to carry on. I wouldn't let myself fall to pieces.

Troy had killed Mum, knowing it would destroy me. I wouldn't give him the satisfaction of sending me into a tailspin. First thing tomorrow, I was going to book a hairdresser's appointment and get them to cut off my hair. Troy had always insisted that I keep it long. He used to love entwining his fingers into it and lifting me on to my tiptoes. I swallowed hard at the memory.

'Thanks very much. I love it,' I said to the stylist when he held up the mirror so that I could see the back.

He'd parted my hair in the centre and cut it to collarbone level. I couldn't believe how light my head felt without the weight of my hair hanging down my back.

'It's a huge change, but it really suits you. And I think it's so lovely that you're donating the hair I cut off to charity,' the stylist replied.

I'd asked him to plait my hair so that I could send it to The Little Princess Trust. The charity made wigs for children and young people who'd lost their hair as a result of cancer treatment and other illnesses.

'Not everyone could carry this off, but you've got such a beautiful face any style would suit you. If I was straight, you'd be just my type!' the stylist joked.

'Aww, thanks,' I replied.

I loved gay men. They were so unthreatening and

complimentary. I felt like a million dollars when I walked out of the salon. The confidence boost was just what I needed and prompted my next move. Troy didn't like me wearing make-up. He especially hated red lipstick. As soon as I stepped out of the hairdressers, I made a beeline for Boots.

I finished applying my newly acquired make-up with a slick of bright red lipstick and stared into the mirror on my bedroom wall. I barely recognised the woman looking back at me.

'Hello, stranger. Long time no see,' Paul said when he walked into the casino and saw me sitting behind my desk. 'When I didn't hear from you, I thought I'd frightened you off, and you'd got yourself another job.'

'No, nothing like that,' I replied.

'I did a double-take when I came in. You look so different with your hair short.'

'Is that a polite way of saying you don't like it?' I quizzed, suddenly feeling self-conscious.

'I love it. It really suits you. So what have you been up to? Have you been away on holiday?' Paul asked.

'I wish.'

'Is Zac around? I need to speak to him. I've got one hundred grand in here that needs cleaning ASAP.' Paul patted the side of a black rucksack he'd placed on the counter.

'I'll call his office. Just a minute.'

Paul stepped to the side so that I could serve the customer approaching the booth. While I counted out his winnings, I noticed Zac appear in the corridor and usher Paul away.

As it was my first week back, Cassandra told me to do eight-hour shifts instead of twelve to break myself into the routine gradually. She was concerned it might be too much for me otherwise. She'd offered to let me have more time off, but I'd declined, preferring to throw myself into work to keep busy and take my mind off things. Millie hadn't finished her shift yet, so I was making my way to the station on my own when I heard somebody call out my name.

'Hey, Lola, wait up,' the man shouted.

My first instinct was to run. Troy was never far from my thoughts, but before I'd had a chance to, a familiar face came into view.

'I was hoping to have a chat with you. Do you fancy going for a quick drink?' Paul asked.

'Okay,' I shrugged. 'Where are your friends?'

'They're still in the casino.'

We walked side by side for a short distance until Paul stopped outside the Red Lion on the corner of the street.

'Will this place do?' Paul asked.

'Yes,' I replied.

The Red Lion didn't have the nicest frontage I'd ever seen, but it served alcohol and was within spitting distance of the station. Paul held open the door for me, and I stepped inside.

'What are you having?' he asked as we stood at the bar.

'A bottle of Kopparberg strawberry and lime, please.'

'Would you like ice in that?' the barman asked.

'No thanks,' I replied.

'I'll have a pint of Stella please, mate,' Paul said.

Once we'd got our drinks, we took a seat at a table in a quiet corner; not that there were many people in the pub, but it was tucked away all the same.

'I just wanted to apologise to you. I hope you didn't think I was grilling you earlier about where you'd been. I was worried I'd scared you off by asking you to get involved with washing the cash.'

'Not at all. I've been thinking of ways you could filter extra money through the doors. As you know, customer accounts are compulsory, and Zac monitors them closely, so it would look less suspicious if you varied the amount you gamble with. Millie might be able to switch some chips that have already been played for ones you haven't used. I didn't want to involve her until I ran it past you first.'

'That's not a bad idea. Let me have a think about it.' Paul paused for a couple of seconds before he continued speaking. 'Millie told me your mum passed away. I'm sorry for your loss.'

His words took me completely by surprise, and I was unable to stop my tears from flowing.

'Oh my God, I'm so sorry; I didn't mean to make you cry. That's the last thing I wanted to do. I always seem to put my foot in it.'

Paul sat opposite me, sipping his pint, looking as though he wished the ground would open up and swallow him. I knew he wasn't trying to be insensitive; he was just offering his condolences. But I was too caught up in the tidal wave of grief to put his mind at rest.

I should have realised this would happen. I couldn't disappear from work without people asking questions. You got to know your regular customers, so they were bound to be wondering where I'd been.

'I'm sorry I had a meltdown. My dad died when I was young, and I'm an only child, so I feel very. alone and vulnerable at the moment,' I said when I managed to compose myself.

I was surprised I'd shared that information with Paul, and I suddenly felt a bit guarded. I was worried he might use it against me in some way.

'You've got nothing to apologise for. You've experienced a lot of heartache for someone your age,' Paul said.

Wasn't that the truth? And he didn't know the half of it.

Paul downed the rest of his pint. 'Same again?'

'No thanks. I'd better get going.'

I'd embarrassed myself quite enough for one day, and if I had another drink, my emotions might run away with themselves again.

'I should go too. The guys are waiting for me at the casino. I'll see you next week, but feel free to call me before then if there's anything I can do,' Paul said as we headed out of the Red Lion.

76

Abbie

I walked into the casino foyer, expecting to find Lola sitting behind the cashier's desk, but a young man was in her place. I flashed him a smile and my ID when I approached the booth.

'I'm DI Kingsly. I'd like to have a quick word with Lola Marshall, please?'

'I'm sorry, but her shift finished a little while ago,' the young man replied.

'I need to speak to her urgently,' I said, pausing for effect. 'Can you give me her address and mobile number?'

'Um... I'm really sorry, but I don't have access to employees' personal information. I'll just get my manager. She'll be able to help you.'

A moment later Cassandra came into view. I recognised her; photos of her adorned every surface of Zac's office but we'd never been introduced so she had no idea who I was.

'Sorry to keep you waiting. How can I help you?' Cassandra asked.

'I need the address and mobile number of Lola Marshall.'
I saw the hesitation on Cassandra's face. 'I need to speak to
her urgently. It's a confidential police matter.'

Cassandra suddenly seemed more willing to help me.
'Of course. Just give me one moment,' she said before she
started scrolling through her phone.

Cassandra swivelled the screen around so that I could
read the details. I wrote them down in my notebook and
as I was heading for the door, something caught my eye. I
was surprised to see the four guys in Zac's company. They
looked very pally as they stood at the roulette table together,
drinks in hands.

So I turned on my heel and listened attentively from
a discreet distance. I felt my blood boil when I saw the
amount they were gambling. Money laundering was
the hardest crime to prevent, especially if you had an inside
source. It looked to me like Zac had been double-dealing
and playing me for a fool. He seemed to have forgotten the
terms of our arrangement, I did him favours, and in return,
he tipped me off when anyone tried to filter money through
the tables. I might be mistaken, but he didn't appear to be
sticking to his side of the bargain. If that was the case, I was
going to have to teach the man a lesson he wouldn't forget
in a hurry.

I'd known Zac for years, but he seemed happy to betray
my trust. He wasn't fawning over the guys because he
enjoyed their company. They had to be greasing his palm.
Money was Peterson's one and only true love. I'd first met
him when I'd come here with Ryan and some of his work
colleagues. All of them were loaded and would happily
lose several months' worth of wages for an average person

on a night of entertainment. Something that hadn't gone unnoticed by the owner.

Ryan was a criminal defence lawyer; we'd met when we were working on the same case. He was defending the low-life scum I'd arrested. When he managed to get the man off the charges, he asked me out to dinner to celebrate. I couldn't believe Ryan had the front to do that. More fool me for accepting. I could have saved myself a lot of heartache if I'd turned him down.

Ryan was highly educated, but he thought he was a cut above the rest of us, swanning around in his handmade suits reeking of designer aftershave. He'd come from humble beginnings, but that was a closely guarded secret. He wanted people to think Mummy and Daddy had a huge detached pile in the home counties because that suited his persona so much more than the truth. His parents were ordinary people and lived in a semi-detached on the outskirts of Basildon. Ryan worked hard to lose his Essex accent, adopting one that was more in keeping with his high-profile role, mimicking his colleagues' plummy sounding vowels. It always used to make me smile because if we ever got into an argument, he'd drop the façade in a heartbeat, and his cockney twang would come to the surface and rear its ugly head. He'd tried to bury his roots, but it just went to show they were never that far away.

Ryan was a high flyer and often made me feel like I wasn't good enough. I got myself into a huge amount of debt, trying to keep up with the lifestyle we were leading. I'd obtained multiple credit cards with crippling interest rates and used one to pay off the other. I'd been going round in circles, but I hadn't wanted to lose face.

I needed to focus on why I'd come here and not get bogged down in the past. So I pushed thoughts of my ex from my head, then stole one last glance at Paul and Zac before I headed out of the casino.

I suspected Lola was either involved with the guys, or at the very least she knew something about the money laundering I was convinced was going on under my nose at the casino. It was time to find out and judging by the last time I spoke to her, I didn't think she'd hold up well to questioning.

Lola's flat was above the shops in Acton town centre, so I parked my car in a nearby space on the high street and walked the short distance. Just as I reached the bottom of the stone steps that led up to Lola's property, I noticed a tall, well-built man ahead of me. I hadn't thought anything of it at first. I just presumed he lived there, but when I rounded the corner, I could see he was acting suspiciously, so I hung back and observed him from the shadows. The bald man pressed his face up to the glass and looked through the window of the first flat he came to. Then he bent down, lifted the letterbox and peered through that as well. A few moments later, he moved on to the next. When he'd checked the five properties out, he began walking back in my direction with his fists clenched, so I legged it back down the stairs and stayed out of sight until he passed by.

I'd thought he was about to break into one of the flats, but he walked away without committing any crime, so I put thoughts of him out of my mind and went back to the purpose of my visit. I stopped outside the white PVC door of flat two and rapped on the knocker. Then a couple of seconds later, I repeated the action. I never understood why people didn't have doorbells. They made life so much easier for everyone. I followed the man's example and flipped the letterbox. My eyes scanned around the inside. It was clear nobody was home and I had better things to do with my Sunday than hang around waiting for Lola to come home. I'd call again another time. At least I had her mobile number and knew where she lived now, so my time hadn't been completely wasted.

77

Lola

I'd walked back from the station on autopilot. My head was all over the place. I'd been hoping to keep Mum's death and my work life separate, but I should have known that was never going to happen. I could already feel the lines blurring between the two. Paul's words of sympathy had caught me off guard and my barriers had come crashing down, exposing my vulnerability. I'd been trying to put on a brave face, but I was struggling to cope with what had happened.

As soon as I opened the front door, something seemed wrong. I cast my eyes around the room from the doorway, but nothing appeared to be out of place. I was in danger of losing the plot. I needed to get a grip, so I pushed my fears aside and stepped inside. I didn't like being on my own. My self-confidence had been beaten out of me and although it was starting to return I had a long way to go yet.

I hung my jacket up on the brass peg by the front door and put my shoes and bag on the wooden rack beneath it.

Then I glanced over my shoulder and scanned the empty space. I couldn't put my finger on what was troubling me, but, like a heart attack victim, I had a sense of impending doom. The atmosphere in the flat seemed off, so I considered going back out again. I felt edgy and Millie wasn't due back for hours, but all the decent shops were closed now thanks to Sunday trading hours. I decided to settle for a long soak in the bath with a glass of wine instead. That might help to soothe my frazzled nerves.

I walked into the bathroom, turned on the hot tap and poured a generous amount of Radox under the stream of water. Then I went back into the kitchen while the bath was filling, took a wine glass and a bottle of Merlot out of the cupboard and unscrewed the top. After I poured myself a large glass, I went to check the water level. It still had a way to go. I liked to be fully submerged on the rare occasion I treated myself to a soak. I might even go all out and have a face mask too, I thought.

I put my glass down on the edge of the sink and started to take my make-up off. The mirror had steamed up so I ran my fingers across the reflective surface. My heart skipped a beat and then started hammering in my chest when the surface cleared and I saw Troy standing in the doorway behind me.

'You don't seem that pleased to see me,' Troy grinned and I knew I was in trouble.

I stared at my ex-boyfriend with hatred in my eyes. I should have known he'd ignore the bail conditions that had been put in place to protect me.

'Wouldn't you like to know how I found you?'

I couldn't answer. Panic had me in its grasp, so I couldn't

think straight. I needed to get away before Troy had an opportunity to hurt me, but he was filling the doorway and I was trapped in the room with a bath full of water. It would be so easy for him to drown me.

'You gave your mum a lovely send-off,' Troy said.

His words hit me full force and I felt my breath catch in my throat. A shiver ran down my spine when I realised he must have been watching me at the funeral.

'I was surprised how easy it was to find you in the end. After all the time I wasted trying to get your address from Dee all I had to do was tail the car you were in and you led me straight to your door,' Troy laughed. 'Did you seriously think I wouldn't come after you?'

My temples felt like they were about to explode. I'd been so stupid and now he was going to make me pay.

'I've waited a long time for this; now you're going to get what's coming to you.' Troy stepped towards me and lunged at me wrapping both hands around my throat. 'You seemed to have forgotten, I can make you do whatever I want. And right now, I want to feel your life seep out of you.'

Troy began to squeeze my neck and when I gasped a smile spread across his face.

'Do you see how easy it would be for me to kill you?'

Troy looked into my eyes as I clawed at his hands with my nails, trying to prise them off, but I couldn't loosen his hold. I could feel myself slipping away and when I began to lose consciousness, he released his grip. I started coughing and spluttering, desperately trying to drag air into my lungs, but after I'd taken a few breaths, Troy tightened his grip again which filled me with terror. I was going to die if I

didn't fight back. In a primal push for surviv[...]
for the glass, smashing it on the basin so that[...]
it as a weapon. I managed to force the jagged ed[...]
stomach. Troy yelled out in pain.

'You fucking bitch!'

Troy let go of me and used his hands to cover the blood seeping from his wound. While he was distracted, I made a break for the door. I staggered out of the bathroom, crossed the open-plan living area as fast as my wobbly legs would allow and flung open the front door. I'd only taken two steps along the communal landing when Troy grabbed me and pulled me around to face him. His eyes were blazing as they bore into me. I tried to lash out at him again, but he began crushing my hand in his until I dropped the broken glass.

'You shouldn't have done that,' Troy shouted before he clasped his hands around my throat again. 'Now you're going to die.'

78

Abbie

I was sitting on my terrace sipping a glass of chilled Chablis, trying to unwind. But I was failing miserably. My mind was whirring as I tried to work out the connection between Lola and the four guys. There was no way I was going to settle until I spoke to her. I needed to question her face to face. People gave away a lot in their expressions so I didn't want to miss potential clues by phoning her.

When I rounded the top of the stairs I saw Lola in the grip of the man I'd spotted earlier. I didn't mess around trying to loosen his hold. Strangulation was one of the most lethal forms of violence and it didn't look as though time was on my side. Lola's skin was pale and she was starting to flop like a rag doll. A thin line existed between unconsciousness and death.

I pulled the gun I always carried out of the inside pocket of my jacket and aimed it at the man's head as I walked towards him. 'Let her go or I'll shoot.'

He looked up at the sound of my voice, reluctantly tearing

his eyes away from his victim. When he realised I had him in my sights he immediately did as I requested, so I stepped past Lola who'd dropped to her knees, gasping for breath, and cuffed him. I helped her up while holding the gun in the small of his back and led the way back to Lola's flat away from curtain twitchers. Not that there appeared to be a soul around. Lola would have been a goner if I hadn't turned up when I had. This piece of scum deserved locking up for good. As soon as I checked Lola was okay, I'd cart him off to the station. I was in no doubt he'd intended to kill her.

'Sit down and don't move a muscle,' I said to the man once I closed the door behind us.

He did as requested without putting up any resistance. It was interesting to see the bully wasn't so brave now that he had a gun pointed at him and no longer had the upper hand. I turned my attention to Lola. I could see she was having difficulty breathing and had a blotchy chest, bloodshot eyes and bruises around her neck.

'What the hell was going on out there?'

Lola placed her hand at the base of her neck. I could see she was experiencing intense pain and having trouble swallowing.

'Do you want me to call an ambulance?'

I was well aware that this type of assault could leave permanent damage to the victim's throat or brain.

'No, thanks,' Lola replied in a raspy voice.

'How do you know him?' I gestured with a flick of my head to the man sitting obediently on the sofa.

'Troy's my ex,' Lola said before she started coughing.

I'd guessed as much. Strangulation was a very personal way to end a person's life. The power of controlling their victim's next breath meant it was frequently used by abusers. I had zero tolerance for partners like this.

I walked over to the sink while keeping the gun aimed at her attacker and got her a glass of water.

'Here you go,' I said, handing it to her.

Lola offered me a weak smile and then lifted the cool liquid to her lips with trembling fingers. But as she tried to swallow it, she scrunched her eyes up as though I'd just forced her to drink razor blades. She was in no condition to talk thanks to the thug she used to go out with.

'I can see you're in pain, so I'll let you rest. I'll get a statement from you when you're feeling better. But I'd advise you to get yourself checked by a doctor to make sure he hasn't done any lasting damage.'

'I will,' Lola croaked.

I was almost certain she wouldn't bother seeking medical assistance, but that was her call. I couldn't force her to take my advice.

'Right, on your feet. You're going off to the cells,' I said as I led Troy out of Lola's flat.

I'd thought he was casing potential properties to break into when I'd stumbled upon him earlier. I hadn't realised he was a psycho ex looking for an opportunity to pounce. He must have stayed in the shadows waiting for Lola to come home. Luckily for her, I'd shown up when I had. I'd saved her life, so surely she'd feel indebted to me. And in my book, the best way to repay a favour was with a favour.

79

Lola

Several hours had passed since Troy had tried to strangle me, and I still couldn't speak properly. I was exhausted, but every time I closed my eyes, I pictured his hate-filled face. If Abbie hadn't arrived when she had, I wouldn't be alive now. I was sure of that. The fact that Troy had tracked me down hadn't come as a surprise, but I couldn't work out why Abbie had suddenly appeared on the scene.

'How are you feeling?' Abbie asked when she came to take my statement.

'I've been better,' I croaked.

'I know it's hard for you to talk, so we'll keep this brief,' Abbie said. 'I ran Troy's name through our database and saw that he'd been released on bail after he murdered your mum, on the understanding that he had to abide by certain conditions.'

Tears pricked the back of my eyes, but I was determined to hold them in.

I nodded. 'He wasn't allowed to contact me and was required to live at his home address.'

'Troy's breached the terms of the agreement. So he'll be brought back to court tomorrow. A judge or magistrates will decide whether to remand him in custody or release him again.'

I felt my breath catch in my throat. 'Are you serious? Is there a chance they'll let him go?'

'Hopefully, he'd be remanded in custody this time,' Abbie replied. 'Rest assured, if they release Troy again, I'll make sure he doesn't come within a million miles of you. I appreciate you need to rest, so we'll leave it at that. I'll be in touch tomorrow when I know the court's decision.'

Abbie walked towards the door.

'Before you go, can I say something?'

'Of course,' Abbie smiled.

'Thank you for saving my life.' My voice cracked with emotion as the words left my mouth.

'My pleasure,' Abbie replied.

'Had you come here to see me?' I asked.

'Yes, I wanted to ask if you could help me with some inquiries regarding Finn McCaskill and his friends, but then I found Troy with his hands around your throat and dealing with the assault had to take priority. We'll talk about it when you're feeling better,' Abbie said, leaving me with my thoughts.

80

Paul

After Millie told me that Lola's mum had died, I attempted to reach out to her, but she seemed to be keeping me at arm's length. She was friendly enough on the face of things, but I could sense if I tried to get closer, her barriers would go up. I'd been hoping things would start to progress between us, but I got the feeling Lola was reluctant to get involved in a relationship for some reason. Maybe she'd had a bad experience.

Things weren't working out the way I'd expected. I'd originally thought Mark would disappear first, and once he was settled, Finn would hand in his notice, telling his colleagues that he was fed up of listening to Mark going on about what a fantastic time he was having, so he'd decided to go and join him. We'd give it another month or two, and then Kevin and I would do the same thing. The four of us had been inseparable for years, so nobody would think anything of the fact that we were relocating to the same place.

None of us really cared where we ended up, we just wanted to go somewhere with a nice climate and a good standard of living. It was stick a pin in a map time by the looks of it. We'd previously agreed that we couldn't go too far wrong if we headed to southern Spain. It seemed to tick all the boxes. The place was flooded with British ex-pats and tourists, so the language barrier shouldn't be too much of a problem as most of the locals spoke English anyway. We'd originally intended to go off in different directions when we left the UK, but the idea of having my closest friends around me when I was leaving my family behind seemed like the sensible thing to do. At least we'd have each other while we got used to our new surroundings.

'Time's running out. The watersports centre reopens in a matter of weeks, so if you're going to take the boat without the owner's permission, you'll need to get on with it,' I said to Mark.

'I was thinking the same thing,' Finn said.

'Why don't we go tomorrow?' Kevin suggested. 'That will give us almost a week's headstart before DI Kingsly realises we haven't shown up at the casino.'

The guys knew that Lola had to inform her every time we ventured over the threshold. Finn and Mark glanced at each other, but neither of them made any comment.

'That sounds like a great idea. You lucky bastards,' I replied, wishing my fear of water wasn't stopping me from joining them.

'I won't be able to get everything organised that quickly. Wednesday would be the earliest we could leave,' Mark said.

'Wednesday it is then,' Finn beamed.

81

Abbie

I'd only intended to give up an hour of my Sunday when I'd slipped over to question Lola. But I hadn't been expecting to find her being strangled by her abusive ex outside her flat and become caught up in their domestic dispute. I'd had to forget my plans and go to her aid. It looked like my good deed was going to pay off; she seemed incredibly grateful when I went back to take her statement.

On the drive back to my flat, I tried to put the pieces of the puzzle together in my mind, but they still didn't fit. I had to work out the connection between the guys, Lola and Zac before time ran out. First thing tomorrow, I'd head to London City Airport and try and catch Finn off guard.

'I'd like to speak to Finn McCaskill,' I said, holding up my warrant card.

'He doesn't work here any more,' the cargo handler replied.

I had to stop myself from letting out a loud yell.

'Sorry?' I questioned, hoping I'd misheard him.

'Finn doesn't work here any more,' the man repeated.

'Can I speak to Stanley Brown in that case?' I tried to keep my tone neutral.

'He's in the office. Follow me,' the man said.

Stanley wrung his hands, and his eyes flicked from side to side as I approached. I could see why Ed was convinced he was our man.

'Your colleague tells me Finn's not working here now.'

'That's right,' Stanley replied.

'Since when?' I quizzed.

'For quite a while. He'd been suffering from PTSD since the robbery,' Stanley said.

I barely managed to hold back my laughter. I could picture Finn clearly yesterday, sitting at the roulette table knocking back shots like they were going out of fashion.

'PTSD?'

'Yes. The airline released him from his contract on medical grounds as he was finding it too traumatic to be here,' Stanley explained.

So Finn had blatantly lied to me when I'd brought him in for questioning and asked if any of his colleagues had started behaving differently since the heist. He'd told me the only person he'd noticed a change in was Stanley which had delighted Ed. No prizes for guessing why he'd done that.

While I listened to his account, I watched the pictures changing on the sophisticated closed-circuit screens that just happened not to be working on the day of the robbery. I felt like slamming my fist down on Stanley's desk in frustration. I briefly considered going along with Ed's theory and framing the old boy for the robbery I knew he hadn't orchestrated just so I'd be able to close the case. I could feel the thieves slipping through my fingers, but without evidence, there was nothing I could do to stop them from getting away.

'When did he leave?' I asked.

'Last week. Finn had been signed off sick for months, so the airline didn't ask him to work the usual notice period.'

Wasn't that a pity?

Stanley had earned a reprieve. I wasn't sure he'd be able to cope with life behind bars, and more importantly, I didn't want to give Ed the satisfaction of saying I told you so if we charged him with masterminding the heist. He'd never stop rubbing my nose in the fact that he'd solved the case even though it was clear in my mind that Stanley had nothing to do with it. Finn and his friends were the ones responsible. McCaskill didn't have PTSD any more than I did. I knew he was a liar, but that was all I had on him. I couldn't prove he was part of the gang that committed the heist, for the moment.

My thoughts turned to Lola. She could be the missing piece of the puzzle I'd been searching for and hold the answers that would tie all the loose ends together. I needed to win her trust so that she'd give up Finn and his friends. There was no better way to get her onside than by giving her some good news.

'Lola? It's DI Kingsly. I just wanted to let you know Troy has been refused bail. He's going to be held in custody until his court hearing.'

'Oh, thank God! You don't know how relieved I am to hear that,' Lola replied.

82

Lola

The corners of my mouth lifted when the phone Paul called me on started ringing.

'I just wanted to let you know the guys are going to France with some of the dosh on Wednesday,' Paul said.

And just like that, my mood took a nosedive, reminding me how fragile my state of mind was. I felt my eyes grow wide, and my smile vanished as a feeling of panic hit me. I was unsure how to react.

'Are you going with them?'

'No. I'm acting as a diversion, but I'll be joining them soon,' Paul smiled.

My heart sank as his words registered. Because my dad died when I was young, I worried that everyone I loved or got close to was going to leave me and that had only intensified since Mum was murdered. I had no right to be put out by his plans. It wasn't as though Paul and I were a couple or romantically involved.

'Are you still there?' Paul asked when I didn't reply.

'Yes.'

I couldn't manage more than a one-word answer. I suddenly felt choked up.

'This might sound like a crazy idea, but why don't you come along for the ride? You'd be doing me a huge favour,' Paul said.

My face broke into a huge grin.

'I can't. I hardly know you.'

'All the more reason to come with me. There's no better way to get acquainted with somebody than going on holiday together. I promise to be on my best behaviour. I'll book separate rooms and everything.'

'What about my job?' I protested half-heartedly.

'What about it? You can get a job in France or Spain or Italy for that matter. Anywhere you like. France is the gateway to Europe,' Paul said.

I couldn't deny he was selling it to me, but I wasn't impulsive by nature. I couldn't just walk out on Cassandra after she'd been so good to me.

'At least think about it. You've got nothing to stay here for. And if you don't like living abroad, you can always come back,' Paul suggested before he ended the call.

I clutched the phone to my chest for a moment to let the conversation sink in.

83

Abbie

Wayne Perry had been arrested multiple times but had only ever been cautioned before. Now he was looking at being put away for a stretch after he'd stabbed the drug dealer he was trying to rob. His fingerprints were all over the weapon used in the attack.

His court date was looming, so I was sure he'd be keen to make all the charges go away. If he agreed to help me out, I could be persuaded to do the same for him. It was surprising how quickly a case could collapse if the key piece of evidence disappeared. I'd be happy to make the knife vanish, but I needed something in return. Was that corrupt, unethical, dishonest? Of course it was. But I'd be lying if I said I hadn't lost evidence or planted some if none existed during the course of my career.

Thanks to my upbringing, I was familiar with blades and firearms. I was no stranger to machetes and sawn-off shotguns. They were the weapons of choice on the streets where I grew up. My uncle had quite a stash of them and happily showed them off at family get-togethers. I'd harboured an ambition to join the force for years before I'd plucked up the courage to tell my family. They didn't have much faith in the police, so I knew how it was going to go down. We'd fallen out when I signed up because we were on opposing sides.

My background shouldn't have stopped me from being a good detective. I was very aware of criminality. It was in my blood. I often got my best results when I walked the thin line between the underworld and the police world. I used my mind and my looks to my advantage; the opposite sex constantly underestimated my IQ. They couldn't see past the blonde hair; Zac Peterson was guilty of that.

Zac liked to keep a corrupt officer in his pocket; we had so many uses, apparently. He'd told me before the fact that I was a woman with the face of an angel was a huge advantage because I aroused less suspicion than a man. His flattery was wasted on me. I was only interested in the monthly retainer he paid to keep me sweet. But if he thought that gave him the right to swindle me, he was very much mistaken.

Informants were the lifeblood of solving cases; without them, you didn't get tipped off to crimes while they were still in the pipeline. He'd made himself redundant when he'd double-crossed me. Zac had served his purpose, so he had to go. I couldn't risk him dropping me in the shit in the act of retaliation. He needed to be taken out of the equation, but I couldn't afford to get blood on my hands, so I'd come up with a different plan. A solution to every problem could be bought with a bribe.

★

'Let's go for a walk,' I said when Wayne opened his front door to me.

He was too startled to reply but pulled the door closed behind him to do as I'd requested, restoring my faith in the fact that most people were submissive to authority under the right circumstances.

'Are you worried about the court case?' I began.

'I'm shitting myself,' Wayne replied.

'Keep this to yourself, but I might be able to get the charges dropped.'

Wayne wasn't sure whether to believe what I was saying. It would be a sorry state of affairs if he couldn't trust a police officer.

'But you'd have to do something for me.'

Plea bargaining rarely failed to loosen people's tongues.

'What do you want me to do?' The eagerness in Wayne's voice was apparent.

'I need you to steal a car.'

'And if I do, you'll drop the charges?' Wayne questioned.

'Consider it done,' I replied with a smile on my face. 'And stay off the gear. I need you to have your wits about you tonight,' were my parting words.

I'd parked near the casino's entrance so that I could see what was going on but not so close to draw attention to myself as I'd left my engine idling. I checked the time on my watch; it was almost two o'clock in the morning. The foyer door opened, and Zac appeared on the pavement and started walking in the direction of home. I pulled up the camera on my phone and filmed him. As he stepped out to cross the road, a car ploughed into him at high speed. He flew ten feet in the air before landing in a crumpled heap. The sound of the thud alerted some passers-by who scrambled to help him. I put my phone on the passenger's seat and pulled away from the kerb, driving after the vehicle that had committed the hit and run.

I'd met a lot of professional criminals over the years, and one thing I'd learned from them was that they wouldn't hesitate to kill somebody who posed a threat to them. The only way to ensure the person's silence was if they took what they knew to the grave.

Wayne had parked in a deserted car park shrouded in darkness five minutes' drive away. It was clear from the huge dent in the bonnet that he'd been involved in a nasty accident. When I pulled up behind him, he jumped out of the driver's seat and legged it towards me, so I lowered the passenger's window.

'Don't touch my car,' I said. I got out, walked around to the boot and opened it. 'Can you give me a hand?'

'What the fuck!' Wayne said, his eyes on stalks.

I'd told Lola a little white lie when I'd said Troy had been remanded in custody. After what he'd done, I didn't want to risk some crackpot judge releasing him into society again, so I'd forced him to get into my boot instead of taking him to the station yesterday. His wrists were still cuffed but I'd also bound his ankles and gaffer-taped his mouth to incapacitate him. Having been without food and water for more than twenty-four hours he was very compliant when I released his ankle restraints so that he'd be able to walk. I placed a hood over his head before Wayne and I hauled him out of the car, led him towards the one involved in the hit and run and forced him on to the back seat.

'Your ordeal will be over very soon. I just need you to wait patiently,' I said to Troy.

'What are you doing?' Wayne asked.

He'd find out soon enough.

'Get changed into these.'

I handed Wayne a plain black sweatshirt and joggers. I'd brought him a spare set of clothes. I didn't want to run the risk of the forensic team linking him to the hit and run. 'Make sure you take everything off, then throw it back into the car.' He looked at me with a horrified expression on his face. Anyone would think I'd never seen a naked man before. As he went to protest, I cut him off with a wave of my hand.

'Listen, I'm not trying to get a cheap thrill here. I'm making sure we've covered your tracks. Just get on with it; we haven't got time to waste.'

To preserve his modesty, I got to work dousing the stolen car with petrol. I couldn't abide men like Troy. Being locked up wouldn't be enough punishment for him. He deserved to die screaming. I'd promised Lola I wouldn't let him come within a million miles of her. Killing him was the only way I could guarantee I kept my word.

As soon as Wayne threw his clothes on the front passenger seat, I poured what was left in the jerry can over the garments. The smell of petrol was overpowering in the confined space. Troy's hooded head jerked in my direction and he began wriggling like a fish on a line as he worked out what was about to happen.

'Stand back,' I said to Wayne.

'What about that guy?' I could see Wayne was terrified.

'What about him?'

I lit a match and threw it on top of Wayne's bomber jacket. It was made from polyester, by the looks of it, so it should go up with no trouble. Troy's days of terrorising women were over. Watching him kicking the backs of the seats while desperately trying to free himself was satisfying, albeit short-lived and he soon succumbed to the effects of the fire. It was a shame Lola couldn't have seen him suffering for herself. But I couldn't run the risk of letting her into my little secret in case she turned out not to be trustworthy.

Wayne and I stood side-by-side in silence, watching the flames take hold. It was strangely soothing seeing the fire licking at the windscreen; pretty soon, the whole interior was like an inferno. At first, the fireball was contained within the metal frame of the car. Wayne jumped when a large bang filled the air around us.

'Let's get out of here,' I said when the heat from the fire became too extreme for us to stay nearby. 'Put those on.' I handed Wayne a pair of gloves. The last thing I wanted was for him to leave his prints all over the inside of my car.

'Did you follow my instructions to the letter?' I asked as we drove away from the burning car.

'Yes,' he replied.

I'd told him not to bring his phone with him because the police would be able to track his movements and to make sure he had an alibi in place just in case he was questioned.

'I'm sure I don't need to tell you that we never mention this incident again.'

I had the video footage of Wayne running Zac over on my phone as an insurance policy just in case I needed it. You could never be too careful where criminals were involved.

Wayne was sitting in the passenger seat like a frightened mouse. It was no wonder he'd got caught when he'd stabbed the drug dealer. He had about as much bottle as a choirboy. He didn't have the right personality to be a crook.

'Oh, and in future, make sure you keep your nose clean,' I said as Wayne opened the passenger's door and stepped out into the night. I'd wanted Zac Peterson's death to look like an accident rather than the work of a hitman. If a pedestrian was mowed down in the early hours of the morning when there weren't a lot of witnesses about to report the incident, it wouldn't raise eyebrows. That sort of thing happened from time to time. The investigating team would conclude that the motorist was more than likely over the limit, driving a stolen vehicle or had no insurance, which was why they hadn't stopped at the scene or phoned the emergency services. Peterson's death would be recorded as a tragic accident. Whereas if I'd had him finished off in a drive-by shooting, I would have been opening a can of worms. And as for Troy, he got what he had coming to him. It made perfect sense to destroy both sets of evidence in one go. There was no point in making more work for myself.

Killing off Zac would have serious consequences for me. Not in the way you might imagine. I wasn't worried that I'd be linked to his murder. I liked to maintain a safe distance from the crimes I committed so that it was virtually impossible to connect me with them. But I'd become reliant on the money he'd fed me over the years and now I'd lost a valuable source of income. I couldn't afford to be without it, so the pressure was really mounting to find the missing millions.

84

Lola

I stripped off my uniform and changed into trackies and a T-shirt before plonking myself down on the sofa. I was enjoying doing shorter shifts, but I didn't like being home alone, especially since Troy had attacked me. Even though Abbie had assured me he was behind bars, I didn't feel safe now that he knew where I lived. Rightly or wrongly, I hadn't told Millie what happened. Troy had murdered my mum when he couldn't get to me so she might think it was too risky for us to share a flat. The idea of that was unbearable. That was how I justified keeping her in the dark. I also hadn't mentioned anything about the conversation I'd had with Paul. There was no point; I couldn't seriously consider going to France with him no matter how appealing he'd made it sound.

Millie wouldn't be back for hours yet, so I started flicking through the channels trying to find something to watch on TV. Every other programme seemed to involve the police catching people in the act of doing something they shouldn't, so I abandoned that and went to start the dinner instead.

While I chopped up vegetables, my mind kept drifting back to Paul and the fact that I might never see him again. I didn't like the thought of that, so I tried to bury it and focus on something else. Anything would do. The conversation I'd had with Abbie suddenly popped into my head. She'd been coming over to ask if I could help her with some inquiries when she'd found Troy with his hands around my throat. The memory of his hands squeezing my flesh sent a shiver down my spine. There was a good chance I'd implicate myself if Abbie started questioning me about Paul and his friends, so I'd need to avoid her at all costs. I felt compelled to help them even though I knew I shouldn't. My head told me to stay out of it, but something was clouding my judgement. Paul had somehow got under my skin, so I didn't want him to get caught and put away.

I looked up from the pile of diced carrots when my pay as you go mobile started to ring. I felt my shoulders slump before I lifted it to my ear.

'Hi, Lola,' Paul said when I answered the phone. 'I've got some news. Is now a good time to talk?'

My heart started pounding beneath my clothes.

'Are the guys still going to France tomorrow?' I blurted out.

'No. That's why I'm phoning. There's been a change of plan. It looks like I'll be around for a while yet.'

My lips stretched into a huge grin.

'How come?'

'Mark went to get the boat ready and found there was a

problem with the engine. It's fixable but it's going to take time to get the parts.'

I knew that wasn't ideal for the guys, but I felt like jumping with joy.

'That doesn't sound good.'

'Tell me about it.' Paul sounded utterly pissed off.

'When do you think the boat will be ready?' I asked with my fingers crossed.

'Who knows, but if it takes too long we'll have lost our window. The centre reopens at the end of the month.'

85

Abbie

'Somebody broke into the evidence room and stole the knife,' I said when Ed walked into my office.

'How the hell could that have happened?' he questioned, giving me a long stare.

The evidence room had key card access and was guarded by a member of staff as well as being covered by CCTV.

'I don't know, but it did. They've got footage of the culprit tasering the officer on duty before using the injured man's card to gain entry,' I replied.

'Where does that leave us?' Ed asked.

'We've had to drop the charges.'

'For fuck's sake!' Ed shouted as he stormed out of my office.

He wasn't a happy bunny, but I was floating on air. Breaking into the evidence room had been easier than I'd thought. I was a seasoned detective and knew the importance of not leaving evidence behind. I fully intended to retire with an unblemished record, having spent years hiding just below the cover of innocence. I had a tough, no-nonsense mentality and was streetwise. Protect and serve was what I outwardly preached. I'd had an impressive track record before I'd turned crooked.

I hadn't always been this way; a thin line existed between honesty and dishonesty. When I'd first started at Hendon Police Training College, I'd thrown myself in headfirst. I did everything by the book. I was independent and fiercely ambitious, which didn't go down well with some of my colleagues.

I used my background experience to help with investigations. I understood the criminal mind more than most and knew how corrupt people thought. I'd grown up rubbing shoulders with some high profile members of southeast London's underworld. They'd started small but had gone on to become professional crooks. When my childhood friends and family realised I was joining up, they'd tried to nurture me into becoming a dirty cop from day one. They'd offered to pay me to be their eyes and ears.

The area I'd come from was a hotbed for criminals and police corruption. Having a close relative that had strayed down the wrong path made me aware of the relationships between the two camps before I'd joined the force. My uncle had had a colourful past. He was disgusted when I signed up and was convinced I'd end up bent, which he reckoned might prove to be useful for some of his less than honest friends. I'd initially been determined to prove him wrong, but before long, I'd succumbed to temptation.

I'd devoted too much of my time to the job, working more hours than was necessary. As a result, my home life suffered, and I ended up paying the ultimate price. The rougher things got at home, the more time I spent working. You get the picture. My love life was falling apart, which had a profound effect on me and my ability to perform at work. There were various reasons why officers turned crooked. Losing the love of my life because of my dedication to my job was the catalyst for me. I couldn't really blame Ryan. Being the live-in partner of an officer wasn't easy. Long made plans could change in the blink of an eye. My ex used to accuse me of putting my job first, and he got fed up with being second best. My relationship ended the same way as those of many of my colleagues; it was a sad fact that police officers have one of the highest rates of divorce of all professions.

I'd resisted venturing off the straight path for a long time and prided myself on the fact that I didn't accept bribes under any circumstances. Not long after Ryan left me, I'd arrested two men who'd assured me their boss would pay me well for my assistance. At first, I refused to help but then the temptation of easy money when I was struggling to make ends meet got the better of me. Earning extra cash had suddenly become essential. Otherwise, I was going to lose my home, which was the only bit of stability I had in my life. Ryan and I had bought a swanky apartment we couldn't afford, and we were mortgaged up to the hilt. The repayments were crippling me since Ryan had packed up his designer suits and left me to foot the bill while he shacked up with my replacement. His new girlfriend had about as much class as a pig in lipstick. What a Prince Charming he turned out to be.

My salary was falling a long way short. It seemed like a natural progression to play the system. A perk of the job was the fact that I had full clearance to access computer data and intelligence systems across the capital. I managed to erase the training that was hardwired into me; my good habits became restricting. Selling sensitive information to criminals was incredibly lucrative, and I needed the money. The first time I accepted a bribe, I met my paymaster in the car park of a service station on the M1. Searching the police's national computer and tracing car registrations in exchange for money seemed harmless enough. Providing confidential police information from victim statements was a new level. I didn't allow myself to think about how that sensitive material might be used in the beginning. I felt bitter towards the establishment that cost me the love of my life. I gave up the best years of my life trying to bring criminals to justice before I developed an if you can't beat them, join them attitude and became part of their tainted world.

Being a shadowy police associate and part of a secret world proved to be beneficial to my career. It had more perks than just financial ones. Criminals would tip me off about rivals' activities, which helped to boost my arrest record no end and saw me rise up the ranks, making me even more valuable to my underworld associates.

The threat of exposure was ever-present. I could land in the shit at any given moment, and the game would be over, which was why I kept private files on anything I uncovered; my records stretched back years. The best way to survive was to get dirt on senior officers. My archives acted as a guarantee. I couldn't be exposed without taking others down with me. That was my trump card, and I kept it close to my chest in case I ever needed to use it. Sheer nerve was a key factor in being crooked.

Crime syndicates were able to thrive because bent coppers acted as their eyes and ears within the force, divulging details of confidential police operations, among other things. Corrupt police and crooks fed off each other. It was essential for criminals to have officers in their pockets so they could operate with impunity. When you looked at it like that, I was just providing a service. They needed me as much as they needed air to breathe.

Wayne had only just been told he was in the clear when rumours began circulating that Zac had been killed on the orders of a serving police officer with connections to powerful criminals. The timing couldn't have been worse as it coincided with a complaint to the independent authority by a low-life piece of scum I'd previously crossed paths with making allegations against me. He'd accused me of being on the take, but there was no tangible evidence against me apart from the word of a convicted criminal. Shit sticks, so it hadn't gone unnoticed by Ed. He was all ears now; he loved a bit of scandal.

'It's shocking about the complaint. Doesn't that man know, as police officers, we have to abide by a strict code of conduct and ethics,' Ed said.

It was either a show of false sympathy or an attempt to bait me, so I didn't deign to respond. I wasn't on trial here. I could sense Ed was suspicious of me; I could see him discreetly studying me out of the corner of his eye.

My would-be accuser didn't know it yet, but he would shortly be imprisoned for murder. A murder he hadn't committed. Once the deed was done, and I'd tampered with the evidence which would later frame him, he'd wish he'd never heard of me, let alone tried to bring me down. I'd make sure his life behind bars was a living hell. Nothing would give me greater pleasure. He'd rue the day he tried to be a whistleblower.

Wayne's earthly time had just run out. I knew people everywhere and had powerful connections and friends in high places. One in particular, who shall remain nameless, paid me a monthly retainer to be on call. I'd sold him confidential information and buried murder allegations in the past, so he owed me a favour, big time.

86

Lola

Paul had given me the green light to confide in him when he'd told me he was involved in the airport heist. I wanted him to know that Troy had tracked me down and tried to strangle me. He also deserved to know the truth about what happened to Mum, but every time I tried to open up, my words lodged in my throat.

I couldn't deny I had a soft spot for Paul, but I was scared to get involved. Since Mum had been murdered, I had even worse trust issues than before, if that was possible. I knew I'd never be able to leave the past behind if I didn't push myself out of my comfort zone. Paul wasn't going to be around for much longer, so if I was going to let him in, it was now or never.

'I've decided to tell Paul about Troy,' I said.

'I think that's a great idea,' Millie beamed, flicking her silken hair over her shoulder.

'Here goes.'

I gave Millie a weak smile before walking into my

bedroom and closing the door so that we could talk in private. I sat down on the edge of the bed and took a couple of deep breaths before reaching for my phone. My heartbeat went into overdrive when his mobile started to ring, and I could feel beads of sweat break out on my upper lip. I clenched my teeth and pointed my chin upwards, channelling my Dunkirk spirit, another trait I'd inherited from my dad.

'Hello,' Paul said.

'There's something I need to tell you.'

'Is everything okay?' Concern coated Paul's words.

'You asked me before what made me come down south and I said work, but that wasn't true. I came to London to get away from Troy, my abusive ex. He used to beat me black and blue.'

'I'd like to get my hands on the fucking coward.'

'The reason I'm telling you this is he turned up at my flat on Sunday and tried to strangle me.' I felt choked up with emotion.

'He did what?' Paul sounded horrified. 'You must have been terrified. Why didn't you say something before now?'

'I didn't feel ready to talk.' I was still shaken up by the experience.

'I understand,' Paul said.

'Troy must have broken into my flat while I was at work. When I let myself in, something didn't feel right, but nothing looked out of place so I brushed it off and went to run a bath. The mirror had steamed up and when I cleared it, he was standing in the doorway. Troy clamped his hands around my throat but I managed to get away. I made it to the communal landing before he caught up with me. I'm sure he would have killed me if Abbie hadn't intervened.' I sniffed back my tears.

'Abbie?' Paul questioned.

'Yeah, I know. I was surprised to see her too.'

'What was she doing at your flat?'

'She wanted to ask me some questions about you and the guys.'

'What did she want to know?'

'She never got around to questioning me. She ended up arresting Troy instead, but I'm guessing it has something to do with the money you're putting through the casino.'

'Jesus Christ. That's all we need.' Paul sounded stressed.

'Don't worry. I won't tell her anything.'

Even though Abbie had saved my life my loyalty lay with Paul and his friends.

'Thanks, Lola, you're a star.' I could tell by the tone of Paul's voice that he was smiling.

'And there's something else.' I paused to compose myself. 'You know my mum died recently.'

'Yes,' Paul replied.

'She didn't pass away peacefully. Troy murdered her because she wouldn't tell him where I'd gone.' My voice broke as the words left my mouth.

'I'm so sorry, Lola. I don't know what to say. That's so awful.'

'The only blessing is because Troy breached his bail conditions when he turned up here, he's going to be held in custody until his court hearing. Hopefully, he'll be put away for a very long time.'

I felt a lot safer knowing that Troy wasn't walking the

streets any more. I'd never have been able to relax if he'd been granted bail again. I would have had to stay doubly alert to remain one step ahead of him. I didn't want to live like that with the constant worry that danger was lurking around every corner.

'I hate the idea of going away and leaving you behind. Do me a favour, please? Seriously consider coming with me,' Paul said and his words tugged at my heartstrings.

87

Lola

Millie and I had been asked to go to Cassandra's office at the start of our shift.

Millie turned to look at me as we walked along the corridor. 'I wonder why she wants to see us?'

'Who knows,' I replied, but I had a feeling it might have something to do with the amount of money Paul and the guys were putting through the casino.

Cassandra had her back to us when we walked into her rose-tinted room. Even before she'd uttered a word, I knew something was wrong. She didn't look herself. She was always so glamorous and well-groomed. Her long dark hair usually tumbled over her shoulders in loose curls, but today it hung in two limp strands on either side of her neck. She'd swapped her boardroom suits for a baggy sweatshirt and jeans and her eyes were red-rimmed and puffy as though she'd been up all night crying.

'I'm afraid I've got some bad news,' Cassandra began, pausing to dab her eyes with a tissue.

I couldn't help noticing her trademark smooth as satin voice sounded hoarse and raspy, much lower in pitch than normal.

'It's Zac,' Cassandra blurted out before she started sobbing.

My heart went out to her. It was clear something terrible had happened.

'He's been in an accident...'

Cassandra's hands flew up and covered her mouth.

'Oh my God! Is he okay?' I asked.

I took a step towards her. Then I paused. I wasn't sure what the etiquette was between boss and employee in a situation like this but she looked like she could do with a hug.

Cassandra shook her head and tears started rolling down her cheeks. 'He's dead.'

Any thoughts of protocol went out of the window and I rushed over to where she was standing and threw my arms around her. Millie was only two paces behind me. We took up position on either side of her as we did our best to comfort her, but she was inconsolable.

'Would you like to sit down?' I said when I felt her legs buckle.

Cassandra didn't reply but Millie and I helped her on to a chair all the same. She reached across her desk and picked up a silver frame containing a photo of her late husband.

'Zac was walking home when he was hit by a car in the early hours of Tuesday morning,' she said running her fingertips across the glass. 'The driver didn't even bother to stop. They left him where he fell. He was taken to hospital, but he died from his injuries.'

Cassandra put the photo down on her desk and turned her tear-stained face towards Millie and me. She looked utterly broken.

'I know exactly what you're going through. Having somebody you love snatched away from you without warning leaves behind the worst pain imaginable,' I said.

'That's so awful. I don't know what to say,' Millie added.

'I'm sorry you've had to witness me being such a mess. I should have cried myself dry by this stage and who knew my nose could produce this much snot?' Cassandra tried to force out a smile to show her appreciation.

I was glad Cassandra had felt comfortable enough to confide in Millie and me. It meant a lot to know that she trusted us and wasn't scared to let us see her when she was so vulnerable. That took a lot of courage.

Cassandra inhaled a deep breath to compose herself. 'I'm not going to be able to run the casino on my own. Zac has left big shoes to fill,' she said.

Zac's death had come as such a shock, it hadn't even occurred to me at this stage that Cassandra had not only lost her husband but her business partner too.

'I'm going to need all the help I can get, so, for starters, I'd like to promote the two of you,' Cassandra smiled. 'I'd love to mentor you and see you reach your true potential. Zac would have loved that too. You both have so much to offer the company. I hope you'll consider my offer.'

Cassandra had reached out to us and I didn't want to let her down. Millie and I couldn't have asked for a better boss. She'd been incredibly sympathetic when Mum had been murdered and had told me to take as much time off as

I needed. I wanted to repay her kindness by being there for her in her hour of need. I could see Millie felt the same way. She'd been so good to both of us.

'Thank you. I'd be delighted to accept,' I replied.

'Same goes for me,' Millie piped up.

88

Abbie

Police corruption wasn't a modern problem. A crooked undercurrent had flowed through the force for centuries. I wasn't alone; hundreds of bent cops were operating within the establishment. Most officers suspected of corruption were allowed to resign or moved departments instead of being prosecuted or disciplined. For obvious reasons, the force was keen to keep the true extent of police corruption under wraps. The powers that be did their very best to cover things up, denying that corruption was an issue rather than tackling it.

'Roman Brady got justice after all. Wayne Perry was found in an alleyway off Monk Street with a bullet in the back of his head,' I said when Ed walked into my office.

'Wasn't that where Roman was stabbed?' Ed questioned.

'Yes, pretty much the same spot by all accounts.'

'Are we on the investigation team?'

'The area's full of villains. I think we'll put it down to an eye for an eye,' I replied.

'You seem very keen to close the case. Is somebody paying you to look the other way?' Ed asked, narrowing his beady eyes.

'What did you just say?' I couldn't swallow my anger.

'You heard,' Ed fired back.

I hadn't accepted a bribe; Wayne's killer was simply repaying a favour. No money had changed hands.

Since Zac had been killed, allegations had been swirling around me. Nobody usually dared to challenge my authority. My partner was going out on a limb, questioning my honesty and integrity. His accusations of corruption had no foundation. He had no evidence to back up his suspicions and support his claim.

The criminals I accepted bribes from knew better than to inform on me. It wasn't the done thing. They knew what side their bread was buttered on. You didn't bite the hand that fed you. They were loyal. It was a shame the same couldn't be said for my colleague.

'Are you deliberately trying to smear my name because you're holding a personal grudge against me? On second thoughts, don't bother to answer that.'

Just the sight of Ed sent fury coursing through my veins.

'I've suspected you were corrupt for some time, now I'm certain. I'm going to make a statement against you.'

Ed should have realised there would be risks involved if he pressed ahead with his plan. I considered saying, sometimes you have to pretend to be crooked to infiltrate a criminal organisation to cover up my unethical practices. But I didn't think he'd fall for that; his style of policing was to follow the rules and regulations down to a T.

Ed was delusional if he thought he could accuse me of

being crooked and get away with it. Who would believe him over me? I felt safe in the knowledge that it was notoriously difficult to catch and prosecute dishonest officers. The golden rule was never admit to anything.

I'd have to put Ed in his place. Who did he think he was confronting me about my less than honest work practices and trying to bring me to justice. It was laughable. Ed had no idea what he was dealing with.

I'd been running crooked operations for years, and it would take a lot more than an overzealous newbie to bring me down. I'd run rings around my superior officers by exploiting the grey areas for longer than I cared to remember. I wasn't going to let Ed land me in hot water. I'd never been the subject of a full-scale inquiry, and I never intended to be. I would do anything necessary to stop him from exposing me.

'I want to talk to you in private,' I said before walking out of my office.

Ed trailed along behind me, doing as he was told for once. I led the way to his car. Once Ed was behind the wheel, I told him to drive to the multi-storey car park close by. The rooftop was deserted; his was the only car on the upper level.

'Get out,' I said, unfastening my seat belt.

'No,' Ed replied.

His skin had paled, and I wondered if he could sense what was coming. He'd placed himself in real danger by challenging me. I reached into the back waistband of my trousers and pulled out a gun.

'I said, get out,' I repeated, pointing the revolver at him.

Ed reluctantly released his white-knuckled grip on the

steering wheel and unclipped his safety belt with trembling fingers. Then he followed my instructions as I frogmarched him over to the edge.

'Climb over the barrier.'

'Yeah right. As if I'm going to do that.'

Ed's bravado was admirable and if he hadn't been trembling like a leaf, I might have been impressed by the pluckiness he was displaying.

'You don't have a choice in the matter,' I replied as I held the gun to his head.

'You'll never get away with this.' Ed's voice quavered when he spoke.

'Hurry up. I haven't got all day.'

I jabbed the barrel of the gun into his cranium as a gentle reminder while he stood in front of me with his hands up. The next thing I knew, he spun around and knocked my gun offline. He'd done some Kung Fu when he was a child, but he was no Bruce Lee and his attempt to disarm me failed. Ed looked unbalanced after his high-speed twirl so I barged him with my right shoulder, hitting him full force which sent him toppling over the safety barrier. I watched him flailing his arms and legs for a couple of seconds with a smile playing on my lips.

Ed landed with a thud moments later, but I didn't feel the slightest bit guilty. When he'd started nosing around in my affairs, he'd signed his own death warrant. I normally preferred to use a third party than get blood on my hands, but sometimes needs must. I stole one last glimpse at Ed before I rushed down the stairwell and out onto the street. He'd attracted quite a crowd by the time I got there.

'Stand back, please,' I said, flashing my lanyard at the passers-by.

Ed was lying on his back, staring straight ahead with sightless eyes. I went through the motions of looking for a pulse in his limp wrist. I knew full well I wouldn't find one, but I had to be seen to be following procedure. The emergency services arrived shortly afterwards and pronounced Ed dead at the scene. I didn't care enough to have a conscience. The corpse of my recently deceased partner was lifted into an open body bag and zipped closed before the gurney was pushed into the ambulance.

Once I was back at the station, I gave the account of how my young partner took his own life because I'd discovered he was crooked and was going to report him. The stress of being exposed was too much for him. I'd tried to talk him down when I'd realised he was going to jump, but I hadn't been able to stop him was the yarn I'd spun.

I almost stopped short at going down that route. But I didn't owe him anything. It was a final kick in the nuts from me, turning the tables on the bastard. It served him right; he should have played by my rules and not tried to turn me over. I'd become an expert at diverting attention away from myself, stitching up my colleagues to keep the heat away from my door long before Ed had been my partner.

89

Lola

'I can't believe Zac's dead,' Millie said.

'I know. Poor Cassandra was beside herself,' I replied.

'Being promoted's going to be a big step for us; we're only just learning the ropes,' Millie continued.

'Tell me about it, but we need to do everything we can to help her through this.'

I cast my eyes to the floor so that Millie wouldn't see the tears that were threatening to spill down my cheeks.

'Are you okay, Lola?' Millie asked.

I should have realised my friend would notice I was upset. I had a lot on my plate at the moment and was feeling a bit overwhelmed.

'Paul told me he's going away for a while.' I could hear the sadness coating my words.

'Oh no. I'm sorry to hear that.'

I hadn't intended to mention this to Millie, but I really needed to hear what she thought about the situation. I was facing a huge dilemma and needed her input. I would have loved to have gone with Paul but I felt tied to Millie and Cassandra too. Even though I had feelings for him, it was early days. I hadn't known him that long. Deciding what to do for the best had become a new kind of mental torture.

'He asked me to go with him.'

Millie's mouth dropped open. 'Really?'

I nodded.

'Lucky you. I'm not even a tiny bit jealous. In fact, I couldn't think of anything worse,' she joked. 'I'm happy for you, Lola. Paul's a great guy.'

'There's nothing going on between us.'

'Not yet, but anyone can see he's got a soft spot for you,' Millie smiled.

I smiled back. 'This probably sounds a bit strange, but I'd feel guilty starting another relationship after everything that's happened. Mum lost her life because of my last partner.'

Millie took hold of my hands and stared into my soul with her brown eyes. 'Listen, Lola, you can't think like that. Nobody deserves happiness more than you do. Don't ever forget that. Your mum wouldn't want you to be stuck in the past. From what you've told me, I'm sure she'd love to see you settle down with somebody nice.'

'Steady on. We haven't even had a date yet, and you're talking about us settling down together,' I laughed.

I was making light of it, but Millie was right. That was all Mum had ever wanted for me. I couldn't change what had happened and didn't want her to have died in vain. I owed it to her memory to move on and not let the bad experience I'd had with Troy control my future.

'What are you going to do?' Millie asked.

'Under the circumstances, I think I'll have to say no,' I replied.

'Seriously?' Millie looked at me with a puzzled expression on her face.

If I didn't know better, I'd think Paul had asked her to talk me around. I felt my shoulders slump.

'Do you want my honest opinion?'

'Yes.' I trusted my friend completely. She always had my best interests at heart.

'After what you've been through, it would do you the world of good to get away for a while.'

Paul had phoned and asked me to meet him in the Red Lion for a quick drink after work. He was sitting at our usual table when I arrived and had already got the drinks in. A bottle of Kopparberg and a pint of Stella were on the table in front of him.

'Thanks for coming,' he said as I sat on the sofa next to him.

'No worries,' I smiled.

We exchanged a quick glance before an anxious feeling rippled through me. Paul seemed troubled somehow.

'I wanted to tell you in person, Mark's managed to fix the boat and all being well, the guys are going to split tomorrow.'

I felt my heart sink, but I knew this day was coming.

'I've bought myself a campervan. You should see the state of it. The back's completely covered with stickers the previous owner picked up on their travels. I'm hoping people will think I'm an experienced road-tripper when I head to France in the old banger very soon. I'm not trying to pressure you, but have you thought any more about coming with me?'

Paul's blue eyes searched mine. I had to get this over with before I lost my nerve.

'It's been an agonising decision, but I can't take you up on your offer,' I blurted out.

Paul let out a sigh. He usually exuded confidence and never hesitated over anything, but he seemed floored by what I'd just told him.

'Don't be offended. You're a great guy, but I barely know you…'

'No need to explain. I get it. It's not what I wanted you to say, but I understand.' Paul wrapped his arms around me and pulled me towards him.

I rested my head on his chest. The sound of his strong, steady heartbeat soothed my frazzled nerves, and the heat of his body made me melt into him. I'd forgotten how good it felt to be held by a man, a man who didn't want to pummel my face with his fists. Paul scooted away from me and looked into my eyes. My heart threatened to leap out of my chest when his lips met mine, but the moment ended all too soon and then we sat side by side in contemplative silence sipping our drinks.

Paul turned to face me and took hold of my hands. 'I want you to know something. I'm falling for you big time. I'm gutted you're not coming with me, but promise me you'll keep in touch.'

I didn't trust myself to speak, so I nodded as I looked up into his handsome face. I couldn't peel my eyes away from him. Something told me this might be the last time I saw him. I didn't know how I felt about that. The idea of having a fairy-tale love story was appealing, but I wasn't convinced that was on the cards for me. Much as I liked Paul, I didn't feel ready to get into another relationship yet. It was way too soon. Aside from that, I couldn't throw away the opportunity Cassandra had given me or desert her when she needed me the most. If it was meant to be between Paul and me things would work themselves out one day.

90

Abbie

Finn's mother looked a bit surprised to see me standing on her doorstep. But she couldn't have been more forthcoming with the information she gave me. Finn had indeed been traumatised by the heist, so he'd decided to take some time out and go backpacking in India with his good friend Mark Gibson. That name was all too familiar to me, and I felt the hairs on the back of my neck stand up.

Mark lived with his parents too in the same street, so that was my next port of call.

'Could you please tell me where Mark was between the hours of 6 a.m. and 10 a.m. on 16th February?' I asked.

Mrs Gibson had shown me into the lounge, offered me a cup of tea and insisted I sit down while we talked.

'Now let me see,' she said, pausing for a moment. 'He was driving a van for a local courier company back then, but his hours changed depending on how much work they had on any given day. If he wasn't already at work, he would have been here.'

'Can you give me his employer's address, please?'

After Mrs Gibson handed me a business card belonging to the firm, I thanked her for her help then made my way to the door.

Two down. Two to go.

'Mrs Best?' I flashed my ID at the fifty-something-year-old woman who answered the door.

'Yes,' she replied.

'Could I come in for a moment, please?'

'Has something happened to one of my boys?' Mrs Best asked.

'No. But I need to ask you some questions about a robbery I'm investigating.'

Without saying a word, Mrs Best turned on her heel and walked down the corridor past an old dog asleep in its basket. I followed a couple of paces behind.

'So what's all this about then?' she asked in a surly tone.

No tea or a comfy seat offered in this house I noted.

'Could you please tell me where your sons were between the hours of 6 a.m. and 10 a.m. on 16th February?' I asked.

'My husband and I aren't early birds. The boys leave for work well before we get up. They have an early start,' Mrs Best said.

'I'll need to verify your account. Where is work exactly?' I questioned.

Mrs Best wouldn't be the first mother to cover for her children. I watched her as she scribbled down the addresses of both of her sons' employers on the back of a brown manila envelope. She handed it to me before ushering me towards the door.

Finn, Mark, Paul and Kevin all had alibis for the time

of the robbery, but as yet, we were only able to confirm Finn's. I got into my car to make the calls. My spirits lifted slightly when I spoke to the foreman on the building site and discovered that Paul was still working there. But they were dashed again when HMP Standford Hill said that Kevin was on holiday.

'Do you know where he's gone?' I asked the voice on the other end of the phone.

'I'm afraid not,' the man replied.

Funny how Mrs Best didn't mention that to me a minute ago, I thought. The men must have realised I was closing in on them and decided to do a runner. What I didn't understand was why Paul hadn't gone with them. Ten million pounds would go a long way in a place like India. I'd have to put him under surveillance so that he didn't give me the slip as well.

Fury bubbled up inside of me as I sat behind the wheel. I'd been so preoccupied getting revenge on Ed, I'd taken my eye off the ball, allowing Finn and his friends an opportunity to slip through the net. I only had myself to blame if they got away, so I quickly put out an alert to all airports and ports.

I didn't believe for one minute the guys had gone to India. It was much more likely that they'd head to the continent as Mark had access to boats and France lay just across the water from where they lived. I'd passed the Isle of Sheppey Sailing Club on the way to their addresses. There had to be somebody there that could help me.

I spun my car around and blue-lighted it to the club a few moments' drive away. I spotted a man in a dingy close to the shore as soon as I drove into the car park. So, I jumped out of the driver's seat and began flagging him down before he headed out to sea.

'I was just about to go fishing. Is something wrong?' the man asked.

'I need you to take me out on the water on police business,' I said, flashing him my ID and my brightest smile. 'I'll make sure you're properly reimbursed.'

'There's no need for that. I'd be delighted to help.'

The ruddy-cheeked man in his mid-sixties was only too happy to oblige. I got into the rigid inflatable boat and we headed away from the shore before he changed his mind.

'I'm looking for three men, late twenties who might be headed to France,' I said looking over my shoulder to where the man was sitting next to the outboard motor. 'In fact, you might know them, they're local lads. Finn McCaskill, Kevin Best and Mark Gibson.'

'I know Mark Gibson, he works at the watersports centre, but the other two names don't ring a bell,' the man replied.

'Can you take the quickest route to France from here?' I asked, holding on to my hair to stop it from flying around.

'Righto. That looks like Mark up ahead. The blond-haired fella,' the man shouted over the noise of the engine. He was pointing to a larger boat in the distance.

'Can you catch up with him?' I asked, as my fingertips caressed the barrel of my gun.

'We'll soon find out. Hold tight!'

He opened up the throttle and the inflatable took off like a rocket. He was driving at higher speed and with more skill and precision than I'd expected a man of his age to be capable of. I had to hold on to the base of the seat to try and steady myself as the waves crashed off the sides, sending salty spray into the air.

Finn and Kevin were sitting side by side at the back of the boat. Mark was at the wheel. He looked over his shoulder as we closed the gap. Then he increased his speed to try and lose us. Streams of white spray were flying out behind his boat. As we closed in again, my driver locked the wheel hard, lifting the right side of the boat out of the water. I lurched sideways towards the waterline before the right side re-engaged with the surface. I blew out a breath. It was a hair-raising pursuit. I'd thought we were about to capsize.

Mark had been paying too much attention to us and started frantically steering when he realised he was on a collision course with another vessel. His mistake had cost him valuable time and our inflatable bounced off the waves until we were in line with him.

I pulled my gun out of my jacket pocket and pointed it at Finn.

'Cut the engine or I'll shoot,' I shouted.

Mark did what I'd asked.

'You're all under arrest. Put your hands up,' I instructed, training my gun on the men. 'Now back up and don't move.'

Using the ladder at the back, I climbed on board the boat.

'I'll let you get back to your fishing trip,' I said without taking my eyes off the gang.

'Righto,' the man replied, turning his dingy around and heading back the way we'd come as though it was the most natural thing in the world for him to chase three men across the sea in an inflatable boat.

But his lack of interest suited me down to the ground. I didn't want him poking his nose into what I was about to do. I always kept a supply of nylon cuffs on me for situations like this. Being outnumbered by three men wasn't ideal so I needed to act fast before they overpowered me.

'Hold your hands out in front of you,' I said waving my gun at the men.

I cuffed each one in turn before using the same restraints on their ankles to incapacitate them. Then I reached into the pockets of Finn, Mark and Kevin's jeans and took out their mobile phones.

'What are your pins?'

The men glanced at each other before giving me the numbers. They were using cheap pay as you go mobiles to communicate with each other so the handsets didn't have any complicated biometric security built-in. I tested the codes to check if they were telling the truth before I put the next stage of my plan into action. Using another restraint, I secured Mark's hands to the wheel.

'You two get over there,' I gestured to the back of the boat. Kevin and Finn began shuffling in slow motion like penguins. 'Hurry up. We haven't got all day.'

As soon as Finn was close to the ladder, I booted the back of his knee, throwing him off balance. He landed in the water and wriggled like a worm as he desperately tried to stay afloat, but he was wasting his time. Without a lifejacket, he was going to sink like a stone.

'What the fuck are you doing?' Kevin yelled.

He tried to swing at me, so I squeezed the trigger and planted a bullet in the centre of his chest. The force sent him flying backwards and he landed on the right-hand side of the boat. His upper body was overhanging the edge making it simple for me to tip him overboard. By the looks of it, he was dead before he hit the water, but I didn't bother to find out.

I turned to face Mark. The colour had seeped from his skin and he was shaking like a leaf.

'I want you to take the boat to wherever you were heading as if none of this has happened. Can you do that for me?' I smiled.

Mark nodded so I released his hands from the cuffs to allow him to steer the boat. I could feel I was getting closer to the money with every minute that passed.

91

Paul

'Are you going to tell me what you and Kevin have been up to?' Mum asked when I came in from work.

Her words startled me, but I tried not to let it show. She stood facing me with her hands on her hips, waiting for me to reply.

'Not sure what you mean,' I shrugged.

Mum narrowed her eyes. 'The police called here today. DI Kingsly wanted to know where you and your brother were on 16th February.'

I scratched my head, then crossed my arms over my chest, hoping I looked puzzled by her question.

'So what have the two of you been up to then?' The frown on Mum's forehead deepened.

'We haven't been up to anything. What's so special about 16th February?' I asked, feigning ignorance.

'I don't know. She didn't say. I was hoping you could fill me in.'

Mum had a nosey streak, so the curiosity must have been killing her.

'Sorry, no can do. The date means nothing to me,' I replied. 'I'm going to jump in the shower.'

Mum's glare was relentless, and as I began to walk away, I could feel her eyes boring into the back of my head. I could tell she didn't believe me, but at least she'd let the matter drop. I hated lying to her, but I couldn't risk telling her what we'd done. I had to keep her in the dark to protect her. I didn't want her to become an accessory to a crime she had nothing to do with.

'By the way,' I said, turning back to face her. 'What did you tell her?'

'I said you'd have been at work. Then she asked me to give her your employers' addresses so she could verify that,' Mum replied.

'Fair enough,' I said, but what I really wanted to do was shout, 'fuck, fuck, fuck!' at the top of my voice.

HMP Standford Hill would tell her Kevin had gone on holiday, so Abbie was bound to pay the family home another visit, desperate to know where he'd gone. Before the others had left for France, we'd agreed to tell our families we were going somewhere different so that if Abbie came sniffing around, we could send her off on a wild goose chase. India seemed like a good bet as it was supposedly easy to disappear there. Missing Westerners weren't a high priority, and police corruption was rife, so we'd be pretty difficult to track down if we were hiding out. With any luck, Abbie wouldn't bother looking as it was so far away.

The plan had been to work our way along the French coastline so that Kevin and the guys could make full use of the boat. I'd follow in my campervan. We weren't going to stay too long in any one place in case the police were trying to trace us. If we kept moving around, we'd be harder to locate. And at some point in the future, we hoped to find ourselves in a sleepy little fishing village on the southern coast of Spain.

I'd intended to wait until I'd heard from the guys before I made a move but now I was scared to stay here in case Abbie came back. I didn't want to be a sitting duck, so I decided to sleep in the van until the call came through. Once Mum and Dad went to bed, I slipped out of the house. I took the coward's way out and left a note on the kitchen table saying I'd gone to join Kevin, Finn and Paul in India and would be back in a couple of weeks, to spare myself the inquisition.

Kevin and I had agreed not to tell our parents we weren't coming back; we wanted them to think we were just going for a holiday. My mum would be heartbroken if she thought there was a chance she was never going to see my brother and me again. But I was sure it wouldn't come to that. One day, when the dust settled, I'd buy Mum and Dad tickets to wherever it was I was living.

I'd told Kevin to make sure he contacted me as soon as they arrived in France. To say I was worried about my brother and my friends' safety was an understatement. The Channel was one of the most heavily trafficked waters in the world, with a constant flow of large ships. And that was before you added strong tidal currents and unpredictable weather into the mix. Mark was an experienced skipper, but

I wouldn't be able to relax until the crossing was over. Kevin had tried to brush aside my concerns before they left; he'd told me not to fret and assured me everything was going to be fine. He reckoned in no time at all, we'd be together again, sipping cocktails by the pool. I kept clinging to that thought, but I had a sinking feeling in the pit of my stomach that something had gone wrong.

92

Abbie

Mark gripped the wheel with white-knuckled hands as he steered the boat towards France. I wasn't sure if I could trust him to stick to the gang's original plan, but he'd witnessed what I'd done to Finn and Kevin when they'd been surplus to requirements. So that should keep him in line. And judging by the look on his face he was too scared to put up any resistance.

The weather had been kind to us and Mark moored the boat in Calais just as the light was starting to fade. Once he'd cut the engine, I cuffed his hands together again just to be on the safe side. He was a strong, young man and would be a handful if he decided to kick off.

To pass the time on the journey, I'd been scrolling through Kevin's phone reading the texts he'd previously sent to Paul so that when the time came, the message I sent would look authentic. The sooner Paul came to France, the sooner this would be over and done with.

I just wanted to let you know we made it!

I'd been expecting Paul to type a reply but instead, the handset began to ring. The call was from a withheld number which I assumed to be Paul's but I couldn't risk allowing Mark to answer it, he'd never be able to hold his nerve. So I had to let it go to voicemail and a few moments later, I listened to the recording.

'Hi Kevin, I'm glad to hear that. Ring me back when you get this message,' Paul said.

What a pity Kevin wouldn't be able to return his call, I thought before I turned my attention back to Mark. His face was ashen and his blue eyes were wide and questioning.

'Let's get down to business. Where's the money?'

'It's in the cabin,' Mark replied.

I'd expected to have to torture that information out of him. The gang had been giving me the run around for months, so I was slightly disappointed that he'd rolled over and submitted without bothering to put up a fight. He must have realised the game was up. And having already lost two of his friends, he was probably under the illusion that being compliant would give him the best chance of survival. I decided to play along. I didn't want to disappoint him.

'Show me where it is,' I said, pointing my gun into the small of his back.

Mark shuffled towards the stairwell, dropped on to his knees and slid down the treads on his stomach. He knew he wouldn't be able to walk down the flight with his ankles bound so he'd taken the initiative. As he got back on his feet, he gestured with a nod of the head to a seated area that ran along the left-hand side of the boat.

'There's a false panel under the cushions. The money's in there,' Mark said.

While keeping my gun trained on Mark, I swiped the rectangular pads out of the way, then pulled the fabric tab attached to the wooden seat base, removing it from the frame. The space below it was cavernous. There was more than enough room for the black holdalls lined up side by side. I unzipped the nearest bag and peered inside. The sight of all that money brought a smile to my face.

93

Paul

I'd just had a text from Kevin saying they'd arrived in Calais. I tried to call him, but it went straight to voicemail. Should I be worried that he didn't pick up? Or were the guys too busy enjoying their new surroundings and the cheap beer to bother checking in with me? I knew deep down which one my money was on. Beer won every time.

There's a bottle of Stella with your name on. Get here as soon as you can

Kevin's text brought a smile to my face. Just as I'd guessed, the guys were too busy boozing to give me a second thought. I didn't need to be asked twice. If I didn't get out of here soon, Abbie would close in on me.

'Hi, Lola. I just wanted to let you know I'm about to board the Channel Tunnel,' I said when I called her from the queue.

'Have a safe journey,' Lola replied.

She was doing her best to sound upbeat but she was failing miserably, which gave me a glimmer of hope that she might start pining for me in the not-too-distant future and decide to join me after all.

'I'll be in touch soon,' I said before I ended the call.

Just over half an hour later I arrived in Calais. It was only a short drive to the marina, so I'd be reunited with the guys very soon. I couldn't wait for the four of us to be back together. It felt really weird being apart from them. As I walked along the jetty towards the boat, I could almost taste the beer. I'd half expected the guys to be waiting on the deck for me, but the wind was picking up so they'd no doubt retreated inside to get drunk.

I opened up the door to the stairwell and spotted Mark sitting at the table. As soon as I saw the look on his face, I knew something was wrong. His tanned skin had visibly paled. I couldn't see the others from where I was standing, so I began to walk down the steps. As soon as I did, Mark's face crumpled and he started sobbing, which took me by surprise.

'What's wrong, mate?' I asked.

I rushed down the last few steps and stood next to him. That was when I noticed the nylon cuffs restraining his wrists and ankles.

'Hello, Paul, I'm so glad you could join us.'

I looked up at the sound of the woman's voice and did a double-take when I saw Abbie metres away pointing a gun at me. I put my hands up in response. But it was just for show. I had no intention of surrendering. What the hell was she doing here? The police hadn't managed to catch us while we were living thirty miles away, so I never thought they'd find us once we made it to foreign soil.

'Now that we have a full house, I can finish the job. I don't like leaving loose ends untied,' Abbie smiled.

'Be careful, mate, she's dangerous. She killed Finn and Kevin,' Mark blurted out.

Mark's words winded me. How could they be dead? The thought of that made me see red. I clenched my jaw and felt my nostrils flare. I needed to disarm her before she had a chance to pull the trigger. I glanced sideways at Mark who read the situation perfectly. He'd received my message without me having to say a word. Realising I needed a distraction, he kicked out his bound legs, booting over a side table and sending a lamp crashing to the floor.

Abbie tore her eyes away from me for a brief moment, giving me just enough time to tackle her. I knocked the gun out of her hand and kicked it across the floor. The two of us scrambled after it. I'd been expecting to overpower Abbie but she was giving me a run for my money. She grabbed the weapon first, so I bent her wrist back in one last-ditch attempt to make her drop it. Abbie was holding on for dear life. When the sound of the shot resonated around the cabin, it took a moment for me to realise the gun had gone off and Abbie was bleeding. My hands sprang away from her. I stood open-mouthed watching the blood seeping across the front of her white shirt. Abbie's eyes bore into mine, then she dropped to the floor. In the struggle, one of us had pulled the trigger. I didn't think it was me, but I couldn't be certain.

'Jesus. I think she's dead,' I said as fear raced around my body. I was too scared to find out for sure.

'Can you cut these ties off?' Mark asked. 'There's a knife in the drawer over there.'

I'd completely forgotten that he was still bound at the wrists and ankles.

'What are we going to do?' Panic was spreading through all of my pores. I couldn't think straight.

'We need to get the boat out on the water. Somebody probably heard the shot and they may well have called the police,' Mark said.

We headed up to the deck leaving Abbie's lifeless body lying in a pool of blood. Mark took charge untying the boat and guiding it out to sea while I stood around like a spare part, dazed and confused, trying to make sense of what had just happened.

'I can't believe Kevin and Finn are dead,' I said.

'I know, mate. I saw them die with my own eyes and it still doesn't seem real.' Mark shook his head.

'Why did that bitch kill them?' I felt my temper spike.

'She was after the money. I think she'd intended to kill us too if she hadn't, you know...' Mark let his sentence trail off. 'I'd seen what she was capable of so I showed her where the dosh was; she could have taken it without luring you here. It was Abbie that sent you the texts from Kevin.'

It was all starting to make sense. Abbie had said now she had a full house, she could finish the job. She obviously didn't want to leave any witnesses behind that could link her to the cash or the innocent people she'd murdered. Even though it wouldn't bring my brother and friend back, I was glad she was dead.

'Are you okay, mate?' Mark asked, bringing me back to my senses.

'I've been better,' I replied.

Mark squeezed the top of my shoulder.

I looked over my shoulder. The marina's lights were barely visible and my nerves had started to get the better of me. 'We're a long way from shore,' I pointed out.

'I know. I had to take her a fair way out. I can't risk anyone seeing me scuttle her. It's a crying shame to sink a beautiful boat like this deliberately,' Mark said. He looked genuinely upset.

A jolt of adrenalin suddenly brought me to life. 'You're going to sink the boat?' I questioned as my heart started hammering in my chest.

Mark nodded. 'We've got no option mate.'

'But it's pitch black out here and the wind's blowing a gale,' I protested.

Mark cut the engine and started filling the inflatable with the holdalls while I sat on the floor of the boat wedged into a corner, frozen with fear.

'Get in the dinghy. I need to open up the seacocks. Once I do that the water will flood the hull pretty quickly. When a boat starts going down, it really gains momentum,' Mark said.

I shuddered at the thought.

'What about Abbie?'

'We'll leave her body on board and she'll go down with the boat,' Mark replied, like a seasoned serial killer. 'Come on, mate, shake a leg. The sooner we get out of here the better.'

I gripped on to the ladder as the boat lurched to and fro, but my legs wouldn't move a muscle. Mark walked over and put my arms through a lifejacket before zipping it up.

'It's okay, nothing bad's going to happen. I promise you. But we need to get away from here before we get caught.'

Mark's words suddenly registered in my brain and I

lowered myself into the dinghy and clung on to the rope running around the side as it was battered by the waves, trying not to overthink the situation. A moment later, Mark was in the inflatable beside me rowing us back towards the lights of the marina. He was struggling to make progress, but I was no use to man nor beast as I sat close to tears at the other end praying that this would soon be over. This was my worst nightmare. Being at the mercy of the sea in the dead of night was terrifying, especially when the dinghy started to take on water as the waves grew in size. I was sure we were going to drown. Then, just when I thought all was lost, the wind changed direction, and we made it back to the safety of the harbour.

'Are you sure there'll be no trace of Abbie or the boat?' I asked once we were on dry land.

Mark nodded his head. We got to work loading the holdalls into the campervan, stashing the money inside the seat cushion pads, under the bunks and the huge over-cab bed before Mark went back and sank the dinghy.

'We need to get away from here. Will you be okay to drive?' Mark asked.

'Yes,' I replied.

'Let's head to Le Touquet. It's a nice resort about an hour away. There's bound to be a campsite with pitches for vans, so we'll look like regular tourists,' Mark said, getting into the passenger's seat.

I glanced over at my friend as I got behind the wheel. Mark and I appeared to have swapped roles. I usually took the lead when decisions needed to be made, but he could see I was in no fit state to take charge so he'd shrugged off the anxiety that so often held him back and stepped up to the plate.

94

Lola

After what I'd been through with Troy, the idea of being in a serious relationship made my blood run cold. I wasn't sure I'd ever feel comfortable enough to trust a member of the opposite sex again. But then I met Paul and my barriers started to come down. Since he'd kissed me and told me he was falling for me, I'd felt like I was walking on air. I never thought I'd hear myself say this, but starting a new relationship might be part of the healing process. There was no fixed time for moving on; recovering from abuse looked different for everyone. I was a romantic at heart and far too young to give up on love. Paul made me feel safe, so I was tempted to dip my toe back into the world of dating, but I kept swinging wildly between joy and fear at the thought of having a boyfriend. I reminded myself that Paul wasn't Troy. It wasn't fair to punish him for my ex's mistakes. But if we were going to give this a go, we'd have to take things slowly. He'd need to let me set the pace.

Trust was the fundamental building block of any relationship. It wasn't easy for me to let my guard down. I was scared of being vulnerable. Leaving my emotional baggage behind was going to be an uphill battle. It would take time, patience, and the right person to win me over.

I'd spent a restless night tossing and turning. I hadn't heard a word from Paul since he'd been about to board the Channel Tunnel and I had a horrible feeling something was wrong. I didn't want to scare him off by being needy, so I'd tried to resist calling him. He was probably just having fun with his friends and had lost track of the time. As the hours rolled by, my discomfort grew. I was an anxious mess, wringing my hands in my lap and checking the time on my watch every fifteen seconds. I couldn't stand it any longer so I dialled his number, but it went to voicemail.

'Hi, Paul. It's me. Give me a call when you get a chance,' I tried to make my message sound breezy, but I knew I'd failed, my voice sounded strained.

Millie was at work and I was alone in the flat. I was literally climbing the walls. I needed to try and keep busy. I was wiping down the kitchen counters for the third time when my mobile began to ring. I almost jumped out of my skin.

'I'm sorry I didn't call you sooner, but the shit's well and truly hit the fan,' Paul said before he told me everything that had happened.

I listened in silence. My stomach was too full of knots to speak. I could scarcely take it all in.

'It wasn't meant to end this way. Mark and I are driving around France in a safe on wheels. We've got ten million pounds stashed inside my knackered campervan and we don't know what to do with it. The money feels tainted after what's happened,' Paul sounded really down.

'I'm sure it does, but Kevin and Finn wouldn't have wanted to lose their lives in vain. They'd want you and Mark to use the cash and finish what you set out to do,' I replied.

'I miss you, Lola. I wish you were here right now,' Paul said.

I missed him too. It was early days, but things were going well between us. I'd taken a gamble by not going to France with him. I hoped I'd done the right thing. Spending time apart would test our commitment to each other. But absence made the heart grow fonder, didn't it?

Paul was such a great guy. He was so kind and fun to be around. Slowly but surely he was restoring my faith in men. I wanted to believe more than anything that in the future, I'd share my life with somebody. If we beat the odds and ended up together, I'd feel like I'd won the relationship jackpot. Only time would tell if Lady Luck was on our side though; fingers crossed, happily ever after was on the cards for us.

Acknowledgements

Thank you to my wonderful editor, Martina Arzu. It has been a pleasure working with you again.

Thanks to all the team at Head of Zeus and everyone involved in the production of this book, especially Peyton Stableford, Izzy Frost, Yvonne Doney, Annabel Walker and Cherie Chapman.

Thank you, Sam Michaels, for everything you've done to support me so far on this journey. Your advice and words of encouragement never fail to lift my spirits.

And finally, special thanks should go to Marc Alan Powers Egan for promoting my books in the fabulous Fostering, Memoirs and Fiction Book Club. All the shares and posts are greatly appreciated.